THE CLARENDON DICKENS

General Editors

JOHN BUTT   KATHLEEN TILLOTSON

THE MYSTERY OF
EDWIN DROOD

No. III.]   **JUNE, 1870.**   [Price One Shilling.

THE MYSTERY OF EDWIN DROOD.

BY CHARLES DICKENS.

WITH ILLUSTRATIONS.

LONDON: CHAPMAN & HALL, 193, PICCADILLY.

Advertisements to be sent to the Publishers, and ADAMS & FRANCIS, 59, Fleet Street, E.C.
[*The right of Translation is reserved.*]

Cover-design for wrapper of monthly parts, by Luke Fildes. From a copy at Dickens House.
(*Reduced*)

CHARLES DICKENS

THE MYSTERY OF
EDWIN DROOD

EDITED BY

MARGARET CARDWELL

OXFORD
AT THE CLARENDON PRESS
1972

Oxford University Press, Ely House, London W. 1

GLASGOW NEW YORK TORONTO MELBOURNE WELLINGTON
CAPE TOWN IBADAN NAIROBI DAR ES SALAAM LUSAKA ADDIS ABABA
DELHI BOMBAY CALCUTTA MADRAS KARACHI LAHORE DACCA
KUALA LUMPUR SINGAPORE HONG KONG TOKYO

© OXFORD UNIVERSITY PRESS 1972

PRINTED IN GREAT BRITAIN
AT THE UNIVERSITY PRESS, OXFORD
BY VIVIAN RIDLER
PRINTER TO THE UNIVERSITY

PREFACE

by the

General Editors

Reprinted from the first volume of the Clarendon edition, Oliver Twist (1966)

THE idea of such an edition of Dickens's works as this volume inaugurates has been in the minds of the general editors for some twenty years; and between 1949 and 1957 we published, both separately and in collaboration, a small selection of the results of extensive preliminary investigations into the manuscript and other materials. Plans for an edition were discussed with the Clarendon Press and with the late Mr. Humphry House in 1955, and since 1958 editorial work has been proceeding on three novels—*Oliver Twist, Martin Chuzzlewit,* and *David Copperfield*—along with further exploration of the problems of the whole series.

Writing in 1957 in the Preface to *Dickens at Work*, we described Dickens studies as having 'hardly passed beyond the early nineteenth-century phase of Shakespeare studies; while the study of his text seems arrested in the early eighteenth century'. It is our hope that this judgement is now outdated. In this edition a critical text is established, a text free from the numerous corruptions that disfigure modern reprints, with an apparatus of variants that will exhibit Dickens's progressive revision, and accompanied by all such assistance as Dickens himself supplied in the shape of prefaces, descriptive headlines, illustrations, and cover-designs from the wrappers of the monthly part-issues, which often foreshadow the drift of the novel as Dickens originally conceived it. The Introductions trace the history of the composition, publication, and revision of each novel, from the first stirrings that can be discovered in letters and manuscript notes down to the appearance of the last edition in the author's lifetime.

The materials available to the editor are very substantial. The manuscript of each novel from *The Old Curiosity Shop* onwards survives complete; and of the three earlier novels in part, with about 45 leaves of *Pickwick Papers*, about 160 leaves of *Nicholas Nickleby*, and 480 leaves (about two-fifths) of *Oliver Twist*. With the trifling exception of a few leaves here and there, these manuscripts are corrected first drafts, and were sent to the printer as copy for press. Many proofs survive as well, though they are mostly the proofs of novels later in time than *The Old Curiosity Shop*.

Thus in many novels it is possible to trace every action of the author's pen, except for the final revisions made in proof, which were presumably retained by the printer and destroyed after publication. In the manuscript it is often possible to decipher rejected readings under erasures. Thus, the first version of a character's name can sometimes be revealed; afterthoughts can be detected, and sometimes, thanks to the different shades of ink employed, even the moment of revision. It is possible also to judge with what degree of accuracy the compositor followed his peculiarly difficult copy, and what attention the author gave to correcting his proofs. When reading proof, Dickens seems not to have referred to his manuscript, since though he corrected most errors of substance, he sometimes let a plausible error pass, and sometimes introduced a new reading—by no means always a superior reading—instead of reverting to what he had originally written. His principal task when part-issue proofs reached him was to adjust the amount he had written to the number of pages available. Sometimes a galley-proof of 'over-matter' attached to his page-proof indicated that he must retrench, and his corrected proofs show how he did it. Occasionally he found that he must add a paragraph or two so as to give his readers full measure, and these additions are attached to the corrected proofs returned to the printer. All deletions required for adjusting the size of an instalment are printed in the textual apparatus, while all additions made for the same purpose are left in the text and recorded in the apparatus. Where an earlier version of a name can be detected in the manuscript, we record it; we have used our judgement in drawing attention in the apparatus to the more interesting first thoughts; and we have restored the true reading where an error was overlooked in proof-correction.

The textual apparatus records all substantive variants between editions printed in Dickens's lifetime. The two books which Dickens revised most carefully and frequently seem to have been *Sketches by Boz* and *Oliver Twist*. The text of the early chapters of *The Old Curiosity Shop* needed adjustment on their being disengaged from *Master Humphrey's Clock* for separate publication. For the other novels, the amount of revision varied according to whether their original appearance was in part-issues or in a periodical; but all underwent some revision for the three collected editions published in Dickens's lifetime, namely the Cheap edition, the Library edition, and the Charles Dickens edition. In these later editions, corruptions appeared, of which the author seems to have been unaware, and these were in due course transmitted to modern reprints. In no instance do these collected editions provide a copy-text for the present edition, though their authoritative readings have been taken into account.

Dickens was never concerned to preserve the evidence of where his instalments began and ended. Nevertheless, these divisions hold an abiding importance, especially for readers interested in Dickens's constructive powers, and in this edition they will either be indicated on the page or set out in tabular form.

Of the Appendixes and supplementary matter, some items, such as the headlines to the Charles Dickens edition, will be provided for all novels;

others, such as the glossary of thieves' cant in *Oliver Twist*, will elucidate some special feature of the novel concerned. Complete transcripts of Dickens's working notes, where these still survive, will be included. No attempt has been made, however, to undertake the immense task of explanatory annotation; and the Introductions will not include a critical appraisal. But we hope that such appraisal will in future be the more firmly based as a result of our labours.

J. B.
K. T.

THE foregoing Preface was jointly written early in 1965. Before his death on 22 November, John Butt had seen the first proofs of the Introduction, text, and Appendixes [of *Oliver Twist*].

K. T.

23 December 1965

Our 'exploration of the problems of the whole series'| included, at an early stage, a preliminary investigation into the text of *Edwin Drood*; Miss Cardwell gave assistance from the outset, and ten years ago was chosen as editor of the novel. Some of its special problems arise from its incompleteness and partly posthumous publication; but this also serves to exclude, after an ascertainable date, any further authorial revision and correction, and helps to expose some plausible readings as contributed, deliberately or unwittingly, by the printers, including those of the Charles Dickens edition. This edition, published five years after the author's death, is the source of most previous modern texts; no editor has hitherto had recourse to the manuscript, which has been left to a few often ill-equipped seekers of keys to the mystery.

Many questions remain unanswerable; but the present text represents Dickens's intentions as closely and fully as possible, and in the Introduction the editor examines afresh all the available evidence for the composition of his last and unfinished novel.

K. T.

June 1971

ACKNOWLEDGEMENTS

My first debt of gratitude is to the General Editors, for stimulating the initial interest and for subsequent encouragement and help in allowing me to draw on their extensive experience.

Madeline House, editor of the Pilgrim edition of Dickens's *Letters*, has also been generous in giving time and expert information, and in allowing me to consult unpublished letters. Mr. Christopher Dickens has kindly given permission for the use of copyright material.

I wish to thank the curators of libraries who have permitted the use of material in their collections: the Director of the Victoria and Albert Museum, for the use of the manuscript, surviving proof-sheets, and publishers' accounts in the Forster collection; the Trustees of Dickens House, particularly for the use of the collection of the late Howard Duffield, with its extensive accumulation of material relevant to *Edwin Drood*; the Director of the British Museum for a letter; the Librarian of the Huntington Library, California, for a letter. For permission to reproduce illustrations, I thank the Director of the Victoria and Albert Museum, the Trustees of Dickens House, and the Editor of the *Dickensian*.

I am indebted to the staff of the libraries in which I have worked, the British Museum, the Victoria and Albert Museum, the University of London, and the Queen's University, Belfast. I owe a special debt of gratitude to the staff of Dickens House, Miss Minards, Miss Pillers and their colleagues. I wish to thank the executors of the late John Watt for permission to consult his notes on *Edwin Drood*, at Dickens House.

It is a pleasure to record my thanks to those who have helped in various ways with advice and information: Harold F. Brooks, Anthony Burton, D. M. Davin, David Farley-Hills, Gordon Wheeler. Nina Burgis has been constantly helpful in discussing problems and answering inquiries.

To Miss M. Brearley and the Governors of the Froebel Institute, for granting study leave, and to the Academic Council of the Queen's University, Belfast, for research grants, I am deeply grateful.

As a research assistant at Bedford College, I began work on the text of *Edwin Drood*, which I was later able to incorporate in a thesis submitted for the London Ph.D. degree in 1969. My thanks are due to the University of London for permission to use material from the thesis in the present edition. I owe the deepest debt of gratitude to my supervisor, Kathleen Tillotson, for her unfailing kindness and support, and for the generosity with which she has shared her knowledge.

M. C.

25 June 1971

GENERAL CONTENTS

EXTRA ILLUSTRATIONS

REFERENCES AND ABBREVIATIONS

N   The Nonesuch edition, *The Letters of Charles Dickens*, ed. Walter
          Dexter (3 vols., 1938).

Forster   John Forster, *The Life of Charles Dickens* (3 vols., 1872–4; second
          edition, revised, 2 vols., 1876). [Quotations from first edition; refer-
          ences by book and section to second edition.]

Dolby   George Dolby, *Charles Dickens as I knew him* (1885).

MS   manuscript

P   proof

70   1st edition, 1870 (Chapman and Hall)

ES   *Every Saturday*, 1870 (Fields, Osgood and Company)

73   Library edition, 1873 (Chapman and Hall)

75   Charles Dickens edition, 1875 (Chapman and Hall)

⟨ ⟩   Deleted in MS

NOTE ON APPENDIX H

THE set of proofs sent to Luke Fildes, Dickens's illustrator, and referred to in the Introduction (p. l), became available only when this edition was already in proof. As it was too late to incorporate the new evidence in the relevant portions of the textual apparatus, this is set out in detail in Appendix H. The parts chiefly affected are pp. 76–146 (chapters x–xvi, Numbers III–IV) and Appendix F.

The proof is in the Gimbel collection, now in the Beinecke Rare Book and Manuscript Library, Yale University Library, to whose Librarian acknowledgement is gratefully made. The editors also wish to thank Gordon Haight for expediting the arrival of the microfilm, and John Cronin and Michael Barnes for assistance in collation.

K. T.

M. C.

INTRODUCTION

Dickens's last complete novel, *Our Mutual Friend*, was published in November 1865. From then until the writing of his latest novel, his time was mainly devoted to the editing of *All the Year Round*, including up to 1867 the production of Christmas Numbers, and to the public readings in England and America—the first 'private' reading of 'Sikes and Nancy' took place on 14 November 1868. According to Dolby he began 'to cast about for a subject for a new book' after the end of the readings, that is, probably in May 1869.[1] If Forster's recollections are accurate, the 'first fancy for the tale' was expressed in a letter in mid July: 'What should you think of the idea of a story beginning in this way?—Two people, boy and girl, or very young, going apart from one another, pledged to be married after many years—at the end of the book. The interest to arise out of the tracing of their separate ways, and the impossibility of telling what will be done with that impending fate.'[2] The centre of interest here is not that of *Edwin Drood*, and as these words are almost identical with those recorded, perhaps several years earlier, in Dickens's 'Book of Memoranda', doubts have been cast on Forster's trustworthiness.[3] It is, however, conceivable that Dickens turned to his 'Memoranda' when planning *Edwin Drood*: the entry concerning the gas-fitter and the 'jistes'[4] is clearly echoed in Mrs. Billickin's candid admission of the weakness of her floor-boards in chapter xxii. If the 'boy and girl' story was Dickens's first fancy for his new book, it was soon superseded. The novel was much in his thoughts at the end of July[5] and by the beginning of August his ideas were taking shape: 'I laid aside the fancy I told you of, and have a very curious and new idea for my new story. Not a communicable idea (or the interest of the book would be gone), but a very strong one, though difficult to work.'[6] In his very next sentence after quoting this, Forster would have us believe that the incommunicable idea was, in fact, almost at once confided to him:

The story, I learnt immediately afterward, was to be that of the murder of a nephew by his uncle; the originality of which was to consist in the review of the murderer's career by himself at the close, when its temptations were to be dwelt upon as if, not he the culprit, but some other man, were the tempted. The last chapters were to be written in the condemned cell, to which his wickedness, all elaborately elicited from him as if told of another, had brought him. Discovery

---

[1] Dolby, pp. 416–17.   [2] Forster, xi. 2.
[3] See Madeline House and Graham Storey, *The Letters of Charles Dickens* (vol. i, 1965), p. xv; and Felix Aylmer, *The Drood Case* (1964), p. 201.
[4] Forster, ix. 7.   [5] Dolby, p. 434.
[6] Forster, xi. 2 (letter of 6 Aug.).

by the murderer of the utter needlessness of the murder for its object, was to follow hard upon commission of the deed; but all discovery of the murderer was to be baffled till towards the close, when, by means of a gold ring which had resisted the corrosive effects of the lime into which he had thrown the body, not only the person murdered was to be identified but the locality of the crime and the man who committed it. So much was told to me before any of the book was written; and it will be recollected that the ring, taken by Drood to be given to his betrothed only if their engagement went on, was brought away with him from their last interview. Rosa was to marry Tartar, and Crisparkle the sister of Landless, who was himself, I think, to have perished in assisting Tartar finally to unmask and seize the murderer.

Forster's summary of the plot has aroused much speculation as to whether this was an accurate recollection of what he had been told, or an account coloured by his own conclusions after reading the book. However, we have other testimony which shows plainly what was the question that was to keep the reader guessing, though the answer can never be known to everyone's satisfaction.

On Friday 20 August Dickens was trying out possible titles for his new novel.[1] The last on his list puts the enigma most pithily: 'Dead? Or alive?' Of the seventeen titles,[2] ten seem designed to suggest this question, making use of such ambiguously suggestive words as 'Loss', 'Disappearance', or just plain 'Mystery'.[3] Two titles, 'The flight of Edwyn Drood' and 'Edwin Drood in hiding', may be a more deliberately misleading way of covering the same question (Was his suspected flight or hiding—the possibility raised in chapter xvi—really death?), or they may be intended more literally as leading to the further mystery: Why was Edwin Drood in hiding? In a sense, this is an aspect of the same question; for the obvious answer would be: Because his uncle had tried to murder him. All the titles so far discussed, except one, direct the attention to one character, Edwin, though, by implication, to his murderer, or would-be murderer, also. The one exception is 'The Mystery in the Drood Family', and it is possible, but does not seem necessary to posit, that there was some further mystery, which Edwin was trying to uncover—or conceal. Four of the remaining titles introduce Jasper, one merely linking him with Edwin—'The Two Kinsmen', three focusing the attention on his behaviour through the greater part of the novel: 'Sworn to avenge it', 'One Object in Life', 'A Kinsman's Devotion'. These are all, of course, perfectly consistent

[1] See Appendix A below. According to Dolby, p. 436, Dickens was for a long while 'sorely puzzled' to find a title that pleased him.

[2] Some of these show variants in spelling only, but they have been counted separately as still showing persistence of ideas.

[3] Cf. Dickens's reply to his sister-in-law's inquiry about the novel's outcome: 'I call my book the Mystery, not the History, of Edwin Drood.' Quoted in 'Edwin Drood, and the Last Days of Charles Dickens', by Kate Perugini, Pall Mall Magazine (June 1906), p. 654.

with Forster's statement and with the story which could be behind the other titles. There is no contradiction, merely a change of emphasis. The last title to be discussed perhaps gives a little more weight to the 'hiding' theory, if indeed it does refer to Edwin: 'Flight And Pursuit' at least suggests the idea of a pursuit ending in the escaper's capture and return. The reference may, of course, be to Jasper's pursuit of Neville, as the surrounding titles, with their words 'Devotion', 'avenge', 'One Object', indicate. Another possibility is that this, the only title not tied to specific characters, was considered as capable of multiple interpretations, not all of them literal, including, for example, Jasper's 'flight' from his real condition.[1] Beyond this idea of the book's theme, and three essential characters, a victim, an avenger, and a suspect to be hunted down, we also have at this early date a glimpse of the clerical setting, in the inclusion among the characters of 'The Dean', 'Mrs Dean', and 'Miss Dean', with the suggestion of gentle fun or satire inherent in the manner of their listing, and an indication of probably less gentle satire to be directed at the self-explanatory character 'Mr Honeythunder' or 'Mr Honeyblast'. This element of satire, present from the start, was perhaps intended as something topical to add body to the central story.[2]

That Dickens's speculations at this point were not confined to the ingredients of the novel or the desired emphasis of its title, but included also the proposed form of the new work, is indicated in a letter to Frederick Chapman written on the same day as the trial titles.[3] Dickens's mind was attracted by two possible alternatives of publication: twelve monthly numbers complete in themselves, and weekly parts in *All the Year Round*.

---

[1] Cf. Charles Collins's comments on Jasper's pursuit of himself (below, Appendix E).

[2] The possible connection of Honeythunder with the Governor Eyre case has been noted, for example by K. J. Fielding in *Charles Dickens. A Critical Introduction* (2nd edn., 1965), p. 175: '. . . whereas Mill, Darwin, and Huxley demanded an inquiry, Dickens allied himself with Tennyson, Carlyle, and Governor Eyre. The pious philanthropist Honeythunder, in *Edwin Drood*, was probably a satire on those who followed Mill.' Durdles's sodden musing over his provision for Deputy, 'a sort of a—scheme of a— National Education' (ch. v), may reflect interest in the debates on Education prior to the 1870 Act, and the brief account of Bazzard's dramatic circle, which the *Athenaeum* reviewer suspected to be, not 'a chance shot', but 'one steadily aimed at a certain society', is perhaps a humorous glance at the 'Syncretic Society' of unacted dramatists and others, which flourished in the early 1840s (see *N*, i. 582). For examination of the local Rochester background, the portraits from life such as Tope and Durdles, and the dating of the story in the 1840s, see Robert Langton, *Charles Dickens and Rochester* (1889); William R. Hughes, *A Week's Tramp in Dickensland* (1891); Edwin Harris, *John Jasper's Gatehouse* (1931), and a pamphlet, *The Rochester of 'Edwin Drood'*, in the Duffield collection at Dickens House; Percy T. Carden, *The Murder of Edwin Drood* (1920), Appendix II. Deputy's 'Widdy widdy wen!' chant is a slight variation of a verse used in a popular children's game: see *English Dialect Dictionary* under 'Widdy-Widdy-Way'. The detail of Cloisterham life creates an impression of authentic and recognizable local background for the more exotic elements introduced by Jasper and the Landlesses.

[3] 20 Aug. 1869, in the collection of N. C. Peyrouton.

Chapman's advice obviously inclined to the former, and within two days
Dickens was writing to Frederick Ouvry to arrange the contract.[1] A
prospective illustrator was found in Wilkie Collins's brother Charles, and
instructions were accordingly sent to Chapman and Hall:

Charles Collins wishes to try his hand at illustrating my new book. I want him
to try the cover first. Please send down to him at Gad's Hill, any of our old green
covers that you may have by you.[2]

According to Dolby, by 27 September the title was decided and a dinner
was given to celebrate.[3]

It is not until October that we hear of the actual writing of the first
Number—Forster records that the summer and autumn of 1869, following
Dickens's breakdown in April, were passed quietly at Gad's Hill[4]—but the
preliminary calendar is not complete without mention of two related
topics, one closely related, the other more curiously: the visits made by
Dickens with his American friends and the publication of *John Acland*.
Contemporary records—those of Dickens himself, and of Fields, Forster,
and Dolby—agree as to the authenticity of the opening scene in Princess
Puffer's den: the description was based on first-hand experience of a visit
to 'Opium Sal', a visit made by Dickens in the company of J. T. Fields,
of the American firm of Fields, Osgood and Co., who were to be the first
American publishers of *Edwin Drood*, George Dolby, the manager of his
latest reading tours, and two officers of some kind who acted as guides.
Dickens's reference to this visit is in a letter dated 5 May 1870, to Sir John
Bowring, the authority whom he consulted on the effects of opium smoking in the east:

I send you many cordial thanks for your note, and the very curious drawing
accompanying it. I ought to tell you, perhaps, that the opium smoking I have
described, I saw (exactly as I have described it, penny ink-bottle and all) down
in Shadwell this last autumn. A couple of the Inspectors of Lodging-Houses
knew the woman and took me to her as I was making a round with them to see
for myself the working of Lord Shaftesbury's Bill.[5]

Several later writers have accepted this autumn dating[6] and it has been
more particularly identified as 9 October, when Fields is known to have
visited Dickens. This is very close to the date at which he must have been
writing the opening chapter, and, as the evidence of Fields and Dolby,
and possibly Forster, suggests an earlier visit, it seems likely that the
autumn visit was in the nature of a refresher, when he had definitely

[1] N, iii. 739–40. [2] N, iii. 742 (letter of 24 Sept.). [3] Dolby, p. 436.
[4] Forster, xii. 1. [5] N, iii. 775.
[6] e.g. Philip Collins, 'Inspector Bucket Visits the Princess Puffer', *Dickensian*, lx
(1964), pp. 88–90. Andrew Lang is an exception: in his Introduction to the Gadshill
edition (1899), p. vii, he speaks of a summer expedition.

decided to incorporate the material in his new book.[1] Of course, Dickens
could have conceived the idea of Jasper as an opium smoker without the
stimulus of visiting an opium den, but it is possible that an earlier visit
had helped, perhaps unconsciously, to form this idea in his mind. The
testimony of Fields is the most definite on the subject of the date, and the
most detailed in its description of the visit. Following a letter dated
Tuesday 25 May, which refers to 'the rendezvous for Monday evening
. . . *at half past eight* . . . with the great Detective', his recollections of the
summer expeditions continue:

Two of these expeditions were made on two consecutive nights, under the
protection of police detailed for the service. On one of these nights we also
visited the lock-up houses, watch-houses, and opium-eating establishments. It
was in one of the horrid opium-dens that he gathered the incidents which he has
related in the opening pages of "Edwin Drood". In a miserable court we found
the haggard old woman blowing at a kind of pipe made of an old penny ink-
bottle. The identical words which Dickens puts into the mouth of this wretched
creature in "Edwin Drood" we heard her croon as we leaned over the tattered bed
on which she was lying. There was something hideous in the way this woman
kept repeating, 'Ye'll pay up according, deary, won't ye?' and the Chinamen
and Lascars made never-to-be-forgotten pictures in the scene. I watched
Dickens intently as he went among these outcasts of London, and saw with what
deep sympathy he encountered the sad and suffering in their horrid abodes.

Fields's memories of these excursions conclude:

Many days and weeks passed over after those June days were ended before we
were to see Dickens again. . . . A small roll of manuscript in his hand led him
soon to confess that a new story was already begun; but this communication
was made in the utmost confidence. . . .[2]

One other visit made by the group in the summer of 1869 may well have
had its bearing on *Edwin Drood*: it certainly shows the same sensitive
reaction. Both Fields and Dolby record a visit to Canterbury during which
Dickens, in particular, was revolted by the apathetic performance of the
service:

The seeming indifference of the officiating clergy jarred most acutely on
Dickens's feelings, for he, who did all things so thoroughly, could not conceive
how (as he afterwards said) any person accepting an office, or a trust so important
as the proper rendering of our beautiful Cathedral Service, could go through

[1] There is ample evidence, both from the recollections of acquaintances and from
Dickens himself, of his frequent visits to this neighbourhood; see, for example, letter
to Wilkie Collins, 8 Dec. 1868 (*N*, iii. 681).
[2] *N*, iii. 727; and James T. Fields, *In and Out of Doors with Charles Dickens* (James R.
Osgood and Co., Boston, 1876), pp. 105–6, 138. (The firm was first Ticknor and Fields,
then Fields, Osgood and Co., then James R. Osgood and Co.) See also Dolby, pp. 416–
19, 434; and Forster, xii. 1.

their duties in this mechanical and slipshod fashion. He returned to this subject on several subsequent occasions.[1]

Closely applicable as this is to *Edwin Drood*, it is likely that if either Dolby or Fields had been consciously influenced by the novel to read more into the experience than was at the time justified, the parallel with Jasper would have been made. From revulsion from a response no longer anything but mechanical, felt by Dickens in respect of the Canterbury clergymen, the imaginative step is easy to the horror of experiencing the deadness in oneself:

I hate it. The cramped monotony of my existence grinds me away by the grain. How does our service sound to you? . . . It often sounds to me quite devilish. I am so weary of it. The echoes of my own voice among the arches seem to mock me with my daily drudging round. No wretched monk who droned his life away in that gloomy place, before me, can have been more tired of it than I am. He could take for relief (and did take) to carving demons out of the stalls and seats and desks. What shall I do? Must I take to carving them out of my heart?

This note sounded in the first Number (ch. ii)—Jasper's keynote—is reinforced in the last chapter as we have it, a point intended as about half-way through the book, and intended also, with its setting and title, 'The Dawn again', to reinvoke the opening vision of Jasper. This time the wording is even more strikingly close to the words of Dolby:

Constantly exercising an Art which brought him into mechanical harmony with others, and which could not have been pursued unless he and they had been in the nicest mechanical relations and unison, it is curious to consider that the spirit of the man was in moral accordance or interchange with nothing around him.

It is a notable feature of Jasper's presentation that his beautiful singing voice is stressed in circumstances which invite the reader to view him in a discreditable light: in the 'unaccountable expedition' chapter (p. 103: 'he sits chanting choir-music in a low and beautiful voice, for two or three hours'), in the Christmas Eve chapter (p. 128: 'Mr. Jasper is in beautiful voice this day. In the pathetic supplication to have his heart inclined to keep this law, he quite astonishes his fellows by his melodious power'), and again in the last chapter, in the opium den (p. 206: 'What a sweet singer you was when you first come! Used to drop your head, and sing yourself off, like a bird!'). Admittedly, the second of these occasions marks a plot necessity, to introduce the reference to the 'large black scarf',

[1] Dolby, p. 426. See also Fields, p. 131. That this was not a new preoccupation for Dickens is attested by an article on 'The Doom of English Wills', *Household Words*, 28 Sept. 1850, in which reference is made to 'the shivering choristers on a winter morning, huddling on their gowns as they drowsily go to scamper through their work . . . the drawling voice, without a heart, that drearily pursues the dull routine . . .'. See *The Uncollected Writings of Charles Dickens*, ed. Harry Stone (2 vols., Bloomington, Ind., 1968; London, 1969), i. 164–6.

but a secondary, and by no means negligible, effect is to emphasize the sinister nature of outward beauty masking inward hatred and discord.

So far, then, we have coming together, before the actual writing of the book begins, the boy and girl element, Dickens's new and curious idea, the 'dead or alive' question, the opium-den setting, and the jarring apprehension of the gulf between delighted awareness of beauty or truth and mere dulled, mechanical acceptance of it.

The story of *John Acland* deserves brief mention as a last and curiously-timed preliminary, one which throws the speculations roused by the trial titles into a better perspective. On 2 September 1869 Dickens wrote to Robert Lytton, the son of Bulwer Lytton, accepting 'most willingly' a story to which he refers as *John Acland*, but of which the full title presumably was *The Murder of John Acland*, for publication in the 'next monthly part' of *All the Year Round*. As often, Dickens proposed certain improvements, one of great interest in relation to *Edwin Drood*:

. . . I think you let the story out too much—prematurely[1]—and this I hope to prevent artfully. I think your title open to the same objection, and therefore propose to substitute:

THE DISAPPEARANCE
OF JOHN ACLAND

This will leave the reader in doubt whether he really *was* murdered, until the end.[2]

On 18 September *The Disappearance of John Acland, A True Story in 13 chapters* duly began: the number for the following week contained chapters 2, 3, and 4; and so it went on through 2, 9, and 16 October until all 13 chapters had appeared, but, although the story is complete, chapters 5–13 are so short as to arouse speculation in the most passive reader. The reason for this hasty end was given in a further letter from Dickens to Lytton, dated 1 October:

I am assured by a correspondent that John Acland has been done before. Said correspondent has evidently read the story—and is almost confident in Chambers's Journal. This is very unfortunate, but of course cannot be helped. . . .

You will of course understand that I do not tell you this by way of complaint. Indeed, I should not have mentioned it at all, but as an explanation to you of my reason for winding the story up (which I have done to-day) as expeditiously as possible. . . . You could not help it any more than I could, and therefore will not be troubled by it any more than I am.[3]

The whole tone of the letter is reassuring and kindly, designed to spare any embarrassment on the part of the young writer,[4] and there is no reason

---

[1] Cf. Dickens's worries about the progress of his own novel, pp. xxv–xxvii below.
[2] *N*, iii. 740.   [3] *N*, iii. 743.
[4] This intention is reiterated in an unpublished letter of 21 Oct. (MS Lytton Papers) in which Dickens expressed his conviction that it was better not to institute a search for the original.

to suspect Dickens's motives in bringing the story to so rapid a conclusion. The important thing is that he had willingly accepted it a month before, and this would seem surprising if he had already determined the identical major interest for his own new story, which he was possibly even then writing and which would obviously appear within a few months. The implication seems clearly to be that, whatever speculations some of the trial titles may arouse, Dickens's chief interest was not a mere plot resolution, one, indeed, which could only rather naïvely be described as 'a very curious and new idea'; that Forster, in fact, was right in his emphasis: 'the originality of which was to consist in the review of the murderer's career by himself at the close, when its temptations were to be dwelt upon as if, not he the culprit, but some other man, were the tempted.' The interest of *Edwin Drood* is in Jasper, the man out of harmony with outwardly harmonious surroundings, who finds consolation in opium dreams, the man whose character we can see growing in the preliminary stages to the novel's writing.[1] This was the view of another contemporary authority, Kate Perugini, whose first husband had designed the cover,[2] expressed in answer to the strong interest which the mere plot question had evoked since her father's death:

If those who are interested in the subject will carefully read what I have quoted [from Forster], they will not be able to detect any word or hint from my father that it was upon the Mystery alone that he relied for the interest and originality of his idea. The originality was to be shown, as he tells us, in what we may call the psychological description the murderer gives us of his temptations, temperament, and character, as if told by another. . . . I do not mean to imply that the mystery itself had no strong hold on my father's imagination; but, greatly as he was interested in the intricacies of that tangled skein, the information he voluntarily gave to Mr. Forster, from whom he had withheld nothing for thirty-three years, certainly points to the fact that he was quite as deeply fascinated and absorbed in the study of the criminal Jasper, as in the dark and sinister crime that has given the book its title. . . .

It was not, I imagine, for the intricate working out of his plot alone, that my father cared to write this story; but it was through his wonderful observation of character, and his strange insight into the tragic secrets of the human heart, that he desired his greatest triumph to be achieved.[3]

While *John Acland* was reaching its abrupt end, *Edwin Drood* was beginning to take shape. On 17 October Dickens wrote to Percy Fitz-

---

[1] There is no resemblance between the two stories in respect of characters, character-relationships, setting, or emphasis of interest. What possible links there are, are purely 'detective plot' features: the mystification of the reader over the question of murder, the production of jewellery in evidence, a broken love affair, the introduction of a young lady of magnetic powers (compare the sympathy which exists between Helena and Neville), the zeal of the murderer in unravelling the case, and the preservation of the body.

[2] See Appendix E below.   [3] Perugini, pp. 643–54.

gerald, 'I am at work upon a new book', and the next day he informed his old friend Macready more specifically:

This leaves me in the preliminary agonies of a new book, which I hope to begin publishing (in twelve numbers, not twenty) next March. The coming readings being all in London, and being, after the first fortnight, only once a week, will divert my attention very little, I hope.[1]

By the third week of October, Number 1 was finished: it was read at Forster's house 'with great spirit' on 26 October,[2] and Fields, too, was privileged to hear in advance the first instalment, 'the concluding lines of which initial pages were then scarcely dry from the pen'.[3] In late October and November there are various references to work on the 'new book';[4] negotiations for its simultaneous publication in America were under way,[5] and then came the first set-back. Charles Collins, whose cover had been pronounced 'well worth £10',[5] was too ill to go on with the work of illustrating. Dickens wrote to Frederic Chapman on Sunday 28 November:

Charles Collins finds that the sitting down to draw, brings back all the worst symptoms of the old illness that occasioned him to leave his old pursuit of painting; and here we are suddenly without an Illustrator! We will use his cover of course, but he gives in altogether as to further subjects.

I knew this only last night and I lose no time in writing to you. There is no time to be lost, and we must immediately consider what is to be done.[6]

Something was done quickly. A letter preserved in the Duffield collection at Dickens House, dated 28 November 1927, from W. H. Chambers to Howard Duffield, in response to a request for information about Fildes, with whom Chambers was personally acquainted, gives the following account of the discovery of a new illustrator for *Edwin Drood*:

It appears that "Millais" the Artist was staying with Dickens at Gadds Hill and a copy of "The Graphic" containing an illustration by Fildes was sent there. The title of this was I think "Houseless and Homeless." Millais rushed into Dickens' room waving the paper over his head exclaiming "I've got him"— "Got who" said Dickens. "A man to illustrate your Edwin Drood." Millais spread the paper on the desk in front of Dickens. "Who is the artist" said Dickens. "A rising young man on the staff of The Graphic" said Millais. "Yes, I'll write to him" Dickens said. Fildes showed the letter to me. It ran, "I see

[1] N, iii. 745-6.   [2] Forster, xii. 1.
[3] Fields, p. 141. If these two writers are correct in their recollections of dates and details, Fields may have heard the reading two days in advance of Forster, on Sunday 24 Oct.
[4] N, iii. 749, 751 (to T. A. Trollope, 4 Nov., and to Mrs. Frances Elliot, 23 Nov.).
[5] N, iii. 748 (to Frederic Chapman, 29 Oct.). There were complications with American publishers; see pp. xxx–xxxii below.
[6] N, iii. 753. See also 759-60 for Dickens's praise of Collins's 'charming cover'. The cover as designed by Collins was subsequently revised by Fildes. See Appendix E below.

from your illustration in The Graphic this week that you are an adept at drawing scamps, send me some specimens of pretty ladies." Fildes did so, and was invited to Gadds Hill.

Other recollections of this incident vary slightly in detail, but corroborate Chambers's account in substance. The actual title of Fildes's illustration was 'Houseless and Hungry', later re-entitled 'The Casuals'. It appeared in the first issue of the *Graphic* on 4 December. It is ironic that this number also contained an announcement which had to be retracted the following week, of the name of Dickens's new illustrator, Charles Collins.

In the meantime, just when Dickens was faced with the problem of finding a new illustrator, came an even more serious set-back, with the arrival of the proofs of the first two Numbers from the printers on 1 December.[1] We have it on the evidence of Fields[2] that Dickens's eagerness to see his work in print never abated with familiarity, but on this occasion pleasure would seem to have been more than outweighed by shock: each of the Numbers was six pages short, a disaster which necessitated renewed planning and extra work during December, a time which he had set aside for other pressing commitments:

When I had written and, as I thought, disposed of the first two Numbers of my story, Clowes informed me to my horror that they were, together, *twelve printed pages too short!!!* Consequently I had to transpose a chapter from number two to number one, and remodel number two altogether! This was the more unlucky, that it came upon me at the time when I was obliged to leave the book, in order to get up the Readings, quite gone out of my mind since I left them off. However, I turned to it and got it done, and both numbers are now in type.[3]

[1] *N*, iii. 753 (to Georgina Hogarth). According to a letter referred to in the House of El Dieff catalogue, n.d. (stamped 7 May 1950), the last part of Number II was sent to the printers on 27 Nov.

[2] Fields, pp. 146–7: '. . . he once told me that all his life long he never got over the thrill of pleasure and interest which accompanied the first sight in type of anything he had written.'

[3] *N*, iii. 754; and Forster, xi. 2 (letter of 22 Dec.). An additional passage was inserted in Number I to make up the necessary length: the account of Rosa's birthday party in ch. iii. The chapter transposed was ch. v, 'Mr. Durdles and Friend', originally ch. viii. An interesting passage was removed from this chapter, presumably in consequence of its changed position, a passage which would have made a much earlier link for the reader between the opium woman, Deputy, and Jasper's life in Cloisterham. See p. 37 and Number Plan for ch. viii, Appendix B below. Dickens obviously decided to postpone Princess Puffer's appearance in Cloisterham, as, with extra pages to find for Number II, he preferred to write new material rather than to introduce her, as he had originally intended, on the night after the dinner party (ch. viii). Perhaps he felt that too many appearances would detract from her effectiveness, turning her into a melodramatic figure of Nemesis and making it the less likely that her discovery of Jasper's identity could be so delayed. Certainly, Christmas Eve (ch. xiv) is the most dramatic occasion for her appearance in Cloisterham (this may have been planned from the start as one of her appearances; see p. xxvi n.), and, in spite of some difficulty in working out a time schedule, the reader will readily believe that Jasper would need a further visit to the opium den after witnessing the fervent parting between Edwin and Rosa at the end of

No wonder that he told Wills two days later, 'I have been so put about', nor that he wrote to J. H. Chamberlain on 31 December, 'The work I have before me the next three months is the virtuous cause to which I am so true, and I sacrifice every tempting engagement to it'.[1] Never had Dickens underwritten a Number by quite so much before—according to Forster 2½ pages had shocked him in *Our Mutual Friend*;[2] nevertheless, the business like way in which he 'turned to it' and worked at speed seems not to have detracted from his enjoyment of the new novel: on New Year's Eve the second Number was read at Forster's house with 'such an overflow of humour' for Mr. Honeythunder's 'boisterous philanthropy' that 'there was no room, then, for anything but enjoyment.'[3] The New Year was, however, to bring the additional burden of the final series of readings, planned for Tuesday 11 January to Tuesday 15 March, twelve readings in all, including the exhausting 'Sikes and Nancy' murder scenes, and Dickens's letters at this time show the strain of carrying on the two kinds of work simultaneously. To Fields, on 14 January, he admitted that the readings disturbed him at his 'book-work'; 'nevertheless I hope, please God, to lose no way on their account',[4] and the same note, of difficulties hopefully borne, was sounded a week later in a letter to W. H. Wills:

I hope, now I have got over the mornings, that I may be able to work at my book. But up to this time the great preparation required in getting the subjects up again, and the twice a week besides, have almost exclusively occupied me.[5]

Throughout the following month the pressure continued. On 26 February Dickens wrote to G. H. Lewes: 'Between my readings, my book, my weekly journal . . . I am really hard put to it occasionally . . .',[6] and Dolby, who saw so much of him at this time, bears witness, like Forster, to the utter prostration which often followed on the 'Sikes and Nancy' reading and the disturbing after-effects of the readings generally.[7] At this time,

ch. xiii. Dickens's words about remodelling Number II altogether are rather exaggerated: a new chapter, 'Birds in the Bush', had to be written, but the existing chapters remained substantially the same. 'Birds in the Bush' was, in fact, overwritten and had to be shortened at proof stage. Dickens had to increase the number of manuscript pages for subsequent Numbers. See p. xlvi below.

[1] *N*, iii. 755, 6.   [2] Forster, ix. 5.   [3] Forster, xii. 1.   [4] *N*, iii. 759–60.
[5] *N*, iii. 761–2 (23 Jan.). In this letter Dickens himself admitted to Wills, as he did also to Dolby, the exhausting effect of the 'Sikes and Nancy' scenes, the first reading of which he had given on Friday 21 Jan. Morning readings were included in the first two weeks for the benefit of the London actors and actresses, who had particularly requested to hear the *Oliver Twist* murder scenes. See Dolby, pp. 400, 441; and Forster, xii. 1.
[6] *N*, iii. 764.
[7] Dolby refers to Dickens's anxiety to have the new book as far forward as possible before the readings began; the strain of the readings, rising pulse, inability to speak a rational or consecutive sentence for ten minutes after the 'Murder' (pp. 441–4). See also Forster, xii. 1. One after-effect of the murder reading Dolby had noted earlier (p. 386); namely, a craving to do the work over again, an experience which may well have influenced Dickens's conception of Jasper's reactions.

too, attention had to be given to examining the work of the prospective illustrator of *Edwin Drood*: Dickens's approval of 'the highly meritorious and interesting specimens of your art that you have had the kindness to send me'¹ augured well for the collaboration with Fildes. Another encouraging sign was Forster's enthusiastic reception of Number II: the value that Dickens placed on his friend's opinion can be heard in his genial report to Fields that Forster thinks it 'a clincher', and this appreciation from one of his closest friends may have helped to sustain him in the careful planning and thought necessary for the writing of the next part:

There is a curious interest steadily working up to No. 5, which requires a great deal of art and self-denial. I think also, apart from character and picturesqueness, that the young people are placed in a very novel situation. So I hope—at Nos. 5 and 6 the story will turn upon an interest suspended until the end.²

Clearly, in spite of the strain, Dickens was able to work at his book. Number III was at the printers' by 13 February—a letter of 18 February to Clowes refers to the last two-thirds of his 'precious child' deposited last Sunday,³ and on 25 February this Number was read to Forster, who records no comment beyond the recollection that Dickens's hand was 'still swollen and painful' at the time.⁴

In March the prospect seemed cheerful: the readings were attracting 'immense audiences'; Dickens was getting on well with his writing, and Fildes was making preparations for a brother-student to engrave his drawings.⁵ Arrangements had been made for a German translation of the novel by Dr. Lehmann of Hamburg;⁶ Number I was advertised in *All the Year Round* on Saturday 19 March;⁷ two days later the fourth Number was 'read admirably' to Forster;⁸ on 26 March Number I was sent to Sir Arthur Helps for the Queen, with a promise of further advance instalments, if desired,⁹ and then, on 31 March, the first Number, for April, was published. By this time Dickens was free from the anxiety of the public

---

¹ Dated in *N*, iii. 760–1, as Wednesday 16 January, but with a note correctly suggesting February as more probable.

² *N*, iii. 759–60 (letter of 14 Jan.). The 'curious interest' may well refer to Edwin's disappearance and the speculations roused in the reader as to Jasper's conscious or unconscious part in it. Dickens did not at first anticipate getting through his material so quickly. See Appendix B below, plans for Nos. III, IV, and V.

³ W. B. Clowes, *Family Business, 1803–1953* [1953], p. 50.

⁴ Forster, xii. 1.

⁵ *N*, iii. 764–5 (to Macready, 2 Mar.); 766 (to Frederic Chapman, 14 Mar.).

⁶ *N*, iii. 767 (17 Mar.).

⁷ It had already been advertised in the *Publishers' Circular* on 1 Mar. and in the *Athenaeum* as early as 26 Feb. The advertisement described it as 'To be completed in TWELVE MONTHLY Numbers, uniform with the Original Editions of 'Pickwick' and 'Copperfield'. The *Athenaeum*'s 'Literary Gossip' in the previous week had given advance announcement of the title.

⁸ Forster, xii. 1.   ⁹ *N*, iii. 768.

readings. In his farewell speech he had made reference to his forthcoming new contact with his audiences:

In but two short weeks from this time I hope that you may enter, in your own homes, on a new series of readings at which my assistance will be indispensable; but from these garish lights I vanish now for evermore . . .[1]

Everything seemed set for success: he had 'great hopes' of his new illustrator; he was hard at work all day, and 'We have been doing wonders with No. I of Edwin Drood. *It has very, very far outstripped every one of its predecessors.*'[2] The writing of the fifth Number was, however, proving difficult: within a week of sounding this confident note he was confessing to Charles Kent: 'For the last week I have been most perseveringly and ding-dong-doggedly at work, making headway but slowly.'[3] Attention has already been drawn to the evidence that Dickens was using up his material more quickly than he had initially planned, and in Forster's view the fifth Number caused him some apprehension on this score. Forster's singling out of the introduction of Datchery as an example of material introduced too early[4] led to some confusion among later critics. Whether Dickens himself specified this instance to his sister-in-law or Forster originated the suggestion as a likely example, what he said was that 'the incidents leading on to the catastrophe' were brought in too early, not that any of them were misplaced with regard to their immediate context.[5] In fact, examination of the manuscript shows that Dickens very deliberately placed the Datchery chapter in its present position, preceding the account of Jasper's proposal. The chapters were planned in the reverse of this order and the page numbering shows that Dickens wrote the whole of the Jasper chapter and two pages of the Datchery chapter before deciding on the

[1] Forster, xii. 1.

[2] *N*, iii. 771 (to Frith, 16 Apr.; to Fields, 18 Apr.). The *Athenaeum*, 9 Apr., carried a notice to the effect that 'Part I having been out of print a few days, a fresh supply is now ready.'

[3] *N*, iii. 772 (25 Apr.).

[4] Forster, xi. 2. According to Forster, Dickens expressed his misgivings to his sister-in-law.

[5] The search for Datchery's identity led to ingenious suppositions as to the misplacing of the chapter, in order that Helena and Grewgious, or an employee of Grewgious, might be considered among likely candidates. The fact that Dickens saw the proofs for Number V (see below, p. xxix) disposes of any suspicion that the chapter was accidentally misplaced. Henry Fielding Dickens, in 'A Chat about Charles Dickens' published in *Harper's Monthly Magazine* (July 1914), emphatically denied that his father's anxiety related specifically to the misplacing of Datchery: 'That is not at all a correct description of what he did in fact say. He never suggested to her that he had introduced Datchery out of his proper place in the book; but that, having regard to the fact that he had still six more numbers to write, the whole story was advancing too rapidly. It was for this reason that he wrote a new scene, the manuscript of which was found among his papers after his death.'

transposition.[1] This makes no appreciable difference to the chronology, as Rosa's flight obviously follows Jasper's proposal:[2] what it does is to avoid an undramatic interpolation breaking the tension of the reader's feeling for Rosa, and draw his notice clearly to the presence of Datchery in Cloisterham at the time of Jasper's scene with Rosa. The right-hand plan for Number V records the change of order; the left-hand plan, with its reference to 'Kinfrederel', suggests the possibility that Datchery's encounter with Deputy was initially planned for Number V, the 'Mystery' Number, whereas Jasper could not have approached Rosa until after Edwin's disappearance, possibly in Number VI, for which no left-hand plan survives.[3]

There is evidence that Dickens was worried about aspects of his story other than the introduction of Datchery. Luke Fildes's letter of 27 October 1905 (printed in the *Times Literary Supplement*, 3 November) reveals that he had questioned Dickens as to the importance of the long scarf, which Jasper wears in Number IV (ch. xiv), as he had previously drawn Jasper wearing a little black tie. After appearing momentarily disconcerted at having revealed too much at too early a stage, Dickens confided to his illustrator that the scarf was necessary, 'for Jasper strangles Edwin Drood with it'. Fildes's recollections clearly suggest that Dickens had not expected the reader so readily to associate Jasper with the role of murderer. Presumably this discussion took place some time in April, while Dickens was working on the fifth Number, and anxiety over the general progress of his story would be a natural consequence.[4] That Dickens was anxious in the later stages of his writing was confirmed by the testimony of his eldest son, Charles Dickens junior, in his Introduction to Macmillan's edition of *Edwin Drood* (1923):

It was during the last walk I ever had with him at Gadshill, and our talk, which had been principally concerned with literary matters connected with *All the*

[1] The pages of 'Shadow on the Sun Dial', intended for ch. xviii, were numbered originally 10–13, subsequently changed to 15–18; the first two pages of 'A Settler in Cloisterham' were originally numbered 14 and 15, and 14 was headed 'Chapter xix'. 'Shadow on the Sun Dial' is about half a page shorter than the other.

[2] If Dickens had ever intended Datchery's appearance to be a consequence of Rosa's fear, he would have had to postpone it until after ch. xx.

[3] An alternative, and perhaps likelier, possibility is that at this early stage of planning the character of Datchery had not yet been conceived; the word 'Kinfrederel' might have been a cue for the opium woman's reappearance in Deputy's company on the night of the Mystery. See Number Plans (Appendix B below), and comment on change in the cover drawing (Appendix E below).

[4] As in the case of Forster's remark concerning Datchery, later critics have read more into Fildes's story than was justified, assuming that some alteration in either text or illustration had to be made. The manuscript shows that no adjustment was made in the writing, and Fildes himself protested that he discussed the problem with Dickens before making his drawing, and then deliberately avoided a scene in which Jasper would have to be shown wearing the noticeable scarf. See *Dickensian*, xxiii (1927), pp. 157–60, article by W. Laurence Gadd.

Year Round, presently drifting to *Edwin Drood*, my father asked me if I did not
think that he had let out too much of his story too soon. I assented, and added,
"Of course, Edwin Drood was murdered?" Whereupon he turned upon me with
an expression of astonishment at my having asked such an unnecessary question,
and said: "Of course; what else do you suppose?"[1]

Dickens had had difficulties with his writing before,[2] but this was his last
novel, unfinished at the time of his death, and in the circumstances it is
perhaps not surprising that rumours as to his difficulties spread. Rudolf
Lehmann, for example, in his *Reminiscences*, affirmed on the authority of
Wills that Dickens had reached a point at which he could see no way to a
solution:

While in the midst of the serial publication of 'The Mystery of Edwin Drood' he
altered the plot and found himself hopelessly entangled, as in a maze of which
he could not find the issue. Mr. Wills had no doubt that the anxiety and subsequent excitement materially contributed to his sudden and premature death.[3]

Dion Boucicault, too,[4] was reported to have been told by Dickens himself
that he did not know how to end the story.[5] Dickens's remark to Boucicault, if authentic, may, however, have been a way of fobbing off too
pertinent inquiries, in the same category as his reproof to Georgina, 'I
call my book the Mystery, not the History, of Edwin Drood'; and there is
nothing in the plans for the novel to corroborate Wills's statement as to the
altered plot. The enigmatic 'Sapsea fragment', discovered by Forster among
Dickens's manuscripts after his death, does, with its introduction of a
character, Poker, in a situation similar to that of Datchery, indicate hesitation and rewriting at the point when the vitally important 'detective'
character was to be introduced, but it can hardly be, as Forster suggests,[6]

---

[1] p. xv.

[2] See, for example, Forster, ix. 5, with respect to *Our Mutual Friend*.

[3] *An Artist's Reminiscences* (1894), pp. 231–2. The Lehmann family had close connec-
tions with Dickens: two of the brothers, Frederick and Rudolf, married two of the
daughters of R. C. Chambers, the third of whom married Wills. The son of Frederick
and Nina, Rudolph Chambers Lehmann, was the editor of *Charles Dickens as Editor*,
Dickens's letters to Wills. A third brother, Emil, was chosen as the translator of *Edwin
Drood* into German. The latter's son, C. F. Lehmann-Haupt, was convinced that there
was no significance in Wills's remark to his uncle. In a letter to Howard Duffield, now
at Dickens House, dated 19 April 1929, he wrote: '. . . there cannot be any doubt that
Wills' utterance is quite authentic. *But* it only shows how far spread the quite erroneous
idea was that Dickens had ever changed the plot of Edwin Drood and found himself
hopelessly entangled . . .'. His chief support for this view seems, however, to have been
founded on nothing more than Mrs. Perugini's statements in her article in the *Pall Mall
Magazine* of 1906.

[4] For Boucicault's connection with *Edwin Drood* see Appendix G below.

[5] Eustace Conway, *Anthony Munday and Other Essays* (N.Y., 1927), p. 95. Conway
gave no source for his statement, which he himself was inclined to discredit as 'hardly
. . . possible'.

[6] Forster, xi. 2. See also Henry Fielding Dickens's comment cited on p. xxv n.

that Dickens was trying, rather belatedly, to delay his catastrophe by opening 'some fresh veins of character incidental to the interest, though not directly part of it . . .', for Poker's introduction is a parallel too close to that of Datchery to be a likely additional interest; the more reasonable assumption would be that this was a first draft later rejected.[1] Even if Forster were correct, this certainly does not amount to the hopeless state which Wills is said to have witnessed.[2]

The comments of Kate Perugini and of Henry Fielding Dickens strike a more positive, optimistic note,[3] but neither Forster nor the letters throw much light on Dickens's reactions in the last stages of the novel's progress, and there is little left to record but the bare facts. Number II was published on 30 April; Number V, including chapter xxi, which was eventually published as part of Number VI, was read to Forster on 7 May;[4] from 30 May onwards Dickens was at Gad's Hill working on Number VI; 31 May saw the publication of Number III, the last published Number that Dickens saw. In the last two or three days of his life he was hard at work on the novel—on 8 June, 'in excellent spirits about his book', he told Georgina and Mamie that he must finish Number VI that day,[5] the following being the day of his weekly visit to the *All the Year Round* office. Contrary to his usual custom, therefore, he worked most of the day, one of his activities being the writing of a letter to a correspondent who had objected to the passage in chapter x of *Edwin Drood* in which Crisparkle is compared to 'the highly-popular lamb who has so long and unresistingly

[1] See p. xlviii and Appendix C below. The striking reminiscence of Datchery is in the indirect manner in which the name of the newcomer is introduced:
Poker: I asked him his name.
"Mr Sapsea," he answered, looking down, "your penetration is so acute, your glance into the souls of your fellow men is so penetrating, that if I was hardy enough to deny that my name is Poker, what would it avail me?"
Datchery: "Take my hat down for a moment from that peg, will you? No, I don't want it; look into it. What do you see written there?"
The waiter read: "Datchery."
"Now you know my name," said the gentleman; "Dick Datchery." (Ch. xviii.)

[2] The idea that Dickens was in difficulties gained currency rapidly in America as well as in England. See R. Shelton MacKenzie, *Life of Charles Dickens* (Philadelphia, 1870), not always a reliable authority; Phebe Hanaford, *The Life and Writings of Charles Dickens* (Boston, 1882), which cites in evidence the London correspondent of the *Scotsman* for 11 June 1870; and F. B. Perkins, *Charles Dickens. His Life and Works* (N.Y., 1870).
[3] Kate Perugini (*Pall Mall Magazine*, June 1906) recalled her father's extraordinary interest in the development of the story, and Henry Fielding Dickens (*Harper's Monthly Magazine*, July 1914) corroborated his sister's view of the unusual clarity and brightness of his brain at the time.
[4] Forster, xii. 1.
[5] *Letters of Charles Dickens*, edited by his sister-in-law and his eldest daughter (1909; 1st edn., 1893), p. 748.

been led to the slaughter'.[1] Later in the same day he was taken ill, and he died on 9 June, leaving the sixth Number some six or seven pages short. The Number Plans give one more chapter heading for Number VI, but beyond that not even a title. Number IV appeared on 30 June. Number V had been set up in proof before Dickens's death, and among the alterations he made were several deletions to reduce the length to the necessary 32 pages. The last Number obviously had to be seen through the press by someone else, presumably Forster and perhaps Charles Dickens junior or Wills. Certain changes were made in the material of V and VI, in order to make up for the deficiency in length of Number VI. The excised passages from Number V were restored, and the extra material thus gained was split between the two Numbers: chapter xx, called in manuscript 'Divers Flights', became chapter xx, 'A Flight' (Number V), and chapter xxi, 'A Recognition' (Number VI).[2] The division was made at the one point where the narrative could reasonably be broken, but, even so, it is noticeably awkward compared with the transitions between previous Numbers. With these modifications of Dickens's intentions, the last Numbers were duly published: V on 31 July, VI on 31 August. Even with the addition of the 4 pages of the new chapter xxi, Number VI was $2\frac{1}{2}$ pages short of the customary 32. The one-volume issue appeared on the same date as the last monthly Number: included in the preliminary leaves which both contained was the following notice, dated 12 August:

All that was left in manuscript of EDWIN DROOD is contained in the Number now published—the sixth. Its last entire page had not been written two hours when the event occurred which one very touching passage in it (grave and sad but also cheerful and reassuring) might seem almost to have anticipated. The only notes in reference to the story that have since been found concern that portion of it exclusively, which is treated in the earlier Numbers. Beyond the clues therein afforded to its conduct or catastrophe, nothing whatever remains; and it is believed that what the author would himself have most desired is done, in placing before the reader without further note or suggestion the fragment of THE MYSTERY OF EDWIN DROOD.

The publishers' agreement for *Edwin Drood* had included, at Dickens's wish, but not, as Forster states, for the first time, a clause relating to the author's possible death, in which contingency Forster was to determine the amount of compensation to be paid to Frederic Chapman. The sum to be paid for *Edwin Drood* was £7,500 for 25,000 copies. Beyond that number

---

[1] *N*, iii. 784 (to John M. Makeham).

[2] Another, less ingenuous, device was adopted in Number V to persuade the readers that they were getting full measure. Whereas the normal number of lines to a printed page was 52 (47 for the opening page of a chapter), chs. xix and xx were printed with pages of 51 lines (45 and 44 for the opening pages; 46 in ch. xvii). The number of lines involved was a mere matter of 16, but this device, combined with that of starting each of these two chapters on a new page, contrary to the usual procedure, gave the impression that Number V was well up to the required length.

profits were to be shared equally between author and publisher, and according to Forster the number reached while Dickens was still alive was 50,000 copies.[1]

Since 1867, Ticknor and Fields, later Fields, Osgood and Company, had been the authorized American publishers of Dickens's works. The sum of £1,000 was paid for advance sheets of *Edwin Drood* for simultaneous publication in America, and the novel duly appeared there for the first time in the weekly magazine *Every Saturday*. According to the Chapman and Hall Accounts in the Forster collection, Victoria and Albert Museum, the monthly Numbers with their accompanying illustrations were sent to America regularly on the 3rd of the month, from March to August, except that on the first occasion, though the advance sheets went on 3 March, the illustrations and wrapper were not sent off until 7 March.[2] The intended arrangement was obviously that each month's portion should be split into weekly parts to appear on the Saturdays subsequent to that month's publication in England, but that there was some misunderstanding about the agreement is indicated in a letter of 14 May 1870 from Dickens to the American firm, pointing out that their projected plan would jeopardize his English copyright:

... I had no idea of your intended plan of republishing Edwin Drood in America when we engaged for the proof sheets ... if pursued, it would entail upon me the loss of copyright in England of *any parts of the book, first published in America*. ... I wanted to do the most for you that I could, without the least reference to any extra gain, consistently with the safety of my property. ...[3]

The publishers of *Every Saturday* obviously at last accepted the justice of Dickens's protest, and, in fact, it is noticeable that in months where the first Saturday came very early, as in April, June, and July, publication was deferred until the following week.[4] This was not the only difficulty Dickens

---

[1] Forster, xi. 2. The original contract for *Edwin Drood* apparently no longer exists. The Duffield collection at Dickens House contains two letters from Chapman and Hall to Duffield, the first, dated 1 Feb. 1926, stating that the contract was locked in the safe and refusing to have it photographed; the second, dated 25 Jan. 1927, explaining that the original agreement no longer exists, that all former contracts with Dickens were rendered obsolete when the firm purchased the whole of his copyrights from Forster and Miss Hogarth, and that the agreements referring to this later transaction are the only ones preserved.

[2] In spite of the promise on 2 April to publish 'all the original engravings', *Every Saturday* omitted some and provided an independent title for others. See List of Editions, p. lii.

[3] *N*, iii. 777. See also letter of 5 June to Edmund Yates (*N*, iii. 783). The middle of May seems rather late to be running into disagreement; Fields, Osgood and Co. were, in fact, persisting in an argument which had started as early as February, when Dickens had met Harold M. Ticknor in London. See Gerald G. Grubb, 'Some Unpublished Correspondence of Dickens and Chapman and Hall', *Boston University Studies in English*, i (Spring 1955), pp. 125-6.   [4] See List of Editions, p. lii.

ran into over his negotiations for American publication. The 1867 agreement with Ticknor and Fields and its accompanying letters had already roused feeling against him in other publishing firms, such as Harper and Brothers and Petersons, who felt either that a slur had been cast on their own financial transactions with Dickens or that their own imagined copyrights had been infringed. The details of this earlier dispute were published in the *Publishers' Circular* of Philadelphia on 1 June 1867, and, with the title 'The Dickens Controversy', in some editions of Shelton MacKenzie's *Life of Charles Dickens*, published by Petersons in 1870.[1] That Petersons were not satisfied to let this dispute drop is indicated by a comment in the 'Literary Gossip' of the *Athenaeum* on 10 September 1870, called forth by a renewed protest from Petersons against the designation of Ticknor and Fields as Dickens's authorized American publishers. The *Athenaeum* writer merely wished to point out that Petersons attached an unusual meaning to the word 'authorized'. Incredible as it may seem after all the controversy in 1867, Dickens subsequently forgot his agreement with Ticknor and Fields and tentatively offered the advance sheets of the next work to Harper and Brothers, who, on seeing an announcement of the new story on 20 November 1869 in a London paper, offered £2,000 for the rights. This offer was provisionally accepted until Fields, who had been staying with Dickens, looked up his own agreement on returning home; whereupon Dickens had to apologize all round. Even then negotiations were not ended: months later, in March 1870, a renewed approach from Harper and Brothers led Dickens once again to apologize for his mistake and to conclude:

You may be quite sure that if I should find myself 'free' to make a new arrangement concerning advance sheets of *The Mystery of Edwin Drood* at any time during the issuing of the book in numbers, I will at once send them to you, and place myself in your hands.[2]

No new arrangement was made, and Harper and Brothers had to content themselves with running an *Edwin Drood* Monthly Supplement to *Harper's Weekly*, from 23 April to 1 October. Fields, Osgood and Company, perhaps not surprisingly, seem to have experienced other pre-publication difficulties: Dickens's letter to Fields of 14 January, recording Forster's verdict on Number II as 'a clincher', begins:

I cannot overcome my instinctive feeling that it would be a very unseemly thing for me to engage in any single combats with the Pirates. I have already announced my own connexion with your house; and it is for you, and not for me,

---

[1] See also William Glyde Wilkins, *First and Early American Editions of the Works of Charles Dickens* (1910); *Dickensian*, v (1909), pp. 209–10.

[2] See Gerald G. Grubb; *N*, iii. 750 (letter incorrectly dated 13 Nov. for 30 Nov.); J. Henry Harper, *The House of Harper* (N.Y. and London, 1912), pp. 261–2.

to make all appeals or protests or other announcements connected with that association. I am quite clear as to my silent part.[1]

In the course of publication, too, on 11 June, they were impelled to issue a notice in *Every Saturday* reminding readers that theirs was the authorized American edition. The firm also issued an edition in one volume in 1870. The text of this seems to be based on the advance sheets (it incorporates, as does *Every Saturday*, misprints not corrected on proof), but it has corrections, where *Every Saturday* was set up from imperfectly corrected copy.[2]

Towards the end of December 1873 *The Mystery of Edwin Drood* was advertised to be published as volume xxx in the Library edition. This edition included the twelve illustrations from 1870, in line with other volumes in the reissue of the Library edition, and was sold at 8s. One or two obvious errors of the text of 1870 were corrected, but about thirty-five errors of substance introduced. In February and March 1875 advertisements for the Charles Dickens edition appeared, and this, with eight illustrations and descriptive headlines (see below, Appendix D), was sold at 3s. 6d. The latter edition was printed from the former and incorporated all its errors, apart from obvious mistakes, as well as introducing over twenty new ones. In each of these editions, *Master Humphrey's Clock*, *Hunted Down*, *Holiday Romance*, and *George Silverman's Explanation* were included with *Edwin Drood*.[3] Clearly neither of these editions has authoritative readings: they have been included in collation as an indication of errors which have been perpetuated in later texts.[4] No copy of the Cheap edition has been found, nor has mention of it been traced in publishers' advertisements between 1870 and 1875; probably it was never included in the series.

The text of the first edition is obviously the authoritative one for *Edwin Drood*, except for the last two chapters, which Dickens did not see in print. Here the manuscript is the guide to Dickens's intentions. In the previous chapters considerable revision had taken place between

[1] *N*, iii. 759–60, quoted incompletely. The Duffield collection contains photographs of the letter, from the Huntington Library (HM FI 1231).

[2] See Appendix F below.

[3] For a general description of these two collected editions, see Introduction to the Clarendon edition of *Oliver Twist* by Kathleen Tillotson, pp. xxix–xxx. As publishers' advertisements of the period clearly indicate, the reissue of the Library edition, with illustrations, is quite distinct from the firm's Illustrated Library edition, a more expensive production, advertisements for which began to appear in September 1873. *The Mystery of Edwin Drood* in the Illustrated Library edition (Mar. 1876, price 10s.) was printed, not from the Library edition, but from the Charles Dickens edition.

[4] The Nonesuch edition, 1937, for example, though said to follow the text of the original edition, contains errors from these later editions; it also contains an erroneous statement in the Preface as to the nature of the proof-revisions and an apparently unfounded assertion as to the survival of proofs for Number IV.

manuscript and Monthly Number: only rarely of substantial effect on the information given to the reader, and this mainly when considerations of length necessitated a change; for example, in chapter v, of which the position was altered, or in chapter xvi, where the suggestion of Jasper's hypnotic powers is slightly increased in two or three brief passages, added primarily, it may be, to give full value of pages to the reader. For the most part, alterations are stylistic: sentences more incisively constructed, contrasting words neatly balanced, ideas more precisely phrased, unpleasing sounds smoothed away. Many of the changes seem to be in the cause of euphony: the public readings may well have rendered Dickens even more acutely sensitive to sound. At the same time that he was giving great care to his choice of words, he was capable of being incredibly careless over his proof-reading, the most notable instance in *Edwin Drood* being in the opening lines of the novel, where 'Tower' printed for 'Town' renders meaningless the word 'its' in the third sentence.

TREATMENT OF THE TEXT OF 70

(1) *Principles of Emendation*

All cases of emended reading have manuscript authority.[1] The problem of restoration has necessarily been different in different parts of the text. For chapters i to xvi, representing Monthly Numbers I to IV, in the absence of proofs it has not been possible to determine whether certain variations between manuscript and 70 were deliberate on Dickens's part or originated in printers' errors which either were unnoticed in the proof-revision or were allowed to stand as acceptable readings. Reinstatement of manuscript readings has therefore been more cautious in this section of the novel than in subsequent chapters. Where the sense of the manuscript version is clearly correct, and where it is inconceivable that Dickens would have made the alteration to the reading of 70, manuscript reading has been restored, notably in the change from 'Tower' to 'Town' in the opening lines and from 'unfounded fears' to 'unformed fears' in chapter x. In each of these instances the manuscript word could easily be misread, and the evidence of the complete collation suggests that Dickens frequently failed to notice printers' mistakes. In less easily decided cases considerable weight has been given to the relative difficulty of the manuscript reading, as, for example, where deletions could cause confusion or where phrases have been inserted above the line and might have been missed by the printer. Admittedly, an argument against this latter type of restoration is that Dickens might at the proof stage have reverted to first thoughts. In one instance a printer's error[2] is not due to misreading

---

[1] A letter from Dickens to the printer corrects the confused reading of 70 at a point where the manuscript folio is missing. See ch. xi, p. 88. The correction obviously came too late to be incorporated in the text.   [2] But see Appendix H below.

of a word: in chapter xvi, the text of 70 has Mr. Crisparkle straining his hawk's eyes for the correction of his 'sight', although it is clearly his 'fancy', as in manuscript, that is at fault. Two lines lower, however, the manuscript has the phrase 'shadowed forth to the sense of sight', where 70 reads 'shadowed forth'. Evidently the printer caught the word 'sight' and substituted it for 'fancy', and Dickens, noting the repetition, deleted 'to the sense of sight', instead of consulting the manuscript (which he rarely did) or recalling what he had originally written, and correcting the first 'sight' to 'fancy'. Often words in the manuscript are difficult to read: when there is doubt as to whether the word intended differs from that printed, the printed word has been retained and the possible variant recorded in a footnote: an exception is in chapter xi (p. 91) where Mr. Grewgious expresses his assumption that Edwin has called on him to sharpen him up in his proceedings. The word before 'proceedings', printed in 70 as 'any', has a blot obscuring the initial letter, and was probably intended as 'my', which is preferable in the context.

If, at a future date, proofs for these chapters become available,[1] renewed scrutiny of the text will be necessary: support for further manuscript restorations may be found; some emendations made here may prove to be unwarranted.

For chapters xvii to xxi, Number V as planned by Dickens, the proof corrected for the printers provides valuable evidence as to the part played by printers' errors in determining changes between manuscript and 70. There are in these pages approximately one hundred such errors, thirty-nine of which were corrected by Dickens to the manuscript reading. In six further cases his correction introduced a new reading. Six of the uncorrected errors occur in passages which were intended for deletion. The printers themselves caught two or three obvious mistakes before publication, but introduced, or accepted, after this proof stage three substantially different readings presumably unauthorized by Dickens,[2] and ignored

[1] See pp. xii, l, and Appendix H below.

[2] In two of these three cases (ch. xvii, pp. 155 and 160) ES agrees with 70, showing that the change was deliberately made and recorded on the copy sent to America. In the third instance (ch. xx, p. 174) ES, which otherwise in this Number has fully corrected proof, agrees with MS and P. There is a curious instance in ch. xviii, p. 163, of a change in punctuation from MS to P. This was unnoticed on P and therefore perpetuated in ES, but someone later restored MS reading in 70, either by coincidence or by recourse to MS. The curious feature of the case is that there was no necessity for a change in 70, as the reading of P is perfectly acceptable. The text of 70 could not have been set up from a second proof seen and corrected by Dickens, as a second proof would omit the passages which he deleted. The change on p. 155 could not have been made at this stage, as it occurs within a deleted passage. The first proof, with Dickens's alterations for the printers, would have to be scrutinized closely by whoever authorized the final form for publication, and it seems likely that the first two of these alterations were made at this stage: the two not found in the American text were presumably made at an even later stage, when two misprints, 'variety' for 'vanity' (p. 152) and 'more' for 'none' (p. 185) were corrected, but not on American copy. See Appendix F below.

Dickens's correction in four cases concerning spelling, punctuation, or a minor alteration not very clearly marked.

For these chapters, then, the distinction is clear between those changes which were deliberately made by Dickens and those which originated in printers' errors. Of the latter, where no correction was made, the manuscript version has been restored.[1] Where a printer's error led to a further alteration by Dickens, the manuscript reading has been restored if it seems unlikely that Dickens would have preferred a change but for the mistake in proof. The manuscript reading has been restored in the three cases where the variant came in at a later stage, as it is scarcely possible that these changes could have been made by Dickens. There are two instances in these chapters where a probable though not certain manuscript reading has been preferred, namely in chapter xviii where Jasper speaks of Mr. Sapsea's recommendation as being 'naturally' (70: 'actually') much more important than his own, and in chapter xxi where the manuscript almost certainly has 'feared' and not 'fancied' as in 70.

In the list of emended readings which follows, and in the footnotes to the text, the symbol P is used to denote proof as printed. This enables the reader to detect printers' errors. Where a divergence is recorded between P and 70, as, for example, on p. 169 of chapter xix, it is to be understood that the alteration came in as a proof-correction, unless a specific note to the contrary is given.

The most important instance of divergence between text of 70 and Dickens's proof-alterations is in the case of the deletions made because of 'over-matter' in the Number. In these cases it has been thought best to follow the practice of 70[2] and retain the passages concerned, recording the deletions as footnotes. This does not introduce great inconsistency as compared with other chapters, as the only other case of substantial deletions in *Edwin Drood* occurs in chapter ix, which was itself written as an addition to make up the required length for the first two Numbers.

In chapters xxii and xxiii, for which Dickens could not have seen the proof, the manuscript alone has authority, and its readings are followed, with one exception. In chapter xxiii, 'It announces itself . . . timidly beginning to spring up' (p. 204), the manuscript reading gives an impossible construction, which Dickens would certainly have revised.[3] In chapter xxii (p. 193) neither reading gives an entirely satisfactory

[1] This sometimes gives a markedly improved reading, notably in the restoration of 'yours' for 'years' in ch. xix, p. 170.

[2] See p. xxix. The present edition also retains the chapter-division made at this stage for 70.

[3] The sub-standard form *yer* (70) has also been retained where on one occasion in ch. xxiii MS has *you*. Readings elsewhere show that Dickens intended *yer* in Deputy's speech, although he sometimes made mistakes even within a single sentence. The form *yer* is consistently used in 70.

construction to Mr. Grewgious's speech and the manuscript reading is accepted.

There are in these two chapters more than fifty printers' errors, involving omissions, misreadings of words or of word order, and normalizing of sub-standard forms of speech.

The following is a list of all substantive emendations, with the emended reading given first and occasional comment added:

Ch. i, p. 1	English Cathedral Town] MS: English Cathedral Tower 70–75 (*twice*)
Ch. i, p. 1	What IS the spike] MS: What is the spike 70–75
Ch. i, p. 2	More than three shillings and sixpence] MS *after* More ⟨nor⟩ three shillings and sixpence: More nor . . . sixpence 70–75
Ch. i, p. 2	remember, too, that] MS: remember that 70–75
Ch. i, p. 2	As he lies on his back, the said Chinaman] MS: Said Chinaman 70–75
Ch. i, p. 3	wild chattering and clattering] MS: chattering and clattering 70–75
Ch. i, p. 3	a-bed in a black hutch] MS: in bed in a black hutch 70–75
Ch. ii, p. 5	"Breathed to that extent would be preferable," the Dean...condescendingly remarks; "would be preferable."] MS: "Breathed to that extent," the Dean ...condescendingly remarks, "would be preferable." 70–75 (*repetition is a characteristic of the Dean's speech*)
Ch. ii, p. 5	asks the Dean] MS: asked the Dean 70–75
Ch. iii, p. 15	in a cold perspiration] MS: in a slow perspiration 70–75
Ch. iii, p. 15	a sprightly Miss Twinkleton whom the young ladies have never seen] MS: a sprightlier Miss Twinkleton than the young ladies have ever seen 70–75
Ch. iv, p. 24	cool, chill autumn evening] MS: cool, chilly autumn evening 70–75
Ch. v, p. 33	introducing gravestone with extinguished torch] MS: introducing gravestone 70–75
Ch. vi, p. 41	glad that he is not to be Mr. Honeythunder himself] MS: glad that he is not Mr. Honeythunder himself 70–75
Ch. vi, p. 42	Plain instructions were then despatched] MS: Instructions were then despatched 70–75
Ch. vi, p. 45	the Vice Treasurer] MS: the sub-Treasurer 70–75 (*see context*)

Ch. vii, p. 48	an immeasurable difference] MS: an unmistakeable difference 70–75
Ch. vii, p. 51	a little less steady] MS: less steady 70–75
Ch. viii, p. 57	is but a few yards from here] MS: is a few yards from here 70–75
Ch. viii, p. 61	I showed you to it] MS: I showed it to you 70 ES: I showed it you 73 75
Ch. ix, p. 63	the beloved young figure] MS: the dead young figure 70–75
Ch. ix, p. 65	what had really taken place] MS: what had taken place 70–75
Ch. ix, p. 69	time moves on] MS: time works on 70–75
Ch. ix, p. 71	Memorandum, 'Wishes.' Exactly. Is there] MS: Memorandum, 'Wishes:' My dear, is there 70–75
Ch. ix, p. 73	"Dear me," said Mr. Grewgious, peering in] MS: "Dear me," said Mr. Grewgious, peeping in 70–75
Ch. x, p. 80	into one great bowl . . . and into the other]MS *not absolutely clear, owing to deletions* (*Dickens may originally have written* another *in the second phrase*): into the great bowl . . . and into the other 70–75
Ch. x, p. 85	*you* are always welcome] MS: you are always welcome 70–75
Ch. x, p. 86	vague and unformed fears] MS: vague and unfounded fears 70–75
Ch. xi, p. 88	that sensitive Constitution, the property of us Britons, the odd fortune of which sacred institution] *letter from Dickens to printer, 28 May 1870* (MS *folio missing*): that sensitive constitution, the property of us Britons. The odd fortune of which sacred institutions 70: that sensitive constitution, the property of us Britons; the odd fortune of which sacred institutions ES: that sensitive constitution, the property of us Britons: the odd fortune of which sacred institutions 73: that sensitive constitution, the property of us Britons: the odd fortune of which sacred institution 75
Ch. xi, p. 90	It is fortunate] MS: It's fortunate 70–75
Ch. xi, p. 91	sharpen me up a bit in my proceedings] MS *blotted, but probable reading*: sharpen me up a bit in any proceedings 70–75

Ch. xi, p. 92   found fault with him in secret nudges] MS: found fault with him 70–75

Ch. xi, p. 93   to flicker over his stolid face] MS: to flicker over his face 70–75

Ch. xi, p. 94   as near the mark] MS: as nearly the mark 70–75

Ch. xi, p. 96   in short dry sentences] MS: in short sentences 70–75

Ch. xii, p. 100   tickling his ears:—figuratively long enough to present a considerable area* for tickling] MS: tickling his ears—figuratively, long enough to present a considerable area for tickling 70 ES: tickling his ears—figuratively—long enough to present a considerable area for tickling 73 75   * surface MS

Ch. xii, p. 104   at that end, too, is a piece] MS: at that end, too, there is a piece 70–75

Ch. xii, p. 107   open an iron gate and enable them] MS: open an iron gate so to enable them 70–75

Ch. xii, p. 111   to grovel in the dust with one defensive leg up, and cry] MS: to grovel in the dust, and cry 70–75

Ch. xiii, p. 112   the finest feelings of our nature] MS: the first feelings of our nature 70–75

Ch. xiv, p. 126   My lungs is weak] MS: My lungs is weakly 70–75

Ch. xv, p. 132   I'll do that little] MS after I'll do ⟨it⟩: I'll do it 70–75

Ch. xv, p. 134   intently watching Neville] MS: intensely watching Neville 70–75

Ch. xvi, p. 142   for the correction of his fancy . . . was remotely shadowed forth to the sense of sight] MS: for the correction of his sight . . . was remotely shadowed forth 70–75

Ch. xvi, p. 146   an expressive look] MS: an impressive look 70–75

Ch. xvii, p. 148   came and went] MS: came and went by P (with by deleted) 70–75

Ch. xvii, p. 148   his name was twice called] MS: his name was called P 70–75

Ch. xvii, p. 149   each short sentence of a word] MS: each short sentiment of a word P 70–75

Ch. xvii, p. 151   a false God of your making] P (with of your making as a proof addition) ES 73 75: a false God MS P: a false God of our making 70

Ch. xvii, p. 151   War is a vast calamity] MS: War is a calamity P 70–75

Ch. xvii, p. 152   He betook himself to] MS: He took himself to P 70–75

Ch. xvii, p. 153   did; and if you had seen] MS: did; if you had seen P 70–75

Ch. xvii, p. 153   when I go out—as I only do—at night] MS: when I go out—as I do—only at night P: when I go out—as I do only—at night 70–75

Ch. xvii, p. 155   mastery of her] MS P: mastery over her 70–75 (*no warrant for change: this is part of a passage deleted in* P)

Ch. xvii, p. 156   I am glad you approved] MS: I am glad you approve P 70–75

Ch. xvii, p. 158   his neckerchief] MS: the neckerchief P 70–75

Ch. xvii, p. 158   without asking permission] MS: without asking your permission P 70–75

Ch. xvii, p. 158   Not at all. I beg you will not think so. I ought to apologize] MS: Not at all. I ought to apologize P 70–75

Ch. xvii, p. 159   the short cut] MS: this short cut P 70–75

Ch. xvii, p. 160   or seem likely to] MS P (*with no alteration*): or seem likely to do it 70–75

Ch. xviii, p. 160   with the view of settling down there] MS: with a view of settling down there P 70–75

Ch. xviii, p. 161   I have no doubts] MS: I have no doubt P 70–75 (*this is part of a passage deleted in* P)

Ch. xviii, p. 161   made a dint in 'is wool] MS: made a dint in his wool P 70–75

Ch. xviii, p. 162   Mr. Datchery . . . directed] MS *no new paragraph*: Mr. Datchery . . . directed *new paragraph* P 70–75 (*sentence deleted in* P)

Ch. xviii, p. 164   whose recommendation is naturally much more important] MS *probable not certain*: whose recommendation is actually much more important P 70–75

Ch. xviii, p. 165   I too am returning home] MS: I am returning home P 70–75

Ch. xviii, p. 165   she must be *im*morally certain] MS: she must be immorally certain P 70–75

Ch. xviii, p. 167   he'll be double welcome] MS: he'll be doubly welcome P 70–75

Ch. xix, p. 169   the lost has long been . . . mourned for, as the dead] MS: the lost has long been . . . mourned for, as dead P 70–75

Ch. xix, p. 169 After several times forming her lips . . . into the shape of some other hesitating reply, and then into none, by turns, she answers] MS: After several times forming her lips . . . into the shape of some other hesitating reply, and then into none, it was, she answers P: After several times forming her lips . . . into the shape of some other hesitating reply, and then into none, she answers 70–75

Ch. xix, p. 169 but I draw no parallel] MS: I will draw no parallel P: I'll draw no parallel 70–75

Ch. xix, p. 169 he suggests] MS: he suggested P 70–75

Ch. xix, p. 170 that is not fair] MS: that's not fair P 70–75

Ch. xix, p. 170 for his sake, but worshipped in torment for yours] MS: for his sake, but worshipped in torment for years P 70–75

Ch. xix, p. 171 I endured all in silence] MS: I endured it all in silence P 70–75

Ch. xix, p. 172 I devoted myself to] MS: I have devoted myself to P 70–75

Ch. xix, p. 172 be he who he might] MS: be he whom he might P 70–75

Ch. xx, p. 174 His self-absorption] MS P (*with no alteration*) ES: Jasper's self-absorption 70 73 75

Ch. xx, p. 174 He had unnecessarily declared] MS: He had even declared P 70–75

Ch. xx, p. 175 restrained herself from giving it] MS: restrained herself from so giving it P (*with* so *deleted*) 70–75

Ch. xx, p. 176 by appealing against it to the honest and true] MS: by appealing to the honest and true P 70–75

Ch. xx, p. 176 whether she would find him] MS: whether she should find him P 70–75

Ch. xx, p. 177 to protect . . . all of us from him. You will?] MS: to protect . . . all of us from him, if you will? P 70–75

Ch. xx, p. 181 This blockhead my master!] MS: This blockhead is my master! P 70–75

Ch. xx, p. 182 Furnival's is specially watched and lighted] MS P (*with alteration to reading of* 70–75): Furnival's is fire-proof and specially watched and lighted 70–75 (*see context. The insertion in* P *was consequent on the preceding deletion*)

Ch. xxi, p. 183   when the clocks struck ten] MS: when the clock struck ten P 70–75

Ch. xxi, p. 183   after having tapped] MS: after having rapped P 70–75

Ch. xxi, p. 183   Oh, is it a dark gentleman?] MS: Is it a dark gentleman? P 70–75

Ch. xxi, p. 184   by the hair of my head] MS: by the hair of the head P 70–75

Ch. xxi, p. 184   either to pick him up, or go down with him] MS: rather to pick him up, or go down with him P ES: to pick him up, or go down with him 70 73 75

Ch. xxi, p. 185   so very unexpected] MS: so unexpected P 70–75

Ch. xxi, p. 186   in the person of any watchman] MS: in the person of a watchman P 70–75

Ch. xxi, p. 186   Fair and softly, dear sir] MS: Fair and softly, sir P 70–75 (*this is part of a passage deleted in* P)

Ch. xxi, p. 186   I begin to understand . . . and I highly approve] MS: I begin to understand . . . and highly approve P 70–75 (*this is part of a passage deleted in* P)

Ch. xxi, p. 187   And she feared] MS *probable not certain*: And she fancied P 70–75

Ch. xxii, p. 189   it is always agreeable] MS: it is only agreeable 70–75

Ch. xxii, p. 189   even if she *hadn't* been conducted] MS: even if she hadn't been conducted 70–75

Ch. xxii, p. 189   his admiral's cabin . . . its flower-garden] MS: his admiral's cabin . . . his flower-garden 70–75

Ch. xxii, p. 190   any new maligning] MS: any more maligning 70–75

Ch. xxii, p. 191   he also held . . . that John Jasper was a brigand *and* a wild beast] MS: and he also held . . . that John Jasper was a brigand and a wild beast 70–75

Ch. xxii, p. 191   she could almost answer for that] MS: she could almost answer for it 70–75

Ch. xxii, p. 191   would seem to be in the threat to you] MS: would seem to be the threat to you 70–75

Ch. xxii, p. 191   with a heightened color] MS: with a greatly heightened color 70–75

Ch. xxii, p. 191   the inside of the state-cabin and the out] MS: the inside of the state-cabin and out 70–75

Ch. xxii, p. 192   The refection that Mr. Tartar produced] MS 75: The reflection that Mr. Tartar produced 70 ES 73

Ch. xxii, p. 193   It has come into my thoughts . . . that the respected lady, Miss Twinkleton, occasionally repairs to London in the recess . . . for interviews with metropolitan parents, if any. Whether . . . we might invite] MS ES: It has come into my thoughts . . . that as the respected lady, Miss Twinkleton, occasionally repairs to London in the recess . . . for interviews with metropolitan parents, if any—whether . . . we might invite 70 73 75

Ch. xxii, p. 193   stated . . . on a brass door-plate, and yet not lucidly stated as to sex] MS: stated . . . on a brass door-plate, and yet not lucidly as to sex 70–75

Ch. xxii, p. 193   out from her own exclusive back parlor] MS: out of her own exclusive back parlor 70–75

Ch. xxii, p. 194   an elder lady] MS: an elderly lady 70–75 (cf. *same error in* Oliver Twist, *ch. xxxiii*)

Ch. xxii, p. 194   be you who you may] MS: be you what you may 70–75

Ch. xxii, p. 195   having been enrobed by her attendant] MS: having been enrolled by her attendant 70–75

Ch. xxii, p. 196   the Archway] MS: the Arching 70–75

Ch. xxii, p. 197   an uncomfortable appearance on it] MS: an uncomfortable appearance 70–75

Ch. xxii, p. 198   re-counting her luggage] MS: recounting her luggage 70–75

Ch. xxii, p. 198   each looking very hard at the last shilling . . . grumblingly descended the doorsteps] MS: each looking very hard at the last shilling grumblingly . . . descended the doorsteps 70–75

Ch. xxii, p. 198   Miss Twinkleton bewildered on a bonnet-box] MS: Miss Twinkleton on a bonnet-box 70–75

Ch. xxii, p. 198   the inference that Miss Twinkleton would set herself] MS: the inference that Miss Twinkleton set herself 70–75

Ch. xxii, p. 199   which I 'ope you will agree with me . . . was a right precaution] MS: which I 'ope you will agree with . . . was a right precaution 70–75

Ch. xxii, p. 199   for the sake of an emphasis at once polite and powerful] MS: for the sake of emphasis at once polite and powerful 70–75

Ch. xxii, p. 200   began Miss Twinkleton again, when again the Billickin neatly stopped her] MS: began Miss Twinkleton, when again the Billickin neatly stopped her 70–75

All but two of the clear instances which appear in 70 of the normalizing by printers of sub-standard forms occur in Mrs. Billickin's speech in chapter xxii, presumably not as a deliberate policy of the proof-reader, as other sub-standard forms were retained. In all these cases the forms shown in manuscript, such as *everywheres*, *Cloist'rham's*, *parlior*, *disapintmink*, *respectin'*, *Chris'en*, *forard*, have been restored.[1] The opium woman's use of *you* and *ye* presents more of a problem, as Dickens's writing is not always clear. He may have intended her to use *you* for the nominative, *ye* in all other cases, but as this practice is not consistently followed, the irregularities of 70 have been preserved where they seem to have manuscript authority.[2] Handwriting presents further problems in the final chapter: on one occasion it is difficult to be sure whether Dickens wrote *always* or *allays* for the opium woman (*always* is the form used for her elsewhere); and it is not clear whether *asides* or *besides* is intended in the one instance of Deputy's use of this word. In each case the reading of 70 has been retained.

The text of 70 contains very few literal misprints, mainly in the nature of patent errors of punctuation. These have been silently corrected.

(2) *Treatment of Accidentals*

Proofs for other novels show that Dickens normally expected the printer to revise his punctuation. The punctuation of 70 has been followed, except in a very few instances where the printers were clearly in error or where a correction on proof shows that Dickens desired a change. Of the latter cases, comprising mainly two or three instances of the insertion of commas, one change is recorded in a footnote, as marking a slight increase in emphasis;[3] otherwise the proof-correction has been silently accepted.

The spelling of 70, where consistent and acceptable in its own time, is retained. Where variant spellings are found, a single form has been preferred, the choice being governed, as in the case of *Oliver Twist*, by Dickens's own preference, or, where he too is inconsistent, by relative frequency in 70. The general policy has been to retain variant spellings

---

[1] pp. 107, 167, 194, 195, 196, 199. This does not apply in earlier cases where there is evidence to suggest that Dickens later preferred the reading of 70, for example, in the case of the opium woman's *of* (70) *o'* (MS) in ch. i. In later chapters manuscript also has *of*. See also note 2 following.

[2] There is a distinct possibility that Dickens gradually changed his conception of the opium woman's speech and came to prefer a less sub-standard form for her. In the first chapter *ye* is regular, and there is indecision over the use of *nor* for *than*: in manuscript Dickens deleted *nor* in favour of *than*, but allowed *nor* to go through in proof. In view of later uses of *than* (ch. xxiii) the word has been restored in ch. i, as *nor* could have been an unnoticed printer's error. The one other occasion in ch. i where manuscript has *than* is no help towards a decision, as Dickens changed the phrase in proof. As with the cases of *of/o'*, it has been difficult to decide whether printers' errors or Dickens's own hesitations were responsible for the final form in 70.   [3] p. 168.

in sub-standard pronunciation if these have the authority of both manuscript and 70, but two examples of sub-standard speech have been
regularized, *kinfreederel* and such forms as *look'ee, hark'ee*. In the latter
case Dickens is consistent, so far as one can judge, but the difficulty of
deciphering his writing led to inconsistencies in 70. The word *kinfreederel*
caused him considerable problems and it was tried in manuscript in a
variety of forms. In this case the spelling of 70 is consistent, except on one
occasion, and the predominant form has here been adopted. One of the
most interesting variants is the change in Durdles's pronunciation from
Jasper to *Jarsper*, which occurs in chapter xii of 70, but is not recorded in
manuscript until it is used for Deputy in chapter xviii. Presumably
Dickens preferred the new spelling wherever it could be inserted.

The use of capitals for nouns such as Cathedral, Gate House, Precincts,
High Street has been regularized according to the dominant form in 70.
(Dickens's practice varies considerably, his writing does not always make
his intention clear, and some of his capitals were removed in 70.) Occasionally a word which is normally printed without a capital is allowed to
retain it where the context makes this desirable. Word-division and
hyphenation have been made consistent, again according to the dominant
form in 70, and this practice has been extended to include colloquial forms
of speech such as *a goin'*, which appears variously as *a goin'*, *a-goin'*,
agoin'. The dropping of the final *g* in such forms is not consistent and this
inconsistency has been allowed to remain, but the apostrophe has been
inserted on all occasions where *g* is dropped. Similarly an apostrophe has
been inserted in the colloquial form *'un*, as this is the more frequent
practice in 70. The occasional misplacing of an apostrophe has been silently
corrected. Full stops have been omitted in chapter headings and in the
descriptive headlines (Appendix D below). The indentation of chapter
openings (usual in 70) has been adapted to modern practice, but not by
editorial intention.

(3) *Selection of Variants*

Deletions in the manuscript are so numerous and frequently so difficult
to decipher that it has been practicable to include only the most important,
such as those recording a decision as to a character's name or a substantial
change of intention. Of the latter, those referring to Edwin's last appearances (pp. 120, 125) and to the opium woman's interest in Jasper (p. 209)
are of interest in view of the unfinished state of the story. Passages
written on verso or on slips pasted over the original are specified, but
beyond this it has not been possible to indicate stages of revision in the
manuscript. There are occasions where *Every Saturday* has some, but not
all, of the changes made between manuscript and 70. This suggests either
gross carelessness in the preparation of copy or the possibility of two
stages of proof-revision. (See Appendix F below.)

All substantive differences between manuscript and text are included; but not spellings, punctuation, capitalization, or changes of form such as *sprang/sprung*, *upward/upwards*, *on/upon*. These have also been omitted from the variants between printed texts, as has the change from *further* to *farther* in 73 and 75.

Obvious errors in the manuscript and literal misprints in *Every Saturday* have been omitted. Literal misprints are rare in 73 and 75. Errors in proof have been recorded, even when proof-correction replaced the original reading, as these give an indication of the frequency of error, and one or two such mistakes were perpetuated in *Every Saturday*.[1] Corrections on the proof sent to Fildes[2] have not been recorded, except in one instance (p. 188) where this proof has an alteration apparently cancelled later.

THE MANUSCRIPT

The autograph manuscript, which was sent to press, is preserved complete, but for one folio comprising the first five paragraphs of chapter xi, in the Forster collection at the Victoria and Albert Museum (47.A.38). The missing folio was probably removed for checking of copy when Dickens had occasion, at the last minute, to draw the printer's attention to an error in the second paragraph.[3] The manuscript of the actual novel covers 157 (minus 1) folios of blue paper, size 9·2 in. by 7·4–7·5 in., now mounted and bound in one volume. The roughness of the inner edges indicates that the original sheets, twice this size, were divided here; hence the slight variation in width. The writing is small and cramped: there are on average about 45 lines to a page, as compared with about 25 in *Oliver Twist*; roughly 27 slips to a 32-page monthly Number, as compared with 30 for *David Copperfield*, and about 95 for early novels. Dickens's necessary readjustments of length, and the contents of each Number, can be seen in the following table:[4]

No. I	23+4½ ('Mr Durdles and Friend' from No. II)	27½	chs. i–iv plus viii, which became v	i–v in 70
No. II	22½−4½+9½ ('Birds in the Bush')	27½	chs. v, vi, vii, which became vi, vii, viii, plus ix	vi–ix in 70
No. III		27	chs. x–xii	x–xii in 70
No. IV		27	chs. xiii–xvi	xiii–xvi in 70
No. V	(as written)	27	chs. xvii–xx (xx split into xx and xxi as printed, and over-matter restored)	xvii–xx in 70
No. VI	(as written)	20	chs. xxi and xxii, which became xxii and xxiii when xxi brought in from No. V	xxi–xxiii in 70

[1] Ch. xxi, p. 185.   [2] See p. l.   [3] See p. 88 n.

[4] Based on the number of manuscript pages to each chapter. Additions and deletions at proof stage within the chapters (see p. 19 n.) are not accounted for here.

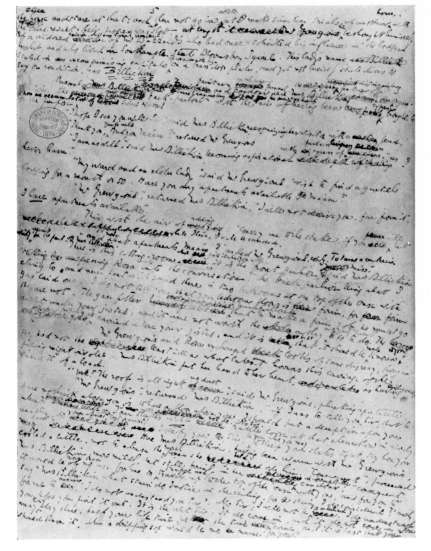

A page of Dickens's manuscript of the novel (Number VI, chapter xxii). Forster collection, Victoria and Albert Museum. (*Reduced*)

The first page of each monthly part is headed with its Number; there are two pages headed 'N.° III', one heading subsequently crossed out, as this was the point at which Dickens had to write another chapter for inclusion in II. Pagination is consecutive within each Number, except that the pages of the additional chapter, ix, are not numbered, except in pencil. The transference at proof stage of the previous chapter, viii, to become v of Number I might have caused Dickens hesitation as to where to start the numbering of the new chapter, and perhaps he left it unnumbered to avoid possible confusion. There are 22 chapters in manuscript (23 in 70).[1] Only 20 slips were written for Number VI: the flourish below the last sentence of manuscript denotes that 'The Dawn again' is complete, and the Number Plan shows that one more chapter was projected for this Number.

The manuscript for the most part is written in blue ink. Occasional marks to the printers and a few corrections are in what was probably black, now faded to brown, and in two passages Dickens had recourse to this colour: in chapter x, from 'And I say now, that I think ill of Mr Neville' (p. 78) to 'a saccharine transfiguration' (p. 79), and in chapter xvii, from 'But I should like you to do it' (p. 153) to 'whether he is adverse or . . .' (p. 154). Comparison with the ink of the 'Sapsea fragment'[2] is of interest here. Deletions, usually in the form of curly lines,[3] are numerous, as are interlinear insertions. Many of the original words are irrecoverable and ascertaining the final reading and word order is frequently difficult. Once or twice a passage for insertion has been written, or a much altered passage rewritten, on the reverse side, and on other occasions a fresh slip has been pasted over the rejected passage.[4] One such slip has been removed to the blank page opposite so that the original can be read, and others are slightly damaged where readers have tried to look beneath in pursuit of clues. There is an instance of Dickens's habit[5] of turning over and starting afresh on the reverse side, if he wished to make an alteration on a page newly begun. The page numbering here indicates that the phrase 'Thessalonians, Ephesians and Galatians', found in isolation on the reverse of p. 26 of Number IV, was tried out as part of a much rewritten passage referring to Cloisterham's understanding of the reading habits of "Natives".[6]

Scattered over the manuscript, usually in pencil or the brown ink, are various compositors' names—Taylor, King, Oxley, Thompson jun., Holiday—and instructions in Dickens's hand to the printers, William Clowes and Sons, such as '(Printer. White line here)', or 'Printer. Please observe that the scraps of Diary at folios 8 and 9, are to be printed in a smaller type.'

---

[1] See p. xxix.   [2] See p. xlviii.
[3] At one point in the 'Sapsea fragment' Dickens wrote 'Delete' over the words below.
[4] See pp. 10, 29, 31, 113, 143, 177, 189, 209.   [5] See Clarendon *Oliver Twist*, p. xlvi.
[6] p. 143, 'always reading tracts of the obscurest meaning, in broken English'.

Preceding the manuscript of the actual novel are the following pages of Memoranda and notes:

(*a*) List of projected titles: ½ page. (See Appendix A below.)

(*b*) Chapter headings for Number VI: ½ page, the right half of the Number Plan. A pencil note records: 'From Mrs. Forster added May 1887.' There is no explanation of what happened to the left half-sheet. (See Appendix B below.)

(*c*) The 'Sapsea fragment': five half-sheets, numbered in ink 6 to 10, at the top centre, Dickens's usual procedure, and breaking off in mid-sentence. Forster does not make it clear that his finding 'Within the leaves of one of Dickens's other manuscripts'[1] was incomplete: in fact his inclusion of a title suggests otherwise. The obvious inference is that the title, 'How Mr. Sapsea Ceased to be a Member of the Eight Club. Told by Himself', was invented by Forster. The first half-sheet begins with a note specifying a new paragraph, but no indication of what went before survives: presumably the preceding pages would have given some explanation of how Mr. Sapsea came to be telling the story. The fragment is written partly in blue, partly in the brown-coloured ink, and, as the latter is found elsewhere only in chapters x and xvii, it seems possible that Dickens was writing, on the latter of these two occasions, a preliminary try-out for chapter xviii, 'A Settler in Cloisterham'. (See p. xxviii and Appendix C below.)

(*d*) The Number Plans. These follow the pattern described by J. Butt and K. Tillotson in *Dickens at Work* (1957):[2] each page has general notes for the contents of the Number on the left half and details of the individual chapters on the right. There is an introductory page headed 'Mystery of Edwin Drood. / Nº Plans'. Eleven pages in all (a double, XI and XII, for the last Number) were prepared; in each case the right-hand half has been headed 'Mystery of Edwin Drood.—Nº [I]'. A blank sheet has been inserted in the place of Number VI, which was not discovered until later. The sheets from VII to XI/XII are, un-fortunately, blank; even Number VI, without its left half, which perhaps had no notes written on it, tells us nothing beyond chapter titles and the fact that there was to have been one more chapter, unnamed, in the Number. The Number Plans of *Edwin Drood* show clearly Dickens's practice at work: the left-hand memoranda were basically for planning ahead; the right-hand for summarizing chapter contents. Some of the left-hand entries here were obviously made well in advance, as a preliminary plan for several Numbers: for example, the notes for Number V, the last in a sequence of three entries, in-dicating a prominent problem in Dickens's calculations, the capacity for

---

[1] Forster, xi. 2.   [2] pp. 25–7.

development inherent in the relationship between Edwin and Rosa. Presumably, before writing a Number, Dickens went back to his left-hand notes to plan in more detail the material finally assigned to the Number. The last group of entries for Number IV was clearly written at a later stage than the initial entries for IV and V. No second stage of planning for V was recorded, and from here onwards even the right-hand notes give the minimum of information. The right-hand notes are sometimes cast in the form of an injunction, indicating preparatory planning: the first entry for chapter iv, 'Connect Jasper with him', is of this nature, and is followed by a reminder of the reason for the move: 'He will want a solemn donkey bye and bye'. In addition to using the chapter notes for this purpose, Dickens apparently went back to them after he had begun writing the Number, to make a note of changes and perhaps even to summarize the contents for future reference.[1] Several changes in chapter titles are recorded: sometimes the notes show the alteration (as in chs. xvii and xx); sometimes merely the final form (as in ch. ii). In chapter i the notes show the change in title, though the alteration was not made in the manuscript which was sent to the printer, and Dickens's emphasis in the chapter note on the change to be made here suggests the possibility that this was a reminder to himself to make the alteration when the proofs came back. The fact that the last entry for chapter xi (originally headed x, before the extra chapter was written for Number II) is squashed in in insufficient space indicates, what the chapter headings for Numbers V and VI confirm, that all the chapters for a Number were listed before any notes were made. These, and other details of planning, can be seen in the reproduction of the Number Plans in Appendix B below.

(e) A list of chapter headings from i to xx (to the end of Number V as written), in the final ordering, not in the order in which they were written.[2] The one discrepancy between this list and that of 70 is that Chapter xx, 'Divers Flights', refers to chapters xx and xxi of 70. The list is written on recto and verso of a single page and is preceded by a page inscribed 'Mystery of Edwin Drood/Chapter Headings'.

THE PROOF

(a) *Proof corrected for the printers*

The proof for Number V only, chapters xvii to xxi (including the first chapter of Number VI as published), is preserved in the Forster collection at the Victoria and Albert Museum (48.E.24). An envelope

---

[1] Since manuscript for a Number was sometimes sent to the printers in stages (see p. xxiv), Dickens would frequently be writing without the preceding chapters at hand for consultation.

[2] 'Mr Durdles and Friend' is listed as ch. v.

bearing in Dickens's hand the direction 'Mr Day—Messrs. Clowes and Sons, Duke Street' accompanies it. Thirty-two pages are in page form, numbered 129 to 160, and these are followed by a galley of over-matter numbered 161, running from 'The gentleman saw a struggling recollection'[1] to the end of the chapter. Presumably for convenience of binding in the volume this galley has been cut in half. In the margin of the galley l.50 and l.100 have been numbered in ink, presumably by the printers. The words 'By Tuesday' are written on the back of the first half in the same ink, which is not that used for proof-corrections. Included in the corrections made by Dickens are several deletions to reduce the length of the Number. These passages were subsequently restored by the printers in order to fill out the material for Number VI.

(b) *Proof sent to Fildes*

This complete proof is in the possession of Colonel Richard Gimbel of Yale University, but unfortunately he was unwilling to make it available for consultation. Two photographs,[2] comprising galley 161, in the Duffield collection at Dickens House, with a pencil note ascribing ownership of the original to Gimbel, show that in printed matter this is identical with the proof in the Victoria and Albert Museum. The proof for Fildes is, however, less fully corrected. An article by Professor Butt in the April 1962 number of the *Yale University Library Gazette* (xxxvi. 4), referring to this proof, indicates that the usual practice of printing over-matter in galley form was also followed at the end of chapter ix.

[1] p. 184.
[2] See also *Yale University Library Gazette*, xxxvii. 2 (Oct. 1962).

Note. Since the death of Colonel Gimbel this proof has come to the Beinecke Library of Yale University; see p. xii, and Appendix H below.

DESCRIPTIVE LIST OF EDITIONS
1870–1875

Introductory note

This list is confined to the two editions of which part appeared in Dickens's lifetime, and the two posthumous editions which are drawn on in the textual apparatus as being the source of errors in all later editions.

1870: First edition in monthly parts and one volume

The Mystery of Edwin Drood. By Charles Dickens. With twelve illustrations by S. L. Fildes, and a portrait. London: Chapman and Hall, 193 Piccadilly. 1870.

Collation: A^4 B–N^8. A1 title, verso imprint of William Clowes and Sons. A2 note dated '12th August, 1870'. A3, 4 Contents and list of illustrations. A3^v and A4^r numbered vi and vii. N7^v (p. 190) imprint of William Clowes and Sons. N8 advt. of Charles Dickens's Works.

Each of the six monthly parts consisted of two sheets, except the last, which contained the preliminary leaves and was two and a half sheets.

Plates: Nos. I–V contained two plates and No. VI four plates, placed together between 'Advertiser' and text. The plates from June onwards bear the signature of C. Roberts, the engraver, as well as that of Fildes. Those for April bear the signature Dalziel as well as Fildes's name or initials; on those for May, only Fildes's name or initials are visible. According to Kitton (*Dickens and His Illustrators* (1899), p. 216) the titles for the illustrations completed after Dickens's death were supplied by Fildes. The two additional plates in Number VI are a portrait of Dickens, signed and dated 1870, engraved by J. H. Baker from a photograph taken in 1868 by Mason and Co., and a vignette of Rochester by Fildes. The monthly parts wrapper, initially sketched by Charles Collins, was redesigned by Fildes.

Binding: Described by Sadleir, *XIX Century Fiction*, i. 105 and Carter, *Binding Variants*, pp. 108–9. Binding of copies containing W. H. Smith's 1872 book catalogue differs slightly from that of copies with Chapman and Hall's advertisement, dated 1870. The third variant binding (C) described by Carter is the rarest and probably the latest of the three.

Copies seen:

(*a*) Unbound parts. Victoria and Albert Museum; British Museum; London University Library; Dickens House; The Queen's University Library, Belfast; copies in possession of the editors.

(*b*) Volume. Victoria and Albert Museum (two copies: one, with the original binding and Forster's book-plate, has the green wrappers bound in; one rebound); London University Library (two copies, one with 1872

catalogue, one rebound); Dickens House (several copies); The Queen's
University Library, Belfast (binding C); three copies in possession of the
editor, one in original binding, one with 1872 catalogue, one rebound.

Publication: In six monthly parts, April to September (31 March to
31 August) 1870, 1s. each, but the price of the September Number was
raised to 1s. 6d. (In some copies 'Eighteenpence' is printed on the cover; in
others it is on a slip pasted over the original price.) The monthly parts,
with their advertisements, are described in Thomas Hatton and Arthur H.
Cleaver, *Bibliography of the Periodical Works of Charles Dickens* (1933).

In one volume on 31 August 1870. 7s. 6d.

'Every Saturday'

Publishers: Fields, Osgood and Company, Boston.

The dates of publication and the accompanying illustrations were as
follows:

No. I	9 April, chs. i and ii	In the Court
	16 April, ch. iii	Under the Trees
	23 April, chs. iv and v	
No. II	7 May, chs. vi and vii	Mr. Jasper Accompanies Miss Rosebud (At the Piano)
	14 May, chs. viii and ix	The Quarrel (On Dangerous Ground)
No. III	11 June, ch. x	By the River (Mr. Crisparkle is Overpaid)
	18 June, ch. xi	
	25 June, ch. xii	Mr. Durdles (Durdles Cautions Mr. Sapsea against Boasting)
No. IV	9 July, chs. xiii and xiv	
	16 July, ch. xv	Mr. Grewgious Breaks the News to Jasper (Mr. Grewgious has his Suspicions)
	23 July, ch. xvi	
No. V	6 August, ch. xvii	
	13 August, chs. xviii and xix	Jasper's Sacrifices
	20 August, ch. xx	Mr. Grewgious experiences a New Sensation
No. VI	3 September, ch. xxi and part of ch. xxii	
	10 September, end of ch. xxii and part of ch. xxiii	
	17 September, rest of ch. xxiii	

Copy seen: Dickens House.

1873: Library edition

The Mystery of Edwin Drood and Other Stories. By Charles Dickens. With Illustrations. London: Chapman and Hall, 193 Piccadilly. 1874.

Collation: A^4 B–Z^8 AA–EE^8 FF^4. $A1$ half-title. $A2$ title, verso imprint of Robson and Sons. $A3$ Contents. $A3^v$ numbered vi. $A4$ lacking [? List of Illustrations].[1] B–Q^8 The Mystery of Edwin Drood. R–Z^8 AA–EE^8 FF^4 Master Humphrey's Clock; Hunted Down; Holiday Romance; George Silverman's Explanation. $FF4^v$ (p. 440) imprint of Robson and Sons.

Note on Printing: Text printed from 1870 (see Introduction, p. xxxii).

Plates: Frontispiece (between $A1$ and $A2$) 'Mr. Crisparkle is Overpaid'; otherwise arranged as in 70, but without the portrait and the Rochester vignette.

Copies: London University Library; British Museum (date-stamp 8 Ja. 74).

Publication: Vol. XXX of the Library edition, dated 1874, but listed in *Publisher's Circular* for December 1873 and in *Athenaeum*, 'List of New Books' for 20 December 1873. 8*s*.

1875: Charles Dickens edition

The Mystery of Edwin Drood, and Other Stories. By Charles Dickens. London: Chapman and Hall, 193, Piccadilly.

Collation: A^4 B–T^8. $A1$ series title. $A2$ title, verso imprint of Virtue and Co. $A3$ Contents. $A4$ title. B^8–L6 The Mystery of Edwin Drood. L7, 8 M–T^8 Master Humphrey's Clock; Hunted Down; Holiday Romance; George Silverman's Explanation. $T8^v$ ([p. 288]) imprint of Virtue and Co.

Note on Printing: Text printed from 1873 (see Introduction, p. xxxii).

Plates: Frontispiece 'Durdles Cautions Mr. Sapsea Against Boasting' and seven illustrations: 'Under The Trees', 'At The Piano', 'On Dangerous Ground', ' "Good-Bye, Rosebud, Darling!" ', 'Mr. Grewgious Has His Suspicions', 'Jasper's Sacrifices', 'Up The River'.

Copy described: British Museum (date-stamp 2 Jy 75).

Publication: 27 February 1875 (*Athenaeum*, 'List of New Books'). 3*s*. 6*d*.

---

[1] Found in this position in most other volumes in the series.

THE MYSTERY

OF

EDWIN DROOD.

BY

CHARLES DICKENS.

WITH TWELVE ILLUSTRATIONS BY S. L. FILDES,
AND A PORTRAIT.

CHAPMAN AND HALL, 193 PICCADILLY.

1870.

[*The right of Translation is reserved.*]

Title-page of the first edition

CONTENTS

THE MYSTERY
OF
EDWIN DROOD,
BY
CHARLES DICKENS.

LONDON:

CHAPMAN & HALL, 193, PICCADILLY.

ILLUSTRATIONS

Vignette Title Page

CHAPTER I

THE DAWN[1]

AN ancient English Cathedral Town?[2] How can the ancient English Cathedral town[3] be here! The well-known massive grey square[4] tower of its old Cathedral? How can that be here! There is no spike of rusty iron in the air, between the eye and it, from any point of the real prospect. What is[5] the spike that intervenes, and who has set it up? Maybe, it is set up by the Sultan's orders for the impaling of a horde of Turkish robbers, one by one. It is so, for cymbals clash, and the Sultan goes by to his palace in long[6] procession. Ten thousand scimitars flash in the sunlight,[7] and thrice ten thousand dancing-girls strew flowers. Then, follow white elephants caparisoned in countless gorgeous colors, and infinite in number and attendants. Still, the Cathedral tower rises in the background, where it cannot be, and still no writhing figure is on the grim spike. Stay! Is the spike so low a thing as the rusty spike on the top of a post of an old bedstead that has tumbled all awry?[8] Some vague period[9] of drowsy laughter must be devoted to the consideration of this possibility.

Shaking from head to foot, the man whose scattered consciousness has thus fantastically pieced itself together, at length rises, supports his trembling frame upon his arms, and looks around.[10] He is in the meanest and closest[11] of small rooms. Through the ragged window-curtain, the light of early day steals in from a miserable court. He lies, dressed, across a large unseemly bed, upon a bedstead that has indeed given way under the weight upon it. Lying, also dressed and also across the bed, not longwise, are a Chinaman, a Lascar, and a haggard woman. The two first are in a sleep or stupor; the last is blowing at a kind of pipe, to kindle it. And as she blows, and shading it with her lean hand, concentrates its red spark of light, it serves in the dim morning as[12] a lamp to show him what he sees of her.

"Another?" says this woman, in a querulous, rattling whisper.[13] "Have another?"

---

[1] THE DAWN] THE PROLOGUE MS   [2] Town] MS Tower 70–75
[3] town] MS tower 70–75   [4] massive grey square] grey square massive MS
[5] is] MS is 70–75   [6] long] long, long, long MS
[7] flash in the sunlight] reflect the sun MS
[8] awry] awry, so that he who is recumbent on the bedstead on the lower side, touches the floor MS
[9] vague period] centuries MS   [10] around] round MS
[11] meanest and closest] meanest, squalidest, and closest MS
[12] as] for MS
[13] querulous, rattling whisper] querulous whisper that rattles MS

He looks about him, with his hand to his forehead.[1]

"Ye've smoked as many as five since ye come in at midnight," the woman goes on, as she chronically complains.[2] "Poor me, poor me, my head is so bad! Them two come in after ye. Ah, poor me, the business is slack, is slack! Few Chinamen about the Docks, and fewer Lascars, and no ships coming in, these say! Here's another ready for ye, deary. Ye'll remember like a good soul, won't ye, that the market price is dreffle high just now? More than[3] three shillings[4] and sixpence for a thimbleful![5] And ye'll remember, too,[6] that nobody but me (and Jack Chinaman t'other side the court; but he can't do it as well as me) has the true secret of mixing it? Ye'll pay up according, deary, won't ye?"

She blows at the pipe as she speaks, and, occasionally bubbling at it, inhales much of its contents.

"Oh me, Oh me, my lungs is weak, my lungs is bad![7] It's nearly ready for ye, deary. Ah, poor me, poor me,[8] my poor hand shakes like to drop off! I see ye coming-to, and I ses to my poor self, 'I'll have another ready for him, and he'll bear in mind the market price of[9] opium, and pay according.'[10] Oh my poor head! I makes my pipes of[9] old penny ink-bottles, ye see, deary—this is one—and I fits in a mouthpiece, this way, and I takes my mixter out of[9] this thimble with this little horn spoon;[11] and so I fills, deary. Ah, my poor nerves! I got Heavens-hard drunk for sixteen year afore I took to this; but this don't hurt me, not to speak of. And it takes away the hunger as well as[12] wittles, deary."

She hands him the nearly-emptied pipe, and sinks back, turning over on her face.

He rises unsteadily from the bed, lays the pipe upon the hearthstone, draws back the ragged curtain, and looks with repugnance at his three companions. He notices that the woman has opium-smoked herself into a strange likeness of the Chinaman. His form of cheek, eye, and temple, and his color, are repeated in her. As he lies on his back, the said[13] Chinaman convulsively wrestles with one of his many Gods, or Devils, perhaps, and snarls horribly. The Lascar laughs and dribbles at the mouth. The hostess is still.

"What visions can *she* have?" the waking man muses, as he turns her face towards him, and stands looking down at it. "Visions of many butchers' shops, and public houses, and much credit? Of an increase of hideous customers, and this horrible bedstead set upright again, and this

[1] with his hand to his forehead] deliriously MS
[2] complains] shivers and complains MS   [3] than] ⟨nor⟩ than MS nor 70–75
[4] three shillings] shilling ES   [5] thimbleful] little thimble full MS
[6] too] MS *om.* 70–75   [7] bad] very bad MS
[8] poor me, poor me] poor me MS   [9] of] o' MS
[10] according] accordin MS   [11] little horn spoon] needle MS
[12] as well as] better than MS
[13] As he lies on his back, the said] MS Said 70–75

IN THE COURT

horrible court swept clean? What can she rise to, under any quantity of opium, higher than that!—Eh?"

He bends down his ear, to listen to her mutterings.

"Unintelligible!"

As he watches the spasmodic shoots and darts that break out of her face and limbs, like fitful lightning out of a dark sky, some contagion in them seizes upon him: insomuch that he has to withdraw himself to a lean arm-chair by the hearth—placed there, perhaps, for such emergencies— and to sit in it, holding tight, until he has got the better of this unclean spirit of imitation.

Then he comes back, pounces on the Chinaman, and, seizing him with both hands by the throat, turns him violently on the bed. The Chinaman clutches the aggressive hands, resists, gasps, and protests.

"What do you say?"

A watchful pause.

"Unintelligible!"

Slowly loosening his grasp as he listens to the incoherent jargon with an attentive frown, he turns to the Lascar and fairly drags him forth upon the floor. As he falls, the Lascar starts into a half-risen attitude, glares with his eyes, lashes about him fiercely with his arms, and draws a phantom knife. It then becomes apparent that the woman has taken posses-sion of his[1] knife, for safety's sake; for, she too starting up, and restrain-ing and expostulating with him, the knife is visible in her dress, not in his, when they drowsily drop back, side by side.

There has been wild[2] chattering and clattering enough between them, but to no purpose. When any distinct word has been flung into the air, it has had no sense or sequence. Wherefore "unintelligible!" is again the comment of the watcher, made with some reassured nodding of his head, and a gloomy smile. He then lays certain silver money on the table, finds his hat, gropes his way down the broken stairs, gives a good-morning to some rat-ridden doorkeeper,[3] a-bed[4] in a black hutch beneath the stairs, and passes out.

That same afternoon, the massive grey square tower of an old Cathedral rises before the sight of a jaded traveller. The bells are going for daily vesper service, and he must needs attend it, one would say, from his haste to reach the open Cathedral door. The choir are getting on their sullied white robes, in a hurry, when he arrives among them, gets on his own robe, and falls into the procession filing in to service. Then, the Sacristan locks the iron-barred gates that divide the sanctuary from the chancel, and all of the procession having scuttled into their places, hide their

---

[1] his] this 73 75   [2] wild] MS om. 70–75
[3] doorkeeper] doorkeeper or what not MS
[4] a-bed] MS in bed 70–75

faces; and then the intoned words, "WHEN THE WICKED MAN——" rise among groins of arches and beams of roof, awakening muttered thunder.[1]

CHAPTER II

A DEAN, AND A CHAPTER ALSO[2]

WHOSOEVER has observed that sedate and clerical bird, the rook,[3] may perhaps have noticed that when he wings his way homeward towards nightfall, in a sedate and clerical company, two rooks[4] will suddenly detach themselves from the rest, will retrace their flight for some distance, and will there[5] poise and linger; conveying to mere men the fancy that it is of some occult importance to the body politic, that this artful couple should pretend to have renounced connexion with it.

Similarly, service being over in the old Cathedral with the square tower, and the choir scuffling out again, and divers venerable persons of rook-like[6] aspect dispersing, two of these latter retrace their steps, and walk together in the echoing Close.

Not only is the day waning, but the year. The low sun is fiery and yet cold behind the monastery ruin, and the Virginia creeper on the Cathedral wall has showered half its deep-red leaves down on the pavement. There has been rain this afternoon, and a wintry shudder goes among the little pools on the cracked uneven flagstones, and through the giant elm trees as they shed a gust of tears. Their fallen leaves lie strewn thickly about. Some of these leaves, in a timid rush, seek sanctuary within the low arched Cathedral door; but two men coming out, resist them, and cast them forth again with their feet; this done, one of the two locks the door with a goodly key, and the other flits away with a folio music-book.

"Mr. Jasper was that, Tope?"[7]

"Yes, Mr. Dean."

"He has stayed late."

"Yes, Mr. Dean. I have stayed for him, your Reverence. He has been took a little poorly."

"Say 'taken,' Tope—to the Dean," the younger rook[3] interposes in a low tone with this touch of correction, as who should say: "You may offer bad grammar to the laity, or the humbler clergy; not[8] to the Dean."

---

[1] thunder] thunders MS

[2] A DEAN, AND A CHAPTER ALSO] ⟨A DEAN AS WELL AS A CHAPTER⟩ A DEAN, AND A CHAPTER ALSO MS

[3] rook] crow MS　　　　[4] rooks] crows MS　　　　[5] there] *possibly* then MS

[6] rook-like] crow-like MS

[7] Tope] ⟨Peptune⟩ Tope MS *and so to the end of ch. iv*

[8] not] but not MS

Mr. Tope, Chief Verger and Showman, and accustomed to be high with excursion parties, declines with a silent loftiness to perceive that any suggestion has been[1] tendered to him.

"And when and how has Mr. Jasper been taken—for, as Mr. Crisparkle has remarked, it is better to say taken—taken—" repeats the Dean; "when and how has Mr. Jasper been Taken——"

"Taken, sir," Tope deferentially murmurs.

"——Poorly, Tope?"

"Why, sir, Mr. Jasper was that breathed——"

"I wouldn't say 'That breathed,' Tope," Mr. Crisparkle interposes, with the same touch as before. "Not English—to the Dean." *Orientale*

"Breathed to that extent would be preferable,"[2] the Dean (not unflattered by this indirect homage), condescendingly remarks; "would be preferable."

"Mr. Jasper's breathing was so remarkably short;" thus discreetly does Mr. Tope work his way round the sunken rock, "when he came in, that it distressed him mightily to get his notes out: which was perhaps the cause of his having a kind of fit on him after a little. His memory grew DAZED." Mr. Tope, with his eyes on the Reverend Mr. Crisparkle, shoots this word out, as defying him to improve upon it: "and a dimness and giddiness crept over him as strange as ever I saw: though he didn't seem to mind it particularly, himself. However, a little time and a little water brought him out of his DAZE." Mr. Tope repeats the word and its emphasis, with the air of saying: "As I *have* made a success, I'll make it again."

"And Mr. Jasper has gone home quite himself, has he?" asks[3] the Dean.

"Your Reverence, he has gone home quite himself. And I'm glad to see he's having his fire kindled up, for it's chilly after the wet, and the Cathedral had both a damp feel and a damp touch this afternoon, and he was very shivery."

They all three look[4] towards an old stone Gate House crossing the Close, with an arched thoroughfare passing beneath it. Through its latticed window, a fire shines out upon the fast darkening scene, involving in shadow the pendent masses of ivy and creeper covering the building's front. As the deep Cathedral bell strikes the hour, a ripple of wind goes through these at their distance, like a ripple of the solemn sound that hums through tomb and tower, broken niche and defaced statue, in the pile close at hand.

"Is Mr. Jasper's nephew with him?" the Dean asks.[5]

"No, sir," replies[6] the Verger, "but expected. There's his own solitary

[1] been] ever been MS   [2] would be preferable] MS *om.* 70–75
[3] asks] MS asked 70–75   [4] look] looked ES
[5] the Dean asks] ⟨asks⟩ the Dean ⟨enquires⟩ enquires MS
[6] replies] replied 73 75

shadow betwixt his two windows—the one looking this way, and the one looking down into the High Street—drawing his own curtains now."

"Well, well," says the Dean, with a sprightly air of breaking up the little conference, "I hope Mr. Jasper's heart may not be too much set upon his nephew. Our affections, however laudable, in this transitory world, should never master us; we should guide them, guide them. I find I am not disagreeably reminded of my dinner, by hearing my dinner-bell. Perhaps Mr. Crisparkle you will, before going home, look in on Jasper?"

"Certainly, Mr. Dean. And tell him that you had the kindness to desire to know how he was?"

"Ay; do so, do so. Certainly. Wished to know how he was. By all means. Wished to know how he was."

With a pleasant air of patronage, the Dean as nearly cocks his quaint hat as a Dean in good spirits may, and directs his comely gaiters towards the ruddy dining-room of the snug old red-brick house where he is at present "in residence" with Mrs. Dean and Miss Dean.

Mr. Crisparkle, Minor Canon, fair and rosy, and perpetually pitching himself head-foremost into all the deep running water in the surrounding country; Mr. Crisparkle, Minor Canon, early riser, musical, classical, cheerful, kind,[1] good-natured, social, contented, and boy-like; Mr. Crisparkle, Minor Canon and good man,[2] lately "Coach" upon the chief Pagan high roads, but since promoted by a patron (grateful for a well-taught son) to his present Christian beat; betakes himself to the Gate House, on his way home to his early tea.

"Sorry to hear from Tope that you have not been well, Jasper."

"Oh, it was nothing, nothing!"

"You look a little worn."

"Do I? Oh, I don't think so. What is better, I don't feel so. Tope has made too much of it I suspect. It's his trade to make the most of everything appertaining to the Cathedral, you know."

"I may tell the Dean—I call expressly from the Dean—that you are all right again?"

The reply, with a slight smile, is: "Certainly; with my respects and thanks to the Dean."

"I'm[3] glad to hear that you expect young Drood."

"I expect the dear fellow every[4] moment."

"Ah! He will do you more good than a doctor, Jasper."

"More good than a dozen doctors. For I love him dearly, and I don't love doctors, or doctors' stuff."

Mr. Jasper is a dark man of some[5] six-and-twenty, with thick, lustrous, well-arranged black hair and whisker.[6] He looks older than he is, as dark men often do. His voice is deep and good, his face and figure are good,

---

¹ kind] *not in* MS   ² and good man] *not in* MS   ³ I'm] I am MS
⁴ every] *possibly* any MS   ⁵ some] ⟨five or⟩ MS   ⁶ whisker] whiskers 73 75

his manner is a little sombre. His room is a little sombre, and may have
had its influence in forming his manner. It is mostly in shadow. Even
when the sun shines brilliantly, it seldom touches the grand piano in
the recess, or the folio music-books on[1] the stand, or the bookshelves
on the wall, or the unfinished picture of a blooming schoolgirl[2] hanging over the chimneypiece; her flowing brown hair tied with a blue
riband, and her beauty remarkable for a quite childish, almost babyish,
touch of saucy discontent, comically conscious of itself. (There is not the
least artistic merit in this picture, which is[3] a mere daub; but it is clear
that the painter has made it humorously—one might almost say, revenge-
fully—like the original.)

"We shall miss you, Jasper, at the 'Alternate Musical Wednesdays'
to-night; but no doubt you are best at home. Good-night. God bless you!
'Tell me, shep-herds te-e-ell me; tell me-e-e, have you seen (have you
seen, have you seen, have you seen) my-y-y Flo-o-ora-a pass this way!' "
Melodiously good Minor Canon the Reverend Septimus[4] Crisparkle thus
delivers himself, in musical rhythm, as he withdraws his amiable[5] face
from the doorway and conveys it down stairs.

Sounds of recognition and greeting[6] pass between the Reverend
Septimus and somebody else, at the stair-foot. Mr. Jasper listens, starts
from his chair, and catches a young fellow in his arms, exclaiming:

"My dear Edwin!"

"My dear Jack! So glad to see you!"

"Get off your greatcoat, bright boy, and sit down here in your own
corner. Your feet are not wet? Pull your boots off. Do pull your boots off."

"My dear Jack, I am as dry as a bone. Don't moddley-coddley, there's
a good fellow. I like anything better than being moddley-coddleyed."

With the check upon him of being unsympathetically restrained in a
genial outburst[7] of enthusiasm, Mr. Jasper stands still, and looks on
intently at the young fellow, divesting himself of his outer[8] coat, hat,
gloves, and so forth. Once for all, a look of intentness and intensity—
a look of hungry, exacting, watchful, and yet devoted affection—is always,
now and ever afterwards, on the Jasper face whenever the Jasper face is
addressed in this direction. And whenever it is so addressed, it is never,
on this occasion or on any other, dividedly addressed; it is always concentrated.

"Now I am right, and now I'll take my corner, Jack. Any dinner,
Jack?"

Mr. Jasper opens a door at the upper end of the room, and discloses

---

[1] on] ⟨on⟩ in MS   [2] schoolgirl] schoolgirl of sixteen at the utmost MS
[3] which is] *not in* MS   [4] Septimus] ⟨Joe⟩ Septimus MS *and so up to p. 40 l. 7*
[5] amiable] ⟨cheerful⟩ honest MS
[6] recognition and greeting] greeting and recognition ES
[7] outburst] burst MS   [8] outer] outward 75

a small inner room pleasantly lighted and prepared, wherein a comely dame is in the act of setting dishes on table.

"What a jolly old Jack it is!" cries the young fellow, with a clap of his hands. "Look here, Jack; tell me; whose birthday is it?"

"Not yours, I know," Mr. Jasper answers, pausing to consider.

"Not mine, you know? No; not mine, *I* know! Pussy's!"

Fixed as the look the young fellow meets, is, there is yet in it some strange power of suddenly including the sketch[1] over the chimney-piece.

"Pussy's, Jack! We must drink Many happy returns to her. Come, uncle; take your dutiful and sharp-set nephew in to dinner."

As the boy (for he is little more) lays a hand on Jasper's shoulder, Jasper cordially and gaily lays a hand on *his* shoulder, and so Marseillaise-wise they go in to dinner.

"And Lord! Here's Mrs. Tope!" cries the boy. "Lovelier than ever!"

"Never you mind me, Master Edwin," retorts the Verger's wife; "I can take care of myself."

"You can't. You're much too handsome. Give me a kiss, because it's Pussy's birthday."

"I'd Pussy you, young man, if I was Pussy, as you call her," Mrs. Tope blushingly retorts, after being saluted. "Your uncle's too much wrapped up in you, that's where it is. He makes so much of you, that it's my opinion you think you've only to call your Pussys by the dozen, to make 'em come."

"You forget, Mrs. Tope," Mr. Jasper interposes, taking his place at table[2] with a genial smile, "and so do you, Ned, that Uncle and Nephew are words prohibited here by common consent and express agreement. For what we are going to receive His holy name be praised!"

"Done like the Dean! Witness, Edwin Drood! Please to carve, Jack, for I can't."

This sally ushers in the dinner. Little to the present purpose, or to any purpose, is said, while it is in course of being disposed of. At length the cloth is drawn, and a dish of walnuts and a decanter of rich-colored sherry are placed upon the table.

"I say! Tell me, Jack," the young fellow then flows on: "do you really and truly feel as if the mention of our relationship divided us at all? *I*[3] don't."

"Uncles as a rule, Ned, are so much older than their nephews," is the reply, "that I have that feeling instinctively."

"As a rule? Ah, may-be! But what is a difference in age of half a dozen years or so?[4] And some uncles, in large families, are even younger than their nephews. By George, I wish it was the case with us!"

¹ sketch] ⟨picture⟩ ⟨sketch⟩ picture MS   ² table] the table 75
³ *I*] I ES   ⁴ half a dozen years or so] less than half a dozen years MS

"Why ?"

"Because if it was, I'd take the lead with you, Jack, and be as wise as Begone dull care that turned a young man grey, and begone dull care that turned an old man to clay.—Halloa, Jack! Don't drink."

"Why not?"

"Asks why not, on Pussy's birthday, and no Happy returns proposed! Pussy, Jack, and many of 'em! Happy returns, I mean."

Laying an affectionate and laughing touch on the boy's extended hand, as if it were at once his giddy head and his light heart, Mr. Jasper drinks the toast in silence.

"Hip, hip, hip, and nine times nine, and one to finish with, and all that, understood. Hooray, hooray, hooray! And now, Jack, let's have a little talk about Pussy. Two pairs of nut-crackers? Pass me one, and take the other." Crack. "How's Pussy getting on, Jack?"

"With her music? Fairly."

"What a dreadfully conscientious fellow you are, Jack. But *I* know Lord bless you! Inattentive, isn't she?"

"She can learn anything, if she will."

"*If* she will? Egad that's it. But if she won't?"

Crack. On Mr. Jasper's part.

"How's she looking, Jack?"

Mr. Jasper's concentrated face again includes the portrait as he returns: "Very like your sketch indeed."

"I *am* a little proud of it," says the young fellow, glancing up at the sketch with complacency, and then shutting one eye, and taking a corrected prospect of it over a level bridge of nut-cracker[1] in the air: "Not badly hit off from memory. But I ought to have caught that expression pretty well, for I have seen it often enough."

Crack. On Edwin Drood's part.

Crack. On Mr. Jasper's part.

"In point of fact," the former resumes, after some silent dipping among his fragments of walnut with an air of pique, "I see it whenever I go to see Pussy. If I don't find it on her face, I leave it there.—You know I do, Miss Scornful Pert. Booh!" With a twirl of the nut-crackers at the portrait.

Crack. Crack. Crack. Slowly, on Mr. Jasper's part.

Crack. Sharply, on the part of Edwin Drood.

Silence on both sides.

"Have you lost your tongue, Jack?"

"Have you found yours, Ned?"

"No, but really;—isn't it, you know, after all?"

Mr. Jasper lifts his dark eyebrows inquiringly.

"Isn't it unsatisfactory to be cut off from choice in such a matter?

[1] nut-cracker] nut-crackers 73 75

There, Jack! I tell you! If I could choose, I would choose Pussy from all the pretty girls in the world."

"But you have not got to choose."

"That's what I complain of. My dead and gone father and Pussy's dead and gone father must needs marry us together by anticipation. Why the— Devil, I was going to say, if it had been respectful to their memory— couldn't they leave us alone?"

"Tut, tut, dear boy," Mr. Jasper remonstrates, in a tone of gentle deprecation.

"Tut, tut? Yes, Jack, it's all very well for *you*. *You* can take it easily. *Your* life is not laid down to scale, and lined and dotted out for you, like a surveyor's plan. *You* have no uncomfortable suspicion that you are forced upon anybody, nor has anybody an uncomfortable suspicion that she is forced upon you, or that you are forced upon her. *You* can choose for yourself. Life, for *you*, is a plum with the natural bloom on; it hasn't been over-carefully wiped off for *you*——"

"Don't stop, dear fellow. Go on."

"Can I anyhow have hurt your feelings, Jack?"

"How can you have hurt my feelings?"

"Good Heaven,[1] Jack, you look frightfully ill! There's a strange film come over your eyes."

Mr. Jasper, with a forced smile, stretches out his right hand, as if at once to disarm apprehension and gain time to get better. After a while he says faintly:

"I have been taking opium for a pain—an agony—that sometimes overcomes me. The effects of the medicine steal over me like a blight or a cloud, and pass. You see them in the act of passing; they will be gone directly. Look away from me. They will go all the sooner."

With a scared[2] face, the younger man complies, by casting his eyes downward at the ashes on the hearth. Not relaxing his own gaze at the fire,[3] but rather strengthening it with a fierce, firm grip upon his elbow-chair, the elder sits for a few moments rigid, and then, with thick drops standing on his forehead, and a sharp catch of his breath, becomes as he was before. On his so subsiding in his chair, his nephew gently and assiduously tends him while he quite recovers. When Jasper is restored, he lays a tender hand upon his nephew's shoulder, and, in a tone of voice less troubled than the purport of his words—indeed with something of raillery or banter in it—thus addresses him:[4]

---

[1] Good Heaven] Good Heavens MS
[2] scared] scared and confounded MS
[3] at the fire] *not in* MS on the fire 75
[4] "I have been taking . . . thus addresses him] *written in* MS *on a fresh slip pasted over the first draft. Subsequent removal of slip to verso of preceding page reveals* "(I have been taking) opium for a pain—an agony—[I] sometimes have. Its effects steal over me like

"There is said to be a hidden skeleton in every house; but you thought there was none in mine, dear Ned."

"Upon my life, Jack, I did think so. However,[1] when I come to consider that even in Pussy's house—if she had one—and in mine—if I had one——"

"You were going[2] to say (but that I interrupted you in spite of myself) what a quiet life mine is. No whirl and uproar around me, no distracting commerce or calculation, no risk, no change of place, myself devoted to the art I pursue, my business my pleasure."

"I really was going to say something of the kind, Jack; but you see, you, speaking of yourself, almost necessarily leave out much that I should have put in. For instance: I should have put in the foreground, your being so much respected as Lay Precentor, or Lay Clerk, or whatever you call it,[3] of this Cathedral; your enjoying the reputation of having done such wonders with the choir; your choosing your society, and holding such an independent position in this queer old place; your gift of teaching (why, even Pussy, who don't like being taught, says there never was such a Master as you are!) and your connexion."

"Yes; I saw what you were tending to. I hate it."

"Hate it, Jack?" (Much bewildered.)

"I hate it. The cramped monotony of my existence grinds me away by the grain. How does our service sound to you?"

"Beautiful! Quite celestial."

"It often sounds to me quite devilish. I am so weary of it! The echoes of my own voice among the arches seem to mock me with my daily drudging round. No wretched monk who droned his life away in that gloomy place, before me, can have been more tired of it than I am. He could take for relief (and did take) to carving demons out of the stalls and seats and desks. What shall I do? Must I take to carving them out of my heart?"

"I thought you had so exactly found your niche in life, Jack," Edwin Drood returns, astonished, bending forward in his chair to lay a sympathetic hand on Jasper's knee, and looking at him with an anxious face.

"I know you thought so. They all think so."

a blight or a cloud, and pass. ⟨There is no cause for alarm⟩ You see them in the act of passing. Put those knives out at the door—both of them!"

"My dear Jack, why?"

"It's going to lighten; they may attract the lightning; put them ⟨away⟩ in the dark."

With a scared and confounded face, the younger man complies. No ⟨lightning⟩ flash ensues, nor was there, for a moment, any passing likelihood of a thunder storm. He gently and assiduously tends his kinsman who by slow degrees recovers and clears away that cloud or blight. When he, (Jasper)—is quite himself and is as it were once more all resolved into that concentrated look, he lays a tender hand upon his nephew's shoulder and thus addresses him

[1] However,] ⟨But truly⟩ However, truly MS

[2] going] going on MS   [3] or Lay Clerk, or whatever you call it] *not in* MS

"Well; I suppose they do," says Edwin, meditating aloud. "Pussy thinks so."

"When did she tell you that?"

"The last time I was here. You remember when. Three months ago."

"How did she phrase it?"

"Oh! She only said that she had become your pupil, and that you were made for your vocation."

The younger man glances at the portrait. The elder sees it in him.

"Anyhow, my dear Ned," Jasper resumes, as he shakes his head with a grave cheerfulness: "I must subdue myself to my vocation: which is much the same thing outwardly. It's too late to find another now. This is a confidence between us."

"It shall be sacredly preserved, Jack."

"I have reposed it in you, because——"

"I feel it, I assure you. Because we are fast friends, and because you love and trust me, as I love and trust you. Both hands, Jack."

As each stands looking into the other's eyes, and as the uncle holds the nephew's hands, the uncle thus proceeds:

"You know now, don't you, that even a poor monotonous chorister and grinder of music—in his niche—may be troubled with some stray sort of ambition, aspiration, restlessness, dissatisfaction, what shall we call it?"

"Yes, dear Jack."

"And you will remember?"

"My dear Jack, I only ask you, am I likely to forget what you have said with so much feeling?"

"Take it as a warning, then."

In the act of having his hands released, and of moving a step back, Edwin pauses for an instant to consider the application of these last words. The instant over, he says, sensibly touched:

"I am afraid I am but a shallow, surface kind of fellow, Jack, and that my headpiece is none of the best. But I needn't say I am young; and perhaps I shall not grow worse as I grow older. At all events, I hope I have something impressible within me, which feels—deeply feels—the disinterestedness of your painfully laying your inner self bare, as a warning to me."

Mr. Jasper's steadiness of face and figure becomes so marvellous that his breathing seems to have stopped.

"I couldn't fail to notice, Jack, that it cost you a great effort, and that you were very much moved, and very unlike your usual self. Of course I knew that you were extremely fond of me, but I really was not prepared for your, as I may say, sacrificing yourself to me, in that way."

Mr. Jasper, becoming a breathing man again without the smallest stage of transition between the two extreme states, lifts his shoulders, laughs, and waves his right arm.

"No; don't put the sentiment away, Jack; please don't; for I am very much in earnest. I have no doubt that that unhealthy state of mind which you have so powerfully described is attended with some real suffering, and is hard to bear. But let me reassure you, Jack, as to the chances of its overcoming Me.[1] I don't think I am in the way of it. In some few months less than another year, you know, I shall carry Pussy off from school as Mrs. Edwin Drood. I shall then go engineering into the East, and Pussy with me. And although we have our little tiffs now, arising out of a certain unavoidable flatness that attends our love-making, owing to its end being all settled beforehand, still I have no doubt of our getting on capitally then, when it's done and can't be helped. In short, Jack, to go back to the old song I was freely quoting at dinner (and who knows old songs better than you!), my wife shall dance and I will sing, so merrily pass the day. Of Pussy's being beautiful there cannot be a doubt;—and when you are good besides, Little Miss Impudence," once more apostrophizing the portrait, "I'll burn your comic likeness and paint your music-master another."

Mr. Jasper, with his hand to his chin, and with an expression of musing benevolence on his face, has attentively watched every animated look and gesture attending the delivery of these words. He remains in that attitude after they are spoken, as if in a kind of fascination attendant on his strong interest in the youthful spirit that[2] he loves so well. Then, he says with a quiet smile:

"You won't be warned, then?"

"No, Jack."

"You can't be warned, then?"

"No, Jack, not by you. Besides that I don't really consider myself in danger, I don't like your putting yourself in that position."

"Shall we go and walk in the churchyard?"

"By all means. You won't mind my slipping out of it for half a moment to the Nuns' House, and leaving a parcel there? Only gloves for Pussy; as many pairs of gloves as she is years old to-day. Rather poetical, Jack?"

Mr. Jasper, still in the same attitude, murmurs: "'Nothing half so sweet in life,' Ned!"

"Here's the parcel in my greatcoat pocket. They must be presented to-night, or the poetry is gone. It's against regulations for me to call at night, but not to leave a packet. I am ready, Jack!"

Mr. Jasper dissolves his attitude, and they go out together.

---

[1] Me] me 73 75   [2] that] *not in* MS

CHAPTER III

THE NUNS' HOUSE

For sufficient reasons which this narrative will itself unfold as it advances, a fictitious name must be bestowed upon the old Cathedral town. Let it stand in these pages as Cloisterham. It was once possibly known to the Druids by another name, and certainly to the Romans by another, and to the Saxons by another, and to the Normans by another; and a name more or less in the course of many centuries can be of little moment to its dusty chronicles.

An ancient city, Cloisterham, and no meet dwelling-place for any one with hankerings after the noisy world. A monotonous, silent city, deriving an earthy flavor throughout, from its Cathedral crypt, and so abounding in vestiges of monastic graves, that the Cloisterham children grow small salad in the dust of abbots and abbesses, and make dirt-pies of nuns and friars; while every ploughman in its outlying fields renders to once puissant Lord Treasurers, Archbishops, Bishops, and such-like, the attention which the Ogre in the story-book desired to render to his unbidden visitor, and grinds their bones to make his bread.

A drowsy city, Cloisterham, whose inhabitants seem to suppose, with an inconsistency more strange than rare, that all its changes lie behind it, and that there are no more to come. A queer moral to derive from antiquity, yet older than any traceable antiquity. So silent are the streets of Cloisterham (though prone to echo on the smallest provocation), that of a summer day the sunblinds of its shops scarce dare to flap in the south wind; while the sun-browned tramps who pass along and stare, quicken their limp a little, that they may the sooner get beyond the confines of its oppressive respectability. This is a feat not difficult of achievement, seeing that the streets of Cloisterham city are little more than one narrow street by which you get into it and get out of it: the rest being mostly disappointing yards with pumps in them and no thoroughfare—exception made of the Cathedral Close, and a paved Quaker settlement, in color and general conformation very like a Quakeress's bonnet, up in a shady corner.

In a word, a city of another and a bygone time is Cloisterham, with its hoarse Cathedral bell, its hoarse rooks[1] hovering about the Cathedral tower, its hoarser and less distinct rooks[1] in the stalls far beneath. Fragments of old wall, saint's chapel, chapter-house, convent, and monastery, have got incongruously or obstructively built into many of its houses and gardens, much as kindred jumbled notions have become incorporated into many of its citizens' minds. All things in it are of the past. Even its single

[1] rooks] crows MS

pawnbroker takes in no pledges, nor has he for a long time, but offers vainly an unredeemed stock for sale, of which the costlier articles are dim and pale old watches apparently in a cold[1] perspiration, tarnished sugar-tongs with ineffectual legs, and odd volumes of dismal books. The most abundant and the most agreeable evidences of progressing life in Cloisterham, are the evidences of vegetable life in its[2] many gardens; even its drooping and despondent little theatre has its poor strip of garden, receiving the foul fiend, when he ducks from its stage into the infernal regions, among scarlet beans or oyster-shells, according to the season of the year.

In the midst of Cloisterham stands the Nuns' House; a venerable brick edifice whose present appellation is doubtless derived from the legend of its conventual uses. On the trim gate enclosing its old courtyard, is a resplendent brass plate flashing forth the legend: "Seminary for Young Ladies. Miss Twinkleton." The house-front is so old and worn, and the brass plate is so shining and staring, that the general result has reminded imaginative strangers of a battered old beau with a large modern eye-glass stuck in his blind eye.

Whether the nuns of yore, being of a submissive rather than a stiff-necked generation, habitually bent their contemplative heads to avoid collision with the beams in the low ceilings of the many chambers of their House; whether they sat in its long low windows, telling their beads for their mortification instead of making necklaces of them for their adorn-ment; whether they were ever walled up alive in odd angles and jutting gables of the building for having some ineradicable leaven of busy mother Nature in them which has kept the fermenting world alive ever since; these may be matters of interest to its haunting ghosts (if any), but con-stitute no item in Miss Twinkleton's half-yearly accounts. They are neither of Miss Twinkleton's inclusive regulars, nor of her extras. The lady who undertakes the poetical department of the establishment at so much (or so little) a quarter, has no pieces in her list of recitals bearing on such unprofitable questions.

As, in some cases of drunkenness, and in others of animal magnetism, there are two states of consciousness which never clash, but each of which pursues its separate course as though it were continuous instead of broken (thus if I hide my watch when I am drunk, I must be drunk again before I can remember where), so Miss Twinkleton has two distinct and separate phases of being. Every night, the moment the young ladies have retired to rest, does Miss Twinkleton smarten up her curls a little, brighten up her eyes a little, and become a sprightly Miss Twinkleton whom the young ladies have never seen.[3] Every night, at the same hour, does Miss Twinkleton

---

[1] cold] MS slow 70–75   [2] its] *om.* 73 75
[3] a sprightly . . . seen] MS *with confusing deletions*   a sprightlier Miss Twinkleton than the young ladies have ever seen 70–75

resume the topics of the previous night, comprehending the tenderer scandal of Cloisterham, of which she has no knowledge whatever by day, and references to a certain season at Tunbridge Wells (airily called by Miss Twinkleton in this state of her existence "The Wells"), notably the season wherein a certain finished gentleman (compassionately called by Miss Twinkleton in this state[1] of her existence, "Foolish Mr. Porters") revealed a homage of the heart, whereof Miss Twinkleton, in her scholastic state of existence, is as ignorant as a granite pillar. Miss Twinkleton's companion in both states of existence, and equally adaptable to either, is one Mrs. Tisher:[2] a deferential widow with a weak back, a chronic sigh, and a suppressed voice,[3] who looks after the young ladies' wardrobes, and leads them to infer that she has seen better days. Perhaps this is the reason why it is an article of faith with the servants, handed down from race to race, that the departed Tisher was a hairdresser.

The pet pupil of the Nuns' House is Miss Rosa Bud, of course called Rosebud; wonderfully pretty, wonderfully childish, wonderfully whimsical. An awkward interest (awkward because romantic) attaches to Miss Bud in the minds of the young ladies, on account of its being known to them that a husband has been chosen for her by will and bequest, and that her guardian is bound down to bestow her on that husband when he comes of age. Miss Twinkleton, in her seminarial state of existence, has combated the romantic aspect of this destiny by affecting to shake her head over it behind Miss Bud's dimpled shoulders, and to brood on the unhappy lot of that doomed little victim. But with no better effect— possibly some unfelt touch of foolish Mr. Porters has undermined the endeavour—than to evoke from the young ladies an unanimous bedchamber cry of "Oh! what a pretending old thing Miss Twinkleton is, my dear!"

The Nuns' House is never in such a state of flutter as when this allotted husband calls to see little Rosebud. (It is unanimously understood by the young ladies that he is lawfully entitled to this privilege, and that if Miss Twinkleton disputed it she would be instantly taken up and transported.) When his ring at the gate bell is expected, or takes place, every young lady who can, under any pretence, look out of window, looks out of window: while every young lady who is "practising," practises out of time; and the French class becomes so demoralized that the Mark goes round as briskly as the bottle at a convivial party in the last century.

On the afternoon of the day next after the dinner of two at the Gate House, the bell is rung with the usual fluttering results.

"Mr. Edwin Drood to see Miss Rosa."

This is the announcement of the parlor-maid in chief. Miss Twinkleton,

---

[1] state] stage 75   [2] Mrs. Tisher] Mrs Tisher, her aide de camp MS
[3] a chronic sigh, and a suppressed voice] a suppressed voice and a chronic sigh MS

with an exemplary air of melancholy on her, turns to the sacrifice, and says: "You may go down, my dear." Miss Bud goes down, followed by all eyes.

Mr. Edwin Drood is waiting in Miss Twinkleton's own parlor: a dainty room, with nothing more directly scholastic in it than a terrestrial and a celestial globe. These expressive machines imply (to parents and guardians) that even when Miss Twinkleton retires into the bosom of privacy, duty may at any moment compel her to become a sort of Wandering Jewess, scouring the earth and soaring through the skies in search of knowledge for her pupils.

The last new maid, who has never seen the young gentleman Miss Rosa is engaged to, and who is making his acquaintance between the hinges of the open door, left open for the purpose, stumbles guiltily down the kitchen stairs, as a charming little apparition with its[1] face concealed by a little silk apron thrown over its head, glides into the parlor.

"Oh! It *is* so ridiculous!" says the apparition, stopping and shrinking. "Don't, Eddy!"

"Don't what, Rosa?"

"Don't come any nearer, please. It *is* so absurd."

"What is absurd, Rosa?"

"The whole thing is. It *is* so absurd to be an engaged orphan;[2] and it *is* so absurd to have the girls and the servants scuttling about after one, like mice in the wainscot; and it *is* so absurd to be called upon!"

The apparition appears to have a thumb in the corner[3] of its mouth while making this complaint.

"You give me an affectionate reception, Pussy, I must say."

"Well, I will in a minute, Eddy, but I can't just yet. How are you?" (very shortly).

"I am unable to reply that I am much the better for seeing you, Pussy, inasmuch as I see nothing of you."

This second remonstrance brings a dark bright pouting eye out from a corner of the apron; but it swiftly becomes invisible again, as the apparition exclaims: "Oh! Good Gracious, you have had half your hair cut off!"

"I should have done better to have had my head cut off, I think," says Edwin, rumpling the hair in question, with a fierce glance at the looking-glass, and giving an impatient stamp. "Shall I go?"

"No; you needn't go just yet, Eddy. The girls would all be asking questions why you went."

"Once for all, Rosa, will you uncover that ridiculous little head of yours and give me a welcome?"

[1] its] *deleted, possibly in error, in* MS
[2] an engaged orphan] an orphan without a will of one's own MS
[3] the corner] a corner MS

The apron is pulled off the childish head, as its wearer replies: "You're very welcome, Eddy. There! I'm sure that's nice. Shake hands. No, I can't kiss you, because I've got an acidulated drop in my mouth."

"Are you at all glad to see me, Pussy?"

"Oh, yes, I'm dreadfully glad.—Go and sit down.—Miss Twinkleton."

It is the custom of that excellent lady, when these visits occur, to appear every three minutes, either in her own person or in that of Mrs. Tisher, and lay an offering on the shrine of Propriety by affecting to look for some desiderated article. On the present occasion, Miss Twinkleton, gracefully gliding in and out, says, in passing: "How do you do, Mr. Drood? Very glad indeed to have the pleasure. Pray excuse me. Tweezers. Thank you!"

"I got the gloves last evening, Eddy, and I like them very much. They are beauties."

"Well, that's something," the affianced replies, half grumbling. "The smallest encouragement thankfully received. And how did you pass your birthday, Pussy?"[1]

"Delightfully! Everybody gave me a present. And we had a feast. And we had a ball at night."

"A feast and a ball, eh? These occasions seem to go off tolerably well without me, Pussy."

"De-lightfully!" cries Rosa, in a quite spontaneous manner, and without the least pretence of reserve.

"Hah! And what was the feast?"

"Tarts, oranges, jellies, and shrimps."

"Any partners at the ball?"

"We danced with one another, of course, sir. But some of the girls made game to be their brothers. It *was* so droll!"

"Did anybody make game to be——"

"To be you? Oh dear yes!" cries Rosa, laughing with great enjoyment. "That was the first thing done."

"I hope she did it pretty well," says Edwin, rather doubtfully.

"Oh! It was excellent!—I wouldn't dance with you, you know."

Edwin scarcely seems to see the force of this; begs to know if he may take the liberty to ask why?

"Because I was so tired of you," returns Rosa. But she quickly adds, and pleadingly too, seeing displeasure in his face: "Dear Eddy, you were just as tired of me, you know."

"Did I say so, Rosa?"

"Say so! Do you ever say so? No, you only showed it. Oh, she did it so well!" cries Rosa, in a sudden ecstacy with her counterfeit betrothed.

"It strikes me that she must be a devilish impudent girl," says Edwin Drood. "And so, Pussy, you have passed your last birthday in this old house."

[1] See p. 19 n.

"Ah, yes!" Rosa clasps her hands, looks down with a sigh, and shakes her head.

"You seem to be sorry, Rosa."

"I am sorry for the poor old place. Somehow, I feel as if it would miss me, when I am gone so far away, so young."

"Perhaps we had better stop short, Rosa?"

She looks up at him with a swift bright look; next moment shakes her head, sighs, and looks down again.

"That is to say, is it Pussy, that we are both resigned?"

She nods her head again, and after a short silence, quaintly bursts out with: "You know we must be married, and married from here, Eddy, or the poor girls will be so dreadfully disappointed!"

For the moment there is more of compassion, both for her and for himself, in her affianced husband's face, than there is of love. He checks the look, and asks:[1] "Shall I take you out for a walk, Rosa dear?"

Rosa dear does not seem at all clear on this point, until her face, which has been comically reflective, brightens. "Oh, yes, Eddy; let us go for a walk! And I tell you what we'll do. You shall pretend that you are engaged to somebody else, and I'll pretend that I am not engaged to anybody, and then we shan't quarrel."

"Do you think that will prevent our falling out, Rosa?"

"I know it will. Hush! Pretend to look out of window.—Mrs. Tisher!"

Through a fortuitous concourse of accidents, the matronly Tisher heaves in sight, says, in rustling through the room like the legendary[2] ghost of a Dowager in silken skirts: "I hope I see Mr. Drood well; though I needn't ask, if I may judge from his complexion? I trust I disturb no one; but there *was* a paper-knife—Oh, thank you, I am sure!" and disappears with her prize.

"One other thing you must do, Eddy, to oblige me," says Rosebud. "The moment we get into the street, you must put me outside, and keep close to the house yourself—squeeze and graze yourself against it."

"By all means, Rosa, if you wish it. Might I ask why?"

"Oh! because I don't want the girls to see you."

"It's a fine day; but would you like me to carry an umbrella up?"

"Don't be foolish, sir. You haven't got polished leather boots on," pouting, with one shoulder raised.

"Perhaps that might escape the notice of the girls, even if they did see me," remarks Edwin, looking down at his boots with a sudden distaste for them.

"Nothing escapes their notice, sir. And then I know what would happen. Some of them would begin reflecting on me by saying (for *they* are free) that they never will on any account engage themselves to

---

[1] And how did you pass your birthday [*p. 18*] . . . checks the look, and asks:] *not in* MS
[2] legendary] *not in* MS

lovers without polished leather boots. Hark! Miss Twinkleton. I'll ask for leave."

That discreet lady being indeed heard without, inquiring of nobody in a blandly conversational tone as she advances: "Eh? Indeed! Are you quite sure you saw my mother-of-pearl button-holder on the work-table in my room?" is at once solicited for walking leave, and graciously accords it. And soon the young couple go out of the Nuns' House, taking all precautions against the discovery of the so vitally defective boots of Mr. Edwin Drood: precautions, let us hope, effective for the peace of Mrs. Edwin Drood that is to be.

"Which way shall we take, Rosa?"

Rosa replies: "I want to go to the Lumps-of-Delight shop."

"To the —— ?"

"A Turkish sweetmeat, sir. My gracious me, don't you understand anything? Call yourself an Engineer, and not know *that*?"

"Why, how should I know it, Rosa?"

"Because I am very fond of them. But oh! I forgot what we are[1] to pretend. No, you needn't know anything about them; never mind."

So, he is gloomily borne off to the Lumps-of-Delight shop, where Rosa makes her purchase, and, after offering some to him (which he rather indignantly declines), begins to partake of it with great zest: previously taking off and rolling up a pair of little pink gloves, like rose-leaves, and occasionally putting her little pink fingers to her rosy lips, to cleanse them from the Dust of Delight that comes off the Lumps.

"Now, be a good-tempered Eddy, and pretend. And so you are engaged?"

"And so I am engaged."

"Is she nice?"

"Charming."

"Tall?"

"Immensely tall!" Rosa being short.

"Must be gawky, I should think," is Rosa's quiet commentary.

"I beg your pardon; not at all," contradiction rising in him. "What is termed a fine woman; a splendid woman."

"Big nose, no doubt," is the quiet commentary again.

"Not a little one, certainly," is the quick reply. (Rosa's being a little one.)

"Long pale nose, with a red knob in the middle. *I* know the sort of nose," says Rosa, with a satisfied nod, and tranquilly enjoying the Lumps.

"You *don't* know the sort of nose, Rosa," with some warmth; "because it's nothing of the kind."

"Not a pale nose, Eddy?"

"No." Determined not to assent.

[1] are] were MS

"A red nose? Oh! I don't like red noses. However; to be sure she can always powder it."

"She would scorn to powder it," says Edwin, becoming heated.

"Would she? What a stupid thing she must be! Is she stupid in everything?"

"No. In nothing."

After a pause, in[1] which the whimsically wicked face has not been unobservant of him, Rosa says:

"And this most sensible of creatures likes the idea of being carried off to Egypt; does she, Eddy?"

"Yes. She takes a sensible interest in triumphs of engineering skill: especially when they are to change the whole condition of an undeveloped country."

"Lor!" says Rosa, shrugging her shoulders, with a little laugh of wonder.

"Do you object," Edwin inquires, with a majestic turn of his eyes downward upon the fairy figure: "do you object, Rosa, to her feeling that interest?"

"Object? My dear Eddy! But really. Doesn't she hate boilers and things?"

"I can answer for her not being so idiotic as to hate Boilers," he returns with angry emphasis; "though I cannot answer for her views about Things; really not understanding what Things are meant."

"But don't she hate Arabs, and Turks, and Fellahs, and people?"

"Certainly not." Very firmly.

"At least, she *must* hate the Pyramids? Come, Eddy?"

"Why should she be such a little—tall, I mean—Goose, as to hate the Pyramids, Rosa?"

"Ah! you should hear Miss Twinkleton," often nodding her head, and much enjoying the Lumps, "bore about them, and then you wouldn't ask. Tiresome old burying-grounds! Isises, and Ibises, and Cheopses, and Pharaohses; who cares about them? And then there was Belzoni or somebody, dragged out by the legs, half choked with bats and dust. All the girls say serve him right, and hope it hurt him, and wish he had been quite choked."

The two youthful figures, side by side, but not now arm-in-arm, wander discontentedly about the old Close; and each sometimes stops and slowly imprints a deeper footstep in the fallen leaves.

"Well!" says Edwin, after a lengthy silence. "According to custom. We can't get on, Rosa."

Rosa tosses her head, and says she don't want to get on.

"That's a pretty sentiment, Rosa, considering."

"Considering what?"

[1] in] during MS

"If I say what, you'll go wrong again."

"*You*'ll go wrong, you mean, Eddy. Don't be ungenerous."

"Ungenerous! I like that!"

"Then I *don't* like that, and so I tell you plainly," Rosa pouts.

"Now, Rosa, I put it to you. Who disparaged my profession, my destination——"

"You are not going to be buried in the Pyramids, I hope?" she interrupts, arching her delicate eyebrows. "You never said you were. If you are, why haven't you mentioned it to me? I can't find out your plans by instinct."

"Now, Rosa; you know very well what I mean, my dear."

"Well then, why did you begin with your detestable red-nosed Giantesses? And she would, she would, she would, she would, she WOULD powder it!" cries Rosa, in a little burst of comical contradictory spleen.

"Somehow or other, I never can come right in these discussions," says Edwin, sighing and becoming resigned.

"How is it possible, sir, that you ever can come right when you're always wrong? And as to Belzoni, I suppose he's dead;—I'm sure I hope he is—and how can his legs, or his chokes concern you?"

"It is nearly time for your return, Rosa. We have not had a very happy walk, have we?"

"A happy walk? A detestably unhappy walk, sir. If I go up stairs the moment I get in and cry till I can't take my dancing-lesson, you are responsible, mind!"

"Let us be friends, Rosa."

"Ah!" cries Rosa, shaking her head and bursting into real tears. "I wish we *could* be friends! It's because we can't be friends, that we try one another so. I am a young little thing, Eddy, to have an old heartache; but I really, really have, sometimes. Don't be angry. I know you have one yourself, too often. We should both of us have done better, if What is to be had been left, What might have been. I am quite a serious little[1] thing now, and not teasing you. Let each of us forbear, this one time, on our own account, and on the other's!"

Disarmed by this glimpse of[2] a woman's nature in the spoilt child, though for an instant disposed to resent it as seeming to involve the enforced infliction of himself upon her, Edwin Drood stands watching her as she childishly cries and sobs, with both hands to the handkerchief at her eyes, and then—she becoming more composed, and indeed beginning in her young inconstancy to laugh at herself for having been so moved—leads her to a seat hard by, under the elm trees.

"One clear word of understanding, Pussy dear. I am not clever out of my own line—now I come to think of it I don't know that I am

[1] serious little] little serious 73 75
[2] of] of the depths of MS

UNDER THE TREES

particularly clever in it—but I want to do right. There is not—there may be—I really don't see my way to what I want to say, but I must say it before we part—there is not any other young——?"

"Oh no, Eddy! It's generous of you to ask me; but no, no, no!"

They have come very near to the Cathedral windows, and at this moment the organ and the choir sound out sublimely. As they sit listening to the solemn swell, the confidence of last night rises in young Edwin Drood's mind, and he thinks how unlike this music is, to that discordance.

"I fancy I can distinguish Jack's voice," is his remark in a low tone in connexion with the train of thought.

"Take me back at once, please," urges his Affianced, quickly laying her light hand upon his wrist. "They will all be coming out directly; let us get away. Oh, what a resounding chord! But don't let us stop to listen to it; let us get away!"

Her hurry is over, as soon as they have passed out of the Close. They go, arm-in-arm now, gravely and deliberately enough, along the old High Street, to the Nuns' House. At the gate, the street being within sight empty, Edwin bends down his face to Rosebud's.

She remonstrates, laughing, and is[1] a childish schoolgirl again.

"Eddy, no! I'm too stickey to be kissed. But give me your hand, and I'll blow a kiss into that."

He does so. She breathes a light breath into it, and asks, retaining it and looking into it:

"Now say, what do you see?"

"See, Rosa?"

"Why, I thought you Egyptian boys could look into a hand and see all sorts of phantoms? Can't you see a happy Future?"

For certain, neither of them sees a happy Present, as the gate opens and closes, and one goes in and the other goes away.

CHAPTER IV

MR. SAPSEA

ACCEPTING the Jackass as the type of self-sufficient stupidity and conceit—a custom, perhaps, like some few other customs, more conventional than fair—then the purest Jackass in Cloisterham is Mr. Thomas Sapsea, Auctioneer.

Mr. Sapsea "dresses at" the Dean; has been bowed to for the Dean, in[2] mistake; has even been spoken to in the street as My Lord, under the

---

[1] is] *not in* MS
[2] in] by ES

impression that he was the Bishop come down unexpectedly, without his chaplain. Mr. Sapsea is very proud of this, and of his voice, and of his style. He has even (in selling landed property), tried the experiment of slightly intoning in his pulpit, to make himself more like what he takes to be the genuine ecclesiastical article. So, in ending a Sale by Public Auction, Mr. Sapsea finishes off with an air of bestowing a benediction on the assembled brokers, which[1] leaves the real Dean—a modest and worthy gentleman—far behind.

Mr. Sapsea has many admirers; indeed, the proposition is carried by a large local majority, even including non-believers in his wisdom, that he is a credit to Cloisterham. He possesses the great qualities of being portentous and dull, and of having a roll in his speech, and another roll in his gait; not to mention a certain gravely flowing action with his hands, as if he were presently going to Confirm the individual with whom he holds discourse. Much nearer sixty years of age than fifty, with a flowing outline of stomach, and horizontal creases in his waistcoat; reputed to be rich; voting at elections in the strictly respectable interest; morally satis-fied that nothing but he himself[2] has grown since he was a baby; how can dunder-headed Mr. Sapsea be otherwise than a credit to Cloisterham, and society?[3]

Mr. Sapsea's premises are in the High Street, over against the Nuns' House. They are of about the period of the Nuns' House, irregularly modernized here and there, as steadily deteriorating generations found, more and more, that they preferred air and light to Fever and the Plague. Over the doorway, is a wooden effigy, about half life-size, representing Mr. Sapsea's father, in a curly wig and toga, in the act of selling. The chastity of the idea, and the natural appearance of the little finger, hammer, and pulpit, have been much admired.

Mr. Sapsea sits in his dull ground-floor sitting-room, giving first on his paved back yard, and then on his railed-off garden. Mr. Sapsea has a bottle of port wine on a table before the fire—the fire is an early luxury, but pleasant on the cool,[4] chill[5] autumn evening—and is characteristically attended by his portrait, his eight-day clock, and his weather-glass. Characteristically, because he would uphold himself against mankind, his weather-glass against weather, and his clock against time.

By Mr. Sapsea's side on the table are a writing-desk and writing materials. Glancing at a scrap of manuscript, Mr. Sapsea reads it to him-self with a lofty air, and then, slowly pacing the room with his thumbs in the arm-holes of his waistcoat, repeats it from memory: so internally, though with much dignity, that the word "Ethelinda" is alone audible.

[1] which] that MS
[2] himself] *not in* MS
[3] and society] to himself, to the Constitution, and to society MS
[4] the cool] a cool ES   [5] chill] MS chilly 70–75

There are three clean wineglasses in a tray on the table. His serving-maid entering, and announcing "Mr. Jasper is come, sir," Mr. Sapsea waves "Admit him" and draws two wineglasses from the rank, as being claimed.

"Glad to see you, sir. I congratulate myself on having the honor of receiving you here for the first time." Mr. Sapsea does the honors of his house in this wise.

"You are very good. The honor is mine and the self-congratulation is mine."[1]

"You are pleased to say so, sir. But I do assure you that it is a satisfaction to me to receive you in my humble home. And that is what I would not say to everybody." Ineffable loftiness on Mr. Sapsea's part accompanies these words, as leaving the sentence to be understood: "You will not easily believe that your society can be a satisfaction to a man like myself; nevertheless,[2] it is."

"I have for some time desired to know you, Mr. Sapsea."

"And I, sir, have long known you by reputation as a man of taste. Let me fill your glass. I will give you, sir," says Mr. Sapsea, filling his own:

> "When the French come over,
> May we meet them at Dover!"

This was a patriotic toast in Mr. Sapsea's infancy, and he is therefore fully convinced of its being appropriate to any subsequent era.

"You can scarcely be ignorant, Mr. Sapsea," observes Jasper, watching the auctioneer with a smile as the latter stretches out his legs before the fire, "that you know the world."

"Well, sir," is the chuckling reply, "I think[3] I know something of it; something of it."

"Your reputation for that knowledge has always interested and surprised me, and made me wish to know you. For, Cloisterham is a little place. Cooped up in it myself, I know nothing beyond it, and feel it to be a very little place."

"If I have not gone to foreign countries, young man," Mr. Sapsea begins, and then stops:—"You will excuse my[4] calling you young man, Mr. Jasper? You are much my junior."

"By all means."

"If I have not gone to foreign countries, young man, foreign countries have come to me. They have come to me in the way of business, and I have improved upon my opportunities. Put it that I take an inventory, or make a catalogue. I see a French clock. I never saw him before, in my

---

[1] The honor . . . is mine] The honour and the self-congratulation are mine MS
[2] nevertheless] but nevertheless MS   [3] I think] *not in* MS
[4] my] me 73 75

life, but I instantly lay my finger on him and say 'Paris!' I see some cups
and saucers of Chinese make, equally strangers to me personally: I put my
finger on them, then and there, and I say 'Pekin, Nankin, and Canton.'
It is the same with Japan, with Egypt, and with bamboo and sandal-wood
from the East Indies; I put my finger on them all. I have put my finger on
the North Pole before now, and said, 'Spear[1] of Esquimaux make, for
half a pint of pale sherry!'"

"Really? A very remarkable way, Mr. Sapsea, of acquiring a knowledge
of men and things."

"I mention it, sir," Mr. Sapsea rejoins, with unspeakable complacency,
"because, as I say, it don't do to boast of what you are; but[2] show how
you came to be it, and then you prove it."

"Most interesting. We were to speak of the late Mrs. Sapsea."

"We were, sir." Mr. Sapsea fills both glasses, and takes the decanter
into safe keeping again. "Before I consult your opinion as a man of taste
on this little trifle"—holding it up—"which is *but* a trifle, and still has
required some thought, sir, some little fever of the brow, I ought perhaps
to describe the character of the late Mrs. Sapsea, now dead three quarters
of a year."

Mr. Jasper, in the act of yawning behind his wineglass, puts down
that screen and calls up a look of interest. It is a little impaired in its
expressiveness by his having a shut-up gape still to dispose of, with
watering eyes.

"Half a dozen years ago, or so," Mr. Sapsea proceeds, "when I had
enlarged my mind up to—I will not say to what it now is, for that might
seem to aim at too much, but up to the pitch of wanting another mind to
be absorbed in it—I cast my eye about me for a nuptial partner. Because,
as I say, it is not good for man to be alone."

Mr. Jasper appears to commit this original idea to memory.

"Miss Brobity at that time kept, I will not call it the rival establishment
to the establishment at the Nuns' House opposite, but I will call it the
other parallel establishment down town. The world did have it that she
showed a passion for attending my sales, when they took place on half-
holidays, or in vacation time. The world did put it about, that she admired
my style. The world did notice that as time flowed by, my style became
traceable in the dictation-exercises of Miss Brobity's pupils. Young man,
a whisper even sprang up in obscure malignity, that one ignorant and
besotted Churl (a parent) so committed himself as to object to it by name.
But I do not believe this. For is it likely that any human creature in his
right senses would so lay himself open to be pointed at, by what I call the
finger of scorn?"

Mr. Jasper shakes his head. Not in the least likely. Mr. Sapsea, in

---

[1] Spear] Bow and arrow MS
[2] but] *not in* MS

a grandiloquent state of absence of mind, seems to refill his visitor's glass, which is full already; and does really refill his own, which is empty.

"Miss Brobity's Being, young man, was deeply imbued with homage to Mind. She revered Mind, when launched, or, as I say, precipitated, on an extensive knowledge of the world. When I made my proposal, she did me the honor to be so overshadowed with a species of Awe, as to be able to articulate only the two words, 'Oh Thou!'—meaning myself. Her limpid blue eyes were fixed upon me, her semi-transparent hands were clasped together, pallor overspread her aquiline features, and, though encouraged to proceed, she never did proceed a word further. I disposed of the parallel establishment, by private contract, and we became as nearly one as could be expected under the circumstances. But she never could, and she never did, find a phrase satisfactory to her perhaps-too-favorable estimate of my intellect. To the very last (feeble action of liver), she addressed me in the same unfinished terms."

Mr. Jasper has closed his eyes as the auctioneer has deepened his voice. He now abruptly opens them, and says, in unison with the deepened voice, "Ah!"—rather as if stopping himself on the extreme verge of adding—"men!"

"I have been since," says Mr. Sapsea, with his legs stretched out, and solemnly enjoying himself[1] with the wine and the fire, "what you behold me; I have been since a solitary mourner; I have been since, as I say, wasting my evening conversation on the desert air. I will not say that I have reproached myself; but there have been times when I have asked myself the question: What if her husband had been nearer on a level with her? If she had not had to look up quite so high, what might the stimulating action have been upon the liver?"

Mr. Jasper says, with an appearance of having fallen into dreadfully low spirits, that he supposes "it[2] was to be."

"We can only suppose so, sir," Mr. Sapsea coincides. "As I say, Man proposes, Heaven disposes. It may or may not be putting the same thought in another form; but that is the way I put it."

Mr. Jasper murmurs assent.

"And now, Mr. Jasper," resumes the auctioneer, producing his scrap of manuscript, "Mrs. Sapsea's monument having had full time to settle and dry, let me take your opinion, as a man of taste, on the inscription I have (as I before remarked, not without some little fever of the brow), drawn out[3] for it. Take it in your own hand. The[4] setting out of the lines requires to be followed with the eye, as well as the contents with the mind."

---

[1] enjoying himself] enjoying himself very much MS
[2] supposes "it] MS "supposes it 70–75
[3] out] up MS
[4] hand. The] hand, as the MS

Mr. Jasper complying, sees and reads as follows:

ETHELINDA,

Reverential Wife of

MR. THOMAS SAPSEA,

AUCTIONEER, VALUER, ESTATE AGENT, &c.,

OF THIS CITY.

Whose Knowledge of the World,

Though somewhat extensive,

Never brought him acquainted with

A SPIRIT

More capable of

LOOKING UP TO HIM.

STRANGER PAUSE

And ask thyself the Question,

CANST THOU DO LIKEWISE?

If Not,

WITH A BLUSH RETIRE.

Mr. Sapsea having risen and stationed himself with his back to the fire, for the purpose of observing the effect of these lines on the countenance of a man of taste, consequently has his face towards the door, when his serving-maid, again appearing, announces, "Durdles is come, sir!" He promptly draws forth and fills the third wineglass, as being now claimed, and replies, "Show Durdles in."

"Admirable!" quoth Mr. Jasper, handing back the paper.

"You approve, sir?"

"Impossible not to approve. Striking, characteristic, and complete."

The auctioneer inclines his head, as one accepting his due and giving a receipt; and invites the entering Durdles to take off that glass of wine (handing the same), for it will warm him.

Durdles is a stonemason; chiefly in the gravestone, tomb, and monument way, and wholly of their color from head to foot. No man is better known in Cloisterham. He is the chartered libertine of the place. Fame trumpets him a wonderful workman—which, for aught that anybody knows, he may be (as he never works); and a wonderful sot—which everybody knows he is. With the Cathedral crypt he is better acquainted than any living authority; it may even be than any dead one. It is said that the intimacy of this acquaintance began in his habitually resorting to that secret place, to lock out the Cloisterham boy-populace, and sleep off the fumes of liquor: he having ready access to the Cathedral, as contractor for rough repairs. Be this as it may, he does know much about it, and, in the demolition of impedimental fragments of wall, buttress, and pavement, has seen strange sights.[1] He often speaks of himself in the third person; perhaps being a little misty as to his own identity when he narrates; perhaps impartially adopting the Cloisterham nomenclature in reference to a character of acknowledged distinction. Thus he will say, touching his strange sights: "Durdles come upon the old chap,"[2] in reference to a buried magnate of ancient time and high degree, "by striking right into the coffin with his pick. The old chap gave Durdles a look with his open eyes, as much as to say 'Is your name Durdles? Why, my man, I've been waiting for you a Devil of a time!' And then he turned to powder." With a two-foot rule always in his pocket, and a mason's hammer all but always in his hand, Durdles goes continually sounding and tapping all about and about[3] the Cathedral; and whenever he says to Tope: "Tope, here's another old 'un in here!" Tope announces it to the Dean as an established discovery.

In a suit of coarse flannel with horn buttons, a yellow neckerchief with draggled ends, an old hat more russet-colored than black, and laced boots of the hue of his stony calling, Durdles leads a hazy, gipsy sort of life, carrying his dinner about with him in a small bundle, and sitting on all manner of tombstones to dine. This dinner of Durdles's has become quite a Cloisterham institution: not only because of his never appearing in public without it, but because of its having been, on certain renowned occasions, taken into custody along with Durdles (as drunk and incapable), and exhibited before the Bench of Justices at the Town Hall. These occasions, however, have been few and far apart: Durdles being as seldom drunk as sober. For the rest, he is[4] an old bachelor, and he[5] lives in a little antiquated hole of a house that was never finished: supposed to be built, so far, of stones stolen from the city wall.[6] To this abode there is an approach, ankle-deep in stone chips, resembling a petrified grove of tombstones, urns, draperies, and broken columns, in all stages of sculpture. Herein, two journeymen incessantly chip, while[7] other two journeymen, who face each other, incessantly saw stone; dipping as regularly in and out of their sheltering sentry-boxes, as if they were mechanical figures emblematical of Time and Death.

To Durdles, when he has[8] consumed his glass of port, Mr. Sapsea entrusts that precious effort of his Muse. Durdles unfeelingly takes out his two-foot rule, and measures the lines calmly, alloying them with stone-grit.

"This is for the monument, is it, Mr. Sapsea?"

[1] strange sights] a strange sight or so MS
[2] he is better acquainted [*p. 28*] . . . come upon the old chap,"] *written on verso in* MS
[3] about and about] about MS   [4] is] is supposed to be MS
[5] he] *om.* ES   [6] wall] wall and overlooking the churchyard MS
[7] while] *not in* MS   [8] has] had 73 75

"The Inscription. Yes." Mr. Sapsea waits for its effect on a common mind.

"It'll come in to a eighth[1] of a inch," says Durdles. "Your servant, Mr. Jasper. Hope I see you well."

"How are you, Durdles?"

"I've got a touch of the Tombatism on me, Mr. Jasper, but that I must expect."

"You mean the Rheumatism," says Sapsea, in a sharp tone. (He is nettled by having his composition so mechanically received.)

"No, I don't. I mean, Mr. Sapsea, the Tombatism. It's another sort from Rheumatism. Mr. Jasper knows what Durdles means. You get among them Tombs afore it's well light on a winter morning, and keep on, as the Catechism says, a walking in the same all the days of your life, and *you*'ll know what Durdles means."

"It is a bitter cold place," Mr. Jasper assents, with an antipathetic shiver.

"And if it's bitter cold for you, up in the chancel, with a lot of live breath smoking out about you, what the bitterness is to Durdles, down in the crypt among the earthy damps there, and the dead breath of the old 'uns," returns that individual, "Durdles leaves you to judge.—Is this to be put in hand at once, Mr. Sapsea?"

Mr. Sapsea, with an Author's anxiety to rush into publication, replies that it cannot be out of hand too soon.

"You had better let me have the key, then," says Durdles.

"Why, man, it is not to be put inside the monument!"

"Durdles knows where it's to be put, Mr. Sapsea; no man better. Ask e'er a man in Cloisterham whether Durdles knows his work."

Mr. Sapsea rises, takes a key from a drawer, unlocks an iron safe let into the wall, and takes from it another key.

"When Durdles puts a touch or a finish upon his work, no matter where, inside or outside, Durdles likes to look at his work all round, and see that his work is a doing him credit," Durdles explains,[2] doggedly.

The key proffered him[3] by the bereaved widower being a large one, he slips his two-foot rule into a side pocket of his flannel trousers made for it, and deliberately opens his flannel coat, and opens the mouth of a large breast pocket within it before taking the key to place in[4] that repository.

"Why, Durdles!" exclaims Jasper, looking on amused. "You are undermined with pockets!"

"And I carries weight in 'em too, Mr. Jasper. Feel those;" producing two other large keys.

"Hand me Mr. Sapsea's likewise. Surely this is the heaviest of the three."

---

[1] a eighth] half a quarter MS   [2] Durdles explains,] explains Durdles MS
[3] him] to him MS   [4] place in] place it in 73 75

"You'll find 'em much of a muchness, I expect," says Durdles. "They all belong to monuments. They all open Durdles's work. Durdles keeps the keys of his work mostly. Not that they're much used."

"By-the-bye," it comes into Jasper's mind to say, as he idly examines the keys; "I have been going to ask you, many a day, and have always forgotten. You know they sometimes call you Stony Durdles, don't you?"

"Cloisterham knows me as Durdles, Mr. Jasper."[1]

"I am aware of that, of course. But the boys sometimes——"

"Oh! If you mind them[2] young Imps of boys——" Durdles gruffly interrupts.

"I don't mind them, any more than you do. But there was a discussion the other day among the choir, whether Stony stood for Tony;" clinking one key against another.

("Take care of the wards, Mr. Jasper.")

"Or whether Stony stood for Stephen;" clinking with a change of keys.

("You can't make a pitch-pipe of 'em, Mr. Jasper.")

"Or whether the name comes from your trade. How stands the fact?"

Mr. Jasper weighs the three keys in his hand, lifts his head from his idly stooping attitude over the fire, and delivers the keys to Durdles with an ingenuous and friendly face.

But the stony one is a gruff one likewise, and that hazy state of his is always an uncertain state, highly conscious of its dignity, and prone to take offence. He drops his two keys back into his pocket one by one, and buttons them up; he takes his dinner-bundle from the chair-back on which he hung it when he came in; he distributes the weight he carries, by tying[3] the third key up in it, as though he were an Ostrich, and liked to dine off cold iron; and he gets out of the room, deigning no word of answer.

Mr. Sapsea then proposes a hit at backgammon, which, seasoned with his own improving conversation, and terminating in a supper of cold roast beef and salad, beguiles the golden evening until pretty late. Mr. Sapsea's wisdom being, in its delivery to mortals, rather of the diffuse than the epigrammatic order, is by no means expended even then; but his visitor intimates that he will come back for more of the precious commodity on future occasions, and Mr. Sapsea lets him off for the present, to ponder on the instalment he carries away.[4]

---

[1] Jasper."] Jasper," is the answer. MS   [2] them] the ⟨m⟩ MS

[3] he distributes the weight he carries, by tying] and, by way of distributing the weight he carries, ties MS

[4] and he gets out of the room . . . away.] *in* MS *the chapter ends* and finally he gets out of the room with the sulky retort: "How does the fact stand, Mr Jasper? The fact stands six on one side to half a dozen on t'other. So fur as Durdles sees the fact with *his* eyes, it has took up about that position as near as may be." *The last part of the chapter, from* But the stoney one *to* may be." *was written on a slip pasted over the original*

CHAPTER V

MR. DURDLES AND FRIEND

JOHN JASPER, on his way home through the Close, is brought to a standstill by the spectacle of Stony Durdles, dinner-bundle and all, leaning his back against the iron railing of the burial-ground enclosing it from the old cloister-arches; and a hideous small boy in rags flinging stones at him as a well-defined mark in the moonlight. Sometimes the stones hit him, and sometimes they miss him, but Durdles seems indifferent to either fortune. The hideous small boy, on the contrary, whenever he hits Durdles, blows a whistle of triumph through a jagged gap convenient for the purpose, in the front of his mouth, where half his teeth are wanting; and whenever he misses him, yelps out "Mulled agin!" and tries to atone for the failure by taking a more correct and vicious aim.

"What are you doing to the man?" demands Jasper, stepping out into the moonlight from the shade.

"Making a cock-shy of him," replies the hideous small boy.

"Give me those stones in your hand."

"Yes,¹ I'll give 'em you down your throat, if you come a ketching hold of me," says the small boy, shaking himself loose, and backing. "I'll smash your eye, if you don't look out!"

"Baby-devil that you are, what has the man done to you?"

"He won't go home."

"What is that to you?"

"He gives me a 'apenny to pelt him home if I ketches him out too late," says the boy. And then chants, like a little savage, half stumbling and half dancing among the rags and laces of his dilapidated boots:

> "Widdy widdy wen!
> I—ket—ches—Im—out—ar—ter—ten.
> Widdy widdy wy!
> Then—E—don't—go—then—I—shy—
> Widdy Widdy Wake-cock warning!"

—with a comprehensive sweep on the last word, and one more delivery² at Durdles.

This would seem to be a poetical note of preparation, agreed upon, as caution to Durdles to stand clear if he can, or to betake himself homeward

John Jasper invites the boy with a beck of his head to follow him (feeling it hopeless to drag him, or coax him) and crosses to the iron railing where the Stony (and stoned) One is profoundly meditating.

CHAPTER V] CHAPTER VIII MS
¹ Yes,] *not in* MS   ² delivery] underhanded delivery MS

"Do you know this thing, this child?" asks Jasper, at a loss for a word[1] that will define this thing.

"Deputy," says Durdles, with a nod.

"Is that its[2]—his—name?"

"Deputy," assents Durdles.

"I'm man-servant up at the Travellers' Twopenny[3] in Gas Works Garding," this thing explains. "All us man-servants at Travellers' Lodgings is named Deputy. When[4] we're chock full and the Travellers is all a-bed I come out for my 'elth." Then withdrawing into the road, and taking aim, he resumes:[5]

> "Widdy widdy wen!
> I—ket—ches—Im—out—ar—ter—"

"Hold your hand," cries Jasper, "and don't throw while I stand so near him, or I'll kill you! Come, Durdles; let me walk home with you to-night. Shall I carry your bundle?"

"Not on any account," replies Durdles, adjusting it.[6] "Durdles was making his reflections here when you come up, sir, surrounded by his works, like a poplar Author.—Your own brother-in-law;" introducing a sarcophagus within the railing, white and cold in the moonlight. "Mrs. Sapsea;" introducing the monument of that devoted wife.[7] "Late Incumbent;" introducing the Reverend Gentleman's broken column. "Departed Assessed[8] Taxes;" introducing a vase and towel, standing on what might represent the cake of soap. "Former pastrycook and muffin-maker, much respected;" introducing gravestone with extinguished torch.[9] "All safe and sound here, sir, and all Durdles's work! Of the common folk that is merely bundled up in turf and brambles, the less said, the better. A poor lot, soon forgot."

"This creature, Deputy, is behind us," says Jasper, looking back. "Is he to follow us?"

The relations between Durdles and Deputy are of a capricious kind; for, on Durdles's turning himself about with the slow gravity of beery soddenness, Deputy makes a pretty wide circuit into the road and stands on the defensive.

"You never cried Widdy Warning before you begun to-night," says Durdles, unexpectedly reminded of, or imagining, an injury.

"Yer lie, I did," says Deputy, in his only form of polite contradiction.[10]

---

[1] a word] any word MS   [2] its] 73 75 it's MS 70 ES

[3] Travellers' Twopenny] Travellers' Twopenny Lodging MS

[4] When] Wen MS   [5] resumes] recommences MS

[6] "Not . . . it] "Not on any account," says Durdles. Jasper pats it, and it clinks. "Not on any account," repeats Durdles, adjusting it MS

[7] wife] wife with inscription finished MS

[8] Assessed] King's MS

[9] with extinguished torch] MS   *om.* 70–75

[10] in his only . . . contradiction] *not in* MS

"Own brother, sir," observes Durdles, turning himself about again, and as unexpectedly forgetting his offence as he had recalled or conceived it; "own brother to Peter the Wild Boy! But I gave him an object in life."

"At which he takes aim?" Mr. Jasper suggests.

"That's it, sir," returns Durdles, quite satisfied; "at which he takes aim. I took him in hand and gave him an object. What was he before? A destroyer.[1] What work did he do? Nothing but destruction. What did he earn by it? Short terms in Cloisterham Jail. Not a person, not a piece of property, not a winder, not a horse, nor[2] a dog, nor[2] a cat, nor[2] a bird, nor[2] a fowl, nor[2] a pig, but what he stoned, for want of an enlightened object. I put that enlightened object before him, and now he can turn his honest halfpenny by the three penn'orth a week."

"I wonder he has no competitors."

"He has plenty, Mr. Jasper, but he stones 'em all away. Now, I don't know what this scheme of mine comes to," pursues Durdles, considering about it with the same sodden gravity; "I don't know what you may precisely call it. It ain't[3] a sort of a—scheme of a—[4]National Education?"

"I should say not," replies Jasper.

"*I* should say not," assents Durdles; "then we won't try to give it a name."

"He still keeps behind us," repeats Jasper, looking over his shoulder; "is he to follow us?"

"We can't help going round by the Travellers' Twopenny, if we go the short way, which is the back way," Durdles answers, "and we'll drop him there."

So they go on; Deputy, as a rear rank of[5] one, taking open order, and invading the silence of the hour and place by stoning every wall, post, pillar, and other inanimate object, by the deserted way.

"Is there anything new down in the crypt, Durdles?" asks John Jasper.[6]

"Anything old, I think you mean," growls[7] Durdles. "It ain't[3] a spot for novelty."

"Any new discovery on your part, I meant."

"There's a old 'un under the seventh pillar on the left[8] as you go down the broken steps of the little underground chapel as formerly[9] was; I make him out (so fur as I've made him out yet) to be one of them old 'uns with a crook. To judge from the size of the passages in the walls, and of[10] the steps and doors, by which they come and went, them crooks must

---

[1] A destroyer] Nothing but a destroyer MS   [2] nor] or MS
[3] ain't] an't MS   [4] scheme of a—] *not in* MS
[5] of] *om.* 75
[6] asks John Jasper] asks John Jasper to have him on his own ground MS
[7] growls] grumbles MS   [8] left] left hand MS   [9] formerly] *not in* MS
[10] of] *not in* MS

have been a good deal in the way of the old 'uns! Two on 'em meeting promiscuous must have hitched one another by the mitre, pretty often, I should say."

Without any endeavour to correct the literality of this opinion, Jasper surveys his companion—covered from head to foot with old mortar, lime, and stone grit—as though he, Jasper, were getting imbued with a romantic interest in his weird life.[1]

"Yours is a curious existence."

Without furnishing the least clue to the question, whether he receives this as a compliment[2] or as quite the reverse, Durdles gruffly answers: "Yours is another."

"Well! Inasmuch as my lot is cast in the same old earthy, chilly, never-changing place, Yes. But there is much more mystery and interest in your connexion with the Cathedral than in mine.[3] Indeed, I am beginning to have some idea of asking you to take me on as a sort of student, or free 'prentice, under you, and to let me go about with you sometimes, and see some of these odd nooks in which you pass your days."

The Stony One replies, in a general way, All right. Everybody knows where to find Durdles, when he's wanted. Which, if not strictly true, is approximately so, if taken to express that Durdles may always be found in a state of vagabondage somewhere.

"What I dwell upon most," says Jasper, pursuing his subject of romantic interest, "is the remarkable accuracy with which you would seem to find out where people are buried.—What is the matter? That bundle is in your way; let me hold it."

Durdles has stopped and backed a little (Deputy, attentive to all[4] his movements, immediately skirmishing into the road) and was looking about for some ledge or corner to place his bundle on, when thus relieved of it.

"Just you give me my hammer out of that," says Durdles, "and I'll show you."

Clink, clink. And his hammer is handed him.

"Now, look'ee here. You pitch your note, don't you, Mr. Jasper?"

"Yes."

"So[5] I sound for mine. I take my hammer, and I tap." (Here he strikes the pavement, and the attentive Deputy skirmishes at a rather wider

---

[1] life.] life; and says to him: MS
[2] compliment] kind of compliment MS
[3] *After* mine. MS *has* As the mental state of Durdles, and of all his sodden tribe, is one hardly susceptible of astonishment in itself, so it is one hardly susceptible of any reasonable interpretation by other minds. But it happens to fall out tonight—just as it might have happened to fall out quite the other way—that Durdles rather likes his position in the dialogue, and chuckles over it.
"Indeed," adds Jasper smiling, "I am beginning   [4] all] *not in* MS
[5] So] *not in* MS

range, as supposing that his head may be in requisition.) "I tap, tap, tap. Solid! I go on tapping. Solid still! Tap again. Halloa! Hollow! Tap again, persevering.[1] Solid in hollow! Tap, tap, tap, to try it better. Solid in hollow; and inside solid, hollow again! There you are! Old 'un crumbled away in stone coffin, in vault!"

"Astonishing!"

"I have even done this," says Durdles, drawing out his two-foot rule, (Deputy meanwhile skirmishing nearer, as suspecting that Treasure may be about to be discovered, which may somehow lead to his own enrichment, and the delicious treat of the discoverers being hanged by the neck, on his evidence, until they are dead). "Say that hammer of mine's a wall— my work.[2] Two; four; and two is six," measuring on the pavement. "Six foot inside that wall is Mrs. Sapsea."

"Not really Mrs. Sapsea?"

"Say Mrs. Sapsea. Her wall's thicker, but say Mrs. Sapsea. Durdles taps that wall represented by that hammer, and says, after good sounding: 'Something betwixt us!' Sure enough, some rubbish has been left in that same six-foot space by Durdles's men!"

Jasper opines that such accuracy "is a gift."

"I wouldn't have it at a gift," returns Durdles, by no means receiving the observation in good part. "I worked it out for myself. Durdles comes by *his* knowledge through grubbing deep for it, and having it up by the roots when it don't want to come.—Halloa you Deputy!"

"Widdy!" is Deputy's shrill response, standing off again.

"Catch that ha'penny. And don't let me see any more of you to-night, after we come to the Travellers' Twopenny."

"Warning!" returns Deputy, having caught the halfpenny, and appearing by this mystic word to express his assent to the arrangement.

They have but to cross what was once the vineyard, belonging to what was once the Monastery, to come into the narrow back lane wherein stands the crazy wooden house of two low stories currently known as the Travellers' Twopenny:—a house all warped and distorted, like the morals of the travellers, with scant remains of a lattice-work porch over the door, and also[3] of a rustic fence before its stamped-out garden; by reason of the travellers being so bound to the premises by a tender sentiment (or so fond of having a fire by the roadside in the course of the day), that they can never be persuaded or threatened into departure, without violently possessing themselves of some wooden forget-me-not, and bearing it off.[4]

The semblance of an inn is attempted to be given to this wretched place by fragments of conventional red curtaining in the windows, which rags are made muddily transparent in the night-season by feeble lights of rush

---

[1] persevering] pretty persevering MS
[2] Say that . . . my work] That hammer of mine's a wall—Durdles's work MS
[3] also] eke MS   [4] off] away MS

or cotton dip burning dully in the close air of the inside.[1] As Durdles and Jasper come near, they are addressed by an inscribed paper lantern over[2] the door, setting forth the purport of the house. They are also addressed by some half-dozen other hideous small boys—whether twopenny lodgers or followers or hangers-on of such, who knows!—who, as if attracted by some carrion-scent of Deputy in the air, start into the moonlight, as vultures might gather in the desert, and instantly fall to stoning him and one another.

"Stop, you young brutes," cries Jasper, angrily, "and let us go by!"

This remonstrance being received with yells and flying stones, according to a custom of late years comfortably established among the police regulations of our English communities, where Christians are stoned on all sides, as if the days of Saint Stephen were revived, Durdles remarks of the young savages, with some point, that "they haven't got an object," and leads the way down the lane.

At the corner of the lane, Jasper, hotly enraged, checks his companion and looks back. All is silent.[3] Next moment, a stone coming rattling at his hat,[4] and a distant yell of "Wake-Cock! Warning!" followed by a crow, as from some infernally-hatched[5] Chanticleer, apprising him under whose victorious[6] fire he stands, he turns the corner into safety, and takes Durdles home: Durdles stumbling among the litter of[7] his stony yard as if he were going to turn head-foremost[8] into one of the unfinished tombs.

[1] of the inside] within MS   [2] over] above ES

[3] As Durdles and Jasper come near . . . All is silent.] *in the place of this passage* MS *has* As Durdles and Jasper come near, a woman is seen crouching and smoking in the cold night air on a seat just outside the door, which stands ajar.

Of a sudden, Jasper stops, and looks at this woman—the lighter-colored figure of Durdles being between himself and her—very keenly.

"Is that Deputy?" she croaks out in a whimpering and feeble way; "where have you been, you young good for nothing wretch?"

"Out for my Elth," returns the hideous sprite.

"I'll claw you," retorts the woman, "when I can lay my fingers on you. I'll be bad for your Elth! (O me, o me, my breath is very short!) I wanted my pipe and my little spoon, and ye'd been and put 'Em on a shelf I couldn't find."

"Wot did yer go to bed for then?" retorts Deputy, quite unabashed. "Who ha' thought yer wos going to get up agin?"

"You. You might ha' known I was like to do it."

"Yer lie!" says Deputy, in his only form of contradiction.

Jasper, touching Durdles on the shoulder, and laying his finger on his lips when that worthy looks round, leads the way onward gingerly enough. He more than once or twice looks back, but utters no word until they have reached the corner of the lane; then he casually remarks in a subdued voice that he is well out of any unseemly quarrel or discussion in such a place, and glances back again. All is still.

[4] hat] hat, and knocking it off MS
[5] infernally-hatched] diabolically hatched MS
[6] victorious] *not in* MS
[7] stumbling among the litter of] tumbling up MS
[8] head-foremost] *not in* MS

John Jasper returns by another way to his Gate House, and entering softly with his key, finds his fire still burning.[1] He takes from a locked press, a peculiar-looking pipe which he fills—but not with tobacco—and, having adjusted the contents of the bowl, very carefully, with a little instrument, ascends an inner staircase of only a few steps, leading to two rooms. One of these is his own sleeping-chamber: the other, is his nephew's.[2] There is a light in each.

His nephew lies asleep, calm and untroubled. John Jasper stands looking down upon him, his unlighted pipe in his hand, for some time, with a fixed and deep attention.[3] Then, hushing his footsteps, he passes to his own room, lights his pipe, and delivers himself to the Spectres[4] it invokes at midnight.

CHAPTER VI

PHILANTHROPY IN MINOR CANON CORNER

THE Reverend Septimus Crisparkle[5] (Septimus, because six little brother Crisparkles before him went out, one by one, as they were born, like six weak little rushlights, as[6] they were lighted),[7] having broken the thin morning ice near Cloisterham Weir with his amiable head, much to the invigoration of his frame, was now assisting his circulation by boxing at a looking-glass with great science and prowess. A fresh and healthy portrait the looking-glass presented of the Reverend Septimus, feinting and dodging with the utmost artfulness, and hitting out from the shoulder with the utmost straightness, while his radiant features teemed with innocence, and soft-hearted benevolence beamed from his[8] boxing-gloves.

It was scarcely breakfast-time yet, for Mrs. Crisparkle—mother, not wife, of the Reverend Septimus—was only just down, and waiting for the urn. Indeed, the Reverend Septimus left off at this very moment to take the pretty old lady's entering face between his boxing-gloves and kiss it. Having done so with tenderness,[9] the Reverend Septimus turned to

[1] burning] burning, and on the hearth some glittering fragments of the late commotion MS

[2] rooms. One ... nephew's] rooms: one, his own sleeping chamber: one, his nephew's MS

[3] his unlighted ... attention] unlighted pipe in hand, for a long time, with a fixed attention MS   [4] Spectres] ghosts and phantoms MS
END OF No. I
CHAPTER VI] CHAPTER V MS

[5] Septimus Crisparkle] ⟨Mr Crisparkle⟩ ⟨Joe⟩ ⟨Arthur⟩ ⟨Joe⟩ Septimus Crisparkle MS
[6] one by one ... as] one by one, like six weak little rushlights, almost as soon as MS
[7] (Septimus ... lighted)] *inserted above line as an afterthought in* MS
[8] his] his very MS   [9] tenderness] the gentlest tenderness MS

again, countering with his left, and putting in his right, in a tremendous manner.

"I say, every morning of my life, that you'll do it at last, Sept," remarked the old lady, looking on; "and so you will."

"Do what, Ma dear?"

"Break the pier-glass, or burst a blood-vessel."

"Neither, please God, Ma dear. Here's wind, Ma. Look at this!"

In a concluding round of great severity, the Reverend Septimus administered and escaped all sorts of punishment, and wound up by getting the old lady's cap into Chancery—such is the technical term used in scientific circles by the learned in the Noble Art—with a lightness of touch that hardly stirred the lightest lavender or cherry riband on it. Magnanimously releasing the defeated, just in time to get his gloves into a drawer and feign[1] to be looking out of window in a contemplative state of mind when a servant entered, the Reverend Septimus then gave place to the urn and other preparations for breakfast. These completed, and the two alone again, it was pleasant to see (or would have been, if there had been any one to see it, which there never was), the old lady standing to say the Lord's Prayer aloud, and her son, Minor Canon nevertheless, standing with bent head[2] to hear it, he being within five years of forty: much as he had stood to hear the same words from the same lips when he was within five months of four.

What is prettier than an old lady—except a young lady—when her eyes are bright, when her figure is trim and compact, when her face is cheerful and calm, when her dress is as the dress of a china shepherdess: so dainty in its colors, so individually assorted to herself, so neatly moulded on her? Nothing is prettier, thought the good Minor Canon frequently, when taking his seat at table opposite his long-widowed mother. Her thought at such times may be condensed into the two words that oftenest did duty together in all her conversations: "My Sept!"

They were a good pair to sit breakfasting together in Minor Canon Corner, Cloisterham. For, Minor Canon Corner was a quiet place in the shadow of the Cathedral, which the cawing of the rooks,[3] the echoing footsteps of rare passers, the sound of the Cathedral bell, or the roll of the Cathedral organ, seemed to render more quiet than absolute silence. Swaggering fighting men had had their centuries of ramping and raving about Minor Canon Corner, and beaten serfs had had their centuries of drudging and dying there, and powerful monks had had their centuries of being sometimes useful and sometimes harmful there, and behold they were all gone out of Minor Canon Corner, and so much the better. Perhaps one of the highest uses of their ever having been there, was, that there might be left behind, that blessed air of tranquillity which pervaded Minor Canon Corner, and that serenely romantic state of the mind—

---

[1] feign] pretend MS   [2] bent head] head bent ES   [3] rooks] crows MS

productive for the most part of pity and forbearance—which is engendered by a sorrowful story that is all told, or a pathetic play that is played out.

Red-brick walls harmoniously toned down in color by time, strong-rooted ivy, latticed windows, panelled rooms, big oaken beams in little places, and stone-walled gardens where annual fruit yet ripened upon monkish trees, were the principal surroundings of pretty old Mrs. Crisparkle and the Reverend Septimus[1] as they sat at breakfast.

"And what, Ma dear," inquired the Minor Canon, giving proof of a wholesome and vigorous appetite, "does the letter say?"

The pretty old lady, after reading it, had just laid it down upon the breakfast-cloth. She handed it over to her son.

Now, the old lady was exceedingly proud of her bright eyes being so clear that she could read writing without spectacles. Her son was also so proud of the circumstance, and so dutifully bent on her deriving the utmost possible gratification from it, that he had invented the pretence that he himself could *not* read writing without spectacles. Therefore he now assumed a pair, of grave and prodigious proportions, which not only seriously inconvenienced his nose and his breakfast, but seriously impeded his perusal of the letter. For, he had the eyes of a microscope and a telescope combined, when they were unassisted.

"It's from Mr. Honeythunder, of course," said the old lady, folding her arms.[2]

"Of course," assented her son. He then lamely read on:

> "Haven of Philanthropy,
> "Chief Offices, London, Wednesday.

" 'DEAR MADAM,

" ' I write in the ——;' In the what's this? What does he write in?"

"In the chair," said the old lady.

The Reverend Septimus took off his spectacles, that he might see her face, as he exclaimed:

"Why, what should he write in?"

"Bless me, bless me, Sept," returned the old lady, "you don't see the context! Give it back to me, my dear."

Glad to get his spectacles off (for they always made his eyes water) her son obeyed: murmuring that his sight for reading manuscript got worse and worse daily.

" 'I write,' " his mother went on, reading very perspicuously and precisely, " 'from the chair, to which I shall probably be confined for some hours.' "

Septimus looked at the row of chairs against the wall, with a half-protesting and half-appealing countenance.

" 'We have,' " the old lady read on with a little extra emphasis, " 'a

---

[1] Septimus] *name settled at this point in* MS   [2] arms] hands MS

meeting of our Convened Chief Composite Committee of Central and
District Philanthropists, at our Head Haven as above; and it is their
unanimous pleasure that I take the chair.'"

Septimus breathed more freely, and muttered: "Oh! If he comes to
that, let him."

"'Not to lose a day's post, I take the opportunity of a long report being
read, denouncing a public miscreant——'"

"It is a most extraordinary thing," interposed the gentle Minor Canon,
laying down his knife and fork to rub his ear in a vexed manner, "that
these Philanthropists are always denouncing somebody. And it is another
most extraordinary thing that they are always so violently flush of
miscreants!"

"'Denouncing a public miscreant!'"—the old lady resumed, "'to get
our little affair of business off my mind. I have spoken with my two wards,
Neville and Helena Landless,[1] on the subject of their defective education,
and they give in to the plan proposed; as I should have taken good care
they did,[2] whether they liked it or not.'"

"And it is another most extraordinary thing," remarked the Minor
Canon in the same tone as before, "that these Philanthropists are so given
to seizing their fellow-creatures by the scruff of the neck, and (as one may
say) bumping them into the paths of peace.—I beg your pardon, Ma dear,
for interrupting."

"'Therefore, dear Madam, you will please prepare your son, the Rev.
Mr. Septimus, to expect Neville as an inmate to be read with, on Monday
next. On the same day Helena will accompany him to Cloisterham, to
take up her quarters at the Nuns' House, the establishment recommended
by yourself and son jointly. Please likewise to prepare for her reception
and tuition there. The terms in both cases are understood to be exactly as
stated to me in writing by yourself, when I opened a correspondence
with you on this subject, after the honor of being introduced to you at
your sister's house in town here. With compliments to the Rev. Mr.
Septimus, I am, Dear Madam, Your affectionate brother (In Philanthropy), LUKE HONEYTHUNDER.'"

"Well, Ma," said Septimus, after a little more rubbing of his ear, "we
must try it. There can be no doubt that we have room for an inmate, and
that I have time to bestow upon him, and inclination too. I must confess
to feeling rather glad that he is not to be[3] Mr. Honeythunder himself.
Though that seems wretchedly prejudiced—does it not?—for I never saw
him. Is he a large man, Ma?"

"I should call him a large man, my dear," the old lady replied after
some hesitation, "but that his voice is so much larger."

[1] Helena Landless] ⟨Olympia Heyridge⟩ ⟨Heyfort⟩ Helena Landless MS *and so up to*
p. 55 ll. 32, 35
[2] they did] that they did MS   [3] to be MS *om.* 70–75

"Than himself?"

"Than anybody."

"Hah!" said Septimus. And finished his breakfast as if the flavor of the Superior Family Souchong, and also of the ham and toast and eggs, were a little on the wane.

Mrs. Crisparkle's sister, another piece of Dresden china, and matching her so neatly that they would have made a delightful pair of ornaments for the two ends of any capacious old-fashioned chimneypiece, and by right[1] should never have been seen apart, was the childless wife of a clergyman holding Corporation preferment in London City. Mr. Honeythunder in his public character of Professor of Philanthropy had come to know Mrs. Crisparkle during the last re-matching of the china ornaments (in other words during her last annual visit to her sister), after a public occasion of a philanthropic nature, when certain devoted orphans of tender years had been glutted with plum buns, and plump bumptiousness. These were all the antecedents known in Minor Canon Corner of the coming pupils.

"I am sure you will agree with me, Ma," said Mr. Crisparkle, after thinking the matter over,[2] "that the first thing to be done, is, to put these young people as much at their ease as possible. There is nothing disinterested in the notion, because we cannot be at our ease with them unless they are at their ease with us. Now, Jasper's nephew is down here at present; and like takes to like, and youth to youth. He is a cordial young fellow, and we will have him to meet the brother and sister at dinner. That's three. We can't think of asking him, without asking Jasper. That's four. Add[3] Miss Twinkleton and the fairy bride that is to be, and that's six. Add our two selves, and that's eight. Would eight at a friendly dinner at all put you out, Ma?"

"Nine would, Sept," returned the old lady, visibly nervous.

"My dear Ma, I particularize eight."

"The exact size of the table and the room, my dear."

So it was settled that way; and when Mr. Crisparkle called with his mother upon Miss Twinkleton, to arrange for the reception of Miss Helena Landless at the Nuns' House, the two other invitations having reference to that establishment were proffered and accepted. Miss Twinkleton did, indeed, glance at the globes, as regretting that they were not formed to be taken out into society; but became reconciled to leaving them behind. Plain[4] instructions were then despatched to the Philanthropist for the departure and arrival, in good time for dinner, of Mr. Neville and Miss Helena; and stock for soup became fragrant in the air of Minor Canon Corner.

In those days there was no railway to Cloisterham, and Mr. Sapsea said

---

[1] by right] *possibly* by rights MS   [2] over] out MS
[3] Add] Now, add MS   [4] Plain] MS   *om.* 70–75

there never would be. Mr. Sapsea said more; he said there never should be. And yet, marvellous to consider, it has come to pass, in these days, that Express Trains don't think Cloisterham worth stopping at, but yell and whirl through it on their larger errands, casting the dust off their wheels as a testimony against its insignificance. Some remote fragment of Main Line to somewhere else, there was, which was going to ruin the Money Market[1] if it failed, and Church and State if it succeeded, and (of course), the Constitution, whether or no; but even that had already so unsettled Cloisterham traffic, that the traffic, deserting the high road, came sneaking in from an unprecedented part of the country by a back stable-way, for many years labelled at the corner: "Beware of the Dog."

To this ignominious avenue of approach, Mr. Crisparkle repaired, awaiting the arrival of a short squat omnibus, with a disproportionate heap of luggage on the roof—like a little Elephant with infinitely too much Castle —which was then the daily service between Cloisterham and external mankind. As this vehicle lumbered up, Mr. Crisparkle could hardly see anything else of it for a large outside passenger seated on the box, with his elbows squared, and his hands on his knees, compressing the driver into a most uncomfortably small compass, and glowering about him with a strongly marked face.

"Is this Cloisterham?" demanded the passenger, in a tremendous voice.

"It is," replied the driver, rubbing himself as if he ached, after throwing the reins to the ostler. "And I never was so glad to see it."

"Tell your master to make his box seat wider then," returned the passenger. "Your master is morally bound—and ought to be legally, under ruinous penalties—to provide for the comfort of his fellow-man."

The driver instituted, with the palms of his hands, a superficial perquisition into the state of his skeleton; which seemed to make him anxious.

"Have I sat upon you?" asked the passenger.

"You have," said the driver, as if he didn't like it at all.

"Take that card, my friend."

"I think I won't deprive you on it," returned the driver, casting his eyes over it with no great favor, without taking it. "What's the good of it to me?"

"Be a Member of that Society," said the passenger.

"What shall I get by it?" asked the driver.

"Brotherhood," returned the passenger, in a ferocious voice.

"Thank'ee," said the driver, very deliberately, as he got down; "my mother was contented with myself, and so am I. I don't want no brothers."

"But you must have them," replied the passenger, also descending, "whether you like it or not. I am your brother."

---

[1] Money Market] shareholders MS

"I say!" expostulated the driver, becoming more chafed in temper; "not too fur! The worm *will*, when[1]——"

But here Mr. Crisparkle interposed, remonstrating aside, in a friendly voice: "Joe, Joe, Joe! Don't forget yourself, Joe, my good fellow!" and then, when Joe peaceably touched his hat, accosting the passenger with: "Mr. Honeythunder?"

"That is my name, sir."

"My name is Crisparkle."

"Reverend[2] Mr. Septimus? Glad to see you, sir. Neville and Helena are inside. Having a little succumbed of late, under the pressure of my public labours, I thought I would take a mouthful of fresh air, and come down with them, and return at night.[3] So you are the Reverend[2] Mr. Septimus, are you?" surveying him on the whole with disappointment, and twisting a double eye-glass by its riband, as if he were roasting it; but not otherwise using it. "Hah! I expected to see you older, sir."

"I hope you will," was the good-humoured reply.

"Eh?" demanded Mr. Honeythunder.

"Only a poor little joke. Not worth repeating."

"Joke? Ay; I never see a joke," Mr. Honeythunder frowningly retorted. "A joke is wasted upon me, sir. Where are they! Helena and Neville, come here! Mr. Crisparkle has come down to meet you."

An unusually handsome lithe young fellow, and an unusually handsome lithe girl; much alike; both very dark, and very rich in color; she, of almost the gipsy type; something untamed about them both; a certain air upon them of hunter and huntress; yet withal a certain air of being the objects of the chase, rather than the followers. Slender, supple, quick of eye and limb; half shy, half defiant; fierce of look; an indefinable kind of pause coming and going on their whole expression, both of face and form, which might be equally likened to the pause before a crouch, or a bound. The rough mental notes made in the first five minutes by Mr. Crisparkle, would have read thus, *verbatim*.

He invited Mr. Honeythunder to dinner, with a troubled mind, (for the discomfiture of the dear old china shepherdess lay heavy on it), and gave his arm to Helena Landless. Both she and her brother, as they walked all together through the ancient streets, took great delight in what he pointed out of the Cathedral and the monastery ruin, and wondered—so his notes ran on—much as if they were beautiful barbaric captives[4] brought from some wild tropical dominion. Mr. Honeythunder walked in the middle of the road, shouldering the natives out of his way, and loudly developing a scheme he had, for making a raid on all the unemployed persons in the United Kingdom, laying them every one by

[1] "not too fur! . . . when] "Don't go *too* fur! The worm *will*, you know! MS
[2] Reverend] Rev. ES   [3] at night] *possibly* tonight MS
[4] barbaric captives] state-captives MS

the heels in jail,[1] and forcing them on pain of prompt extermination to become Philanthropists.

Mrs. Crisparkle had need of her own share of philanthropy when she beheld this very large and very loud excrescence on the little party. Always something in the nature of a Boil upon the face of society, Mr. Honeythunder expanded into an inflammatory Wen in Minor Canon Corner. Though it was not literally true, as was facetiously charged against him by public unbelievers, that he called aloud to his fellow-creatures: "Curse your souls and bodies, come here and be blessed!" still his philanthropy was of that gunpowderous sort that the difference between it and animosity was hard to determine. You were to abolish military force, but you were first to bring all commanding officers who had done their duty, to trial by court martial for that offence, and shoot[2] them. You were to abolish war, but were to make converts by making war upon them, and charging them with loving war as the apple of their eye. You were to have no capital punishment, but were first to sweep off the face of the earth all legislators, jurists, and judges, who were of the contrary opinion. You were to have universal concord, and were to get it by eliminating all the people who wouldn't, or conscientiously couldn't, be concordant. You were to love your brother as yourself, but after an indefinite[3] interval of maligning him (very much as if you hated him), and calling him all manner of names. Above all things, you were to do nothing in private, or on your own account. You were to go to the offices of the Haven of Philanthropy, and put your name down as a Member and a Professing Philanthropist. Then, you were to pay up your subscription, get your card of membership and your riband and medal, and were evermore to live upon a platform, and evermore to say what Mr. Honeythunder said, and what the Treasurer said, and what the Vice Treasurer[4] said, and what the Committee said, and what the sub-Committee said, and what the Secretary said, and what the Vice Secretary said. And this was usually said in the unanimously carried resolution under hand and seal, to the effect: "That this assembled[5] Body of Professing Philanthropists views, with indignant[6] scorn and contempt, not unmixed with utter detestation and loathing[7] abhorrence,"—in short, the baseness of all those who do not belong to it, and pledges itself to make as many obnoxious statements as possible about[8] them, without being at all particular as to facts.[9]

The dinner was a most doleful breakdown. The Philanthropist deranged the symmetry of the table, sat himself in the way of the waiting, blocked up the thoroughfare, and drove Mr. Tope (who assisted the

[1] jail] jails MS   [2] shoot] hang or shoot MS
[3] indefinite] uncertain MS   [4] Vice Treasurer] MS sub-Treasurer 70–75
[5] assembled] not in MS   [6] indignant] not in MS
[7] loathing] not in MS   [8] about] concerning MS
[9] without being at all particular as to facts] this, or a similar phrase, was deleted in MS

parlor-maid), to the verge of distraction by passing plates and dishes[1] on, over his own head. Nobody could talk to anybody, because he held forth to everybody at once, as if the company had no individual existence, but were a Meeting. He impounded the Reverend Mr.[2] Septimus, as an official personage to be addressed, or kind of human peg to hang his oratorical hat on, and fell into the exasperating habit, common among such orators, of impersonating him as a wicked and weak opponent. Thus, he would ask: "And will you, sir, now stultify yourself by telling me"—and so forth, when the innocent man had not opened his lips, nor meant to open them. Or he would say: "Now see, sir, to what a position you are reduced. I will leave you no escape. After exhausting all the resources of fraud and falsehood, during years upon years; after exhibiting a combination of dastardly meanness with[3] ensanguined daring, such as the world has not often witnessed; you have now the hypocrisy to bend the knee before the most degraded of mankind, and to sue and whine and howl for mercy!" Whereat the unfortunate Minor Canon would look, in part indignant and in part perplexed: while his worthy mother sat bridling, with tears in her eyes, and the remainder of the party lapsed into a sort of gelatinous state, in which there was no flavor or solidity, and very little resistance.

But the gush of philanthropy that burst forth when the departure of Mr. Honeythunder began to impend, must[4] have been highly gratifying to the feelings of that distinguished man. His coffee was produced, by the special activity of Mr. Tope, a full hour before he wanted it. Mr. Crisparkle sat with his watch in his hand, for about the same period, lest he should overstay his time. The four young people were unanimous in believing[5] that the Cathedral clock struck three quarters, when it actually struck but one. Miss Twinkleton estimated the distance to the omnibus at[6] five-and-twenty minutes' walk, when it was really five. The affectionate kindness of the whole circle hustled him into his greatcoat, and shoved him out into the moonlight, as if he were a fugitive traitor with whom they sympathized,[7] and a troop of horse were at the back door. Mr. Crisparkle and his new charge, who took him to the omnibus, were so fervent[8] in their apprehensions of his catching cold, that they shut him up in it instantly and left him, with still half an hour to spare.

---

[1] and dishes] *not in* MS   [2] Mr.] *not in* MS
[3] with] and MS   [4] must] ⟨must⟩ should MS
[5] believing] ⟨believing⟩ holding MS   [6] at] as MS
[7] with whom they sympathized] *not in* MS   [8] fervent] ardent and fervent MS

CHAPTER VII

MORE CONFIDENCES THAN ONE

"I KNOW very little of that gentleman, sir," said Neville to the Minor Canon as they turned back.

"You know very little of your guardian?" the Minor Canon repeated.

"Almost nothing."

"How came he——"

"To *be* my guardian? I'll tell you, sir. I suppose you know that we come (my sister and I) from Ceylon?"

"Indeed, no."

"I wonder at that. We lived with a stepfather there. Our mother died there, when we were little children. We have had a wretched existence. She made him our guardian, and he was a miserly wretch who grudged us food to eat, and clothes to wear. At his death, he passed us over to this man; for no better reason that I know of, than his being a friend or connexion of his, whose name was always in print and catching his attention."

"That was lately, I suppose?"

"Quite lately, sir. This stepfather of ours was a cruel brute as well as a grinding one. It was[1] well he died when he did, or I might have killed him."

Mr. Crisparkle stopped short in the moonlight and looked at his hopeful pupil in consternation.

"I surprise you, sir?" he said, with a quick change to a submissive manner.

"You shock me; unspeakably shock me."

The pupil hung his head for a little while, as they walked on, and then said: "You never saw him beat your sister. I have seen him beat mine, more than once or twice, and I never forgot it."

"Nothing," said Mr. Crisparkle, "not even a beloved and beautiful sister's tears under dastardly ill-usage;" he became less severe, in spite of himself, as his indignation rose; "could justify those horrible expressions that you used."

"I am sorry I used them, and especially to you, sir. I beg to recall them. But permit me to set you right on one point. You spoke of my sister's tears. My sister would have let him tear her to pieces, before she would have let him believe that he could make her shed a tear."

Mr. Crisparkle reviewed[2] those mental notes of his, and was neither at all surprised to hear it, nor at all disposed to question it.

CHAPTER VII] CHAPTER VI MS

[1] was] is 73 75   [2] reviewed] *possibly* hastily reviewed MS; *deletions not clear*

"Perhaps you will think it strange, sir"—this was said in a hesitating voice—"that I should so soon ask you to allow me to confide in you, and to have the kindness to hear a word or two from me in my defence?"

"Defence?" Mr. Crisparkle repeated. "You are not on your defence, Mr. Neville."

"I think I am, sir. At least I know I should be, if you were better acquainted with my character."

"Well, Mr. Neville," was the rejoinder. "What if you leave me to find it out?"

"Since it is your pleasure, sir," answered the young man, with a quick change in his manner to sullen disappointment: "since it is your pleasure to check me in my impulse, I must submit."

There was that in the tone of this short speech which made the conscientious man to whom it was addressed, uneasy. It hinted to him that he might, without meaning it, turn aside a trustfulness beneficial to a mis-shapen young mind and perhaps to his own power of directing and improving it. They were within sight of the lights in his windows, and he stopped.

"Let us turn back and take a turn or two up and down, Mr. Neville, or you may not have time to finish what you wish to say to me. You are hasty in thinking that I mean to check you. Quite the contrary.[1] I invite your confidence."

"You have invited it, sir, without knowing it, ever since I came here. I say 'ever since,' as if I had been here a week! The truth is, we came here (my sister and I) to quarrel with you, and affront you, and break away again."

"Really?" said Mr. Crisparkle, at a dead loss for anything else to say.

"You see, we could not know what you were beforehand, sir; could we?"

"Clearly not," said Mr. Crisparkle.

"And having liked no one else with whom we have ever been brought into contact, we had made up our minds not to like you."

"Really?" said Mr. Crisparkle again.

"But we do like you, sir, and we see an immeasurable[2] difference between your house and your reception of us, and anything else we have ever known. This—and my happening to be alone with you—and everything around us seeming so quiet and peaceful after Mr. Honeythunder's departure—and Cloisterham being so old and grave and beautiful, with the moon shining on it—these things inclined me[3] to open my heart."

"I quite understand, Mr. Neville. And it is salutary to listen to such influences."

"In describing my own imperfections, sir, I must ask you not to suppose that I am describing my sister's. She has come out of the disadvantages

---

[1] Quite the contrary] Quite the contrary, quite the contrary MS
[2] immeasurable] MS unmistakeable 70–75
[3] inclined me] made me inclined MS

of our miserable life, as much better than I am, as that Cathedral tower is higher than those chimnies."

Mr. Crisparkle in his own breast was not so sure of this.

"I have had, sir, from my earliest remembrance, to suppress a deadly and bitter[1] hatred. This has made me secret and revengeful. I have been always tyrannically held down by the strong hand. This has driven me, in my weakness, to the resource of being false and mean. I have been stinted of education, liberty, money, dress, the very necessaries of life, the commonest[2] pleasures of childhood, the commonest[2] possessions of youth. This has caused me to be utterly wanting in I don't know what emotions, or remembrances, or good instincts—I have not even a name for the thing, you see!—that you have had to work upon in other young men to whom you have been accustomed."

"This is evidently true. But this is not encouraging," thought Mr. Crisparkle as they turned again.

"And to finish with, sir: I have been brought up among abject and servile dependants, of an inferior race, and I may easily have contracted some affinity with them. Sometimes, I don't know but that it may be a drop of what is tigerish in their blood."

"As in the case of that remark just now," thought Mr. Crisparkle.

"In a last word of reference to my sister, sir (we are twin children), you ought to know, to her honor, that nothing in our misery ever subdued her, though it often cowed me. When we ran away from it (we ran away four times in six years, to be soon brought back and cruelly punished), the flight was always of her planning and leading. Each time she dressed as a boy, and showed the daring of a man. I take it we were seven years old when we first decamped; but I remember, when I lost the pocket-knife with which she was to have cut her hair short, how desperately she tried to tear it out, or bite it off. I have nothing further to say, sir, except that I hope you will bear with me and make allowance for me."

"Of that, Mr. Neville, you may be sure," returned the Minor Canon. "I don't preach more than I can help, and I will not repay your confidence with a sermon. But I entreat you to bear in mind, very seriously and steadily, that if I am to do you any good, it can only be with your own assistance; and that you can only render that, efficiently, by seeking aid from Heaven."

"I will try to do my part, sir."

"And, Mr. Neville, I will try to do mine. Here is my hand on it. May God bless our endeavours!"

They were now standing at his house door, and a cheerful sound of voices and laughter was heard within.

"We will take one more turn before going in," said Mr. Crisparkle, "for I want to ask you a question. When you said you were in a changed

---

[1] bitter] most bitter MS   [2] the commonest] and the commonest MS

mind concerning me, you spoke, not only for yourself, but for your sister too."

"Undoubtedly I did, sir."

"Excuse me, Mr. Neville, but I think you have had no opportunity of communicating with your sister, since I met you. Mr. Honeythunder was very eloquent; but perhaps I may venture to say, without ill-nature, that he rather monopolized the occasion. May you not have answered for your sister without sufficient warrant?"

Neville shook his head with a proud smile.

"You don't know, sir, yet, what a complete understanding can exist between my sister and me, though no spoken word—perhaps hardly as much as a look—may have passed between us. She not only feels as I have described, but she very well knows that I am taking this opportunity of speaking to you, both for her and for myself."

Mr. Crisparkle looked in his face, with some incredulity; but his face expressed such absolute and firm conviction of the truth of what he said, that Mr. Crisparkle looked at the pavement, and mused, until they came to his door again.

"I will ask for one more turn, sir, this time," said the young man with a rather heightened color rising in his face. "But for Mr. Honeythunder's —I think you called it eloquence, sir?" (somewhat slyly).

"I—yes, I called it eloquence," said Mr. Crisparkle.

"But for Mr. Honeythunder's eloquence, I might have had no need to ask you what I am going to ask you. This Mr. Edwin Drood, sir: I think that's the name?"

"Quite correct," said Mr. Crisparkle. "D-r-double o-d."

"Does he—or did he—read with you, sir?"

"Never, Mr. Neville. He comes here visiting his relation, Mr. Jasper."

"Is Miss Bud his relation too, sir?"

("Now, why should he ask that, with sudden superciliousness!" thought Mr. Crisparkle.) Then he explained, aloud, what he knew of the little story of their betrothal.

"Oh! *That*'s it, is it?" said the young man. "I understand his air of proprietorship now!"

This was said so evidently to himself, or to anybody rather than Mr. Crisparkle, that the latter instinctively felt[1] as if to notice it would be almost tantamount to noticing a passage in a letter which he had read by chance over the writer's shoulder. A moment afterwards they re-entered the house.[2]

Mr. Jasper was seated at the piano as they came into[3] his drawing-room, and was accompanying Miss Rosebud while she sang. It was a consequence of his playing the accompaniment without notes, and of her being

---

[1] instinctively felt] felt instinctively MS   [2] the house] his house MS
[3] came into] entered MS

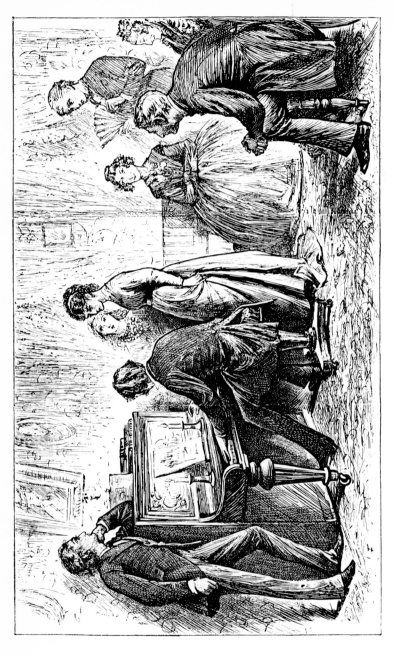

AT THE PIANO

a heedless little creature very apt to go wrong, that he followed her lips most attentively, with his eyes as well as hands; carefully[1] and softly hinting the key-note from time to time. Standing with an arm drawn round her, but with a face far more intent on Mr.[2] Jasper than on her singing, stood Helena, between whom and her brother an instantaneous recognition passed, in which Mr. Crisparkle saw, or thought he saw, the understanding that had been spoken of, flash out. Mr. Neville then took his admiring station, leaning against the piano, opposite the singer; Mr. Crisparkle sat down by the china shepherdess; Edwin Drood gallantly furled and unfurled Miss Twinkleton's fan; and[3] that lady passively claimed that sort of exhibitor's proprietorship in the accomplishment on view, which Mr. Tope, the Verger, daily claimed in the Cathedral service.

The song went on. It was[4] a sorrowful strain of parting, and the fresh young voice was very plaintive and tender.[5] As Jasper watched[6] the pretty lips, and ever and again hinted the one[7] note, as though it were a low whisper from himself, the voice became a little[8] less steady, until all at once the singer broke into a burst of tears, and shrieked out, with her hands over her eyes: "I can't bear this! I am frightened! Take me away!"

With one swift turn of her lithe figure, Helena laid the little beauty on a sofa, as if she had never caught her up. Then, on one knee beside her, and with one hand upon her rosy mouth, while with the other she appealed to all the rest, Helena[9] said to them: "It's nothing; it's all over; don't speak to her for one minute, and she is well!"

Jasper's hands had, in the same instant, lifted themselves from the keys, and were now poised above them, as though he waited to resume. In that attitude he yet sat quiet: not even looking round, when all the rest had changed their places and were reassuring one another.

"Pussy's not used to an audience; that's the fact," said Edwin Drood. "She got nervous, and couldn't hold out. Besides, Jack, you are such a conscientious master, and require so much, that I believe you make her afraid of you. No wonder."

"No wonder," repeated Helena.

"There, Jack, you hear! You would be afraid of him, under similar circumstances, wouldn't you, Miss Landless?"[10]

"Not under any circumstances," returned Helena.

Jasper brought down his hands, looked over his shoulder, and begged to thank Miss Landless for her vindication of his character. Then he fell to dumbly playing, without striking the notes, while his little pupil was

---

[1] carefully] skilfully MS   [2] Mr.] *possibly deleted in* MS
[3] and] while MS
[4] service./The song . . . It was] Service; and the song went on./It was MS
[5] very plaintive and tender] ⟨tender and⟩ very plaintive MS
[6] As Jasper watched] As Jasper—unwinking—watched MS
[7] the one] *possibly* that one MS   [8] a little] MS *om.* 70–75
[9] Helena] she MS   [10] Landless] ⟨Heyridge⟩ Landless MS

taken to an open window for air, and was otherwise petted and restored. When she was brought back, his place was empty. "Jack's gone, Pussy," Edwin told her. "I am more than half afraid he didn't like to be charged with being the Monster who had frightened you." But she answered never a word, and shivered, as if they had made her a little too cold.

Miss Twinkleton now opining that indeed these were late hours, Mrs. Crisparkle, for finding ourselves outside the walls of the Nuns' House, and that we who undertook the formation of the future wives and mothers of England[1] (the last words in a lower voice, as requiring to be communicated in confidence) were really bound (voice coming up again) to set a better example than one of rakish habits, wrappers were put in requisition, and the two young cavaliers volunteered to see the ladies home. It was soon done, and the gate of the Nuns' House closed upon them.

The boarders had retired, and only Mrs. Tisher in solitary vigil awaited the new pupil. Her bedroom being within Rosa's, very little introduction or explanation was necessary, before she was placed in charge of her new friend, and left for the night.

"This is a blessed relief, my dear," said Helena.[2] "I have been dreading all day, that I should be brought to bay at this time."

"There are not many of us," returned Rosa, "and we are good-natured girls; at least the others are; I can answer for them."

"I can answer for you," laughed Helena, searching the lovely little face with her dark fiery eyes, and tenderly caressing the small figure. "You will be a friend to me, won't you?"

"I hope so. But the idea of my being a friend to you seems too absurd, though."

"Why?"

"Oh! I am such a mite of a thing, and you are so womanly and handsome. You seem to have resolution and power enough to crush me. I shrink into nothing by the side of your presence even."

"I am a neglected creature, my dear, unacquainted with all accomplishments, sensitively conscious that I have everything to learn, and deeply ashamed to own my ignorance."

"And yet you acknowledge everything to me!" said Rosa.

"My pretty one, can I help it? There is a fascination in you."

"Oh! Is there though?" pouted Rosa, half in jest and half in earnest. "What a pity Master Eddy doesn't feel it more!"

Of course her relations towards that young gentleman had been already imparted, in Minor Canon Corner.

"Why, surely he must love you with all his heart!" cried Helena, with an earnestness that threatened to blaze into ferocity if he didn't.

[1] Nuns' House, and ... England] Nuns' House—Hem!—and...England—Hem!— MS

[2] Helena] ⟨Olympia⟩ Helena Landless MS

"Eh? Oh, well, I suppose he does," said Rosa, pouting again; "I am sure I have no right to say he doesn't. Perhaps it's my fault. Perhaps I am not as nice to him as I ought to be. I don't think I am. But it *is* so ridiculous!"

Helena's eyes demanded what was.

"*We* are," said Rosa, answering as if she had spoken. "We are such a ridiculous couple. And we are always quarrelling."

"Why?"

"Because we both know we are ridiculous, my dear!" Rosa gave that answer as if it were the most conclusive answer in the world.

Helena's masterful look was intent upon her face for a few moments, and then she impulsively put out both her hands and said:

"You will be my friend and help me?"

"Indeed, my dear, I will," replied Rosa, in a tone of affectionate childishness that went straight and true to her heart; "I will be as good a friend as such a mite of a thing can be to such a noble creature as you.[1] And be[2] a friend to me, please; for[3] I don't understand myself; and I want a friend who can understand me, very much indeed."

Helena Landless kissed her, and retaining both her hands, said:

"Who is Mr. Jasper?"

Rosa turned aside her head in answering: "Eddy's uncle, and my music-master."

"You do not love him?"

"Ugh!" She put her hands up to her face, and shook with fear or horror.

"You know that he loves you?"

"Oh, don't, don't, don't!" cried Rosa, dropping on her knees, and clinging to her new resource. "Don't tell me of it! He terrifies me.[4] He haunts my thoughts, like a dreadful ghost. I feel that I am never safe from him. I feel as if he could pass in through the wall when he is spoken of." She actually did look round, as if she dreaded to see him standing in the shadow behind her.

"Try to tell me more about it, darling."

"Yes, I will, I will. Because you are so strong. But hold me the while, and stay with me afterwards."

"My child! You speak as if he had threatened you in some dark way."

"He has never spoken to me about—that. Never."

"What has he done?"

"He has made a slave of me with his looks. He has forced me to understand him, without his saying a word; and he has forced me to keep silence, without his uttering a threat. When I play, he never moves his

---

[1] as you] *not in* MS   [2] be] be you MS   [3] for] *om.* 75
[4] terrifies me] terrifies me so MS

eyes from my hands. When I sing, he never moves his eyes from my lips. When he corrects me, and strikes a note, or a chord, or plays a passage, he himself is in the sounds, whispering that he pursues me as a lover, and commanding me to keep his secret. I avoid his eyes, but he forces me to see them without looking at them. Even when a glaze comes over them (which is sometimes the case), and he seems to wander away into a frightful sort of dream in which[1] he threatens most, he obliges me to know it, and to know that he is sitting close at my side,[2] more terrible to me then[3] than ever."

"What is this imagined threatening, pretty one? What is threatened?"[4]

"I don't know. I have never even dared to think or wonder what it is."

"And was this all, to-night?"

"This was all; except that to-night when he watched my lips so closely as I was singing, besides feeling terrified I felt ashamed and passionately hurt. It was as if he kissed me, and I couldn't bear it, but cried out. You must never breathe this to any one. Eddy is devoted to him. But you said to-night that you would not be afraid of him, under any circumstances, and that[5] gives me—who am so much[6] afraid of him—courage to tell only you. Hold me! Stay with me! I am too frightened[7] to be left by myself."

The lustrous gipsy-face drooped over the clinging arms and bosom, and the wild black hair fell down protectingly over the childish form. There was a slumbering gleam of fire in the intense dark eyes, though they were then softened with compassion and admiration. Let whomsoever it most concerned, look well[8] to it!

CHAPTER VIII

DAGGERS DRAWN

THE two young men, having seen the damsels, their charges, enter the courtyard of the Nuns' House, and finding themselves coldly stared at by the brazen door-plate, as if the battered old beau with the glass in his eye were insolent, look at one another, look along the perspective of the moonlit street, and slowly walk away together.

"Do you stay here long, Mr. Drood?" says Neville.

"Not this time," is the careless answer. "I leave for London again, to-morrow.[9] But I shall be here, off and on, until next Midsummer; then

---

[1] in which] when MS   [2] side] side, with a dropped jaw MS
[3] then] om. 73 75
[4] threatened?"] threatened?" asked ⟨Olympia⟩ Helena. MS
[5] that] it MS   [6] much] not in MS
[7] too frightened] too much frightened MS   [8] well] not in MS
CHAPTER VIII] CHAPTER VII MS
[9] to-morrow] tomorrow morning MS

I shall take my leave of Cloisterham, and England too; for many a long day, I expect."

"Are you going abroad?"

"Going to wake up Egypt a little," is the condescending answer.

"Are you reading?"

"Reading!" repeats Edwin Drood, with a touch of contempt. "No. Doing, working, engineering. My small patrimony was left a part of the capital of the Firm I am with, by my father, a former partner; and I am a charge upon the Firm until I come of age; and then I step into my modest share in the concern. Jack—you met him at dinner—is, until then, my guardian and trustee."

"I heard from Mr. Crisparkle of your other good fortune."

"What do you mean by my other good fortune?"

Neville has made his remark in a watchfully advancing, and yet furtive and shy manner, very expressive of that peculiar air already noticed, of being at once hunter and hunted. Edwin has made his retort with an abruptness not at all polite. They[1] stop and interchange a rather heated look.

"I hope," says Neville, "there is no offence, Mr. Drood, in my innocently referring to your betrothal?"

"By George!" cries Edwin, leading on again at a somewhat quicker pace. "Everybody in this chattering old Cloisterham refers to it. I wonder no Public House has been set up, with my portrait for the sign of The Betrothed's Head. Or Pussy's portrait. One or the other."

"I am not accountable for Mr. Crisparkle's mentioning the matter to me, quite openly," Neville begins.

"No; that's true; you are not," Edwin Drood assents.

"But," resumes Neville, "I am accountable for mentioning it to you. And I did so, on the supposition that you could not fail to be highly proud of it."

Now, there are these two curious touches of human nature working the secret springs of this dialogue. Neville Landless is already enough impressed by Little Rosebud, to feel indignant that Edwin Drood (far below her) should hold his[2] prize so lightly. Edwin Drood is already enough impressed by Helena, to feel indignant that Helena's brother (far below her) should dispose of him so coolly, and put him out of the way so entirely.[3]

However, the last remark had better be answered. So, says Edwin:

"I don't know, Mr. Neville" (adopting that mode of address from Mr. Crisparkle), "that what people are proudest of, they usually talk most about; I don't know either, that what they are proudest of, they most like other people to talk about. But I live a busy life, and I speak

<hr/>

[1] They] So they MS   [2] his] this MS
[3] entirely] completely MS

under correction by you readers, who ought to know everything, and I dare say do."

By this time they have[1] both become savage; Mr. Neville out in the open; Edwin Drood under the transparent cover of a popular tune, and a stop now and then to pretend[2] to admire picturesque effects in the moonlight before him.

"It does not seem to me very civil in you," remarks Neville, at length, "to reflect upon a stranger who comes here, not having had your advantages, to try to make up for lost time. But, to be sure, I[3] was not brought up in 'busy life,' and my ideas of civility were formed among Heathens."

"Perhaps, the best civility, whatever kind of people we are brought up among," retorts Edwin Drood, "is to mind our own business. If you will set me that example, I promise to follow it."

"Do you know that you take a great deal too much upon yourself," is the angry rejoinder; "and that in the part of the world I come from, you would be called to account for it?"

"By whom, for instance?" asks Edwin Drood, coming to a halt, and surveying the other with a look of disdain.[4]

But, here a startling right hand is laid on Edwin's shoulder, and Jasper stands between them. For, it would seem that he, too, has strolled round by the Nuns' House, and has come up behind them on the shadowy side of the road.

"Ned, Ned, Ned!" he says. "We must have no more of this. I don't like this. I have overheard high words between you two. Remember, my dear boy, you are almost in the position of host[5] to-night. You belong, as it were, to the place, and in a manner represent it towards a stranger. Mr. Neville is a stranger, and you should respect[6] the obligations of hospitality. And, Mr. Neville:" laying his left hand on the inner shoulder of that young gentleman, and thus walking on between them, hand to shoulder on either side: "you will pardon me; but I appeal to you to govern your temper too. Now, what is amiss? But why ask! Let there be nothing amiss, and the question is superfluous. We are all three on a good understanding, are we not?"

After a silent struggle between the two young men who shall speak last, Edwin Drood strikes in with: "So far as I am concerned, Jack, there is no anger in me."

"Nor in me," says Neville Landless, though not so freely; or perhaps so carelessly. "But if Mr. Drood knew all that lies behind me, far away from here, he might know better how it is that sharp-edged words have sharp[7] edges to wound me."

---

[1] have] had 75   [2] pretend] feign MS   [3] I] I MS
[4] disdain] great disdain MS   [5] host] host here MS
[6] you should respect] really you should bear in mind MS *very difficult to read*
[7] sharp] very sharp MS

"Perhaps," says Jasper, in a smoothing manner, "we had better not qualify our good understanding. We had better not say anything having the appearance of a remonstrance or condition; it might not seem generous. Frankly and freely, you see there is no anger in Ned. Frankly and freely, there is no anger in you, Mr. Neville?"

"None at all, Mr. Jasper." Still, not quite so frankly or so freely; or, be it said once again, not quite so carelessly perhaps.

"All over then! Now, my bachelor Gate House is but[1] a few yards from here, and the heater is on the fire, and the wine and glasses[2] are on the table, and it is not a stone's throw from Minor Canon Corner. Ned, you are up and away to-morrow.[3] We will carry Mr. Neville in with us, to take a stirrup-cup."

"With all my heart, Jack."

"And with all mine, Mr. Jasper." Neville feels it impossible to say less, but would rather not go. He has an impression upon him that he has lost hold of his temper; feels that Edwin Drood's coolness, so far from being infectious, makes him red hot.[4]

Mr. Jasper, still walking in the centre, hand to shoulder on either side, beautifully turns the refrain of a drinking-song, and they all go up to his rooms.[5] There, the first object visible, when he adds the light of a lamp to that of the fire, is the portrait over the chimneypiece. It is not an object calculated to improve the understanding between the two young men, as rather awkwardly reviving the subject of their difference. Accordingly, they both glance at it consciously, but say nothing. Jasper, however (who would appear from his conduct to have gained but an imperfect[6] clue to the cause of their late high words), directly calls attention to it.

"You recognize that picture, Mr. Neville?" shading the lamp to throw the light upon it.

"I recognize it, but it is far from flattering the original."

"Oh, you are hard upon it! It was done by Ned, who made me a present of it."

"I am sorry for that, Mr. Drood." Neville apologizes, with a real intention to apologize; "if I had known I was in the artist's presence——"

"Oh, a joke, sir, a mere joke," Edwin cuts in, with a provoking yawn. "A little humouring of Pussy's points! I'm going to paint her gravely, one of these days, if she's good."

The air of leisurely patronage and indifference with which this is said, as the speaker throws himself back in a chair and clasps his hands at the back of his head, as a rest for it, is very exasperating to the excitable and excited Neville. Jasper looks observantly from the one to the other,

---

[1] but] MS *om.* 70–75
[2] heater . . . and the wine and glasses] kettle . . . and the glasses MS
[3] to-morrow] tomorrow morning early MS   [4] red hot] blaze MS
[5] rooms] room MS   [6] an imperfect] a very imperfect MS

slightly smiles, and turns his back to mix[1] a jug of mulled wine at the fire. It seems to require much mixing and compounding.[2]

"I suppose, Mr. Neville," says Edwin, quick to resent the indignant protest against himself in the face of young Landless, which is fully as visible as the portrait, or the fire, or the lamp: "I suppose that if you painted the picture of your lady love——"

"I can't paint," is the hasty interruption.

"That's your misfortune, and not your fault. You would if you could. But if you could, I suppose you would make her (no matter what she was in reality), Juno, Minerva, Diana, and Venus, all in one. Eh?"

"I have no lady love, and I can't say."

"If I were to try my hand," says Edwin, with a boyish boastfulness getting up in him, "on a portrait of Miss Landless—in earnest, mind you; in earnest—you should see what I could do!"

"My sister's consent to sit for it being first got, I suppose? As it never will be got, I am afraid I shall never see what you can do. I must bear the loss."

Jasper turns round from the fire, fills a large goblet glass for Neville, fills a large goblet glass for Edwin, and hands each his own; then fills for himself, saying:

"Come, Mr. Neville, we are to drink to my Nephew, Ned. As it is his foot that is in the stirrup—metaphorically—our stirrup-cup is to be devoted to him. Ned, my dearest fellow, my love!"

Jasper[3] sets the example of nearly emptying his glass, and Neville follows it. Edwin Drood says "Thank you both very much," and follows the double example.

"Look at him!" cries Jasper, stretching out his hand admiringly and tenderly, though rallyingly[4] too. "See where he lounges so easily, Mr. Neville! The world is all before him where to choose. A life of stirring work and interest, a life of change and excitement, a life of domestic ease and love! Look at him!"

Edwin Drood's face has become quickly and remarkably flushed by[5] the wine; so has the face of Neville Landless. Edwin still sits thrown back in his chair, making that rest of clasped hands for his head.

"See how little he heeds it all!" Jasper proceeds in a bantering vein. "It is hardly worth his while to pluck[6] the golden fruit that hangs ripe on the tree for him. And yet consider the contrast, Mr. Neville. You and I have no prospect of stirring work and interest, or of change and excitement, or of domestic ease and love. You and I have no prospect (unless you are more fortunate than I am, which may easily[7] be), but the tedious, unchanging round of this dull place."

---

[1] mix] make MS   [2] compounding] blending MS   [3] Jasper] He MS
[4] rallyingly] rallying MS   [5] by] with 73 75   [6] pluck] go and pluck MS
[7] easily] very easily MS

ON DANGEROUS GROUND

"Upon my soul, Jack," says Edwin, complacently, "I feel quite apologetic for having my way smoothed as you describe. But you know what I know, Jack, and it may not be so very easy as it seems, after all. May it, Pussy?" To the portrait, with a snap of his thumb and finger. "We have got to hit it off yet; haven't we, Pussy? You know what I mean, Jack."

His speech has become thick and indistinct. Jasper, quiet and self-possessed, looks to Neville, as expecting his answer or comment. When Neville[1] speaks, *his* speech is also thick and indistinct.

"It might have been better for Mr. Drood to have known some hardships," he says, defiantly.

"Pray," retorts Edwin, turning merely[2] his eyes in that direction, "pray why might it have been better for Mr. Drood to have known some hardships?"

"Ay," Jasper assents with an air of interest; "let us know why?"

"Because they might have made him more sensible," says Neville, "of good fortune that is not by any means necessarily the result of his own merits."

Mr. Jasper quickly looks to his nephew for his rejoinder.

"Have *you* known hardships, may I ask?" says Edwin Drood, sitting upright.

Mr. Jasper quickly looks to the other for his retort.

"I have."

"And what have they made *you* sensible of?"

Mr. Jasper's play of eyes between the two, holds good throughout the dialogue, to the end.

"I have told you once before to-night."

"You have done nothing of the sort."

"I tell you I have. That you take a great deal too much upon yourself."

"You added something else to that, if I remember?"

"Yes, I did say something else."

"Say it again."

"I said that in the part of the world I come from, you would be called to account for it."

"Only there?" cries Edwin Drood, with a contemptuous laugh. "A long way off, I believe? Yes; I see! That part of the world is at a safe distance."

"Say here, then," rejoins the other, rising in a fury. "Say anywhere! Your vanity is intolerable, your conceit is beyond endurance, you talk as if you were some rare and precious prize, instead of a common boaster. You are a common fellow, and a common boaster."

"Pooh, pooh," says Edwin Drood, equally furious, but more collected; "how should you know? You may know a black common fellow, or a

---

¹ Neville] *he* MS   ² turning merely] merely turning MS

black common boaster, when you see him (and no doubt you have a large acquaintance that way); but you are no judge of white men."

This insulting allusion to his dark skin infuriates Neville to that violent degree, that he flings the dregs of his wine at Edwin Drood, and is in the act of flinging the goblet after it, when his arm is caught in the nick of time by Jasper.

"Ned, my dear fellow!"[1] he cries in a loud voice; "I entreat you, I command you, to be still!" There has been a rush of all the three, and a clattering of glasses and overturning of chairs. "Mr. Neville, for shame! Give this glass to me. Open your hand, sir. I WILL have it!"

But Neville throws him off, and pauses for an instant, in a raging passion, with the goblet yet in his uplifted hand. Then, he dashes it down under the grate, with such force that the broken splinters fly out again in a shower; and he leaves the house.

When he first emerges into the night air, nothing around him is still or steady; nothing around him shows like what it is; he only knows that he stands with a bare head in the midst of a blood-red whirl, waiting to be struggled with, and to struggle to the death.

But, nothing happening, and the moon looking down upon him as if he were dead after a fit of wrath,[2] he holds his steam-hammer beating head and heart, and staggers away. Then, he becomes half conscious of having heard himself bolted and barred out, like a dangerous animal; and thinks what shall he do?

Some wildly passionate ideas of the river, dissolve under the spell of the moonlight on the Cathedral and the graves,[3] and the remembrance of his sister, and the thought of what he owes to the good man who has but that very day won his confidence and given him his pledge. He repairs to Minor Canon Corner, and knocks softly at the door.

It is Mr. Crisparkle's custom to sit up last of the early household, very softly touching his piano and practising his favorite parts in concerted vocal music. The south wind that goes where it lists, by way of Minor Canon Corner on a still night, is not more subdued than Mr. Crisparkle at such times, regardful of the slumbers of the china shepherdess.

His knock is immediately answered by Mr. Crisparkle himself. When he opens the door, candle in hand, his cheerful face falls, and disappointed amazement is in it.

"Mr. Neville! In this disorder! Where have you been?"

"I have been to Mr. Jasper's, sir. With his nephew."

"Come in."

The Minor Canon props him by the elbow with a strong hand (in a

---

[1] my dear fellow] my dear fellow, my boy MS

[2] wrath] wrath, and the old Cathedral and the old graves regarding him so solemnly MS

[3] on the Cathedral and the graves] *not in* MS

strictly scientific manner, worthy of his morning trainings), and turns him
into his own little book-room, and shuts the door.

"I have begun ill, sir. I have begun dreadfully ill."

"Too true. You are not sober, Mr. Neville."

"I am afraid I am not, sir, though I can satisfy you at another time that
I have had very little[1] indeed to drink, and that it overcame me in the
strangest and most sudden manner."

"Mr. Neville, Mr. Neville," says the Minor Canon, shaking his head
with a sorrowful smile; "I have heard that said[2] before."

"I think—my mind is much confused, but I think—it is equally true
of Mr. Jasper's nephew, sir."

"Very likely," is the dry rejoinder.

"We quarrelled, sir. He insulted me most grossly. He had heated that
tigerish blood I told you of to-day, before then."

"Mr. Neville," rejoins the Minor Canon, mildly, but firmly: "I request
you not to speak to me with that clenched right hand. Unclench it, if
you please."

"He goaded me, sir," pursues the young man, instantly obeying, "beyond my power of endurance. I cannot say whether or no he meant it at
first, but he did it. He certainly meant it at last. In short, sir," with an
irrepressible outburst, "in the passion into which he lashed me, I would
have cut him down if I could, and I tried to do it."

"You have clenched that hand again," is Mr. Crisparkle's quiet commentary.[3]

"I beg your pardon, sir."

"You know your room, for I showed you to it[4] before dinner; but I will
accompany you to it once more. Your arm, if you please. Softly, for the
house is all a-bed."

Scooping his hand into the same scientific elbow-rest as before, and
backing it up with the inert strength of his arm, as skilfully as a Police
Expert, and with an apparent repose quite unattainable by Novices, Mr.
Crisparkle conducts his pupil to the pleasant and orderly old room prepared for him. Arrived there, the young man throws himself into a chair,
and, flinging his arms upon his reading-table, rests his head upon them
with an air of wretched self-reproach.

The gentle Minor Canon has had it in his thoughts to leave the room,
without a word. But, looking round at the door, and seeing this dejected
figure, he turns back to it, touches it with a mild hand, and says "Good-
night!" A sob is his only acknowledgment. He might have had many
a worse; perhaps, could have had few better.

---

[1] very little] a very little 73 75
[2] said] not in MS
[3] commentary.] commentary. "Please again to unclench it." MS
[4] you to it] MS after deletions it to you 70 ES it you 73 75

Another soft knock at the outer door, attracts his attention as he goes down stairs. He opens it to Mr. Jasper, holding in his hand the pupil's hat.

"We have had an awful scene with him," says Jasper, in a low voice.

"Has it been so bad as that?"

"Murderous!"

Mr. Crisparkle remonstrates: "No, no, no. Do not use such strong words."

"He[1] might have laid my dear boy dead at my feet. It is no fault of his, that he did not. But that I was, through the mercy of God, swift and strong with him, he would have cut him down on my hearth."

The phrase smites home. "Ah!" thinks Mr. Crisparkle. "His own words!"[2]

"Seeing what I have seen to-night, and hearing what I have heard," adds Jasper, with great earnestness, "I shall never know peace of mind when there is danger of those two coming together with no one else to interfere. It was horrible. There is something of the tiger in his dark blood."

"Ah!" thinks Mr. Crisparkle.[3] "So he said!"

"You, my dear sir," pursues Jasper, taking his hand, "even you, have accepted a dangerous charge."[4]

"You need have no fear for me, Jasper," returns Mr. Crisparkle, with a quiet smile. "I have none for myself."

"I have none for myself," returns Jasper, with an emphasis on the last pronoun, "because I am not, nor am I in the way of being, the object of his hostility.[5] But you may be, and my dear boy has been. Good-night!"

Mr. Crisparkle goes in, with the hat that has so easily, so almost imperceptibly, acquired the right to be hung up in his hall; hangs it up; and goes thoughtfully[6] to bed.

[1] He] I repeat, murderous. He MS
[2] Mr. Crisparkle. "His own words!"] Mr Crisparkle with an inward shiver. "His ⟨very⟩ words!" MS
[3] Mr. Crisparkle] Mr Crisparkle ⟨with another inward shiver⟩ MS
[4] charge] charge. You must sometimes—no doubt, often—have to put yourself in opposition to this fierce nature and suppress it. After what I have seen tonight, I am fearful even for you MS
[5] hostility] vindictive hostility MS
[6] thoughtfully] sadly MS

CHAPTER IX

BIRDS IN THE BUSH

Rosa, having no relation that she knew of in the world, had, from the seventh year of her age, known no home but the Nuns' House, and no mother but Miss Twinkleton. Her remembrance of her own mother was of a pretty little creature like herself (not much older than herself it seemed to her), who had been brought home in her father's arms, drowned. The fatal accident had happened at a party of pleasure. Every fold and color in the pretty summer dress, and even the long wet hair, with scattered petals of ruined flowers still clinging to it, as the beloved¹ young figure, in its sad, sad beauty lay upon the bed, were fixed indelibly in Rosa's recollection. So were the wild despair and the subsequent bowed-down grief of her poor young father, who died broken-hearted on the first anniversary of that hard day.

The betrothal of Rosa grew out of the soothing of his year of mental distress² by his fast friend and old college companion, Drood: who likewise had been left a widower in his youth. But he, too, went the silent road into which all earthly pilgrimages merge, some sooner, and some later; and thus the young couple had come to be as they were.

The atmosphere of pity surrounding the little orphan girl when she first came to Cloisterham, had never cleared away. It had taken brighter hues as she grew older, happier, prettier;³ now it had been golden, now roseate, and now azure; but it had always adorned her with some soft light of its own. The general desire to console and caress her, had caused her to be treated in the beginning as a child much younger than her years; the same desire had caused her to be still petted when she was a child no longer. Who should be her favorite, who should anticipate this or that small present, or do her this or that small service; who should take her home for the holidays; who should write to her the oftenest when they were separated, and whom she would most rejoice to see again when they were reunited; even these gentle rivalries were not without their slight dashes of bitterness in the Nuns' House. Well for the poor Nuns in their day, if they hid no harder strife under their veils and rosaries!

Thus Rosa had grown to be an amiable, giddy, wilful, winning little creature; spoilt, in the sense of counting upon kindness⁴ from all around her; but not in the sense of repaying it with indifference. Possessing an exhaustless well of affection in her nature, its sparkling waters had

---

CHAPTER IX] *in* MS *the next chapter is* CHAPTER VIII. MR DURDLES AND FRIEND. *On the page after this chapter, the heading* Nº III *is deleted and* CHAPTER IX. BIRDS IN THE BUSH *follows*

¹ beloved] MS dead 70–75   ² distress] agony MS
³ prettier] lovelier MS   ⁴ kindness] kindnesses MS

freshened and brightened the Nuns' House for years, and yet its depths had never yet been moved: what might betide when that came to pass; what developing changes might fall upon the heedless head, and light heart then; remained to be seen.

By what means the news that there had been a quarrel between the two young men over-night, involving even some kind of onslaught by Mr. Neville upon Edwin Drood, got into Miss Twinkleton's establishment before breakfast, it is impossible to say. Whether it was brought in by the birds of the air, or came blowing in with the very air itself, when the casement windows were set open; whether the baker brought it kneaded into the bread, or the milkman delivered it as part of the adulteration of his[1] milk; or the housemaids, beating the dust out of their mats against the gateposts, received it in exchange deposited on the mats by the town atmosphere; certain it is that the news permeated every gable of the old building before Miss Twinkleton was down, and that Miss Twinkleton herself received it through Mrs. Tisher, while yet in the act of dressing; or (as she might have expressed the phrase to a parent or guardian of a mythological turn), of sacrificing to the Graces.

Miss Landless's brother had thrown a bottle at Mr. Edwin Drood.

Miss Landless's brother had thrown a knife at Mr. Edwin Drood.

A knife became suggestive of a fork, and Miss Landless's brother had thrown a fork at Mr. Edwin Drood.

As in the governing precedent[2] of Peter Piper, alleged to have picked the peck[3] of pickled pepper, it was held physically desirable to have evidence of the existence of the peck of pickled pepper which Peter Piper was alleged to have picked: so, in this case, it was held psychologically important to know Why Miss Landless's brother threw a bottle, knife, or fork—or bottle, knife, *and* fork—for the cook had been given to understand it was all three—at Mr. Edwin Drood?

Well, then. Miss Landless's brother had said he admired Miss Bud. Mr. Edwin Drood had said to Miss Landless's brother that he had no business to admire Miss Bud. Miss Landless's brother had then "up'd" (this was the cook's exact information), with the bottle, knife, fork, and decanter (the decanter now coolly flying at everybody's head, without the least introduction), and thrown them all at Mr. Edwin Drood.

Poor little Rosa put a forefinger into each of her ears when these rumours began to circulate, and retired into a corner, beseeching not to be told any more;[4] but Miss Landless, begging permission of Miss Twinkleton to go and speak with her brother, and pretty plainly showing that she would take it if it were not given, struck out the more definite course of going to Mr. Crisparkle's for accurate intelligence.

---

[1] his] the MS   [2] precedent] precedence 75   [3] the peck] ⟨the⟩ a peck MS
[4] beseeching . . . any more] rocking herself to and fro, and beseeching not to be told things that made people either ridiculous or dreadful MS

When she came back (being first closeted with Miss Twinkleton, in order that anything objectionable in her tidings might be retained by that discreet filter), she imparted to Rosa only, what had really[1] taken place; dwelling with a flushed cheek on the provocation her brother had received, but almost limiting it to that last gross affront as crowning "some other words between them," and, out of consideration for her new friend, passing lightly over the fact that the other words had originated in her lover's taking things in general so very easily. To Rosa direct, she brought a petition from her brother that she would forgive him; and, having delivered it with sisterly earnestness, made an end of the subject.

It was reserved for Miss Twinkleton to tone down the public mind of the Nuns' House. That lady, therefore, entering in a stately manner what plebeians might have called the school-room, but what, in the patrician language of the head of the Nuns' House, was euphuistically, not to say round-aboutedly, denominated "the apartment allotted to study," and saying with a forensic air, "Ladies!" all rose. Mrs. Tisher at the same time grouped[2] herself behind her chief, as representing Queen Elizabeth's first historical female friend at Tilbury Fort. Miss Twinkleton then proceeded to remark that Rumour, Ladies, had been represented by the Bard of Avon—needless were it to mention the immortal SHAKESPEARE, also called the Swan of his native river, not improbably with some reference to the ancient superstition that that bird of graceful plumage (Miss Jennings will please stand upright) sang sweetly on the approach of death, for which we have no ornithological authority,—Rumour, Ladies, had been represented by that bard—hem!—[3]

"who drew
The celebrated Jew,"

as painted full of tongues. Rumour in Cloisterham (Miss Ferdinand will honor me with her attention) was no exception to the great limner's portrait of Rumour elsewhere. A slight *fracas* between two young gentlemen occurring last night within a hundred miles of these peaceful walls (Miss Ferdinand, being apparently incorrigible, will have the kindness to write out this evening, in the original language, the first four fables of our vivacious neighbour, Monsieur La Fontaine) had been very grossly exaggerated by Rumour's voice. In the first alarm and anxiety arising from our sympathy with a sweet young friend, not wholly to be dissociated from one of the gladiators in the bloodless arena in question (the impropriety of Miss Reynolds's appearing to stab herself in the band with a pin, is far too obvious, and too glaringly unlady-like, to be pointed out), we descended from our maiden elevation to discuss this uncongenial

[1] really] MS *om.* 70–75
[2] rose. Mrs. Tisher . . . grouped] rose: Mrs Tisher . . . grouping MS
[3] hem!—] *not in* MS

and this unfit theme. Responsible inquiries having assured us that it was but one of those "airy nothings" pointed at by the Poet (whose name and date of birth Miss Giggles will supply within half an hour), we would now discard the subject, and concentrate our minds upon the grateful labours of the day.

But the subject so survived all day, nevertheless, that Miss Ferdinand got into new trouble by surreptitiously clapping on a paper moustache at dinner-time, and going through the motions of aiming a water-bottle at Miss Giggles, who drew a table-spoon in defence.

Now, Rosa thought of this unlucky quarrel a great deal, and thought of it with an uncomfortable feeling that she was involved in it, as cause, or consequence, or what not, through being in a false position altogether as to her[1] marriage engagement. Never free from such uneasiness when she was with her affianced husband, it was not likely that she would be free from it when they were apart. To-day, too, she was cast in upon herself, and deprived of the relief of talking freely with her new friend, because the quarrel had been with Helena's brother, and Helena undisguisedly[2] avoided the subject as a delicate and difficult one to herself. At this critical time, of all times, Rosa's guardian was announced as having come to see her.

Mr. Grewgious had been well selected for his trust, as a man of incorruptible integrity, but certainly for no other appropriate quality discernible on the surface. He was an arid,[3] sandy man, who, if he had been put into a grinding-mill, looked as if he would have ground immediately into high-dried snuff. He had a scanty flat crop of hair, in color and consistency like some very mangy yellow fur tippet;[4] it was so unlike hair, that it must have been a wig, but for the stupendous improbability of anybody's voluntarily sporting such a head. The little play of feature that his face presented, was cut deep into it, in a few hard curves that made it more like work; and he had certain notches in his forehead, which looked as though Nature had been about to touch them into sensibility or refinement, when she had impatiently thrown away the chisel, and said: "I really cannot be worried to finish off this man; let him go as he is."

With too great length[5] of throat at his upper end, and too much ankle-bone and heel at his lower; with an awkward and hesitating manner; with a shambling walk, and with what is called a near sight—which perhaps prevented his observing how much white cotton stocking he displayed to the public eye, in contrast with his black suit—Mr. Grewgious still had some strange capacity in him of making on the whole an agreeable impression.

---

[1] her] that MS   [2] undisguisedly] evidently MS

[3] an arid] a weazen arid MS

[4] mangy yellow fur tippet] common yellow fur tippet, or the mane of the cheapest description of toy-horse MS   [5] length] a length MS

Mr. Grewgious was discovered by his ward, much discomfited by being in Miss Twinkleton's company in Miss Twinkleton's own sacred room. Dim forebodings of being examined in something, and not coming well out of it, seemed to oppress the poor gentleman when found in these circumstances.

"My dear, how do you do? I am glad to see you. My dear, how much improved you are. Permit me to hand you a chair, my dear."

Miss Twinkleton rose at her little writing-table, saying, with general sweetness, as to the polite Universe: "Will you permit me to retire?"

"By no means, madam, on my account. I beg that you will not move."

"I must entreat permission to *move*," returned Miss Twinkleton, repeating the word with a charming grace; "but I will not withdraw, since you are so obliging. If I wheel my desk to this corner window, shall I be in the way?"

"Madam! In the way!"

"You are very kind. Rosa, my dear, you will be under no restraint, I am sure."

Here Mr. Grewgious, left by the fire with Rosa, said again: "My dear, how do you do? I am glad to see you, my dear." And having waited for her to sit down, sat down himself.

"My visits," said Mr. Grewgious, "are, like those of the angels—not that I compare myself to an angel."

"No, sir," said Rosa.

"Not by any means," assented Mr. Grewgious. "I merely refer to my visits, which are few and far between. The angels are, we know very well, up stairs."

Miss Twinkleton looked round with a kind of stiff stare.

"I refer, my dear," said Mr. Grewgious, laying his hand on Rosa's, as the possibility thrilled through his frame of his otherwise seeming to take the awful liberty of calling Miss Twinkleton my dear; "I refer to the other young ladies."

Miss Twinkleton resumed her writing.

Mr. Grewgious, with a sense of not having managed his opening point quite as neatly as he might have desired, smoothed his head from back to front as if he had just dived, and were pressing the water out—this smoothing action, however superfluous, was habitual with him—and took a pocket-book from his coat pocket, and a stump of black-lead pencil from his waistcoat pocket.[1]

"I made," he said, turning the leaves: "I made a guiding memorandum or so—as I usually do, for I have no conversational powers whatever[2]— to which I will, with your permission, my dear, refer. 'Well and happy.' Truly. You are well and happy, my dear? You look so."

"Yes, indeed, sir," answered Rosa.

"For which," said Mr. Grewgious, with a bend of his head towards the corner window, "our warmest acknowledgments are due, and I am sure are rendered, to the maternal kindness and the constant care and consideration of the lady whom I have now the honor to see before me."

This point, again, made but a lame departure from Mr. Grewgious, and never got to its destination; for, Miss Twinkleton, feeling that the courtesies required her to be by this time quite outside the conversation, was biting the end of her pen, and looking upward, as waiting for the descent of an idea from any member of the Celestial Nine who might have one to spare.

Mr. Grewgious smoothed his smooth head again, and then made another reference to his pocket-book; lining out 'well and happy' as disposed of.

"'Pounds, shillings, and pence' is my next note. A dry subject for a young lady, but an important subject too. Life is pounds, shillings, and pence. Death is——" A sudden recollection of the death of her two parents seemed to stop him, and he said in a softer tone, and evidently inserting the negative as an after-thought: "Death is *not* pounds, shillings, and pence."

His voice was as hard and dry as himself, and Fancy might have ground it straight, like himself, into high-dried snuff. And yet, through the very limited means of expression that he possessed, he seemed to express kindness. If Nature had but finished him off, kindness might have been recognizable in his face at this moment. But if the notches in his forehead wouldn't fuse together, and if his face would work and couldn't play, what could he do, poor man!

"'Pounds, shillings, and pence.' You find your allowance always sufficient for your wants, my dear?"

Rosa wanted for nothing, and therefore it was ample.

"And you are not in debt?"

Rosa laughed at the idea of being in debt. It seemed, to her inexperience, a comical vagary of the imagination. Mr. Grewgious stretched his near sight to be sure that this was her view of the case. "Ah!" he said, as comment, with a furtive glance towards Miss Twinkleton, and lining out 'pounds, shillings, and pence': "I spoke of having got among the angels! So I did!"

Rosa felt what his next memorandum would prove to be, and was blushing and folding a crease in her dress with one embarrassed hand, long before he found it.

"'Marriage.' Hem!" Mr. Grewgious carried his smoothing hand down over his eyes and nose, and even chin, before drawing his chair a little nearer, and speaking a little more confidentially: "I now touch, my dear, upon the point that is the direct cause of my troubling you with the present visit. Otherwise, being a particularly Angular man, I should not have intruded here. I am the last man to intrude into a sphere for which I am so entirely unfitted. I feel, on these premises, as if I was a bear—with the cramp—in a youthful Cotillon."

His ungainliness gave him enough of the air of his simile to set Rosa off laughing heartily.[1]

"It strikes you in the same light," said Mr. Grewgious, with perfect calmness. "Just so. To return to my memorandum. Mr. Edwin has been to and fro here, as was arranged. You have mentioned that,[2] in your quarterly letters to me. And you like him, and he likes you."

"I *like* him very much, sir," rejoined Rosa.

"So I said, my dear," returned her guardian, for whose ear the timid emphasis was much too fine. "Good. And you correspond."

"We write to one another," said Rosa, pouting, as she recalled their epistolary differences.

"Such is the meaning that I attach to the word 'correspond' in this application, my dear," said Mr. Grewgious. "Good. All goes well, time moves[3] on, and at this next Christmas-time it will become necessary, as a matter of form, to give the exemplary lady in the corner window, to whom we are so much indebted, business notice of your departure in the ensuing half-year. Your relations with her, are far more than business relations no doubt; but a residue of business remains in them, and business is business ever.[4] I am a particularly Angular man," proceeded Mr. Grewgious, as if it suddenly occurred to him to mention it, "and I am not used to give anything away. If, for these two reasons, some competent Proxy would give *you* away, I should take it very kindly."

Rosa intimated, with her eyes on the ground, that she thought a substitute might be found, if required.

"Surely, surely," said Mr. Grewgious. "For instance, the gentleman who teaches Dancing here—he would know how to do it with graceful propriety. He would advance and retire in a manner satisfactory to the feelings of the officiating clergyman, and of yourself, and the bridegroom, and all[5] parties concerned. I am—I am a particularly Angular man," said Mr. Grewgious, as if he had made up his mind to screw it out at last: "and should only blunder."

Rosa sat still and silent. Perhaps her mind had not got quite so far as the ceremony yet, but was lagging on the way there.

"Memorandum, 'Will.' Now, my dear," said Mr. Grewgious, referring to his notes, disposing of 'marriage' with his pencil, and taking a paper from his pocket: "although I have before possessed you with the contents of your father's will, I think it right at this time to leave a certified copy of it in your hands. And although Mr. Edwin is also aware of its contents,

---

[1] heartily] ⟨heartily, in spite of herself⟩ until she cried MS
[2] that] that, my dear MS   [3] moves] MS works 70–75
[4] ever] still MS   [5] all] of all MS

I think it right at this time likewise to place a certified copy of it in Mr. Jasper's hands[1]——"

"Not in his own?" asked Rosa, looking up quickly. "Cannot the copy go to Eddy himself?"

"Why, yes, my dear, if you particularly wish it; but I spoke of Mr. Jasper as being his trustee."

"I do particularly wish it, if you please," said Rosa, hurriedly and earnestly; "I don't like Mr. Jasper to come between us, in any way."

"It is natural, I suppose," said Mr. Grewgious, "that your young husband should be all in all. Yes. You observe that I say, I suppose. The fact is, I am a particularly Unnatural man, and I don't know from my own knowledge."

Rosa looked at him with some wonder.

"I mean," he explained, "that young ways were never my ways. I was the only offspring of parents far advanced in life, and I half believe I was born advanced in life myself. No personality is intended towards the name you will so soon change, when I remark that while the general growth of people seem to have come into existence, buds, I seem to have come into existence a chip. I was a chip—and a very dry one—when I first became aware of myself. Respecting the other certified copy, your wish shall be complied with. Respecting your inheritance, I think you know all. It is an annuity of two hundred and fifty pounds. The savings upon that annuity, and some other items to your credit, all duly carried to account, with vouchers, will place you in possession of a lump-sum of money, rather exceeding Seventeen Hundred Pounds. I am empowered to advance[2] the cost of your preparations for your marriage out of that fund. All is told."

"Will you please tell me," said Rosa, taking the paper with a prettily knitted brow, but not opening it: "whether I am right in what I am going to say? I can understand what you tell me, so very much better than what I read in law-writings. My poor papa and Eddy's father made their agreement together, as very dear and firm and fast friends, in order that we, too, might be very dear and firm and fast friends after them?"

"Just so."

"For the lasting good of both of us, and the lasting happiness of both of us?"

"Just so."

"That we might be to one another even much more than they had been to one another?"

"Just so."

"It was not bound upon Eddy, and it was not bound upon me, by any forfeit, in case——"

"Don't be agitated, my dear. In the case that it brings tears into your affectionate[1] eyes even to picture to yourself—in the case of your not marry-ing one another—no, no forfeiture on either side. You would then have been my ward until you were of age. No worse would have befallen you. Bad enough perhaps!"

"And Eddy?"[2]

"He would have come into his partnership derived from his father, and into[3] its arrears to his credit (if any), on attaining his majority, just as now."

Rosa with her perplexed face and knitted brow, bit the corner of her attested copy, as she sat with her head on one side, looking abstractedly on[4] the floor, and smoothing it with her foot.

"In short," said Mr. Grewgious, "this betrothal is a wish, a sentiment, a friendly project, tenderly expressed on both sides. That it was strongly felt, and that there was a lively hope that it would prosper, there can be no doubt. When you were both children, you began to be accustomed to it, and it *has* prospered. But circumstances alter cases; and I made this visit to-day, partly, indeed principally, to discharge myself[5] of the duty of telling you, my dear, that two young people can only be betrothed in marriage (except as a matter of convenience, and therefore mockery and misery), of their own free will, their own attachment, and their own assurance (it may or may[6] not prove a mistaken one, but we must take our chance of that), that they are suited to each other and will make each other happy. Is it to be supposed, for example, that if either of your fathers were[7] living now, and had any mistrust on that subject, his mind would not be changed by the change of circumstances involved in the change of your years?[8] Untenable, unreasonable, inconclusive, and pre-posterous!"

Mr. Grewgious said all this, as if he were reading it aloud; or, still more, as if he were repeating a lesson. So expressionless of any approach to spontaneity were his face[9] and manner.

"I have now, my dear," he added, blurring out 'will' with his pencil, "discharged myself of what is doubtless a formal duty in this case, but still a duty in such a case. Memorandum, 'Wishes.' Exactly. Is[10] there any wish of yours that I can further?"

Rosa shook her head, with an almost plaintive air of hesitation in want of help.

"Is there any instruction that I can take from you with reference to your affairs?"

"I—I should like to settle them with Eddy first, if you please," said Rosa, plaiting the crease in her dress.

---

[1] affectionate] *not in* MS   [2] Eddy] Eddy, then MS
[3] into] *not in* MS   [4] on] at MS   [5] myself] myself once for all MS
[6] may] it may 75   [7] were] was MS   [8] involved . . . years] *not in* MS
[9] face] uncompleted face MS   [10] Exactly. Is] MS My dear, is 70–75

"Surely, surely," returned Mr. Grewgious. "You two[1] should be of one mind in all things. Is the young gentleman expected shortly?"

"He has gone away only this morning. He will be back at Christmas."

"Nothing could happen better. You will, on his return at Christmas, arrange all matters of detail with him; you will then communicate with me; and I will discharge myself (as a mere business acquittance) of my business responsibilities towards the accomplished lady in the corner window. They will accrue at that season." Blurring pencil once again. "Memorandum, 'Leave.' Yes. I will now, my dear, take my leave."

"Could I," said Rosa, rising, as he jerked out of his chair in his ungainly way: "could I ask you, most kindly to come to me at Christmas, if I had anything particular to say to you?"

"Why, certainly, certainly," he rejoined; apparently—if such a word can be used of one who had no apparent lights or shadows about him— complimented by the question. "As a particularly Angular man, I do not fit smoothly into the social circle, and consequently I have no other engagement at Christmas-time than to partake, on the twenty-fifth, of a boiled turkey and celery sauce with a—with a particularly Angular clerk I have the good fortune to possess, whose father, being a Norfolk farmer, sends him up (the turkey up), as a present to me, from the neighbourhood of Norwich. I should be quite proud of your wishing to see me, my dear. As a professional Receiver of rents, so very few people *do* wish to see me, that the novelty would be bracing."

For his ready acquiescence, the grateful Rosa put her hands upon his shoulders, stood on tiptoe, and instantly kissed him.

"Lord bless me!" cried Mr. Grewgious. "Thank you, my dear! The honor is almost equal to the pleasure. Miss Twinkleton, Madam, I have had a most satisfactory conversation with my ward, and I will now release you from the incumbrance of my presence."

"Nay, sir," rejoined Miss Twinkleton, rising with a gracious condescension: "say not incumbrance. Not so, by any means. I cannot permit you to say so."[2]

"Thank you, Madam. I have read in the newspapers," said Mr. Grewgious, stammering a little, "that when a distinguished visitor (not that I am one: far from it), goes to a school (not that this is one: far from it), he asks for a holiday, or some sort of grace. It being now the afternoon in the—College[3]—of which you are the eminent head, the young ladies might gain nothing, except in name, by having the rest of the day allowed them. But if there is any young lady at all under a cloud, might I solicit—— ?"

"Ah, Mr. Grewgious, Mr. Grewgious!" cried Miss Twinkleton, with a chastely-rallying forefinger. "Oh, you gentlemen, you gentlemen! Fie

---

[1] two] *not in* MS   [2] to say so] *not in* MS
[3] the—College] the a—College MS

for shame, that you are so hard upon us poor maligned disciplinarians of
our sex, for your sakes! But as Miss Ferdinand is at present weighed down
by an incubus"—Miss Twinkleton might have said a pen-and-ink-ubus
of writing out Monsieur La Fontaine—"go to her Rosa, my dear, and tell
her the penalty is remitted, in deference to the intercession of your
guardian, Mr. Grewgious."

Miss Twinkleton here achieved a curtsey, suggestive of marvels happening to her respected legs, and which she came out of nobly, three
yards behind her starting-point.[1]

As he held it incumbent upon him to call on Mr. Jasper before leaving
Cloisterham, Mr. Grewgious[2] went to the Gate House, and climbed its
postern stair. But Mr. Jasper's door being closed, and presenting on a
slip of paper the word "Cathedral," the fact of its being service-time was
borne into the mind of Mr. Grewgious. So, he[3] descended the stair again,
and, crossing the Close, paused at the great western folding-door of the
Cathedral, which stood open on the fine and bright, though short-lived,
afternoon, for the airing of the place.

"Dear me," said Mr. Grewgious, peering[4] in, "it's like looking down the
throat of Old Time."

Old Time heaved a mouldy sigh from tomb and arch and vault; and
gloomy shadows began to deepen in corners; and damps began to rise
from green patches of stone; and jewels, cast upon[5] the pavement of the
nave from stained glass by the declining sun, began to perish. Within the
grill-gate of the chancel, up the steps surmounted loomingly by the fast
darkening organ, white robes could be dimly seen, and one feeble voice,
rising and falling in a cracked monotonous mutter, could at intervals be
faintly heard. In the free outer air,[6] the river, the green pastures, and the
brown arable lands, the teeming[7] hills and dales, were reddened by the
sunset: while the distant little windows in windmills and farm home-
steads, shone, patches of bright beaten gold. In the Cathedral,[8] all became
grey, murky,[9] and sepulchral, and the cracked monotonous mutter went
on like a dying voice, until the organ and the choir burst forth, and drowned
it in a sea of music. Then, the sea fell, and the dying voice made another
feeble effort,[10] and then the sea rose high, and beat its life out, and lashed
the roof, and surged among the arches, and pierced the heights of the great
tower; and then the sea was dry, and all was still.[11]

---

[1] *After* starting-point. MS *has* Plunged into a state of hopeless angularity by the
spectacle, Mr Grewgious got out of the presence how he could. ⟨and that was disgrace-
fully⟩

[2] Mr. Grewgious] he MS   [3] So, he] He MS
[4] peering] MS peeping 70–75   [5] cast upon] reflected on MS
[6] In the free outer air] Outside MS   [7] teeming] *not in* MS
[8] In the Cathedral] Inside MS   [9] murky] dusky MS
[10] effort] effort for it MS
[11] and then the sea . . . still] and then, lo the sea . . . still and silent MS

Mr. Grewgious had by that time walked to the chancel-steps, where he met the living waters coming out.[1]

"Nothing is the matter?" Thus Jasper accosted him,[2] rather quickly. "You have not been sent for?"

"Not at all, not at all. I came down of my own accord.[3] I have been to my pretty ward's, and am now homeward bound again."[4]

"You found her thriving?"

"Blooming indeed. Most blooming. I merely came to tell her, seriously, what a betrothal by deceased parents is."

"And what is it—according to your judgment?"

Mr. Grewgious noticed the whiteness of the lips that asked the question, and put it down to the chilling account of the Cathedral.

"I merely came to tell her that it could not be considered binding, against any such reason for its dissolution as a want of affection, or want of[5] disposition to carry it into effect, on the side of either party."[6]

"May I ask, had you any especial reason for telling her that?"

Mr. Grewgious answered[7] somewhat sharply: "The especial reason of doing[8] my duty, sir. Simply that." Then he added: "Come, Mr. Jasper; I know your affection for your nephew, and that you are quick to feel on his behalf. I assure you that this implies not the least doubt of, or disrespect to, your nephew."[9]

"You could not," returned Jasper, with a friendly pressure of his arm, as they walked on side by side, "speak more handsomely."[10]

Mr. Grewgious pulled off his hat to smooth his head, and, having smoothed it, nodded it contentedly, and put his hat on again.

"I will wager," said Jasper, smiling—his lips were still so white that he was conscious of it, and bit and moistened them while speaking: "I will wager that she hinted no wish to be released from Ned."

"And you will win your wager, if you do," retorted Mr. Grewgious.[11]

---

[1] After coming out. MS has Among the dirty linen that was already being unbuttoned behind with all the expedition compatible with a feint of following Mr Tope and his mace in procession round the corner was the robe of Mr Jasper. He threw it to a boy (who sadly wanted "getting up" by some laundress) and he and Mr Grewgious walked out of the Cathedral, talking as they went.

[2] Thus Jasper accosted him] Jasper began MS

[3] After accord. MS has I have had it in my mind to come down, off and on, this long time. But more off than on, I am ashamed to say."/"Are you going to—?"

[4] After again. MS has I felt that I ought in politeness to report myself to you before I went."/"Thank you.

[5] want of] not in MS

[6] party] surviving party MS

[7] answered] shrugged his shoulders as he answered MS

[8] doing] resolving to do MS

[9] nephew] nephew. Duty in the abstract must be done, even if it did; but it did not, and it does not. I like your nephew very much. I hope you are satisfied MS

[10] handsomely.] handsomely. Can I be less than satisfied? MS

[11] After Grewgious. MS has Jasper laid that friendly pressure on his arm again.

"We should allow some margin for little maidenly delicacies in a young[1] motherless creature, under such circumstances, I suppose;[2] it is not in my line; what do you think?"

"There can be no doubt of it."

"I am glad you say so. Because," proceeded Mr. Grewgious, who had all this time very knowingly felt his way round to action on his remembrance of what she had said of Jasper himself: "because she seems to have some little delicate instinct that all preliminary arrangements had best be made between Mr. Edwin Drood and herself, don't you see? She don't want us, don't you know?"

Jasper touched himself on the breast, and said, somewhat indistinctly: "You mean me."

Mr. Grewgious touched himself on the breast, and said: "I mean us.[3] Therefore, let them have their little discussions and councils together, when Mr. Edwin Drood comes back here at Christmas, and then you and I will step in, and put the final touches to the business."

"So, you settled with her that you would come back at Christmas?"[4] observed Jasper. "I see! Mr. Grewgious, as you quite fairly said just now, there is such an exceptional attachment between my nephew and me, that[5] I am more sensitive for the dear, fortunate, happy, happy fellow than for myself. But it is only right that the young lady should be considered, as you have pointed out, and that I should accept my cue from you. I accept it. I understand that at Christmas they will complete their

[1] young] little MS

[2] circumstances, I suppose] circumstances," observed Mr Grewgious: "at least I suppose we should MS

[3] *After* us. MS *has* Jasper looked at him steadily, smiled, and said nothing. Mr Grewgious had an impression that he was shaking his head; but stopping to look at him steadily in return, found that he was not shaking his head.
"Therefore," said Mr Grewgious in a cosily arranging manner, "let

[4] Christmas] that time MS

[5] observed Jasper. "I see! . . . my nephew and me, that] observed Jasper.
"Eh?" said the other, expressionlessly innocent. But not without adding internally: "This is a very quick watch-dog!"
"So you settled with her that you would come back at Christmas," repeated Jasper.
"At Christmas? Certainly. O dear yes, I settled with her that I would come back at Christmas," replied Mr Grewgious, as if the question had previously lain between Lady Day, Midsummer Day, and Michaelmas.
By this time, sometimes walking very slowly and sometimes standing still, they had reached the Gate House.
"Will you not walk up," said Jasper, "and refresh?"
"Thank you, no. I have a horse and chaise here, and have not too much time to get across and catch the new railroad."
Jasper pressed his hand.
"Mr Grewgious, as you quite fairly said just now, my affection for my dear boy makes me quick to feel in his behalf, and I cannot allow any approach to a slight to be put upon him. There is such an exceptional attachment between him and me that MS

preparations for May, and that their[1] marriage will be put in final train
by themselves,[2] and that nothing will remain for us but to[3] put ourselves
in train also, and have everything ready for our formal release[4] from our
trusts, on Edwin's birthday."

"That is my understanding," assented[5] Mr. Grewgious, as they shook
hands to part. "God bless them both!"

"God save them both!" cried Jasper.[6]

"I said, bless them," remarked the former, looking back over his
shoulder.

"I said, save them," returned the latter. "Is there any difference?"

CHAPTER X

SMOOTHING THE WAY

IT has been often enough remarked that women have a curious power of
divining the characters of men, which would seem to be innate and instinctive; seeing that it is arrived at through no patient process of reasoning,
that it can give no satisfactory or sufficient account of itself, and that it
pronounces in the most confident manner even against accumulated observation[7] on the part of the other sex. But it has not been quite so often
remarked that this power (fallible, like every other human attribute), is for
the most part absolutely incapable of self-revision; and that when it has
delivered an adverse opinion which by all human lights is subsequently
proved to have failed, it is undistinguishable from prejudice, in respect of
its determination not to be corrected. Nay, the very possibility of contradiction or disproof, however remote, communicates to this feminine
judgment from the first, in nine cases out of ten, the weakness attendant
on the testimony of an interested witness: so personally and strongly does
the fair diviner connect herself with her divination.

"Now, don't you think, Ma dear," said the Minor Canon to his mother
one day as she sat at her knitting in his little book-room, "that you are
rather hard on Mr. Neville?"

"No, I do not, Sept," returned the old lady.

"Let us discuss it, Ma."

"I have no objection to discuss it, Sept. I trust, my dear, I am always
open to discussion." There was a vibration in the old lady's cap, as though

---

[1] their] the MS
[2] by themselves] not in MS   [3] for us but to] but for us to MS
[4] our formal release] the formal release of ourselves MS
[5] assented] returned MS   [6] Jasper] Mr Jasper MS
END OF No. II
CHAPTER X] CHAPTER ⟨I⟩X MS
[7] accumulated observation] experience and accumulated observation MS

she internally added: "and I should like to see the discussion that would change *my* mind!"

"Very good, Ma," said her conciliatory son. "There is nothing like being open to discussion."

"I hope not, my dear," returned the old lady, evidently shut to it.

"Well! Mr. Neville, on that unfortunate occasion, commits himself under provocation."

"And under mulled wine," added the old lady.

"I must admit the wine. Though I believe the two young men were much alike in that regard."

"I don't!" said the old lady.

"Why not, Ma?"

"Because I *don't*," said the old lady. "Still, I am quite open to discussion."

"But, my dear Ma, I cannot see how we are to discuss, if you take that line."

"Blame Mr. Neville for it, Sept, and not me," said the old lady, with stately severity.

"My dear Ma! Why Mr. Neville?"

"Because," said Mrs. Crisparkle, retiring on first principles, "he came home intoxicated, and did great discredit to this house, and showed great disrespect to this family."

"That is not to be denied, Ma. He was then, and he[1] is now, very sorry for it."

"But for Mr. Jasper's well-bred consideration in coming up to me next day, after service, in the nave itself, with his gown[2] still on, and expressing his hope that I had not been greatly alarmed or had my rest violently broken, I believe I might never have heard of that disgraceful transaction," said the old lady.

"To be candid, Ma, I think I should have kept it from you if I could: though I had not decidedly made up my mind. I was following Jasper out, to confer with him on the subject, and to consider the expediency of his and my jointly hushing the thing up on all accounts, when I found him speaking to you. Then it was too late."

"Too late, indeed, Sept. He was still as pale as gentlemanly ashes at what had taken place in his rooms over-night."

"If I *had* kept it from you, Ma,[3] you may be sure it would have been for your peace and quiet, and for the good of the young men,[4] and in my best discharge of my duty according to my lights."[5]

The old lady immediately walked across the room and kissed him; saying, "Of course, my dear Sept, I am sure of that."

---

[1] he] *not in* MS   [2] gown] surplice MS
[3] Ma] Ma dear MS   [4] men] *possibly* man MS
[5] lights."] lights," observed the Minor Canon. MS

"However, it became the town-talk," said Mr. Crisparkle, rubbing his ear, as his mother resumed her seat, and her knitting, "and passed out of my power."

"And I said then, Sept," returned the old lady, "that I thought ill of Mr. Neville. And I say now, that I think ill of Mr. Neville. And I said then, and I say now, that I hope Mr. Neville may come to good, but I don't believe he will." Here the cap vibrated again, considerably.

"I am sorry to hear you say so, Ma——"

"I am sorry to say so, my dear," interposed the old lady, knitting on firmly, "but I can't help it."

"—For," pursued the Minor Canon, "it is undeniable that Mr. Neville is exceedingly industrious and attentive, and that he improves apace, and that he has—I hope I may say—an attachment to me."

"There is no merit in the last article, my dear," said the old lady, quickly; "and if he says there is, I think the worse of him for the boast."

"But, my dear Ma, he never said there was."

"Perhaps not," returned the old lady; "still, I don't see that it greatly signifies."

There was no impatience in the pleasant look with which Mr. Crisparkle contemplated the pretty old piece of china as it knitted; but there was, certainly, a humorous sense of its not being a piece of china to argue with very closely.

"Besides, Sept. Ask yourself what he would be without his sister. You know what an influence she has over him; you know what a capacity she has; you know that whatever he reads with you, he reads with her. Give her her fair share of your praise, and how much do you leave for him?"

At these words Mr. Crisparkle fell into a little reverie, in which he thought of several things. He thought of the times he had seen the brother and sister together in deep converse over one of his own old college books; now, in the rimy mornings, when he made those sharpening pilgrimages to Cloisterham Weir; now, in the sombre evenings, when he faced the wind at sunset, having climbed his favorite outlook, a beetling fragment of monastery ruin; and the two studious figures passed below him along the margin of the river, in which the town fires and lights already shone, making the landscape bleaker.[1] He thought how the consciousness had stolen upon him that in teaching one, he was teaching two; and how he had almost insensibly adapted his explanations to both minds—that with which his own was daily in contact, and that which he only approached through it. He thought of the gossip that had reached him from the Nuns' House, to the effect that Helena, whom he had mistrusted as so proud and fierce, submitted herself to the fairy bride (as he called her), and learnt from her what she knew. He thought of the picturesque alliance between those two, externally so very different. He thought—perhaps most of all—

---

[1] bleaker] bleak MS

could it be that these things were yet but so many weeks old, and had become an integral part of his life?

As, whenever the Reverend Septimus fell a musing, his good mother took it to be an infallible sign that he "wanted support," the blooming old lady made all haste to the dining-room closet, to produce from it the support embodied in a glass of Constantia and a home-made biscuit. It was a most wonderful closet, worthy of Cloisterham and of Minor Canon Corner. Above it, a portrait of Handel in a flowing wig beamed down at the spectator, with a knowing air of being up to the contents of the closet, and a musical air of intending to combine all its harmonies in one delicious fugue. No common closet with a vulgar door on hinges, openable all at once, and leaving nothing to be disclosed by degrees, this rare closet had a lock in mid-air, where two perpendicular slides met: the one falling down, and the other pushing up. The upper slide, on being pulled down (leaving the lower a double[1] mystery), revealed deep shelves of pickle-jars, jam-pots, tin canisters, spice-boxes, and agreeably outlandish vessels of blue and white, the luscious lodgings of preserved tamarinds and ginger. Every benevolent inhabitant of this retreat had his name inscribed upon his stomach. The pickles, in a uniform of rich brown double-breasted buttoned coat, and yellow or sombre[2] drab continuations, announced their portly forms, in printed capitals, as Walnut, Gherkin, Onion, Cabbage, Cauliflower, Mixed, and other members of that noble family. The jams, as being of a less masculine temperament, and as wearing curlpapers, announced themselves in feminine caligraphy, like a soft whisper, to be Raspberry, Gooseberry, Apricot, Plum, Damson, Apple, and Peach.[3] The scene closing on these charmers, and the lower slide ascending, oranges were revealed, attended by a mighty japanned sugar-box, to temper their acerbity if unripe. Home-made biscuits waited at the Court of these Powers, accompanied by a goodly fragment of plum-cake, and various slender ladies' fingers, to be dipped into sweet wine and kissed. Lowest of all, a compact leaden vault enshrined the sweet wine and a stock of cordials: whence issued whispers of Seville Orange, Lemon, Almond, and Carraway-seed. There was a crowning air upon this closet of closets, of having been for ages hummed through by the Cathedral bell and organ, until those venerable bees had made sublimated honey of everything in store; and it was always observed that every dipper among the shelves (deep, as has been noticed, and swallowing up head, shoulders, and elbows), came forth again mellow-faced, and seeming to have undergone a saccharine transfiguration.

The Reverend Septimus yielded himself up quite as willing a victim to a nauseous medicinal herb-closet, also presided over by the china shepherdess, as to this glorious cupboard. To what amazing infusions of

---

[1] a double] *probably* as a double MS   [2] sombre] *word not legible in* MS
[3] Peach] Pear ES

gentian, peppermint, gilliflower, sage, parsley, thyme, rue, rosemary, and dandelion, did his courageous stomach submit itself! In what wonderful wrappers enclosing layers of dried leaves, would he swathe his rosy and contented face, if his mother suspected him of a toothache! What botanical blotches would he cheerfully stick upon his cheek, or forehead, if the dear old lady convicted him of an imperceptible pimple there! Into this herbaceous penitentiary, situated on an upper staircase-landing: a low and narrow whitewashed cell, where bunches of dried leaves hung from rusty hooks in the ceiling, and were spread out upon shelves, in company with portentous bottles: would the Reverend Septimus submissively be led, like the highly-popular lamb who has so long and unresistingly been led to the slaughter, and there would he, unlike[1] that lamb, bore nobody but himself. Not even doing that much, so that the old lady were busy and pleased, he would quietly[2] swallow what was given him, merely taking a corrective dip of hands and face into one great bowl of dried rose-leaves, and into the other[3] great bowl of dried lavender, and then would go out,[4] as confident in the sweetening powers of Cloisterham Weir and a wholesome mind, as Lady Macbeth was hopeless of those of all the seas that roll.

In the present instance the good Minor Canon took his glass of Constantia with an excellent grace, and, so supported to his mother's satisfaction, applied himself to the remaining duties of the day. In their orderly and punctual progress they brought round vesper service and twilight. The Cathedral being very cold, he set off for a brisk trot after service; the trot to end in a charge at his favorite fragment of ruin, which was to be carried by storm, without a pause for breath.

He carried it in a masterly manner, and, not breathed even then, stood looking down upon the river. The river at Cloisterham is sufficiently near the sea to throw up oftentimes a quantity of seaweed. An unusual quantity had come in with the last tide, and this, and the confusion of the water, and the restless dipping and flapping of the noisy gulls, and an angry light out seaward beyond the brown-sailed barges that were turning black, foreshadowed a stormy night. In his mind he was contrasting the wild and noisy sea with the quiet harbour of Minor Canon Corner, when Helena and Neville Landless passed below him. He had had the two together in his thoughts all day, and at once climbed down to speak to them together. The footing was rough in an uncertain light for any tread save that of a good climber; but the Minor Canon was as good a climber as most men, and stood beside them before many good climbers would have been half-way down.

[1] unlike] *un*like MS   [2] quietly] *not in* MS
[3] one great bowl . . . the other] MS *not absolutely clear, owing to deletions (Dickens may originally have written* another *in the second phrase*) the great bowl . . . the other 70–75
[4] go out] go out pleasantly MS

"A wild evening, Miss Landless! Do you not find your usual walk with
your brother too exposed and cold for the time of year? Or at all events,
when the sun is down, and the weather is driving in from the sea?"

Helena thought not. It was their favorite walk. It was very retired.

"It is very retired," assented Mr. Crisparkle, laying hold of his opportunity straightway, and walking on with them. "It is a place of all others
where one can speak without interruption, as I wish to do. Mr. Neville,
I believe you tell your sister everything that passes between us?"

"Everything, sir."

"Consequently," said Mr. Crisparkle, "your sister is aware that I have
repeatedly urged you to make some kind of apology for that unfortunate
occurrence which befell, on the night of your arrival here."

In saying it he looked to her, and not to him; therefore it was she, and
not he, who[1] replied:

"Yes."

"I call it unfortunate, Miss Helena," resumed Mr. Crisparkle, "foras-
much as it certainly has engendered a prejudice against Neville. There is
a notion about, that he is a dangerously passionate fellow, of an uncon-
trollable and furious temper: he is really avoided as such."

"I have no doubt he is, poor fellow," said Helena, with a look of proud
compassion at her brother, expressing a deep sense of his being ungener-
ously treated. "I should be quite sure of it, from your saying so; but what
you tell me[2] is confirmed by suppressed hints and references that I meet
with every day."

"Now," Mr. Crisparkle again resumed, in a tone of mild though firm
persuasion, "is not this to be regretted, and ought it not to be amended?
These are early days of Neville's in Cloisterham, and I have no fear of his
outliving[3] such a prejudice, and proving himself to have been misunder-
stood. But how much wiser to take action at once, than to trust to uncertain time! Besides; apart from its being politic, it is right. For there
can be no question that Neville was wrong."

"He was provoked," Helena submitted.

"He was the assailant," Mr. Crisparkle submitted.

They walked on in silence, until Helena raised her eyes to the Minor
Canon's face, and said, almost reproachfully: "Oh, Mr. Crisparkle, would
you have Neville throw himself at young Drood's feet, or at Mr. Jasper's,
who maligns him every day! In your heart you cannot mean it. From your
heart you could not do it, if his case were yours."

"I have represented to Mr. Crisparkle, Helena," said Neville, with a
glance of deference towards his tutor, "that if I could do it from my heart,
I would. But I cannot, and I revolt from the pretence. You forget, however, that to put the case to Mr. Crisparkle as his own, is to suppose Mr.
Crisparkle to have done what I did."

[1] he, who] he that ES   [2] me] us MS   [3] his outliving] his not outliving ES

"I ask his pardon," said Helena.

"You see," remarked Mr. Crisparkle, again laying hold of his opportunity, though with a moderate and delicate touch, "you both instinctively acknowledge that Neville did wrong! Then why stop short, and not otherwise acknowledge it?"

"Is there no difference," asked Helena, with a little faltering in her manner, "between submission to a generous spirit, and submission to a base or trivial one?"

Before the worthy Minor Canon was quite ready with his argument in reference to this nice distinction, Neville struck in:

"Help me to clear myself with Mr. Crisparkle, Helena. Help me to convince him that I cannot be the first to make concessions[1] without mockery and falsehood. My nature must be changed before I can do so, and it is not changed. I am sensible of inexpressible affront, and deliberate aggravation of inexpressible affront, and I am angry. The plain truth is, I am still as angry when I recall that night as I was that night."

"Neville," hinted the Minor Canon, with a steady countenance, "you have repeated that former action of your hands, which I so much dislike."

"I am sorry for it, sir, but it was involuntary. I confessed that I was still as angry."

"And I confess," said Mr. Crisparkle, "that I hoped for better things."

"I am sorry to disappoint you, sir, but it would be far worse to deceive you, and I should deceive you grossly if I pretended that you had softened me in this respect. The time may come when your powerful influence will do even that with the difficult pupil whose antecedents you know; but it has not come yet. Is this so, and in spite of my struggles against myself, Helena?"

She, whose dark eyes were watching the effect of what he said on Mr. Crisparkle's face, replied—to Mr. Crisparkle: not to him: "It is so." After a short pause, she answered the slightest look of inquiry conceivable, in her brother's eyes, with as slight an affirmative bend of her own head; and he went on:

"I have never yet had the courage to say to you, sir, what in full openness I ought to have said when you first talked with me on this subject. It is not easy to say, and I have been withheld by a fear of its seeming ridiculous, which is very strong upon me down to this last moment, and might, but for my sister, prevent my being quite open with you even now. —I admire Miss Bud, sir, so very much, that I cannot bear her being treated with conceit or indifference; and even if I did not feel that I had an injury against young Drood on my own account, I should feel that I had an injury against him on hers."

Mr. Crisparkle, in utter amazement, looked at Helena for corroboration, and met in her expressive face full[2] corroboration, and a plea for advice.

---

[1] concessions] concessions here MS   [2] full] with full MS

"The young lady of whom you speak is, as you know, Mr. Neville, shortly to be married," said Mr. Crisparkle, gravely; "therefore your admiration, if it be of that special nature which you seem to indicate, is outrageously¹ misplaced. Moreover, it is monstrous that you should take upon yourself to be the young lady's champion against her chosen husband. Besides, you have seen them only once. The young lady has become your sister's friend; and I wonder that your sister, even on her behalf, has not checked you in this irrational and culpable fancy."

"She has tried, sir, but uselessly. Husband or no husband, that fellow is incapable of the feeling with which I am inspired towards the beautiful young creature whom he treats like a doll. I say he is as incapable of it, as he is unworthy of her. I say she is sacrificed in being bestowed upon him. I say that I love her, and despise and hate him!" This with a face so flushed, and a gesture so violent, that his sister crossed to his side, and caught his arm, remonstrating, "Neville, Neville!"

Thus recalled to himself, he quickly became sensible of having lost the guard he had set upon his passionate tendency, and covered his face with his hand, as one repentant,² and wretched.

Mr. Crisparkle, watching him attentively, and at the same time meditating how to proceed, walked on for some paces in silence. Then he spoke:

"Mr. Neville, Mr. Neville, I am sorely grieved to see in you more³ traces of a character as sullen, angry, and wild, as the night now closing in. They are of too serious an aspect to leave me the resource of treating the infatuation you have disclosed, as undeserving⁴ serious consideration. I give it very serious consideration, and I speak to you accordingly. This feud between you and young Drood must not go on. I cannot permit it to go on, any longer, knowing what I now know⁵ from you, and you living under my roof. Whatever prejudiced and unauthorized constructions your blind and envious wrath may put upon his character, it is a frank, good-natured character. I know I can trust to it for that. Now, pray observe what I am about to say. On reflection, and on your sister's representation, I am willing to admit that, in making peace with young Drood, you have a right to be met half way. I will engage that you shall be, and even that young Drood shall make the first advance. This condition fulfilled, you will pledge me the honor of a Christian gentleman that the quarrel is for ever at an end on your side. What may be in your heart when you give him your hand, can only be known to the Searcher of all hearts; but it will never go well with you, if there be any treachery there. So far, as to that; next as to what I must again speak of as your infatuation. I

¹ outrageously] completely MS
² repentant] ashamed, repentant MS
³ more] new MS   ⁴ undeserving] undeserving of MS
⁵ know] *possibly* have MS

understand it to have been confided to me, and to be known to no other person save your sister and yourself. Do I understand aright?"

Helena answered in a low voice: "It is only known to us three who are here together."

"It is not at all known to the young lady, your friend?"

"On my soul, no!"

"I require you, then, to give me your similar and solemn pledge, Mr. Neville, that it shall remain the secret it is, and that you will take no other action whatsoever upon it than endeavouring (and that most earnestly) to erase it from your mind. I will not tell you that it will soon pass; I will not tell you that it is the fancy of the moment; I will not tell you that such caprices have their rise and fall among the young and ardent every hour; I will leave you undisturbed in the belief that it has few parallels or none, that it will abide with you a long time, and that it will be very difficult to conquer. So much the more weight shall I attach to the pledge I require from you, when it is unreservedly given."

The young man twice or thrice essayed to speak, but failed.

"Let me leave you with your sister, whom it is time you took home," said Mr. Crisparkle. "You will find me alone in my room by-and-bye."

"Pray do not leave us yet," Helena implored him. "Another minute."

"I should not," said Neville, pressing his hand upon his face, "have needed so much as another minute, if you had been less patient with me, Mr. Crisparkle, less considerate of me, and less unpretendingly good and true. Oh, if in my childhood I had[1] known such a guide!"

"Follow your guide now, Neville," murmured Helena, "and follow him to Heaven!"

There was that in her tone which broke the good Minor Canon's voice, or it would have repudiated her exaltation of him. As it was, he laid a finger on his lips, and looked towards her brother.

"To say that I give both pledges, Mr. Crisparkle, out of my innermost heart, and to say that there is no treachery in it, is to say nothing!" Thus Neville, greatly moved. "I beg your forgiveness for my miserable lapse into a burst of passion."

"Not mine, Neville, not mine. You know with whom forgiveness lies, as the highest attribute conceivable. Miss Helena, you and your brother are[2] twin children. You came into this world with the same dispositions, and you passed your younger days together surrounded by the same adverse circumstances. What you have overcome in yourself, can you not overcome in him? You see the rock that lies in his course. Who but you can keep him clear of it?"

"Who but you, sir?" replied Helena. "What is my influence, or my weak wisdom, compared with yours!"

"You have the wisdom of Love," returned the Minor Canon, "and it

---

[1] had] had but MS   [2] are] were MS

MR. CRISPARKLE IS OVERPAID

was the highest wisdom ever known upon this earth, remember. As to mine—but the less said of that commonplace commodity the better. Good-night!"

She took the hand he offered her, and gratefully and almost reverently raised it to her lips.

"Tut!" said the Minor Canon, softly, "I am much overpaid!" And turned away.

Retracing his steps towards the Cathedral Close, he tried, as he went along in the dark, to think out the best means of bringing to pass what he had promised to effect, and what must somehow be done. "I shall probably be asked to marry them," he reflected, "and I would they were married and gone! But this presses first." He debated principally, whether he should write to young Drood, or whether he should speak to Jasper. The consciousness of being popular with the whole Cathedral establishment inclined him to the latter course, and the well-timed sight of the lighted Gate House decided him to take it. "I will strike while the iron is hot," he said, "and see him now."

Jasper was lying asleep on a couch before the fire, when, having ascended the postern stair, and received no answer to his knock at the door, Mr. Crisparkle gently turned the handle and looked in. Long afterwards he had cause to remember how Jasper sprang from the couch in a delirious state between sleeping and waking, crying[1] out: "What is the matter? Who did it?"

"It is only I, Jasper. I am sorry to have disturbed you."

The glare of his eyes settled down into a look of recognition, and he moved a chair or two, to make a way to the fireside.

"I was dreaming at a great rate, and am glad to be disturbed from an indigestive after-dinner sleep. Not to mention that *you*[2] are always welcome."

"Thank you. I am not confident," returned Mr. Crisparkle as he sat himself down in the easy chair placed for him, "that my subject will at first sight be quite as welcome as myself; but I am a minister of peace, and I pursue my subject in the interests of peace. In a word, Jasper, I want to establish peace between these two young fellows."

A very perplexed expression took hold of Mr.[3] Jasper's face; a very perplexing expression too, for Mr. Crisparkle could make nothing of it.

"How?" was Jasper's inquiry, in a low and slow voice, after a silence.

"For the 'How' I come to you. I want to ask you to do me the great favor and service of interposing with your nephew (I have already interposed with Mr. Neville), and getting him to write you a short note, in his lively way, saying that he is willing to shake hands. I know what a good-natured fellow he is, and what influence you have with him. And without

---

[1] crying] and crying 73 75   [2] *you*] MS you 70–75
[3] Mr.] *not in* MS

in the least defending Mr. Neville, we must all admit that he was bitterly stung."

Jasper turned that perplexed face towards the fire. Mr. Crisparkle continuing to observe it, found it even more perplexing than before, inasmuch as it seemed to denote (which could hardly be) some close internal calculation.

"I know that you are not prepossessed in Mr. Neville's favor," the Minor Canon was going on, when Jasper stopped him:

"You have cause to say so. I am not, indeed."

"Undoubtedly, and I admit his lamentable violence of temper, though I hope he and I will get the better of it between us. But I have exacted a very solemn promise from him as to his future demeanour towards your nephew, if you do kindly interpose; and I am sure he will keep it."

"You are always[1] responsible and trustworthy, Mr. Crisparkle. Do you really feel sure that you can answer for him so confidently?"

"I do."

The perplexed and perplexing look vanished.

"Then you relieve my mind of a great dread, and a heavy weight," said Jasper; "I will do it."

Mr. Crisparkle, delighted[2] by the swiftness and completeness of his success, acknowledged it in the handsomest terms.

"I will do it," repeated Jasper, "for the comfort of having your guarantee against my vague and unformed[3] fears. You will laugh—but do you keep a Diary?"

"A line for a day; not more."

"A line for a day would be quite as much as my uneventful life would need, Heaven knows,"[4] said Jasper, taking a book from a desk; "but that[5] my Diary is, in fact, a Diary of Ned's life too. You will laugh at this entry; you will guess when it was made:

'Past midnight.—After what I have just now seen, I have a morbid dread upon me of some horrible consequences resulting to my dear boy, that I cannot reason with or in any way contend against. All my efforts are vain. The demoniacal passion of this Neville[6] Landless, his strength in his fury, and his savage rage for the destruction of its object, appal me. So profound is the impression, that twice since have I[7] gone into my dear boy's room, to assure myself of his sleeping safely, and not lying dead in his blood.'

"Here is another entry next morning:

'Ned up and away. Light-hearted and unsuspicious as ever. He laughed when I cautioned him, and said he was as good a man as Neville[6] Landless any day.

[1] always] unusually MS   [2] delighted] quite enraptured MS
[3] unformed] MS unfounded 70–75   [4] Heaven knows,] *not in* MS
[5] that] *not in* MS   [6] Neville] Edwin MS
[7] have I] I have 73 75

I told him that might be, but he was not as bad a man. He continued to make light of it, but I travelled with him as far as I could, and left him most unwillingly. I am unable to shake off these dark intangible presentiments of evil—if feelings founded upon staring facts are to be so called.'

"Again and again," said Jasper, in conclusion, twirling the leaves of the book before putting it by, "I have relapsed into these moods, as other entries show. But I have now your assurance at my back, and shall put it in my book, and make it an antidote to my black humours."

"Such an antidote, I hope," returned Mr. Crisparkle, "as will induce you before long to consign the black humours to the flames. I ought to[1] be the last to find any fault with you this evening, when you have met my wishes so freely; but I must say, Jasper, that your devotion to your nephew has made you exaggerative here."

"You are my witness," said Jasper, shrugging his shoulders, "what my state of mind honestly was, that night, before I sat down to write, and in what words I expressed it. You remember objecting to a word I used, as being too strong? It was a stronger word than any in my Diary."

"Well, well. Try the antidote," rejoined Mr. Crisparkle, "and may it give you a brighter and better view of the case! We will discuss it no more, now. I have to thank you for myself, and I thank you sincerely."

"You shall find," said Jasper, as they shook hands, "that I will not do the thing you wish me to do, by halves. I will take care that Ned, giving way at all, shall give way thoroughly."

On the third day after this conversation, he called on Mr. Crisparkle with the following letter:

"MY DEAR JACK,

"I am touched by your account of your interview with Mr. Crisparkle, whom I much respect and esteem. At once I openly say that I forgot myself on that occasion quite as much as Mr. Landless did, and that I wish that bygone to be a bygone, and all to be right again.

"Look here, dear old boy. Ask Mr. Landless to dinner on Christmas Eve (the better the day the better the deed), and let there be only we three, and let us shake hands all round there and then, and say no more about it.
                    "My Dear Jack,
                              "Ever your most affectionate,
                                        "EDWIN DROOD.

"P.S.—Love to Miss Pussy at the next music-lesson."

"You expect Mr. Neville, then?" said Mr. Crisparkle.
"I count upon his coming," said Mr. Jasper.

----

[1] ought to] should MS

CHAPTER XI

A PICTURE AND A RING

Behind the most ancient part of Holborn, London, where certain gabled houses some centuries of age still stand looking on the public way, as if disconsolately looking for the Old Bourne that has long run dry, is a little nook composed of two irregular quadrangles, called Staple Inn. It is one of those nooks, the turning into which out of the clashing street, imparts to the relieved pedestrian the sensation of having put cotton in his ears, and velvet soles on his boots. It is one of those nooks where a few smoky sparrows twitter in smoky trees, as though they called to one another, "Let us play at country," and where a few feet of garden mould and a few yards of gravel enable them to do that refreshing violence to their tiny understandings. Moreover, it is one of those nooks which are legal nooks; and it contains a little Hall, with a little lantern in its roof: to what obstructive purposes devoted, and at whose expense, this history knoweth not.

In the days when Cloisterham took offence at the existence of a railroad afar off, as menacing that sensitive Constitution, the property of us Britons, the odd fortune of which sacred institution[1] it is to be in exactly equal degrees croaked about, trembled for, and boasted of, whatever happens to anything, anywhere in the world: in those days no neighbouring architecture of lofty proportions had arisen to overshadow Staple Inn. The westering sun bestowed bright glances on it, and the south-west wind blew into it unimpeded.

Neither wind nor sun, however, favored Staple Inn, one December afternoon towards six o'clock, when it was filled with fog, and candles shed murky and blurred rays through the windows of all its then-occupied sets of chambers; notably, from a set of chambers in a corner house in the little inner quadrangle, presenting in black and white over its ugly portal the mysterious inscription:

P

J   T

1747.

In which set of chambers, never having troubled his head about the inscription, unless to bethink himself at odd times on glancing up at it, that

CHAPTER XI *One folio of* MS, *comprising the first five paragraphs of this chapter, is missing*

[1] Constitution . . . us Britons, the odd . . . institution] *corrected by Dickens in a letter to the printer, 28 May 1870, now in the Dickens collection at the University of Texas*
constitution, the property of us Britons. The odd fortune of which sacred institutions 70
constitution, the property of us Britons; the odd fortune of which sacred institutions ES
constitution, the property of us Britons: the odd fortune of which sacred institutions 73
constitution, the property of us Britons: the odd fortune of which sacred institution 75

haply it might mean Perhaps John Thomas, or Perhaps Joe Tyler, sat Mr. Grewgious writing by his fire.

Who could have told, by looking at Mr. Grewgious, whether he had ever known ambition or disappointment? He had been bred to the Bar, and had laid himself out for chamber practice; to draw deeds; "convey the wise it call," as Pistol says. But Conveyancing and he had made such a very indifferent marriage of it that they had separated by consent—if there can be said to be separation where there has never been coming together.

No. Coy Conveyancing would not come to Mr. Grewgious. She was wooed, not won, and they went their several ways. But an Arbitration being blown towards him by some unaccountable wind, and he gaining great credit in it as one indefatigable in seeking out right and doing right, a pretty fat Receivership was next blown into his pocket by a wind more traceable to its source. So, by chance, he had found his niche. Receiver and Agent now, to two rich estates, and deputing their legal business, in an amount worth having, to a firm of solicitors on the floor below, he had snuffed out his ambition (supposing him to have ever lighted it) and had settled down with his snuffers for the rest of his life under the dry vine and fig-tree of P. J. T., who planted in seventeen-forty-seven.

Many accounts and account-books, many files of correspondence, and several strong boxes, garnished Mr. Grewgious's room. They can scarcely be represented as having lumbered it, so conscientious and precise was their orderly arrangement. The apprehension of dying suddenly, and leaving one fact or one figure with any incompleteness or obscurity attaching to it, would have stretched Mr. Grewgious stone dead any day. The largest fidelity to a trust was the life-blood of the man. There are sorts of life-blood that course more quickly, more gaily, more attractively; but there is no better sort in circulation.

There was no luxury in his room. Even its comforts were limited to its being dry and warm, and having a snug though faded fireside. What may be called its private life was confined to the hearth, and an easy chair, and an old-fashioned occasional round table that was brought out upon the rug after business hours, from a corner where it elsewise remained turned up like a shining mahogany shield. Behind it, when standing thus on the defensive, was a closet, usually containing something good to drink. An outer room was the clerk's room; Mr. Grewgious's sleeping-room was across the common stair; and he held some not empty cellarage at[1] the bottom of the common stair. Three hundred days in the year, at least, he crossed over to the hotel in Furnival's Inn for his dinner, and after dinner crossed back again, to make the most of these simplicities until it should become broad business day once more, with P. J. T., date seventeen-forty-seven.

As Mr. Grewgious sat and wrote by his fire that afternoon, so did the

[1] at] in the black basement at MS

clerk of Mr. Grewgious sit and write by *his* fire. A pale, puffy-faced, dark-haired person of thirty, with big dark eyes that wholly wanted lustre, and a dissatisfied doughy complexion, that seemed to ask to be sent to the baker's, this attendant was a mysterious being, possessed of some strange power over Mr. Grewgious. As though he had been called into existence, like a fabulous Familiar, by a magic spell which had failed when required to dismiss him, he stuck tight to Mr. Grewgious's stool, although Mr. Grewgious's comfort and convenience would manifestly have been advanced by dispossessing him. A gloomy person with tangled locks, and a general air of having been reared under the shadow of that baleful tree of Java which has given shelter to more lies than the whole botanical kingdom, Mr. Grewgious, nevertheless, treated him with unaccountable consideration.

"Now, Bazzard," said Mr. Grewgious, on the entrance of his clerk: looking up from his papers as he arranged them for the night: "what is in the wind besides fog?"

"Mr. Drood," said Bazzard.

"What of him?"

"Has called," said Bazzard.

"You might have shown him in."

"I am doing it," said Bazzard.

The visitor came in accordingly.

"Dear me!" said Mr. Grewgious, looking round his pair of office candles. "I thought you had called and merely left your name, and gone. How do you do, Mr. Edwin? Dear me, you're choking!"

"It's this fog," returned Edwin; "and it makes my eyes smart, like cayenne pepper."

"Is it really so bad as that? Pray undo your wrappers. It is[1] fortunate I have so good a fire; but Mr. Bazzard has taken care of me."

"No I haven't," said Mr. Bazzard at the door.

"Ah! Then it follows that I must have taken care of myself without observing it," said Mr. Grewgious. "Pray be seated in my chair. No. I beg! Coming out of such an atmosphere, in *my* chair."

Edwin took the easy chair in the corner; and the fog he had brought in with him, and the fog he took off with his greatcoat and neck-shawl, was speedily licked up by the eager fire.

"I look," said Edwin, smiling, "as if I had come to stop."

"—By-the-bye," cried Mr. Grewgious; "excuse my interrupting you; do stop. The fog may clear in an hour or two. We can have dinner in from just across Holborn. You had better take your cayenne pepper here than outside; pray stop and dine."

"You are very kind," said Edwin, glancing about him, as though attracted by the notion of a new and relishing sort of gipsy-party.

---

[1] It is] MS It's 70–75

"Not at all," said Mr. Grewgious; "*you* are very kind to join issue with a bachelor in chambers, and take pot-luck. And I'll ask," said Mr. Grewgious, dropping his voice, and speaking with a twinkling eye, as if inspired with a bright thought: "I'll ask Bazzard. He mightn't like it else. Bazzard!"

Bazzard reappeared.

"Dine presently with Mr. Drood and me."

"If I am ordered to dine, of course I will, sir," was the gloomy answer.

"Save the man!" cried Mr. Grewgious. "You're not ordered; you're invited."

"Thank you, sir," said Bazzard; "in that case I don't care if I do."

"That's arranged. And perhaps you wouldn't mind," said Mr. Grewgious, "stepping over to the hotel in Furnival's, and asking them to send in materials for laying the cloth. For dinner we'll have a tureen of the hottest and strongest soup available, and we'll have the best made-dish that can be recommended, and we'll have a joint (such as a haunch of mutton), and we'll have a goose, or a turkey, or any little stuffed thing of that sort that may happen to be in the bill of fare—in short, we'll have whatever there is on hand."

These liberal directions Mr. Grewgious issued with his usual air of reading an inventory, or repeating a lesson, or doing anything else by rote. Bazzard, after drawing out the round table, withdrew to execute them.

"I was a little delicate, you see," said Mr. Grewgious, in a lower tone, after his clerk's departure, "about employing him in the foraging or commissariat department. Because he mightn't like it."

"He seems to have his own way, sir," remarked Edwin.

"His own way?" returned Mr. Grewgious. "Oh dear no! Poor fellow, you quite mistake him. If he had his own way, he wouldn't be here."

"I wonder where he would be!" Edwin thought. But he only thought it, because Mr. Grewgious came and stood himself with his back to the other corner of the fire, and his shoulder-blades against the chimneypiece, and collected his skirts for easy conversation.

"I take it, without having the gift of prophecy, that you have done me the favor of looking in to mention that you are going down yonder—where I can tell you, you are expected—and to offer to execute any little commission from me to my charming ward, and perhaps to sharpen me up a bit in my[1] proceedings? Eh, Mr. Edwin?"

"I called, sir, before going down, as an act of attention."

"Of attention!" said Mr. Grewgious. "Ah! of course, not of impatience?"

"Impatience, sir?"

Mr. Grewgious had meant to be arch—not that he in the remotest degree expressed that meaning—and had brought himself into scarcely supportable proximity with the fire, as if to burn the fullest effect of his

[1] my] MS *blotted, but probable reading* any 70–75

archness into himself, as other subtle impressions are burnt into hard metals. But his archness suddenly flying before the composed face and manner of his visitor, and only the fire remaining, he started and rubbed himself.

"I have lately been down yonder," said Mr. Grewgious, rearranging his skirts; "and that was what I referred to, when I said I could tell you you are¹ expected."

"Indeed, sir! Yes; I knew that Pussy was looking out for me."

"Do you keep a cat down there?" asked Mr. Grewgious.

Edwin colored a little, as he explained: "I call Rosa Pussy."

"Oh, really," said Mr. Grewgious, smoothing down his head; "that's very affable."

Edwin glanced at his face, uncertain whether or no he seriously objected to the appellation. But Edwin might as well have glanced at the face of a clock.

"A pet name, sir," he explained again.

"Umps,"² said Mr. Grewgious, with a nod. But with such an extraordinary compromise between an unqualified assent and a qualified dissent, that his visitor was much disconcerted.

"Did PRosa——" Edwin began, by way of recovering himself.

"PRosa?" repeated Mr. Grewgious.

"I was going to say Pussy, and changed my mind;—did she tell you anything about the Landlesses?"

"No," said Mr. Grewgious.³ "What is the Landlesses? An estate? A villa? A farm?"

"A brother and sister. The sister is at the Nuns' House, and has become a great friend of P——"

"PRosa's," Mr. Grewgious struck in, with a fixed face.

"She is a strikingly handsome girl, sir, and I thought she might have been described to you, or presented to you, perhaps?"

"Neither," said Mr. Grewgious. "But here is Bazzard."

Bazzard returned, accompanied by two waiters—an immoveable waiter, and a flying waiter; and the three brought in with them as much fog as gave a new roar to the fire. The flying waiter, who had brought everything on his shoulders, laid the cloth with amazing rapidity and dexterity; while the immoveable waiter, who had brought nothing, found fault with him in secret nudges.⁴ The flying waiter then highly polished all the glasses he had brought, and the immoveable waiter looked through them. The flying waiter then flew across Holborn for the soup, and flew back again, and then took another flight for the made-dish, and flew back again, and then took another flight for the joint and poultry, and flew back again, and

¹ are] were MS   ² Umps] Umphs ES
³ Mr. Grewgious] Mr Grewgious, sharply MS
⁴ in secret nudges] MS   om. 70–75

between whiles took supplementary flights for a great variety of articles, as it was discovered from time to time that the immoveable waiter had forgotten them all.[1] But let the flying waiter cleave the air as he might, he was always reproached on his return by the immoveable waiter for bringing fog with him, and being out of breath. At the conclusion of the repast, by which time the flying waiter was severely blown, the immoveable waiter gathered up the tablecloth under his arm with a grand air, and having sternly (not to say with indignation) looked on at the flying waiter while he set clean[2] glasses round, directed a valedictory glance towards Mr. Grewgious, conveying: "Let it be clearly understood between us that the reward is mine, and that Nil is the claim of this slave,"[3] and pushed the flying waiter before him out of the room.

It was like a highly finished miniature painting representing My Lords of the Circumlocutional[4] Department, Commandership-in-Chief of any sort,[5] Government. It was quite an edifying little picture to be hung on the line in the National Gallery.

As the fog had been the proximate cause of this sumptuous repast, so the fog served for its general sauce. To hear the outdoor clerks, sneezing, wheezing, and beating their feet on the gravel was a zest far surpassing Doctor Kitchener's. To bid, with a shiver, the unfortunate flying waiter shut the door before he had opened it, was a condiment of a profounder flavor than Harvey. And here let it be noticed, parenthetically, that the leg of this young man in its application to the door, evinced the finest sense of touch: always preceding himself and tray (with something of[6] an angling air about it), by some seconds: and always lingering after he and the tray had disappeared, like Macbeth's leg when accompanying him off the stage with reluctance to the assassination of Duncan.

The host had gone below to the cellar, and had brought up bottles of ruby, straw-colored, and golden, drinks, which had ripened long ago in lands where no fogs are, and had since lain slumbering in the shade. Sparkling and tingling after so long a nap, they pushed at their corks to help the corkscrew (like prisoners helping rioters to force their gates), and danced out gaily. If P. J. T. in seventeen-forty-seven, or in any other year of his period, drank such wines—then, for a certainty, P. J. T. was Pretty Jolly Too.

Externally, Mr. Grewgious showed no signs of being mellowed by these glowing vintages. Instead of his drinking them, they might have been poured over him in his high-dried snuff form, and run to waste, for any lights and shades they caused to flicker over his stolid[7] face. Neither was his manner influenced. But, in his wooden way, he had observant eyes for Edwin; and when, at the end of dinner, he motioned Edwin back to

---

[1] all] *not in* MS [2] clean] the clean 73 75 [3] slave] young man MS
[4] Circumlocutional] Circumlocution 75 [5] of any sort] *not in* MS
[6] something of] *not in* MS [7] stolid] MS *om.* 70–75

his own easy chair in the fireside corner, and Edwin luxuriously sank[1] into it after very brief remonstrance, Mr. Grewgious, as he turned his seat round towards the fire too, and smoothed his head and face, might have been seen looking at his visitor between his smoothing fingers.

"Bazzard!" said Mr. Grewgious, suddenly turning to him.

"I follow you, sir," returned Bazzard; who had done his work of consuming meat and drink, in a workmanlike manner, though mostly in speechlessness.

"I drink to you, Bazzard; Mr. Edwin, success to Mr. Bazzard!"

"Success to Mr. Bazzard!" echoed Edwin, with a totally unfounded appearance of enthusiasm, and with the unspoken addition:—"What in, I wonder!"

"And May!" pursued Mr. Grewgious—"I am not at liberty to be definite—May!—my conversational powers are so very limited that I know I shall not come well out of this—May!—it ought to be put imaginatively, but I have no imagination—May!—the thorn of anxiety is[2] as near[3] the mark as I am likely to get—[4]May it come out at last!"

Mr. Bazzard with a frowning smile at the fire, put a hand into his tangled locks, as if the thorn of anxiety were there; then into his waistcoat, as if it were there; then into his pockets, as if it were there. In all these movements he was closely followed by the eyes of Edwin, as if that young gentleman expected to see the thorn in action. It was not produced, however, and Mr. Bazzard merely said: "I follow you, sir, and I thank you."

"I am going," said Mr. Grewgious, jingling his glass on the table, with one hand, and bending aside under cover of the other, to whisper to Edwin, "to drink to my ward. But I put Bazzard first. He mightn't like it else."

This was said with a mysterious wink; or what would have been a wink if, in Mr. Grewgious's hands, it could have been quick enough. So Edwin winked responsively, without the least idea what he meant by doing so.

"And now," said Mr. Grewgious, "I devote a bumper to the fair and fascinating Miss Rosa. Bazzard, the fair and fascinating Miss Rosa!"

"I follow you, sir," said Bazzard, "and I pledge you!"

"And so do I!" said Edwin.

"Lord bless me!" cried Mr. Grewgious, breaking the blank silence which of course ensued: though why these pauses *should* come upon us when we have performed any small social rite, not directly inducive of self-examination or mental despondency, who can tell! "I am a particularly Angular man, and yet I fancy (if I may use the word, not having a morsel of fancy), that I could draw a picture of a true lover's state of mind, to-night."

"Let us follow you, sir," said Bazzard, "and have the picture."

"Mr. Edwin will correct it where it's wrong," resumed Mr. Grewgious,

---

[1] luxuriously sank] sank luxuriously 73 75   [2] is] is, I think, MS
[3] near] MS nearly 70–75   [4] get—] get—Mr Edwin, MS

"and will throw in a few touches from the life. I dare say it is wrong in many particulars, and wants many touches from the life, for I was born a Chip, and have neither soft sympathies nor soft experiences. Well! I hazard the guess that the true lover's mind is completely permeated by the beloved object of his affections. I hazard the guess that her dear name is precious to him, cannot be heard or repeated without emotion, and is preserved sacred. If he has any distinguishing appellation of fondness for her, it is reserved for her, and is not for common ears. A name that it would be a privilege to call her by, being alone with her own bright self,[1] it would be a liberty, a coldness, an insensibility, almost a breach of good faith, to flaunt elsewhere."

It was wonderful to see Mr. Grewgious sitting bolt upright, with his hands on his knees, continuously chopping this discourse out of himself: much as a charity boy with a very good memory might get his catechism said: and evincing no correspondent emotion whatever, unless in a certain occasional little tingling perceptible at the end of his nose.

"My picture," Mr. Grewgious proceeded, "goes on to represent (under correction from you, Mr. Edwin,) the true lover as ever impatient to be in the presence or vicinity of the beloved object of his affections; as caring very little for his ease in any other society; and as constantly seeking that. If I was to say seeking that, as a bird seeks its nest, I should make an ass of myself, because that would trench upon what I understand to be poetry; and I am so far from trenching upon poetry at any time, that I never, to my knowledge, got within ten thousand miles of it. And I am besides totally unacquainted with the habits of birds, except the birds of Staple Inn, who seek their nests on ledges, and in gutter-pipes and chimneypots, not constructed for them by the beneficent hand of Nature. I beg, therefore, to be understood as foregoing the bird's-nest. But my picture does represent the true lover as having no existence separable from that of the beloved object of his affections, and as living at once a doubled life and a halved life. And if I do not clearly express what I mean by that, it is either for the reason that having no conversational powers, I cannot express what I mean, or that having no meaning, I do not mean what I fail to express. Which, to the best of my belief, is not the case."

Edwin had turned red and turned white, as certain points of this picture came into the light. He now sat looking at the fire, and bit his lip.

"The speculations of an Angular man," resumed Mr. Grewgious, still sitting and speaking exactly as before, "are probably erroneous on so globular a topic. But I figure to myself (subject, as before, to Mr. Edwin's correction), that there can be no coolness, no lassitude, no doubt, no indifference, no half fire and half smoke state of mind, in[2] a real lover. Pray am I at all near the mark in my picture?"

As abrupt in his conclusion as in his commencement and progress, he

[1] self] face MS   [2] in] of MS

jerked this inquiry at Edwin, and stopped when one might have supposed him in the middle of his oration.

"I should say, sir," stammered Edwin, "as you refer the question to me——"

"Yes," said Mr. Grewgious, "I refer it to you, as an authority."

"I should say then, sir," Edwin went on, embarrassed, "that the picture you have drawn, is generally correct; but I submit that perhaps you may be rather hard upon the unlucky lover."

"Likely so," assented Mr. Grewgious, "likely so. I am a hard man in the grain."

"He may not show," said Edwin, "all he feels; or he may not——"

There he stopped so long, to find the rest of his sentence, that Mr. Grewgious rendered his difficulty a thousand times the greater, by unexpectedly striking in with:

"No to be sure; he *may* not!"

After that, they all sat silent; the silence of Mr. Bazzard being occasioned by slumber.

"His responsibility is very great though," said Mr. Grewgious, at length, with his eyes on the fire.

Edwin nodded assent, with *his* eyes on the fire.

"And let him be sure that he trifles with no one," said Mr. Grewgious; "neither with himself, nor with any other."

Edwin bit his lip[1] again, and still sat looking at the fire.

"He must not make a plaything of a treasure. Woe betide him if he does! Let him take that well to heart," said Mr. Grewgious.

Though he said these things in short dry[2] sentences, much as the supposititious charity boy just now referred to, might have repeated a verse or two from the Book of Proverbs, there was something dreamy (for so literal a man) in the way in which he now shook his right forefinger at the live coals in the grate, and again fell silent.

But not for long. As he sat upright and stiff in his chair, he suddenly rapped his knees, like the carved image of some queer Joss or other coming out of its reverie, and said: "We must finish this bottle, Mr. Edwin. Let me help you. I'll help Bazzard, too, though he *is* asleep. He mightn't like it else."

He helped them both, and helped himself, and drained his glass, and stood it bottom upward on the table, as though he had just caught a bluebottle in it.

"And now, Mr. Edwin," he proceeded, wiping his mouth and hands upon his handkerchief: "to a little piece of business. You received from me, the other day, a certified copy of Miss Rosa's father's will. You knew its contents before, but you received it from me as a matter of business.

[1] lip] lips ES
[2] dry] MS   *om.* 70–75

I should have sent it to Mr. Jasper, but for Miss Rosa's wishing it to come straight to you, in preference. You received it?"

"Quite safely, sir."

"You should have acknowledged its receipt," said Mr. Grewgious, "business being business all the world over. However, you did not."

"I meant to have acknowledged it when I first came in this evening, sir."

"Not a business-like acknowledgment," returned Mr. Grewgious; "however, let that pass. Now, in that document you have observed a few words of kindly allusion to its being left to me to discharge a little trust, confided to me in conversation, at such time as I in my discretion may think best."

"Yes, sir."

"Mr. Edwin, it came into my mind just now, when I was looking at the fire, that I could, in my discretion, acquit myself of that trust at no better time than the present. Favor me with your attention, half a minute."

He took a bunch of keys from his pocket, singled out by the candle-light the key he wanted, and then, with a candle in his hand, went to a bureau or escritoire, unlocked it, touched the spring of a little secret drawer, and took from it an ordinary ring-case made for a single ring. With this in his hand, he returned to his chair. As he held it up for the young man to see, his hand trembled.

"Mr. Edwin, this rose of diamonds and rubies delicately set in gold, was a ring belonging to Miss Rosa's mother. It was removed from her dead hand, in my presence, with such distracted grief as I hope it may never be my lot to contemplate again. Hard man as I am, I am not hard enough for that. See how bright these stones shine!" opening the case. "And yet the eyes that were so much brighter, and that so often looked upon them with a light and a proud heart, have been ashes among ashes, and dust among dust, some years! If I had any imagination (which it is needless to say I have not), I might imagine that the lasting beauty of these stones was almost cruel."

He closed the case again as he spoke.

"This ring was given to the young lady who was drowned so early in her beautiful and happy career, by her husband, when they first plighted their faith to one another. It was he who removed it from her unconscious hand, and it was he who, when his death drew very near, placed it in mine. The trust in which I received it, was, that, you and Miss Rosa growing to manhood and womanhood, and your betrothal prospering and coming to maturity, I should give it to you to place upon her finger. Failing those desired results, it was to remain in my possession."

Some trouble was in the young man's face, and some indecision was in the action of his hand, as Mr. Grewgious, looking steadfastly at him, gave him the ring.

"Your placing it on her finger," said Mr. Grewgious, "will be the solemn seal upon your strict fidelity to the living and the dead. You are going to her, to make the last irrevocable preparations for your marriage. Take it with you."

The young man took the little case, and placed it in his breast.

"If anything should be amiss, if anything should be even slightly wrong, between you; if you should have any secret consciousness that you are committing yourself to this step for no higher reason than because you have long been accustomed to look forward to it; then," said Mr. Grewgious, "I charge you once more, by the living and by the dead, to bring that ring back to me!"

Here Bazzard awoke himself by his own snoring; and, as is usual in such cases, sat apoplectically staring at vacancy, as defying vacancy to accuse him of having been asleep.

"Bazzard!" said Mr. Grewgious, harder than ever.

"I follow you, sir," said Bazzard, "and I have been following you."

"In discharge of a trust, I have handed Mr. Edwin Drood a ring of diamonds and rubies. You see?"

Edwin reproduced the little case, and opened it; and Bazzard looked into it.

"I follow you both, sir," returned Bazzard, "and I witness the trans-action."

Evidently anxious to get away and be alone, Edwin Drood now resumed his outer clothing, muttering something about time and appointments. The fog was reported no clearer (by the flying waiter, who alighted from a speculative flight in the coffee interest), but he went out into it; and Bazzard, after his manner, "followed" him.

Mr. Grewgious, left alone, walked[1] softly and slowly to and fro, for an hour and more. He was restless to-night, and seemed dispirited.

"I hope I have done right," he said. "The appeal to him seemed neces-sary. It was hard to lose the ring, and yet it must have gone from me very soon."

He closed the empty little drawer with a sigh, and shut and locked the escritoire, and came back to the solitary fireside.

"Her ring," he went on. "Will it come back to me? My mind hangs about her ring very uneasily to-night.[2] But that is explainable. I have had it so long, and I have prized it so much! I wonder——"

He was in a wondering mood[3] as well as a restless; for, though he checked himself at that point, and took another walk, he resumed his wondering when he sat down again.

"I wonder (for the ten thousandth time, and what a weak fool I, for what can[4] it signify now!) whether he confided the charge of their orphan

---

[1] walked] took off his shoes, and walked MS   [2] to-night] *not in* MS
[3] mood] mood, tonight, MS
[4] what a weak . . . can] more fool I, for what does MS

child to me, because he knew——Good God, how like her mother she has become!

"I wonder whether he ever so much as suspected that some one doted on her, at a hopeless, speechless distance, when he struck in and won her. I wonder whether it ever crept into his mind who that unfortunate some one was!

"I wonder whether I shall sleep to-night! At all events, I will shut out the world with the bedclothes, and try."

Mr. Grewgious crossed the staircase to his raw and foggy bedroom, and was soon ready for bed. Dimly catching sight of his face in the misty looking-glass, he held his candle to it for a moment.

"A likely some one, *you*, to come into anybody's thoughts in such an aspect!" he exclaimed. "There, there, there! Get to bed, poor man, and cease to jabber!"

With that, he extinguished his light, pulled up the bedclothes around him, and with another sigh shut out the world. And yet there are such unexplored romantic nooks in the unlikeliest men, that even old tinderous and touch-woody P. J. T. Possibly Jabbered Thus, at some odd times, in or about seventeen-forty-seven.

CHAPTER XII

A NIGHT WITH DURDLES

WHEN Mr. Sapsea has nothing better to do, towards evening, and finds the contemplation of his own profundity becoming a little monotonous in spite of the vastness of the subject, he often takes an airing in the Cathedral Close and thereabout. He likes to pass the churchyard with a swelling air of proprietorship, and to encourage in his breast a sort of benignant-landlord feeling, in that he has been bountiful towards that meritorious tenant, Mrs. Sapsea, and has publicly given her a prize. He likes to see a stray face or two looking in through the railings, and perhaps reading his inscription. Should he meet a stranger coming from the churchyard with a quick step, he is morally convinced that the stranger is "with a blush retiring," as monumentally directed.

Mr. Sapsea's importance has received enhancement, for he has become[1] Mayor of Cloisterham. Without mayors and many of them, it cannot be disputed that the whole framework of society—Mr. Sapsea is confident that he invented that forcible figure—would fall to pieces. Mayors have been knighted for "going up" with addresses: explosive machines intrepidly discharging shot and shell into the English Grammar. Mr.

[1] he has become] it is settled that he will be the next MS

Sapsea may "go up" with an address. Rise, Sir Thomas Sapsea! Of such is the salt of the earth.

Mr. Sapsea has improved the acquaintance of Mr. Jasper, since their first meeting to partake of port, epitaph, backgammon, beef, and salad. Mr. Sapsea has been received at the Gate House with kindred hospitality; and on that occasion Mr. Jasper seated himself at the piano, and sang to him, tickling his ears:—figuratively long[1] enough to present a considerable area[2] for tickling. What Mr. Sapsea likes in that young man, is, that he is always ready to profit by the wisdom of his elders, and that he is sound, sir, at the core. In proof of which, he sang to Mr. Sapsea that evening, no kickshaw ditties, favorites with national enemies, but gave him the genuine[3] George the Third home-brewed; exhorting him (as "my brave boys") to reduce to a smashed condition all other islands but this island, and all continents, peninsulas, isthmuses, promontories, and other geographical forms of land soever, besides sweeping the seas in all directions. In short, he rendered it pretty clear that Providence made a distinct mistake in originating so small a nation of hearts of oak, and so many other verminous peoples.

Mr. Sapsea, walking slowly this moist evening near the churchyard with his hands behind him, on the look out for a blushing and retiring stranger, turns a corner, and comes instead into the goodly presence of the Dean, conversing with the Verger and Mr. Jasper. Mr. Sapsea makes his obeisance, and is instantly stricken far more ecclesiastical than any Archbishop of York, or Canterbury.

"You are evidently going to write a book about us, Mr. Jasper," quoth the Dean; "to write a book about us. Well! We are very ancient, and we ought to make a good book. We are not so richly endowed in possessions as in age; but perhaps you will put *that* in your book, among other things, and call attention to our wrongs."

Mr. Tope, as in duty bound, is greatly entertained by this.

"I really have no intention at all, sir," replies Jasper, "of turning author, or archæologist. It is but a whim of mine. And even for my whim, Mr. Sapsea here is more accountable than I am."

"How so, Mr. Mayor?"[4] says the Dean, with a nod of good-natured recognition of his Fetch. "How is that, Mr. Mayor?"[4]

"I am not aware," Mr. Sapsea remarks, looking about him for information, "to what the Very Reverend the Dean does me the honor of referring." And then falls to studying his original in minute points of detail.

"Durdles," Mr. Tope hints.

[1] ears:—figuratively long] MS ears—figuratively, long 70 ES ears—figuratively—long 73 75
[2] area] surface MS
[3] the genuine] the hearty genuine MS   [4] Mr. Mayor] Mr Sapsea MS

"Ay!" the Dean echoes; "Durdles, Durdles!"[1]

"The truth is, sir," explains Jasper, "that my curiosity in the man was first really stimulated by Mr. Sapsea. Mr. Sapsea's knowledge of mankind, and power of drawing out whatever is recluse or odd around him, first led to my bestowing a second thought upon the man: though of course I had met him constantly about. You would not be surprised by this, Mr. Dean, if you had seen Mr. Sapsea deal with him in his own parlor, as I did."

"Oh!" cries Sapsea, picking up the ball thrown to him with ineffable complacency and pomposity; "yes, yes. The Very Reverend the Dean refers to that? Yes. I happened to bring Durdles and Mr. Jasper together. I regard Durdles as a Character."

"A character, Mr. Sapsea, that with a few skilful touches you turn inside out," says Jasper.

"Nay, not quite that," returns the lumbering auctioneer. "I may have a little influence over him, perhaps; and a little insight into his character, perhaps. The Very Reverend the Dean will please to bear in mind that I have seen the world." Here Mr. Sapsea gets a little behind the Dean, to inspect his coat-buttons.[2]

"Well!" says the Dean, looking about him to see what has become of his copyist:[3] "I hope, Mr. Mayor,[4] you will use your study and knowledge of Durdles to the good purpose of exhorting him not to break our worthy and respected Choir Master's neck; we cannot afford it; his head and voice are much too valuable to us."

Mr. Tope is again highly entertained, and, having fallen into respectful convulsions of laughter, subsides into a deferential murmur, importing that surely[5] any gentleman would deem it a pleasure and an honor[6] to have his neck broken, in return for such a compliment from such a source.

"I will take it upon myself, sir," observes Sapsea, loftily, "to answer for Mr. Jasper's neck. I will tell Durdles to be careful of it. He will mind what *I* say. How is it at present endangered?" he inquires, looking about him with magnificent patronage.

"Only by my making a moonlight expedition with Durdles among the tombs, vaults, towers, and ruins," returns Jasper. "You remember suggesting when you brought us together, that, as a lover of the picturesque, it might be worth my while?"

"*I* remember!" replies the auctioneer. And the solemn idiot really believes that he does remember.

"Profiting by your hint," pursues Jasper, "I have had some day-rambles with the extraordinary old fellow, and we are to make a moonlight hole-and-corner exploration to-night."

[1] Durdles, Durdles] Durdles, Durdles, Durdles MS
[2] coat-buttons] coat-skirts MS   [3] looking about . . . copyist] *not in* MS
[4] Mr. Mayor] Mr Sapsea MS
[5] surely] *the word appears to be deleted in* MS   [6] an honor] honor MS

"And here he is," says the Dean.

Durdles, with his dinner-bundle in his hand, is indeed beheld slouching towards them. Slouching nearer, and perceiving the Dean, he pulls off his hat, and is slouching away with it under his arm, when Mr. Sapsea stops him.

"Mind you take care of my friend," is the injunction Mr. Sapsea lays upon him.

"What friend o' yourn is dead?" asks Durdles.[1] "No orders has come in for any friend o' yourn."

"I mean my live friend, there."

"Oh! Him?" says Durdles. "He can take care of himself, can Mister Jarsper."[2]

"But do you take care of him too," says Sapsea.

Whom Durdles (there being command in his tone), surlily surveys from head to foot.

"With submission to his Reverence the Dean, if you'll mind what concerns you, Mr. Sapsea, Durdles he'll mind what concerns him."

"You're out of temper," says Mr. Sapsea, winking to the company to observe how smoothly he will manage him. "My friend concerns me, and Mr. Jasper is my friend. And you are my friend."

"Don't[3] you get into a bad habit of boasting," retorts Durdles, with a grave cautionary nod. "It'll grow upon you."[4]

"You are out of temper," says Sapsea again; reddening, but again winking to the company.

"I own to it," returns Durdles; "I don't like liberties."

Mr. Sapsea winks a third wink to the company, as who should say: "I think you will agree with me that I have settled *his* business;" and stalks out of the controversy.

Durdles then gives the Dean a good-evening, and adding, as he puts his hat on, "You'll find me at home, Mister Jarsper,[5] as agreed, when you want me; I'm a going home to clean myself," soon slouches out of sight. This going home to clean himself is one of the man's incomprehensible compromises with inexorable facts; he, and his hat, and his boots, and his clothes, never showing any trace of cleaning, but being uniformly in one condition of dust and grit.

The lamplighter now dotting the quiet Close with specks of light, and running at a great rate up and down his little ladder with that object—his little ladder under the sacred shadow of whose inconvenience generations

---

[1] asks Durdles] asks Durdles, in reply MS
[2] Mister Jarsper] ⟨Mr Jasper⟩ Mister Jasper MS
[3] Don't] I? Don't MS *the word* I *was inserted as an afterthought*
[4] you] you. You'll be boasting, before long, that His Reverence the Dean is your friend. And if you don't check yourself we shall have you, next, claiming the Bishop MS
[5] Jarsper] Jasper MS

DURDLES CAUTIONS MR. SAPSEA AGAINST BOASTING

had grown up, and which all Cloisterham would have stood aghast at the idea of abolishing—the Dean withdraws to his dinner, Mr. Tope to his tea, and Mr. Jasper to his piano. There, with no light but that of the fire, he sits chanting choir-music in a low and beautiful voice, for two or three hours; in short, until it has been for some time dark, and the moon is about to rise.

Then, he closes his piano softly, softly changes his coat for a pea-jacket with a goodly wicker-cased bottle in its largest pocket, and, putting on a low-crowned flap-brimmed hat, goes softly out. Why does he move so softly to-night? No outward reason is apparent for it. Can there be any sympathetic reason crouching darkly within him?[1]

Repairing to Durdles's unfinished house, or hole in the city wall, and seeing a light within it, he softly picks his course among the gravestones, monuments, and stony lumber of the yard, already touched here and there, sidewise, by the rising moon. The two journeymen have left their two great saws sticking in their blocks of stone; and two skeleton journeymen out of the Dance of Death might be grinning in the shadow of their sheltering sentry-boxes, about to slash away at cutting out the gravestones of the next two people destined[2] to die in Cloisterham. Likely enough, the two think little of that now, being alive, and perhaps merry. Curious, to make a guess at the two;—or say at one[3] of the two!

"Ho! Durdles!"

The light moves, and he appears with it at the door. He would seem to have been "cleaning himself" with the aid of a bottle, jug, and tumbler; for no other cleansing instruments are visible in the bare brick room with rafters overhead and no plastered ceiling, into which he shows his visitor.

"Are you ready?"

"I am ready, Mister Jarsper.[4] Let the old 'uns come out if they dare, when we go among their tombs. My spirits[5] is ready for 'em."

"Do you mean animal spirits, or ardent?"

"The one's the t'other," answers Durdles, "and I mean 'em both."

He takes a lantern from a hook, puts a match or two in his pocket wherewith to light it, should there be need,[6] and they go out together, dinner-bundle and all.

Surely an unaccountable sort of expedition! That Durdles himself, who is always prowling among old graves and ruins, like a Ghoule—that he should be stealing forth to climb, and dive, and wander without an object, is nothing extraordinary; but that the Choir Master or any one else should hold it worth his while to be with him, and to study moonlight effects in

---

[1] any . . . within him] some . . . within him, though there is none visible without MS
[2] destined] doomed MS
[3] Curious, to . . . or say at one] Curious now, to . . . or even at one MS Curious, to . . . or say one 73 75
[4] Jarsper] Jasper MS
[5] spirits] spirit 73 75
[6] need] need of it MS

such company, is another affair.¹ Surely an unaccountable sort of expedition therefore!

"'Ware that there mound by the yard gate, Mister Jarsper."²

"I see it. What is it?"

"Lime."

Mr. Jasper stops, and waits for him to come up, for he lags behind. "What you call quick-lime?"

"Ay!" says Durdles; "quick enough to eat your boots. With a little handy stirring, quick enough to eat your bones."

They go on, presently passing the red windows of the Travellers' Twopenny, and emerging into the clear moonlight of the Monks' Vineyard. This crossed, they come to Minor Canon Corner: of which the greater part lies in shadow until the moon shall rise higher in the sky.

The sound of a closing house door strikes their ears, and two men come out. These are Mr. Crisparkle and Neville. Jasper, with a strange and sudden smile upon his face, lays the palm of his hand upon the breast of Durdles, stopping him where he stands.

At³ that end of Minor Canon Corner the shadow is profound in the existing state of the light: at that end, too, is⁴ a piece of old dwarf wall, breast high, the only remaining boundary of what was once a garden, but is now the thoroughfare. Jasper and Durdles would have turned this wall in another instant; but, stopping so short, stand behind it.

"Those two are only sauntering," Jasper whispers; "they will go out into the moonlight soon. Let us keep quiet here, or they will detain us, or want to join us, or what not."

Durdles nods assent, and falls to munching some fragments from his bundle. Jasper folds his arms upon the top of the wall, and, with his chin resting on them, watches. He takes no note whatever of the Minor Canon, but watches Neville, as though his eye were⁵ at the trigger of a loaded rifle, and he had covered him, and were going to fire. A sense of destructive power is so expressed in his face, that even Durdles pauses in his munching, and looks at him, with an unmunched something in his cheek.

Meanwhile Mr. Crisparkle and Neville walk to and fro, quietly talking together. What they say, cannot be heard consecutively; but Mr. Jasper has already distinguished his own name more than once.

"This is the first day of the week," Mr. Crisparkle can be distinctly heard to observe, as they turn back; "and the last day of the week is Christmas Eve."

"You may be certain of me, sir."

The echoes were favorable at those points, but as the two approach, the sound of their talking becomes confused again. The word "confidence," shattered by the echoes, but still capable of being pieced together, is

¹ affair] matter MS   ² Jarsper] Jasper MS   ³ At] Now, at MS
⁴ is] MS there is 70–75   ⁵ were] was MS

uttered by Mr. Crisparkle. As they draw still nearer, this fragment of a reply[1] is heard: "Not deserved yet, but shall be, sir." As they turn[2] away again, Jasper again hears his own name, in connexion with the words from Mr. Crisparkle: "Remember that I said I answered for you confidently." Then the sound of their talk becomes confused again; they halting for a little while, and some earnest action on the part of Neville succeeding. When they move once more, Mr. Crisparkle is seen to look up at the sky, and to point before him. They then slowly disappear; passing out into the moonlight at the opposite end of the Corner.

It is not until they are gone, that Mr. Jasper moves. But then he turns to Durdles, and bursts into a fit of laughter. Durdles, who still has that suspended something in his cheek, and who sees nothing to laugh at, stares at him until Mr. Jasper[3] lays his face down on his arms to have his laugh out. Then Durdles bolts the something, as if desperately resigning himself to indigestion.

Among those secluded nooks there is very little stir or movement after dark. There is little enough in the high-tide of the day, but there is next to none at night. Besides that the cheerfully frequented High Street lies nearly parallel to the spot (the old Cathedral rising between the two), and is the natural channel in which the Cloisterham traffic flows,[4] a certain awful hush pervades the ancient pile, the cloisters, and the churchyard, after dark,[5] which not many people care to encounter. Ask the first hundred citizens of Cloisterham, met at random in the streets at noon, if they believed in ghosts, they would tell you no; but put them to choose at night between these eerie Precincts and the thoroughfare of shops, and you would find that ninety-nine declared for the longer round and the more frequented way. The cause of this is not to be found in any local superstition that attaches to the Precincts—albeit a mysterious lady, with a child in her arms and a rope dangling from her neck, has been seen flitting about there by sundry witnesses as intangible as herself—but it[6] is to be sought in the innate shrinking of dust with the breath of life in it, from dust out of which the breath of life has passed; also, in the widely diffused, and almost as widely unacknowledged, reflection: "If the dead do, under any circumstances, become visible to the living, these are such likely surroundings for the purpose that I, the living, will get out of them as soon as I can."

Hence, when Mr. Jasper and Durdles pause to glance around them, before descending into the crypt by a small side door of which the latter has a key, the whole expanse of moonlight in their view is utterly deserted. One might fancy that the tide of life was stemmed by Mr. Jasper's own Gate House. The murmur of the tide is heard beyond; but no wave passes[7]

---

[1] reply] reply to him MS   [2] turn] turned ES   [3] Mr. Jasper] he MS
[4] flows] runs MS   [5] dark] sunset MS   [6] it] *not in* MS
[7] passes] passed ES

the archway, over which his lamp burns red behind his curtain, as if the building were a Lighthouse.

They enter, locking themselves in, descend the rugged steps, and are down in the crypt. The lantern is not wanted, for the moonlight strikes in at the groined windows, bare of glass, the broken frames for which cast[1] patterns on the ground. The heavy pillars which support the roof engender masses of black shade, but between them there are lanes of light. Up and down these lanes, they walk, Durdles discoursing of the "old 'uns" he yet counts on disinterring, and slapping a wall, in which he considers "a whole family on 'em" to be stoned and earthed up, just[2] as if he were a familiar friend of the family. The taciturnity of Durdles is for the time overcome by Mr. Jasper's wicker bottle, which circulates freely;—in the sense, that is to say, that its contents enter freely into Mr. Durdles's circulation, while Mr. Jasper only rinses his mouth once, and casts forth the rinsing.

They are to ascend the great Tower. On the steps by which they rise to the Cathedral, Durdles pauses for new store of breath. The steps are very dark, but out of the darkness they can see the lanes of light they have traversed. Durdles seats himself upon a step.[3] Mr. Jasper seats himself upon another. The odour from the wicker bottle (which has somehow passed into Durdles's keeping), soon intimates that the cork has been taken out; but this is not ascertainable through the sense of sight, since neither can descry the other. And yet, in talking, they turn to one another, as though their faces could commune together.

"This is good stuff, Mister Jarsper!"[4]

"It is very good stuff, I hope. I bought it on purpose."

"They don't show, you see, the old 'uns don't, Mister Jarsper!"[4]

"It would be a more confused world than it is, if they could."

"Well, it *would* lead towards a mixing of things," Durdles acquiesces: pausing on the remark, as if the idea of ghosts had not previously presented itself to him in a merely inconvenient light, domestically, or chronologically. "But do you think there may be ghosts of other things, though not of men and women?"

"What things? Flower-beds and watering-pots? Horses and harness?"[5]

"No. Sounds."

"What sounds?"

"Cries."

"What cries do you mean? Chairs to mend?"

"No.[6] I mean screeches. Now, I'll tell you, Mister Jarsper.[7] Wait a bit

---

[1] frames . . . cast] framing . . . casts MS   [2] just] *not in* MS
[3] Durdles . . . step.] As Durdles . . . step, MS   [4] Jarsper] Jasper MS
[5] Horses and harness?] Horses and harness? Pigs and sties? MS
[6] No] No, I don't MS
[7] Mister Jarsper] Mister Jasper MS   Mr. Jarsper 73 75

till I put the bottle right." Here the cork is[1] evidently taken out again, and replaced again. "There! *Now* it's right! This time last year, only a few days later, I happened to have been doing what was correct[2] by the season, in the way of giving it the welcome it had a right to expect, when them town-boys set on me at their worst. At length I gave 'em the slip, and turned in here. And here I fell asleep. And what woke me? The ghost of a cry. The ghost of one terrific[3] shriek, which shriek was followed by the ghost of the howl of a dog: a long dismal woeful howl, such as a dog gives when a person's dead. That was *my* last Christmas Eve."

"What do you mean?" is the very abrupt, and, one might say, fierce retort.

"I mean that I made inquiries everywheres[4] about, and that no living ears but mine heard either that cry or that howl. So I say they was both ghosts; though why they came to me, I've never made out."

"I thought you were another kind of man," says Jasper, scornfully.

"So I thought, myself," answers Durdles with his usual composure; "and yet I was picked out for it."

Jasper had risen suddenly, when he asked him what he meant, and he now says, "Come; we shall freeze here; lead the way."

Durdles complies, not over-steadily; opens the door at the top of the steps with the key he has already used; and so emerges[5] on the Cathedral level, in a passage at the side of the chancel. Here, the moonlight is so very bright again that the colors of the nearest stained-glass window are thrown upon their faces. The appearance of the unconscious Durdles, holding the door open for his companion to follow, as if from the grave, is ghastly enough, with a purple band across his face, and a yellow splash upon his brow; but he bears the close scrutiny of his companion in an insensible way, although it is prolonged while the latter fumbles among his pockets for a key confided to him that will open an iron gate and[6] enable them to pass to the staircase of the great tower.

"That and the bottle are enough for you to carry," he says, giving it to Durdles; "hand your bundle to me; I am younger and longer-winded than you." Durdles hesitates for a moment between bundle and bottle; but gives the preference to the bottle as being by far the better company, and consigns the dry weight to his fellow-explorer.

Then they go up the winding staircase of the great tower, toilsomely, turning and turning, and lowering their heads to avoid the stairs above, or the rough stone pivot around which they twist. Durdles has lighted his lantern, by drawing from the cold hard wall a spark of that mysterious fire which lurks in everything, and, guided by this speck, they clamber

---

[1] is] was MS   [2] correct] right MS
[3] terrific] most terrific MS   [4] everywheres] MS everywhere 70–75
[5] so emerges] ⟨so⟩ emerges first MS *deletion of* so *is not absolutely certain*
[6] and] MS so to 70–75

up among the cobwebs and the dust. Their way lies through strange places. Twice or thrice they emerge into level low-arched galleries, whence they can look down into the moonlit nave; and where Durdles, waving his lantern, shows[1] the dim angels' heads upon the corbels of the roof, seeming to watch their progress. Anon, they turn into narrower and steeper staircases, and the night air begins to blow upon them, and the chirp of some startled jackdaw or frightened rook precedes the heavy beating of wings in a confined space, and the beating down of dust and straws upon their heads. At last, leaving their light behind a stair—for it blows fresh up here—they look down on Cloisterham, fair to see in the moonlight: its ruined habitations and sanctuaries of the dead, at the tower's base: its moss-softened red-tiled roofs and red-brick houses of the living, clustered beyond: its river winding down from the mist on the horizon, as though that were its source, and already heaving with a restless knowledge[2] of its approach towards the sea.

Once again, an unaccountable expedition this! Jasper (always moving softly with no visible reason) contemplates the scene, and especially that stillest part of it which the Cathedral overshadows. But he contemplates Durdles quite as curiously, and Durdles is by times conscious of his watchful eyes.

Only by times, because Durdles is growing drowsy. As aëronauts lighten the load they carry, when they wish to rise, similarly Durdles has lightened the wicker bottle in coming up. Snatches of sleep surprise him on his legs, and stop him in his talk. A mild fit of calenture seizes him, in which he deems that the ground, so far below, is on a level with the tower, and would as lief walk off the tower into the air as not. Such is his state when they begin to come down. And as aëronauts make themselves heavier when they wish to descend, similarly Durdles charges himself with more liquid from the wicker bottle, that he may come down the better.

The iron gate attained and locked—but not before Durdles has tumbled twice, and cut an eyebrow open once—they descend into the crypt again, with the intent of issuing forth as they entered. But, while returning among those lanes of light, Durdles becomes so very uncertain, both of foot and speech, that he half drops, half throws himself down, by one of the heavy pillars, scarcely less heavy than itself,[3] and indistinctly appeals to his companion for forty winks of a second each.

"If you will have it so, or must have it so," replies Jasper, "I'll not leave you here. Take them, while I walk to and fro."

Durdles is asleep at once; and in his sleep he dreams a dream.

It is not much of a dream, considering the vast extent of the domains of dreamland, and their wonderful productions; it[4] is only remarkable

---

[1] shows] waves 73 75
[2] heaving with a restless knowledge] lashing and heaving with the knowledge MS
[3] itself] it MS   [4] it] *possibly* and it MS

for being unusually restless, and unusually real. He dreams of lying there, asleep, and yet counting his companion's footsteps as he walks to and fro. He dreams that the footsteps die away into distance of time and of space, and that something touches him, and that something falls from his hand. Then something clinks and gropes about, and he dreams that he is alone for so long a time, that the lanes of light take new directions as the moon advances in[1] her course. From succeeding unconsciousness, he passes into a dream of slow uneasiness from cold; and painfully awakes to a perception of the lanes of light—really changed, much as he had dreamed—and Jasper walking among them, beating his hands and feet.

"Halloa!" Durdles cries out, unmeaningly alarmed.

"Awake at last?" says Jasper, coming up to him. "Do you know that your forties have stretched into thousands?"

"No."

"They have though."

"What's the time?"

"Hark! The bells[2] are going in the tower!"

They strike four quarters, and then the great bell strikes.

"Two!" cries Durdles, scrambling up;[3] "why didn't you try to wake me, Mister Jarsper?"[4]

"I did. I might as well have tried to wake the dead:—your own family of dead, up in the corner there."

"Did you touch me?"

"Touch you? Yes. Shook you."

As Durdles recalls that touching something in his dream, he looks down on the pavement, and sees the key of the crypt door lying close to where he himself lay.

"I dropped you, did I?" he says, picking it up, and recalling that part of his dream. As he gathers himself[5] again into an upright position, or into a position as nearly upright as he ever maintains, he is again conscious of being watched by his companion.[6]

"Well?" says Jasper, smiling. "Are you quite ready? Pray don't hurry."

"Let me get my bundle right, Mister Jarsper,[7] and I'm with you."

As he ties it afresh, he is once more conscious that he is very narrowly observed.

"What do you suspect me of, Mister Jarsper?"[4] he asks, with drunken displeasure. "Let them as has any suspicions of Durdles, name 'em."

"I've no suspicions of you, my good Mr. Durdles; but I have suspicions that my bottle was filled with something stiffer than either of us supposed.

---

[1] in] ⟨in⟩ on MS
[2] Hark! The bells] Hark!" Jasper answers. "The quarter bells MS
[3] scrambling up] scrambling up unsteadily MS   [4] Jarsper] Jasper MS
[5] himself] himself up 73 75   [6] watched by his companion] closely watched MS
[7] Mister Jarsper] Mr Jasper MS

And I also have suspicions,"[1] Jasper adds, taking it from the pavement and turning it bottom upward, "that it's empty."

Durdles condescends to laugh at this. Continuing to chuckle when his laugh is over, as though remonstrant with himself on his drinking powers, he rolls to the door and unlocks it. They both pass out, and Durdles relocks it, and pockets his key.

"A thousand thanks for a curious and interesting night," says Jasper, giving him his hand; "you can make your own way home?"

"I should think so!" answers Durdles. "If you was to offer Durdles the affront to show him his way home, he wouldn't go home.

> Durdles[2] wouldn't go home till morning,
> And *then* Durdles[2] wouldn't go home,

Durdles wouldn't." This, with the utmost defiance.

"Good-night, then."

"Good-night, Mister Jarsper."[3]

Each is turning his own way, when a sharp whistle rends the silence, and the jargon is yelped out:

> "Widdy widdy wen!
> I—ket—ches—Im—out—ar—ter—ten.
> Widdy widdy wy!
> Then—E—don't—go—then—I—shy—
> Widdy Widdy Wake-cock warning!"

Instantly afterwards, a rapid fire of stones rattles at the Cathedral wall, and the hideous small boy is beheld opposite, dancing in the moonlight.

"What! Is that baby-devil on the watch there!"[4] cries Jasper in a fury: so quickly roused, and so violent, that he seems an older devil himself. "I shall shed the blood of that[5] Impish wretch! I know I shall do it!" Regardless of the fire,[6] though it hits him more than once, he rushes at Deputy, collars him, and tries to bring him across. But Deputy is not to be so easily brought across. With a diabolical insight into the strongest part of his position, he is no sooner taken by the throat than he curls up his legs, forces his assailant to hang him, as it were, and gurgles in his throat, and screws his body, and twists, as already undergoing the first agonies of strangulation. There is nothing for it but to drop him. He instantly gets himself together, backs over to Durdles, and cries to his assailant, gnashing the great gap in front of his mouth with rage and[7] malice:

"I'll blind yer, s'elp me! I'll stone yer eyes out, s'elp me! If I don't

---

[1] suspicions . . . suspicions] my suspicions . . . my suspicions MS

[2] Durdles] He MS   [3] Jarsper] Jasper MS

[4] there] *not in* MS ES *deletions in* MS *at this point; original wording probably* ⟨Is that young demon there?⟩   [5] that] the MS *partly deleted*

[6] fire] fire of stones MS   [7] rage and] *not legible as such in* MS

have yer eyesight, bellows me!" At the same time dodging behind Durdles, and snarling at Jasper, now from this side of him, and now from that: prepared, if pounced upon, to dart away in all manner of curvilinear directions, and, if run down after all, to grovel in the dust with one defensive leg up,[1] and cry: "Now, hit me when I'm down! Do it!"

"Don't hurt the boy, Mister Jarsper,"[2] urges Durdles, shielding him. "Recollect yourself."

"He followed us to-night, when we first came here!"

"Yer lie, I didn't!" replies Deputy, in his one form of polite contradiction.

"He has been prowling near us ever since!"

"Yer lie, I haven't," returns Deputy. "I'd only jist come out for my 'elth when I see you two a coming out of the Kinfreederel.[3] If—

"I—ket—ches—Im—out—ar—ter—ten,"

(with the usual rhythm and dance, though dodging behind Durdles), "it ain't *my* fault, is it?"

"Take him home, then," retorts Jasper, ferociously, though with a strong check upon himself, "and let my eyes be rid of the sight of[4] you!"

Deputy, with another sharp whistle, at once expressing his relief, and his commencement of a milder stoning of Mr. Durdles, begins stoning that respectable gentleman home, as if he were a reluctant ox. Mr. Jasper goes to his Gate House, brooding. And thus, as everything comes to an end, the unaccountable expedition comes to an end—for the time.

CHAPTER XIII

BOTH AT THEIR BEST

Miss Twinkleton's establishment was about to undergo a serene hush. The Christmas recess was at hand. What had once, and at no remote period, been called, even by the erudite Miss Twinkleton herself, "the half;" but what was now called, as being more elegant, and more strictly[5] collegiate, "the term;" would expire to-morrow. A noticeable relaxation of discipline had for some few days pervaded the Nuns' House. Club suppers had occurred in the bedrooms, and a dressed tongue had been carved with a pair of scissors, and handed round with the curling-tongs. Portions of marmalade had likewise been distributed on a service of plates constructed of curlpaper; and cowslip wine had been quaffed from the

---

[1] with one defensive leg up] MS *om.* 70–75   [2] Jarsper] Jasper MS
[3] Kinfreederel] Kinfreedle MS *after many deletions*   [4] the sight of] *not in* MS
END OF No. III
[5] strictly] chastely MS

small squat measuring glass in which little Rickitts (a junior of weakly constitution), took her steel drops daily. The housemaids had been bribed with various fragments of riband, and sundry pairs of shoes, more or less down at heel, to make no mention of crumbs in the beds; the airiest costumes had been worn on these festive occasions; and the daring Miss Ferdinand had even surprised the company with a sprightly solo on the comb-and-curlpaper, until suffocated in her own pillow by two flowing-haired executioners.

Nor were these the only tokens of dispersal. Boxes appeared in the bedrooms (where they were capital at other times), and a surprising amount of packing took place, out of all proportion to the amount packed. Largesse, in the form of odds and ends of cold cream and pomatum, and also of hairpins, was freely distributed among the attendants. On charges of inviolable secresy, confidences were interchanged respecting golden youth of England expected to call, "at home," on the first opportunity. Miss Giggles (deficient in sentiment) did indeed profess that she, for her part, acknowledged such homage by making faces at the golden youth; but this young lady was outvoted by an immense majority.

On the last night before a recess, it was always expressly made a point of honor that nobody should go to sleep, and that ghosts should be encouraged by all possible means. This compact invariably broke down, and all the young ladies went to sleep very soon, and got up very early.

The concluding ceremony came off at twelve o'clock on the day of departure; when Miss Twinkleton, supported by Mrs. Tisher, held a Drawing-Room in her own apartment (the globes already covered with brown holland), where glasses of white wine, and plates of cut pound-cake were discovered on the table. Miss Twinkleton then said, Ladies, another revolving year had brought us round to that festive period at which the finest[1] feelings of our nature bounded in our—— Miss Twinkleton was annually going to add "bosoms," but annually stopped on the brink of that expression, and substituted "hearts." Hearts; our hearts. Hem! Again a revolving year, ladies, had brought us to a pause in our studies—let us hope our greatly advanced studies—and, like the mariner in his bark, the warrior in his tent, the captive in his dungeon, and the traveller in his various conveyances, we yearned for home. Did we say, on such an occasion, in the opening words of Mr. Addison's impressive tragedy:

> "The dawn is overcast, the morning lowers,
> And heavily in clouds brings on the day,
> The great, th' important day——"?

Not so. From horizon to zenith all was *couleur de rose*, for all was redolent of our relations and friends. Might *we* find *them* prospering as *we* expected; might *they* find *us* prospering as *they* expected! Ladies, we

[1] finest] MS first 70–75

"GOOD-BYE, ROSEBUD, DARLING!"

would now, with our love to one another, wish one another good-bye, and happiness, until we met[1] again. And when the time should come for our resumption of those pursuits which (here a general[2] depression set in all round), pursuits which, pursuits which;—then let us ever remember what was said by the Spartan General, in words too trite for repetition, at the battle it were superfluous to specify.[3]

The handmaidens of the establishment, in their best caps, then handed the trays, and the young ladies sipped and crumbled, and the bespoken coaches[4] began to choke the street. Then, leave-taking was not long about, and Miss Twinkleton, in saluting each young lady's cheek, confided to her an exceedingly neat letter, addressed to her next friend at law, "with Miss Twinkleton's best compliments" in the corner. This missive she handed with an air as if it had not the least connexion with the bill, but were something in the nature of a delicate and joyful surprise.

So many times had Rosa seen such dispersals, and so very little did she know of any other Home, that she was contented to remain where she was, and was even better contented than ever before, having her latest friend with her. And yet her latest friendship had a blank place in it of which she could not fail to be sensible. Helena Landless, having been a party to her brother's revelation about Rosa, and having entered into that compact of silence with Mr. Crisparkle, shrank from any allusion to Edwin Drood's name. Why she so avoided it, was mysterious to Rosa, but she perfectly perceived the fact. But for the fact, she might have relieved her own little perplexed heart of some of its doubts and hesitations, by taking Helena into her confidence. As it was, she had no such vent: she could only ponder on her own difficulties, and wonder more and more why this avoidance of Edwin's name should last, now that she knew—for so much Helena had told her—that a good understanding was to be re-established between the two young men, when Edwin came down.

It would have made a pretty picture, so many pretty girls kissing Rosa in the cold porch of the Nuns' House, and that sunny little creature peeping out of it (unconscious of sly faces carved on spout and gable peeping at her), and waving farewells to the departing coaches, as if she represented the spirit of rosy youth abiding in the place to keep it bright and warm in its desertion. The hoarse High Street became musical with the cry, in various silvery voices, "Good-bye, Rosebud, Darling!" and the effigy of Mr. Sapsea's father over the opposite doorway, seemed to say to mankind: "Gentlemen, favor me with your attention to this charming little[5] last lot left behind, and bid with a spirit worthy of the occasion!" Then the staid street, so unwontedly sparkling, youthful, and fresh for a few rippling moments, ran dry, and Cloisterham was itself again.

[1] met] meet ES   [2] a general] general MS
[3] let us ever . . . specify] *in MS written on verso, with many deletions*
[4] coaches] flies MS   [5] little] *not in* MS

If Rosebud in her bower now waited Edwin Drood's coming with an uneasy heart, Edwin for his part was uneasy too. With far less force of purpose in his composition than the childish beauty, crowned by acclamation fairy queen of Miss Twinkleton's establishment, he had a conscience, and Mr. Grewgious had pricked it. That gentleman's steady convictions of what was right and what was wrong in such a case as his, were neither to be frowned aside, nor laughed aside. They would not be moved. But for the dinner in Staple Inn, and but for the ring he carried in the breast pocket of his coat, he would have drifted into their wedding-day without another pause for real thought, loosely trusting that all would go well, left alone. But that serious putting him on his truth to the living and the dead had brought him to a check. He must either give the ring to Rosa, or he must take it back. Once put into this narrowed way of action, it was curious that he began to consider Rosa's claims upon him more unselfishly than he had ever considered them before, and began to be less sure of himself than he had ever been in all his easy-going days.

"I will be guided by what she says, and by how we get on," was his decision, walking from the Gate House to the Nuns' House. "Whatever comes of it, I will bear his words in mind, and try to be true to the living and the dead."

Rosa was dressed for walking. She expected him. It was a bright frosty day, and Miss Twinkleton had already graciously sanctioned fresh air. Thus they got out together before it became necessary for either Miss Twinkleton, or the Deputy High Priest, Mrs. Tisher, to lay even so much as one of those usual offerings on the shrine of Propriety.

"My dear Eddy," said Rosa, when they had turned out of the High Street, and had[1] got among the quiet walks in the neighbourhood of the Cathedral and the river: "I want to say something very serious to you. I have been thinking about it for a long, long time."

"I want to be serious with you too, Rosa dear. I mean to be serious and earnest."

"Thank you, Eddy. And you will not think me unkind because I begin, will you? You will not think I speak for myself only, because I speak first? That would not be generous, would it? And I know you are generous!"

He said, "I hope I am not ungenerous to you, Rosa." He called her Pussy no more. Never again.

"And there is no fear," pursued Rosa, "of our quarrelling, is there? Because, Eddy," clasping her hand[2] on his arm, "we have so much reason to be very lenient to each other!"

"We will be, Rosa."

"That's a dear good boy! Eddy, let us be courageous. Let us change to brother and sister from this day forth."

"Never be husband and wife?"

[1] had] *not in* MS   [2] hand] hands MS

"Never!"

Neither spoke again for a little while. But after that pause he said, with some effort:

"Of course I know that this has been in both our minds, Rosa, and of course I am in honor bound to confess freely that it does not originate with you."

"No, nor with you, dear," she returned, with pathetic earnestness. "It has[1] sprung up between us. You are not truly happy in our engagement; I am not truly happy in it. Oh, I am so sorry, so sorry!" And there she broke into tears.

"I am deeply sorry too, Rosa. Deeply sorry for you."

"And I for you, poor boy! And I for you!"

This pure young feeling, this gentle and forbearing feeling of each towards the other, brought with it its reward in a softening light that seemed to shine on their position. The relations between them did not look wilful, or capricious, or a failure, in such a light; they became elevated into something more self-denying, honorable, affectionate, and true.

"If we knew yesterday," said Rosa, as she dried her eyes, "and we did know yesterday, and on many, many yesterdays, that we were far from right together[2] in those relations which were not of our own[3] choosing, what better could we do to-day than change them? It is natural that we should be sorry, and you see how sorry we both are; but how much better to be sorry now than then!"

"When, Rosa?"

"When it would be too late. And then we should be angry, besides."

Another silence fell upon them.

"And you know," said Rosa, innocently, "you couldn't like me then; and you can always like me now, for I shall not be a drag upon you, or a worry to you. And I can always like you now, and your sister will not tease or trifle with you. I often did when I was not your sister, and I beg your pardon for it."

"Don't let us come to that, Rosa; or I shall want more pardoning than I like to think of."

"No, indeed, Eddy; you are too hard, my generous boy, upon yourself. Let us sit down, brother, on these ruins, and let me tell you how it was with us. I think I know, for I have considered about it very much since you were here, last time. You liked me, didn't you? You thought I was a nice little thing?"

"Everybody thinks that, Rosa."

"Do they?" She knitted her brow musingly for a moment, and then flashed out with the bright little induction: "Well; but say they do. Surely

---

[1] It has] That 75   [2] together] *not in* MS
[3] own] *not in* MS

it was not enough that you should think of me, only as other people did; now, was it?"

The point was not to be got over. It was not enough.

"And that is just what I mean; that is just how it was with us," said Rosa. "You liked me very well, and you had grown used to me, and had¹ grown used to the idea of our being married. You accepted the situation as an inevitable kind of thing, didn't you? It was to be, you thought, and why discuss or dispute it."

It was new and strange to him to have himself presented to himself so clearly, in a glass of her holding up. He had always patronized her, in his superiority to her share of woman's wit. Was that but another instance of something radically amiss in the terms on which they had been gliding towards a life-long bondage?

"All this that I say of you, is true of me as well, Eddy. Unless it was, I might not be bold enough to say it. Only, the difference between us was, that by little and little there crept into my mind a habit of thinking about it, instead of dismissing it. My life is not so busy as yours, you see, and I have not so many things to think of. So I thought about it very much, and I cried about it very much too (though that was not your fault, poor boy); when all at once my guardian came down, to prepare for my leaving the Nuns' House. I tried to hint to him that I was not quite settled in my mind, but I hesitated and failed, and he didn't understand me. But he is a good, good man. And he put before me so kindly, and yet so strongly, how seriously we ought to consider, in our circumstances, that I resolved to speak to you the next moment we were alone and grave. And if I seemed to come to it easily just now, because I came to it all at once, don't think it was so really, Eddy, for Oh, it was very, very hard, and Oh, I am very, very sorry!"

Her full heart broke into tears again. He put his arm about her waist, and they walked by the river side together.

"Your guardian has spoken to me too, Rosa dear. I saw him before I left London." His right hand was in his breast, seeking the ring; but he checked it as he thought: "If I am to take it back, why should I tell her of it?"

"And that made you more serious about it, didn't it, Eddy? And if I had not spoken to you, as I have, you would have spoken to me? I hope you can tell me so? I don't like it to be *all* my doing, though it *is*² so much better for us."

"Yes, I should have spoken; I should have put everything before you; I came intending to do it. But I never could have spoken to you as you have spoken to me, Rosa."

"Don't say you mean so coldly or unkindly, Eddy, please, if you can help it."

¹ had] *not in* MS   ² *is*] *possibly* is MS

"I mean so sensibly and delicately, so wisely and affectionately."

"That's my dear brother!" She kissed his hand in a little rapture. "The dear girls will be dreadfully disappointed," added Rosa, laughing, with the dew-drops[1] glistening in her bright eyes. "They have looked forward to it so, poor pets!"

"Ah! But I fear[2] it will be a worse disappointment to Jack," said Edwin Drood, with a start. "I never thought of Jack!"

Her swift and intent look at him as he said the words, could no more be recalled than a flash of lightning can. But it appeared as though she would have instantly recalled it, if she could; for she looked down, confused, and breathed quickly.

"You don't doubt its being a blow to Jack, Rosa?"

She merely replied, and that, evasively and hurriedly: Why should she? She had not thought about it. He seemed, to her, to have so little to do with it.

"My dear child! Can you suppose that any one so wrapped up in another—Mrs. Tope's expression: not mine—as Jack is in me, could fail to be struck all of a heap by such a sudden and complete change in my life? I say sudden, because it will be sudden to *him*, you know."

She nodded twice or thrice, and her lips parted as if she would have assented. But she uttered no sound, and her breathing was no slower.

"How shall I tell Jack!" said Edwin, ruminating. If he had been less occupied with the thought, he must have seen her singular emotion. "I never thought of Jack. It must be broken to him, before the town crier knows it. I dine with the dear fellow to-morrow and next day—Christmas Eve and Christmas Day—but it would never do to spoil his feast days. He always worries about me, and moddley-coddleys[3] in the merest trifles. The news is sure to overset him. How on earth shall this be broken to Jack!"

"He must be told, I suppose?" said Rosa.

"My dear Rosa! Who ought to be in our confidence, if not Jack?"

"My guardian promised to come down, if I should write and ask him. I am going to do so. Would you like to leave it to him?"

"A bright idea!" cried Edwin. "The other trustee. Nothing more natural. He comes down, he goes to Jack, he relates what we have agreed upon, and he states our case better than we could. He has already spoken feelingly to you, he has already spoken feelingly to me, and he'll put the whole thing feelingly to Jack. That's it! I am not a coward, Rosa, but to tell you a secret, I am a little afraid of Jack."

"No, no! You are not afraid of him?" cried Rosa, turning white and clasping her hands.

[1] the dew-drops] dew drops MS
[2] I fear] *deletion of these words seems to be intended in* MS
[3] and moddley-coddleys] molly-coddles MS and molly-coddles ES

"Why, sister Rosa, sister Rosa, what do you see from the turret?" said Edwin, rallying her. "My dear girl!"

"You frightened me."

"Most unintentionally, but I am as sorry as if I had meant to do it. Could you possibly suppose for a moment, from any loose way of speaking of mine, that I was literally afraid of the dear fond[1] fellow? What I mean is, that he is subject to a kind of paroxysm, or fit—I saw him in it once— and I don't know but that so great a surprise, coming upon him direct from me whom he is so wrapped up in, might bring it on perhaps. Which —and this is the secret I was going to tell you—is another reason for your guardian's making the communication. He is so steady, precise, and exact, that he will talk Jack's thoughts into shape,[2] in no time: whereas with me Jack is always impulsive and hurried, and, I may say, almost womanish."

Rosa seemed convinced. Perhaps from her own very different point of view of "Jack," she felt comforted and protected by the interposition of Mr. Grewgious between herself and him.

And now, Edwin Drood's right hand closed again upon the ring in its little case, and again was checked by the consideration: "It is certain, now, that I am to give it back to him; then why should I tell her of it?" That pretty sympathetic nature which could be so sorry for him in the blight of their childish hopes of happiness together, and could so quietly find itself alone in a new world to weave fresh wreaths of such flowers as it might prove to bear, the old world's flowers being withered, would be grieved by those sorrowful jewels; and to what purpose? Why should it be? They were but a sign of broken joys and baseless projects; in their very beauty, they were (as the unlikeliest of men had said), almost a cruel satire on the loves, hopes, plans, of humanity, which are able to forecast nothing, and are so much brittle dust. Let them be. He would restore them to her guardian when he came down; he in his turn would restore them to the cabinet from which he had unwillingly taken them; and there, like old letters or old vows, or other[3] records of old aspirations come to nothing, they would be disregarded, until, being valuable, they were sold into circulation again, to repeat their former round.

Let them be. Let them lie unspoken of, in his breast. However distinctly or indistinctly he entertained these thoughts, he arrived at the conclusion, Let them be. Among the mighty store of wonderful chains that are for ever forging, day and night, in the vast iron-works of time and circum- stance, there was one chain forged in the moment of that small conclusion, riveted to the foundations of heaven and earth, and gifted with invincible force to hold and drag.

They walked on by the river. They began to speak of their separate plans. He would quicken his departure from England, and she would remain where she was, at least as long as Helena remained. The poor dear

girls should have their disappointment broken to them gently, and, as the
first preliminary, Miss Twinkleton should be confided in by Rosa, even
in advance of the reappearance of Mr. Grewgious. It should be made clear
in all quarters that she and Edwin[1] were the best of friends. There had
never been so serene an understanding between them since they were first
affianced.[2] And yet there was one reservation on each side; on hers, that
she intended through her guardian to withdraw herself immediately from
the tuition of her music-master; on his, that he did already entertain some
wandering speculations whether it might ever come to pass that he would
know more of Miss Landless.

The bright frosty day declined as they walked and spoke together.
The sun dipped in the river far behind them, and the old city lay red
before them, as their walk drew to a close. The moaning water cast its
seaweed duskily at their feet, when they turned to leave its margin; and
the rooks hovered above[3] them with hoarse cries, darker splashes in the
darkening air.

"I will prepare Jack for my flitting soon," said Edwin, in a low voice,
"and I will but see your guardian when he comes, and then go before they
speak together. It will be better done without my being by. Don't you
think so?"

"Yes."

"We know we have done right, Rosa?"

"Yes."

"We know we are better so, even now?"

"And shall be far, far, better so, by-and-bye."

Still, there was that lingering tenderness in their hearts towards the old
positions they were relinquishing, that they prolonged their parting.
When they came among the elm trees by the Cathedral, where they had
last sat together, they stopped, as by consent, and Rosa raised her face
to his, as she had never raised it in the old days;—for they were old
already.

"God bless you, dear! Good-bye!"

"God bless you, dear! Good-bye!"

They kissed each other, fervently.

"Now, please take me home, Eddy, and let me be by myself."

"Don't look round, Rosa," he cautioned her, as he drew her arm
through his, and led her away. "Didn't you see Jack?"

"No! Where?"

"Under the trees. He saw us, as we took leave of each other. Poor
fellow! he little thinks we have parted. This will be a blow to him, I am
much afraid!"

[1] she and Edwin] they MS
[2] affianced] affianced children MS *but Dickens may have intended to delete* children
[3] above] around MS

She hurried on, without resting, and hurried on until they had passed under the Gate House into the street; once there, she asked:

"Has he followed us? You can look without seeming to. Is he behind?"

"No. Yes! he is! He has just passed out[1] under the gateway. The dear sympathetic old fellow likes to keep us in sight. I am afraid he will be bitterly disappointed!"

She pulled hurriedly at the handle[2] of the hoarse old bell, and the gate soon opened. Before going in, she gave him one last wide wondering look, as if she would have asked him with imploring emphasis: "Oh![3] don't you understand?" And out of that look he vanished from her view.[4]

CHAPTER XIV

WHEN SHALL THESE THREE MEET AGAIN?

CHRISTMAS EVE in Cloisterham. A few strange faces in the streets; a few other faces, half strange and half familiar, once the faces of Cloisterham children, now the faces of men and women who come back from the outer world at long intervals to find the city wonderfully shrunken in size, as if it had not washed by any means well in the meanwhile. To these, the striking of the Cathedral clock, and the cawing of the rooks from the Cathedral tower, are like voices of their nursery time. To such as these, it has happened in their dying hours afar off, that they have imagined their chamber floor to be strewn with the autumnal leaves fallen from the elm trees in the Close: so have the rustling sounds and fresh scents of their earliest impressions, revived, when the circle of their lives was very nearly traced, and the beginning and the end were drawing close together.

Seasonable tokens are about. Red berries shine here and there in the lattices of Minor Canon Corner; Mr. and Mrs. Tope are daintily sticking sprigs of holly into the carvings and sconces of the Cathedral stalls, as if they were sticking them into the coat-buttonholes of the Dean and Chapter. Lavish profusion is in the shops: particularly in the articles of currants, raisins, spices, candied peel, and moist sugar. An unusual air of gallantry and dissipation is abroad; evinced in an immense bunch of mistletoe hanging in the greengrocer's shop doorway, and a poor little Twelfth Cake, culminating in the figure of a Harlequin—such a very poor

---

[1] out] *not in* MS

[2] hurriedly at the handle] very hurriedly at the pendent handle MS hurriedly at the pendent handle ES

[3] Oh!] *not in* MS

[4] *There was considerable alteration in* MS *before this final sentence was written. Beneath the deletions can be read* ⟨and never looked upon him⟩ ⟨and never thought [that he was to?] vanish from her view⟩

little Twelfth Cake, that one would rather call it a Twenty Fourth Cake,
or a Forty Eighth Cake—to be raffled for at the pastrycook's, terms one
shilling per member. Public amusements are not wanting. The Wax-Work
which made so deep an impression on the reflective mind of the Emperor
of China[1] is to be seen by particular desire during Christmas Week only,
on the premises of the bankrupt livery-stable keeper[2] up the lane; and a
new grand comic Christmas pantomime is to be produced at the Theatre:
the latter heralded by the portrait of Signor Jacksonini the clown, saying
"How do you do to-morrow?" quite as large as life, and almost as miserably. In short, Cloisterham is up and doing: though from this description
the High School and Miss Twinkleton's are to be excluded. From the
former establishment, the scholars have gone home, every one of them
in love with one of Miss Twinkleton's young ladies (who knows nothing
about it); and only the handmaidens flutter occasionally in the windows of
the latter. It is noticed, by-the-bye, that these damsels become, within the
limits of decorum, more skittish when thus entrusted with the concrete
representation of their sex, than when dividing the representation with
Miss Twinkleton's young ladies.

Three are to meet at the Gate House to-night. How does each one of
the three get through the day?

Neville[3] Landless, though absolved from his books for the time by Mr.
Crisparkle—whose fresh nature is by no means insensible to the charms
of a holiday—reads and writes in his quiet room, with a concentrated air,
until it is two hours past noon. He then sets himself to clearing his table,
to arranging his books, and to tearing up and burning his stray papers. He
makes a clean sweep of all untidy accumulations, puts all his drawers in
order, and leaves no note or scrap of paper[4] undestroyed, save such
memoranda as bear directly on his studies. This done, he turns to his
wardrobe, selects a few articles of ordinary wear—among them, change
of stout shoes and socks for walking—and packs these in a knapsack. This
knapsack is new, and he bought it in the High Street yesterday. He also
purchased, at the same time and at the same place, a heavy walking-stick:
strong in the handle for the grip of the hand, and iron-shod. He tries this,
swings it, poises it, and lays it by, with the knapsack, on a window-seat.
By this time his arrangements are complete.

He dresses for going out, and is in the act of going—indeed has left his
room, and has met the Minor Canon on the staircase, coming out of his
bedroom upon the same story—when he turns back again for his walking-
stick, thinking he will carry it now. Mr. Crisparkle, who has paused on

[1] reflective mind of the Emperor of China] ⟨Crowned Heads of Europe⟩ Emperor of China MS
[2] on the premises of . . . keeper] at the bankrupt livery stable-keeper's MS
[3] Neville] ⟨Edwin⟩ Neville MS   [4] paper] writing MS

the staircase, sees it in his hand on his immediately reappearing, takes it from him, and asks him with a smile how he chooses a stick?

"Really I don't know that I understand the subject," he answers. "I chose it for its weight."

"Much too heavy, Neville; *much* too heavy."

"To rest upon in a long walk, sir?"

"Rest upon?" repeats Mr. Crisparkle, throwing himself into pedestrian form. "You don't rest upon it; you merely balance with it."

"I shall know better, with practice, sir. I have not lived in a walking country, you know."

"True," says Mr. Crisparkle. "Get into a little training, and we will have a few score miles together. I should leave you nowhere now. Do you come back before dinner?"

"I think not, as we dine early."

Mr. Crisparkle gives him a bright nod and a cheerful good-bye: expressing (not without intention), absolute confidence and ease.

Neville repairs to the Nuns' House, and requests that Miss Landless may be informed that her brother is there, by appointment. He waits at the gate, not even crossing the threshold; for he is on his parole not to put himself in Rosa's way.

His sister is at least as mindful of the obligation they have taken on themselves, as he can be, and loses not a moment in joining him. They meet affectionately, avoid lingering there, and walk towards the upper inland country.

"I am not going to tread upon forbidden ground, Helena," says Neville, when they have walked some distance and are turning; "you will understand in another moment that I cannot help referring to—what shall I say—my infatuation."

"Had you not better avoid it, Neville? You know that I can hear nothing."

"You can hear, my dear, what Mr. Crisparkle has heard, and heard with approval."

"Yes; I can hear so much."

"Well, it is this. I am not only unsettled and unhappy myself, but I am conscious of unsettling and interfering with other people. How do I know that, but for my unfortunate presence, you, and—and—the rest of that former party, our engaging guardian excepted, might be dining cheerfully in Minor Canon Corner to-morrow? Indeed it probably would be so. I can see too well that I am not high in the old lady's opinion, and it is easy to understand what an irksome clog I must be upon the hospitalities of her orderly house—especially at this time of year—when I must be kept asunder from this person, and there is such a reason for my not being brought into contact with that person, and an unfavorable reputation has preceded me with such another person, and so on. I have put this very

gently to Mr. Crisparkle, for you know his self-denying ways; but still I
have put it. What I have laid much greater stress upon at the same time,
is, that I am engaged in a miserable struggle with myself, and that a little
change and absence may enable me to come through it the better. So, the
weather being bright and hard, I am going on a walking expedition, and
intend taking myself out of everybody's way (my own included, I hope),
to-morrow morning."

"When to come back?"

"In a fortnight."

"And going quite alone?"

"I am much better without company, even if there were any one but
you to bear me company, my dear Helena."

"Mr. Crisparkle entirely agrees, you say?"

"Entirely. I am not sure but that at first he was inclined to think it
rather a moody scheme, and one that might do a brooding mind harm.
But we took a moonlight walk, last Monday night, to talk it over at leisure,
and I represented the case to him as it really is. I showed him that I do
want to conquer myself, and that, this evening well got over, it is surely
better that I should be away from here just now, than here. I could hardly
help meeting certain people walking together here, and that could do no
good, and is certainly not the way to forget. A fortnight hence, that chance
will probably be over, for the time; and when it again arises for the last
time, why, I can again go away. Further, I really do feel hopeful of bracing
exercise and wholesome fatigue. You know that Mr. Crisparkle allows
such things their full weight in the preservation of his own sound mind
in his own sound body, and that his just spirit is not likely to maintain one
set of natural laws for himself and another for me. He yielded to my view
of the matter, when convinced that I was honestly in earnest, and so, with
his full consent, I start to-morrow morning. Early enough to be not only
out of the streets, but out of hearing of the bells, when the good people
go to church."

Helena thinks it over, and thinks well of it. Mr. Crisparkle doing so,
she would do so; but she does originally, out of her own mind, think well
of it, as a healthy project, denoting a sincere endeavour, and an active
attempt at self-correction. She is inclined to pity him, poor fellow, for
going away solitary on the great Christmas festival; but she feels it much
more to the purpose to encourage him. And she does encourage him.

He will write to her?

He will write to her every alternate day, and tell her all his adventures.

Does he send clothes on, in advance of him?

"My dear Helena, no. Travel like a pilgrim, with wallet and staff. My
wallet—or my knapsack—is packed, and ready for strapping on; and here
is my staff!"

He hands it to her; she makes the same remark as Mr. Crisparkle, that it is very heavy; and gives it back to him, asking what wood it is? Iron-wood.

Up to this point, he has been extremely cheerful. Perhaps, the having to carry his case with her, and therefore to present it in its brightest aspect, has roused his spirits. Perhaps, the having done so with success, is followed by a revulsion. As the day closes in, and the city lights begin to spring up before them, he grows depressed.

"I wish I were not going to this dinner, Helena."

"Dear Neville, is it worth while to care much about it? Think how soon it will be over."

"How soon it will be over," he repeats, gloomily. "Yes. But I don't like it."

There may be a moment's awkwardness, she cheeringly represents to him, but it can only last a moment. He is quite sure of himself.

"I wish I felt as sure of everything else, as I feel of myself," he answers her.

"How strangely you speak, dear! What do you mean?"

"Helena, I don't know. I only know that I don't like it. What a strange dead weight there is in the air!"

She calls his attention to those copperous clouds beyond the river, and says that the wind is rising. He scarcely speaks again, until he takes leave of her, at the gate of the Nuns' House. She does not immediately enter, when they have parted, but remains looking after him along the street. Twice, he passes the Gate House, reluctant to enter. At length, the Cathedral clock chiming one quarter, with a rapid turn he hurries in.

And so *he* goes up the postern stair.

Edwin Drood passes a solitary day. Something of deeper moment than he had thought, has gone out of his life; and in the silence of his own chamber he wept for it last night. Though the image of Miss Landless still hovers in the background of his mind, the pretty little affectionate creature, so much firmer and wiser than he had supposed, occupies its stronghold. It is with some misgiving of his own unworthiness that he thinks of her, and of what they might have been to one another, if he had been more in earnest some time ago; if he had set a higher value on her; if, instead of accepting his lot in life[1] as an inheritance of course, he had studied the right way to its appreciation and enhancement. And still, for all this, and though there is a sharp heartache in all this, the vanity and caprice of youth sustain that handsome figure of Miss Landless in the background of his mind.

That was a curious look of Rosa's when they parted at the gate. Did it mean that she saw below the surface of his thoughts, and down into their twilight depths? Scarcely that, for it was a look of astonished and keen

[1] lot in life] fortune MS fortune in life ES

inquiry. He decides that he cannot understand it, though it was remark-ably[1] expressive.

As he only waits for Mr. Grewgious now, and will depart immediately after having seen him, he takes a sauntering leave of the ancient city and its neighbourhood. He recalls the time when Rosa and he walked here or there, mere children, full of the dignity of being engaged. Poor children! he thinks, with a pitying sadness.

Finding that his watch has stopped, he turns into the jeweller's shop, to have it wound and set. The jeweller is knowing on the subject of a bracelet, which he begs leave to submit, in a general and quite aimless way. It would suit (he considers) a young bride, to perfection; especially if of a rather diminutive style of beauty. Finding the bracelet but coldly looked at, the jeweller invites attention to a tray of rings for gentlemen; here is a style of ring, now, he remarks—a very[2] chaste signet—which gentlemen are much given to purchasing, when changing their condition. A ring of a very responsible appearance. With the date of their wedding-day engraved inside, several gentlemen have preferred it to any other kind of memento.

The rings are as coldly viewed as the bracelet. Edwin tells the tempter that he wears no jewellery but his watch and chain, which were his father's; and his shirt-pin.

"That I was aware of," is the jeweller's reply, "for Mr. Jasper dropped in for a watch-glass the other day, and, in fact, I showed these articles to him, remarking that if he *should* wish to make a present to a gentleman relative, on any particular occasion— But he said with a smile that he had an inventory in his mind of all the jewellery his gentleman relative ever wore; namely, his watch and chain, and his shirt-pin." Still (the jeweller considers) that might not apply to all times, though applying to the present time. "Twenty minutes past two, Mr. Drood, I set your watch at. Let me recommend you not to let it run down, sir."

Edwin takes his watch, puts it on, and goes out, thinking: "Dear old Jack! If I were to make an extra crease in my neck-cloth, he would think it worth noticing!"

He strolls about and about, to pass the time until the dinner hour. It somehow happens that Cloisterham seems reproachful to him to-day; has fault to find with him, as if he had not used it well; but is far more pensive with him than angry. His wonted carelessness is replaced by a wistful looking at, and dwelling upon, all the old landmarks. He will soon be far away, and may never see them again, he thinks. Poor youth! Poor youth![3]

As dusk draws on, he paces the Monks' Vineyard. He has walked to and fro, full half an hour by the Cathedral chimes, and it has closed in dark,

---

[1] remarkably] so remarkably MS   [2] a very] very MS
[3] Poor youth! Poor youth!] ⟨He⟩ Poor youth! ⟨He little, little knows how near a cause he has for thinking so.⟩ Poor youth! MS

before he becomes quite aware of a woman crouching on the ground near[1] a wicket gate in a corner. The gate commands a cross bye-path, little used in the gloaming; and the figure must have been there all the time, though he has but gradually and lately made it out.

He strikes into that path, and walks up to the wicket. By the light of a lamp near it, he sees that the woman is of a haggard appearance, and that her weazen chin is resting on her hands, and that her eyes are staring— with an unwinking, blind sort of steadfastness—before her.

Always kindly, but moved to be unusually kind this evening, and having bestowed kind words on most of the children and aged people he has met, he at once bends down, and speaks to this woman.[2]

"Are you ill?"

"No, deary," she answers, without looking at him, and with no departure from her strange blind stare.

"Are you blind?"

"No, deary."

"Are you lost, homeless, faint? What is the matter, that you stay here in the cold so long, without moving?"

By slow and stiff efforts, she appears to contract her vision until it can rest upon him; and then a curious film passes over her, and she begins to shake.

He straightens himself, recoils a step, and looks down at her in a dread amazement; for he seems to know her.

"Good Heaven!" he thinks, next moment. "Like Jack that night!"

As he looks down at her, she looks up at him, and whimpers: "My lungs is weak;[3] my lungs is dreffle bad. Poor me, poor me, my cough is rattling dry!" And coughs in confirmation, horribly.

"Where do you come from?"

"Come from London, deary." (Her cough still rending her.)

"Where are you going to?"

"Back to London, deary. I came here, looking for a needle in a haystack, and I ain't found it. Look'ee, deary; give me three and sixpence, and don't you be afeard for me. I'll get back to London then, and trouble no one. I'm in a business.—Ah, me! It's slack, it's slack, and times is very bad!— but I can make a shift to live by it."

"Do you eat opium?"

"Smokes it," she replies with difficulty, still racked by her cough. "Give me three and sixpence, and I'll lay it out well, and get back. If you don't give me three and sixpence, don't give me a brass farden. And if you do give me three and sixpence, deary, I'll tell you something."

He counts the money from his pocket, and puts it in her hand. She instantly clutches it tight, and rises to her feet with a croaking laugh of satisfaction.

[1] near] by MS   [2] this woman] the woman MS   [3] weak] MS weakly 70-75

"Bless ye! Hark'ee, dear gen'lm'n. What's your Chris'en name?"

"Edwin."

"Edwin, Edwin, Edwin," she repeats, trailing off into a drowsy repetition of the word; and then asks suddenly: "Is the short of that name, Eddy?"

"It is sometimes called so," he replies, with the color starting to his face.

"Don't sweethearts call it so?" she asks, pondering.

"How should I know!"

"Haven't you a sweetheart, upon my soul?"

"None."

She is moving away with another "Bless ye, and thank'ee, deary!" when he adds: "You were to tell me something; you may as well do so."

"So I was, so I was. Well, then. Whisper. You be thankful that your name ain't Ned."

He looks at her, quite steadily, as he asks: "Why?"

"Because it's a bad name to have just now."

"How a bad name?"

"A threatened name. A dangerous name."

"The proverb says that threatened men live long," he tells her, lightly.

"Then Ned—so threatened is he, wherever he may be while I am[1] a talking to you, deary—should live to all eternity!" replies the woman.

She has leaned forward, to say it in his ear, with her forefinger shaking before his eyes, and now huddles herself together, and with another "Bless ye, and thank'ee!" goes away in the direction of the Travellers' Lodging House.

This is not an inspiriting close to a dull day. Alone, in a sequestered place, surrounded by vestiges of old time and decay, it rather has a tendency to call a shudder into being. He makes for the better lighted streets, and resolves as he walks on to say nothing of this to-night, but to mention it to Jack (who alone calls him Ned), as an odd coincidence, to-morrow; of course only as a coincidence, and not as anything better worth remembering.

Still, it holds to him, as many things much better worth remembering never did. He has another mile or so, to linger out before the dinner-hour; and, when he walks over the bridge and by the river, the woman's words are in the rising wind, in[2] the angry sky, in the troubled water, in[2] the flickering lights. There is some solemn echo of them, even in the Cathedral chime, which strikes a sudden surprise to his heart as he turns in under the archway of the Gate House.

And so *he* goes up the postern stair.

John Jasper passes a more agreeable[3] and cheerful day than either of his guests. Having no music-lessons to give in the holiday season, his time is

---

[1] I am] I'm MS   [2] in] and in MS
[3] agreeable] *not clear in* MS; *could be* equable

his own, but for the Cathedral services. He is early among the shopkeepers, ordering little table luxuries that his nephew likes. His nephew will not be with him long, he tells his provision-dealers, and so must be petted and made much of. While out on his hospitable preparations, he looks in on Mr. Sapsea; and mentions that dear Ned, and that inflammable young spark of Mr. Crisparkle's, are to dine at the Gate House to-day, and make up their difference. Mr. Sapsea is by no means friendly towards the inflammable young spark. He says that his complexion is "Un-English." And when Mr. Sapsea has once declared anything to be Un-English, he considers that thing everlastingly sunk in the bottomless pit.

John Jasper is truly sorry to hear Mr. Sapsea speak thus, for he knows right well that Mr. Sapsea never speaks without a meaning, and that he has a subtle trick of being right. Mr. Sapsea (by a very remarkable co-incidence) is of exactly that opinion.

Mr. Jasper is in beautiful voice this day. In the pathetic supplication to have his heart inclined to keep this law, he quite astonishes his fellows by his melodious power. He has never sung difficult music with such skill and harmony, as in this day's Anthem. His nervous temperament is occasionally prone to take difficult music a little too quickly; to-day, his time is perfect.

These results are probably attained through a grand composure of the spirits. The mere mechanism of his throat is a little tender, for he wears, both with his singing-robe and with his ordinary dress, a large black scarf of strong close-woven silk, slung loosely round his neck. But his composure is so noticeable, that Mr. Crisparkle speaks of it[1] as they come out from Vespers.

"I must thank you, Jasper, for the pleasure with which I have heard you to-day. Beautiful! Delightful! You could not have so outdone yourself, I hope, without being wonderfully well."

"I *am* wonderfully well."

"Nothing unequal," says the Minor Canon, with a smooth motion of his hand: "nothing unsteady, nothing forced, nothing avoided; all thoroughly done in a masterly manner, with perfect self-command."

"Thank you. I hope so, if it is not too much to say."

"One would think, Jasper, you had been trying a new medicine for that occasional indisposition of yours."

"No, really? That's well observed; for I have."

"Then stick to it, my good fellow," says Mr. Crisparkle, clapping him on the shoulder with friendly encouragement, "stick to it."

"I will."

"I congratulate you," Mr. Crisparkle pursues, as they come out of the Cathedral, "on all accounts."

"Thank you again. I will walk round to the Corner with you, if you

[1] of it] of it to himself MS

don't object; I have plenty of time before my company come; and I want to say a word to you, which I think you will not be displeased to hear."

"What is it?"

"Well. We were speaking, the other evening, of my black humours."

Mr. Crisparkle's face falls, and he shakes his head deploringly.

"I said, you know, that I should make you an antidote to those black humours; and you said you hoped I would consign them to the flames."

"And I still hope so, Jasper."

"With the best reason in the world! I mean to burn this year's Diary at the year's end."

"Because you——?" Mr. Crisparkle brightens greatly as he thus begins.[1]

"You anticipate me. Because I feel that I have been out of sorts, gloomy, bilious, brain-oppressed, whatever it may be. You said I had been exaggerative. So I have."

Mr. Crisparkle's brightened face brightens still more.

"I couldn't see it then, because I *was* out of sorts; but I am in a healthier state now, and I acknowledge it with genuine pleasure. I made a great deal of a very[2] little; that's the fact."

"It does me good," cries Mr. Crisparkle, "to hear you say it!"

"A man leading a monotonous life," Jasper proceeds, "and getting his nerves, or his stomach, out of order, dwells upon an idea until it loses its proportions. That was my case with the idea in question. So I shall burn the evidence of my case, when the book is full, and begin the next volume with a clearer vision."

"This is better," says Mr. Crisparkle, stopping at the steps of his own door to shake hands, "than I could have hoped!"

"Why, naturally," returns Jasper. "You had but little reason to hope that I should become more like yourself. You[3] are always training yourself to be, mind and body, as clear as crystal, and you always are, and never change; whereas, I am a muddy, solitary, moping weed. However, I have got over that mope. Shall I wait, while you ask if Mr. Neville has left for my place? If not, he and I may walk round together."

"I think," says Mr. Crisparkle, opening the entrance door with his key, "that he left some time ago; at least I know he left, and I think he has not come back. But I'll inquire. You won't come in?"

"My company wait," says[4] Jasper, with a smile.

The Minor Canon disappears, and in a few moments returns. As he thought, Mr. Neville has not come back; indeed, as he remembers now, Mr. Neville said he would probably go straight to the Gate House.

"Bad manners in a host!" says Jasper. "My company will be there before me! What will you bet that I don't find my company embracing?"

---

[1] begins] begins, and is cut short MS   [2] a very] very MS
[3] yourself. You] yourself; because you MS   [4] says] said 75

"I will bet—or I would, if I ever[1] did bet," returns Mr. Crisparkle, "that your company will have a gay entertainer this evening."[2]

Jasper nods, and laughs Good-night!

He retraces his steps to the Cathedral door, and turns down past it to the Gate House. He sings, in a low voice and with delicate expression, as he walks along. It still seems as if a false note were not within his power to-night, and as if nothing could hurry or retard him. Arriving thus, under the arched entrance of his dwelling, he pauses for an instant in the shelter to pull off that great black scarf, and hang it in a loop upon his arm. For that brief time, his face is knitted and stern. But it immediately clears,[3] as he resumes his singing, and his way.

And so *he* goes up the postern stair.

The red light burns steadily all the evening in the Lighthouse on the margin of the tide of busy life. Softened sounds and hum of traffic pass it and flow on irregularly into the lonely Precincts; but very little else goes by, save violent rushes of wind. It comes on to blow a boisterous gale.

The Precincts are never particularly well lighted; but the strong blasts of wind blowing out many of the lamps (in some instances shattering the frames too, and bringing the glass rattling to the ground), they are unusually dark to-night. The darkness is augmented and confused, by flying dust from the earth, dry twigs from the trees, and great ragged fragments from the rooks' nests up in the tower. The trees themselves so toss and creak, as this tangible part of the darkness madly whirls about, that they seem in peril of being torn out of the earth: while ever and again a crack, and a rushing fall, denote that some large branch has yielded to the storm.

No such power of wind has blown for many a winter night. Chimneys topple in the streets, and people hold to posts and corners, and to one another, to keep themselves upon their feet. The violent rushes abate not, but increase in frequency and fury until at midnight, when the streets are empty, the storm goes thundering along them, rattling at all the latches, and tearing at all the shutters, as if warning the people to get up and fly with it, rather than have the roofs brought down upon their brains.

Still, the red light burns steadily. Nothing is steady but the red light.

All through the night, the wind blows, and abates not. But early in the morning when there is barely enough light in the east to dim the stars, it begins to lull. From that time, with occasional wild charges, like a wounded monster dying, it drops and sinks; and at full daylight it is dead.

It is then seen that the hands of the Cathedral clock are torn off; that lead from the roof has been stripped away, rolled up, and blown into the Close; and that some stones have been displaced upon the summit of the great tower. Christmas morning though it be, it is necessary to send up

---

[1] I ever] ever I 73 75   [2] this evening] *not in* MS
[3] clears] *possibly* clears again MS *blotted*

workmen, to ascertain the extent of the damage done. These, led by Durdles, go aloft; while Mr. Tope and a crowd of early idlers gather down in Minor Canon Corner, shading their eyes and watching for their appearance up there.

This cluster is suddenly broken and put aside by the hands of Mr. Jasper; all the gazing eyes are brought down to the earth by his loudly inquiring of Mr. Crisparkle, at an open window:

"Where is my nephew?"

"He has not been here. Is he not with you?"

"No. He went down to the river last night, with Mr. Neville, to look at the storm, and has not been back. Call Mr. Neville!"

"He left this morning, early."

"Left this morning, early? Let me in, let me in!"

There is no more looking up at the tower, now.[1] All the assembled eyes are turned on Mr. Jasper, white, half dressed, panting, and clinging to the rail before the Minor Canon's house.

CHAPTER XV

IMPEACHED

NEVILLE LANDLESS had started so early and walked at so good a pace, that when the church bells began to ring in Cloisterham for morning service, he was eight miles away. As he wanted his breakfast by that time, having set forth on a crust of bread, he stopped at the next roadside tavern to refresh.

Visitors in want of breakfast—unless they were horses or cattle, for which class of guests there was preparation enough in the way of water-trough and hay—were so unusual at the sign of The Tilted Wagon, that it took a long time to get the wagon into the track of tea and toast and bacon. Neville, in the interval, sitting in a sanded parlor, wondering in how long a time after he had gone, the sneezy fire of damp fagots would begin to make somebody else warm.

Indeed, The Tilted Wagon, as a cool establishment on the top of a hill, where the ground before the door was puddled with damp hoofs and trodden straw; where a scolding landlady slapped a moist baby (with one red sock on and one wanting), in the bar; where the cheese was cast aground upon a shelf, in company with a mouldy tablecloth and a green-handled knife, in a sort of cast-iron canoe; where the pale-faced bread shed tears of crumb over its shipwreck in another canoe; where the family linen, half washed and half dried, led a public life of lying about; where everything to drink was drunk out of mugs, and everything else was

[1] now] *possibly deleted in* MS

suggestive of a rhyme to mugs; The Tilted Wagon, all these things considered, hardly kept its painted promise of providing good entertainment for Man and Beast. However, Man, in the present case, was not critical, but took what entertainment he could get, and went on again after a longer rest than he needed.

He stopped at some quarter of a mile from the house, hesitating whether to pursue the road, or to follow a cart-track between two high hedgerows, which led across the slope of a breezy heath, and evidently struck into the road again by-and-bye. He decided in favor of this latter track, and pursued it with some toil; the rise being steep, and the way worn into deep ruts.

He was labouring along, when he became aware of some other pedestrians behind him. As they were coming up at a faster pace than his, he stood aside, against one of the high banks, to let them pass. But their manner was very curious. Only four of them passed. Other four slackened speed, and loitered as intending to follow him when he should go on. The remainder of the party (half a dozen perhaps), turned, and went back at a great rate.

He looked at the four behind him, and he looked at the four before him. They all returned his look. He resumed his way. The four in advance went on, constantly looking back; the four in the rear came closing up.

When they all ranged out from the narrow track upon the open slope of the heath, and this order was maintained, let him diverge as he would to either side, there was no longer room to doubt that he was beset by these fellows. He stopped, as a last test; and they all stopped.

"Why do you attend upon me in this way?" he asked the whole body. "Are you a pack of thieves?"

"Don't answer him," said one of the number; he did not see which. "Better be quiet."[1]

"Better be quiet?"[1] repeated Neville. "Who said so?"

Nobody replied.

"It's good advice, whichever of you skulkers gave it," he went on angrily. "I will not submit to be penned in between four men there, and four men there. I wish to pass, and I mean to pass, those four in front."

They were all standing still: himself included.

"If eight men, or four men, or two men, set upon one," he proceeded, growing more enraged, "the one has no chance but to set his mark upon some of them. And by the Lord I'll do that little,[2] if I am interrupted any further!"

Shouldering his heavy stick, and quickening his pace, he shot on to pass the four ahead. The largest and strongest man of the number changed swiftly to the side on[3] which he came up, and dexterously closed with him and went down with him; but not before the heavy stick had descended smartly.

[1] quiet] quite quiet MS   [2] that little] MS after ⟨it⟩ it 70–75   [3] on] by MS

"Let him be!" said this man in a suppressed voice, as they struggled together on the grass. "Fair play! His is the build of a girl to mine, and he's got a weight strapped to his back besides. Let him alone. I'll manage him."

After a little rolling about, in a close scuffle which caused the faces of both to be besmeared with blood, the man took his knee from Neville's chest, and rose, saying: "There! Now take him arm-in-arm, any two of you!"

It was immediately done.

"As to our being a pack of thieves, Mr. Landless," said the man, as he spat out some blood, and wiped more from his face: "you know better than that, at midday. We wouldn't have touched you, if you hadn't forced us. We're going to take you round to the high road, anyhow, and you'll find help enough against thieves there, if you want it. Wipe his face somebody; see how it's a trickling down him!"

When his face was cleansed, Neville recognized in the speaker, Joe, driver of the Cloisterham omnibus, whom he had seen but once, and that on the day of his arrival.

"And what I recommend you for the present, is, don't talk, Mr. Landless. You'll find a friend waiting for you, at the high road—gone ahead by the other way when we split into two parties—and you had much better say nothing till you come up with him. Bring that stick along, somebody else, and let's be moving!"

Utterly bewildered, Neville stared around him and said not a word. Walking between his two conductors, who held his arms in theirs, he went on, as in a dream, until they came again into the high road, and into the midst of a little group of people. The men who had turned back, were among the group; and its central figures were Mr. Jasper and Mr. Crisparkle. Neville's conductors took him up to the Minor Canon, and there released him, as an act of deference to that gentleman.

"What is all this, sir? What is the matter? I feel as if I had lost my senses!" cried Neville, the group closing in around him.

"Where is my nephew?" asked Mr. Jasper, wildly.

"Where is your nephew?" repeated Neville. "Why do you ask me?"

"I ask you," retorted Jasper, "because you were the last person in his company, and he is not to be found."

"Not to be found!" cried Neville, aghast.

"Stay, stay," said Mr. Crisparkle. "Permit me, Jasper. Mr. Neville, you are confounded; collect your thoughts; it is of great importance that you should collect your thoughts; attend to me."

"I will try, sir, but I seem mad."

"You left Mr. Jasper's[1] last night, with Edwin Drood?"

"Yes."

---

[1] Mr. Jasper's] Mr. Jasper 73 75

"At what hour?"

"Was it at twelve o'clock?" asked Neville, with his hand to his confused head, and appealing to Jasper.

"Quite right," said Mr. Crisparkle; "the hour Mr. Jasper has already named to me. You went down to the river together?"

"Undoubtedly. To see the action of the wind there."

"What followed? How long did you stay there?"

"About ten minutes; I should say not more. We then walked together to your house, and he took leave of me at the door."

"Did he say that he was going down to the river again?"

"No. He said that he was going straight back."

The bystanders looked at one another, and at Mr. Crisparkle. To whom, Mr. Jasper, who had been intently[1] watching Neville, said: in a low distinct suspicious voice: "What are those stains upon his dress?"

All eyes were turned towards the blood upon his clothes.

"And here are the same stains upon this stick!" said Jasper, taking it from the hand of the man who held it. "I know the stick to be his, and he carried it last night. What does this mean?"

"In the name of God, say what it means, Neville!" urged Mr. Crisparkle.

"That man and I," said Neville, pointing out his late adversary, "had a struggle for the stick just now, and you may see the same marks on him, sir. What was I to suppose, when I found myself molested by eight people? Could I dream of the true reason when they would give me none at all?"

They admitted that they had thought it discreet to be silent, and that the struggle had taken place. And yet the very men who had seen it, looked darkly at the smears which the bright cold air had already dried.

"We must return, Neville," said Mr. Crisparkle; "of course you will be glad to come back to clear yourself?"

"Of course, sir."

"Mr. Landless will walk at my side," the Minor Canon continued, looking around him. "Come, Neville!"

They set forth on the walk back; and the others, with one exception, straggled after them at various distances. Jasper walked on the other side of Neville, and never quitted that position. He was silent, while Mr. Crisparkle more than once repeated his former questions, and while Neville repeated his former answers; also, while they both hazarded some explanatory conjectures. He was obstinately silent, because Mr. Crisparkle's manner directly appealed to him to take some part in the discussion, and no appeal would move his fixed[2] face. When they drew near to the city, and it was suggested by the Minor Canon that they might do well in calling on the Mayor at once, he assented with a stern nod; but he spake no word until they stood in Mr. Sapsea's parlor.

---

[1] intently] MS intensely 70-75   [2] fixed] ⟨lowering⟩ ⟨brooding⟩ lowering MS

Mr. Sapsea being informed by Mr. Crisparkle of the circumstances under which they desired to make a voluntary statement before him, Mr. Jasper broke silence by declaring that he placed his whole reliance, humanly speaking, on Mr. Sapsea's penetration. There was no conceivable reason why his nephew should have suddenly absconded, unless Mr. Sapsea could suggest one, and then he would defer. There was no intelligible likelihood of his having returned to the river, and been accidentally drowned in the dark, unless it should appear likely to Mr. Sapsea, and then again he would defer. He washed his hands as clean as he could, of all horrible suspicions, unless it should appear to Mr. Sapsea that some such were inseparable from his last companion before his disappearance (not on good terms with previously), and then, once more, he would defer. His own state of mind, he being[1] distracted with doubts, and labouring under dismal apprehensions, was not to be safely trusted; but Mr. Sapsea's was.

Mr. Sapsea expressed his opinion that the case had a dark look; in short (and here his eyes rested full on Neville's countenance), an Un-English complexion. Having made this grand point, he wandered into a denser haze and maze of nonsense than even a mayor might have been expected to disport himself in, and came out of it with the brilliant discovery that to take the life of a fellow-creature was to take something that didn't belong to you. He wavered whether or no he should at once issue his warrant for the committal of Neville Landless to jail, under circumstances of grave suspicion; and he might have gone so far as to do it but for the indignant protest of the Minor Canon: who undertook for the young man's remaining in his own house, and being produced by his own hands, whenever demanded. Mr. Jasper then understood Mr. Sapsea to suggest that the river should be dragged, that its banks should be rigidly examined, that particulars of the disappearance should be sent to all outlying places and to London, and that placards and advertisements should be widely circulated imploring Edwin Drood, if for any unknown reason he had withdrawn himself from his uncle's home and society, to take pity on that loving kinsman's sore bereavement and distress, and somehow inform him that he was yet alive. Mr. Sapsea was perfectly understood, for this was exactly his meaning (though he had said nothing about it); and measures were taken towards all these ends immediately.

It would be difficult to determine which was the more oppressed with horror and amazement: Neville Landless, or John Jasper. But that Jasper's position forced him to be active, while Neville's forced him to be passive, there would have been nothing to choose between them. Each was bowed down and broken.

With the earliest light of the next morning, men were at work upon the river, and other men—most of whom volunteered for the service—were

---

[1] being] *not in* MS

examining the banks. All the livelong day, the search went on; upon the river, with barge and pole, and drag and net; upon the muddy and rushy shore, with jack-boot,[1] hatchet, spade, rope, dogs, and all imaginable appliances. Even at night, the river was specked with lanterns, and lurid with fires; far-off creeks, into which the tide washed as it changed, had their knots of watchers, listening to the lapping of the stream, and looking out for any burden it might bear; remote shingly causeways near the sea, and lonely points off which there was a race of water, had their unwonted flaring cressets and rough-coated figures when the next day dawned; but no trace of Edwin Drood revisited the light of the sun.

All that day, again, the search went on. Now, in barge and boat; and now ashore among the osiers, or tramping amidst mud and stakes and jagged stones in low-lying places, where solitary watermarks and signals of strange shapes showed like spectres, John Jasper worked and toiled. But to no purpose; for still no trace of Edwin Drood revisited the light of the sun.

Setting his watches for that night again, so that vigilant eyes should be kept on every change of tide, he went home exhausted. Unkempt and disordered, bedaubed with mud that had dried upon him, and with much of his clothing torn to rags, he had but just dropped into his easy chair, when Mr. Grewgious stood before him.

"This is strange news," said Mr. Grewgious.

"Strange and fearful news."

Jasper had merely lifted up his heavy eyes to say it, and now dropped them again as he drooped, worn out, over one side of his easy chair.

Mr. Grewgious smoothed his head and face, and stood looking at the fire.

"How is your ward?" asked Jasper, after a time, in a faint, fatigued voice.

"Poor little thing! You may imagine her condition."

"Have you seen his sister?" inquired Jasper, as before.

"Whose?"

The curtness of the counter-question, and the cool slow manner in which, as he put it, Mr. Grewgious moved his eyes from the fire to his companion's face, might at any other time have been exasperating. In his depression and exhaustion, Jasper merely opened his eyes to say: "The suspected young man's."

"Do you suspect him?" asked Mr. Grewgious.

"I don't know what to think. I cannot make up my mind."

"Nor I," said Mr. Grewgious. "But as you spoke of him as the suspected young man, I thought you _had_ made up your mind.—I have just left Miss Landless."

"What is her state?"

<hr>

[1] jack-boot] jack-boots 75

"Defiance of all suspicion, and unbounded faith in her brother."

"Poor thing!"

"However," pursued Mr. Grewgious, "it is not of her that I came to speak. It is of my ward. I have a communication to make that will surprise you. At least, it has surprised me."

Jasper, with a groaning sigh, turned wearily in his chair.

"Shall I put it off till to-morrow?" said Mr. Grewgious. "Mind! I warn you, that I think it will surprise you!"

More attention and concentration came into John Jasper's eyes as they caught sight of Mr. Grewgious smoothing his head again, and again looking at the fire; but now, with a compressed and determined mouth.

"What is it?" demanded Jasper, becoming upright in his chair.

"To be sure," said Mr. Grewgious, provokingly slowly and internally, as he kept his eyes on the fire: "I might have known it sooner; she gave me the opening; but I am such an exceedingly Angular man, that it never occurred to me; I took all for granted."

"What is it?" demanded Jasper, once more.

Mr. Grewgious, alternately opening and shutting the palms of his hands as he warmed them at the fire, and looking fixedly at him sideways, and never changing either his action or his look in all that followed, went on to reply.

"This young couple, the lost youth and Miss Rosa, my ward, though so long betrothed, and so long recognizing their betrothal, and so near being married——"

Mr. Grewgious saw a staring white face, and two quivering white lips, in the easy chair, and saw two muddy hands gripping its sides. But for the hands, he might have thought he had never seen the face.

"—This young couple came gradually to the discovery, (made on both sides pretty equally, I think), that they would be happier and better, both in their present and their future lives, as affectionate friends, or say rather as brother and sister, than as husband and wife."

Mr. Grewgious saw a lead-colored face in the easy chair, and on its surface dreadful starting drops or bubbles, as if of steel.

"This young couple formed at length the healthy resolution of interchanging their discoveries, openly, sensibly, and tenderly. They met for that purpose. After some innocent and generous talk, they agreed to dissolve their existing, and their intended, relations, for ever and ever."

Mr. Grewgious saw a ghastly figure rise, open-mouthed, from the easy chair, and lift its outspread hands towards its head.

"One of this young couple, and that one your nephew, fearful, however, that in the tenderness of your affection for him you would be bitterly disappointed by so wide a departure from his projected life, forbore to tell you the secret, for a few days, and left it to be disclosed by me, when I should come down to speak to you, and he would be gone. I speak to you, and he IS[1] gone."

Mr. Grewgious saw the ghastly figure throw back its head, clutch its hair with its hands, and turn with a writhing action from him.

"I have now said all I have to say: except that this young couple parted, firmly,[2] though not without tears and sorrow, on the evening when you last saw them together."

Mr. Grewgious heard a terrible shriek, and saw no ghastly figure, sitting or standing; saw nothing but a heap of torn and miry clothes upon the floor.

Not changing his action even then, he opened and shut the palms of his hands as he warmed them, and looked down at it.

CHAPTER XVI

DEVOTED

WHEN John Jasper recovered from his fit or swoon, he found himself being tended by Mr. and Mrs. Tope, whom his visitor had summoned for the purpose. His visitor, wooden of aspect, sat stiffly in a chair, with his hands upon his knees, watching his recovery.

"There! You've come to, nicely now, sir," said the tearful Mrs. Tope; "you were thoroughly worn out, and no wonder!"

"A man," said Mr. Grewgious, with his usual air of repeating a lesson, "cannot have his rest broken, and his mind cruelly tormented, and his body overtaxed by fatigue, without being thoroughly worn out."

"I fear I have alarmed you?" Jasper apologized faintly, when he was helped into his easy chair.

"Not at all, I thank you," answered Mr. Grewgious.

"You are too considerate."

"Not at all, I thank you," answered Mr.[3] Grewgious again.

"You must take some wine, sir," said Mrs. Tope, "and the jelly that I had[4] ready for you, and that you wouldn't put your lips to at noon, though I warned you what would come of it, you know, and you not breakfasted; and you must have a wing of the roast fowl that has[5] been put back twenty times if it's been put back once. It shall all be on table in five minutes, and this good gentleman belike will stop and see you take it."

This good gentleman replied with a snort, which might mean yes, or no, or anything, or nothing, and which Mrs. Tope would have found

---

[1] IS] is 73 75   [2] parted, firmly] firmly parted MS
[3] Mr.] *om.* 73 75   [4] had] had got MS *probable not certain*
[5] that has] that's MS

MR. GREWGIOUS HAS HIS SUSPICIONS

highly mystifying, but that her attention was divided by the service of the table.

"You will take something with me?" said Jasper, as the cloth was laid.

"I couldn't get a morsel down my throat, I thank you," answered Mr. Grewgious.

Jasper both ate and drank almost voraciously. Combined with the hurry in his mode of doing it, was an evident indifference to the taste of what he took, suggesting that he ate and drank to fortify himself against any other failure of the spirits, far more than to gratify his palate. Mr. Grewgious in the meantime sat upright, with no expression in his face, and a hard kind of imperturbably polite protest all over him: as though he would have said, in reply to some invitation to discourse: "I couldn't originate the faintest approach to an observation on any subject whatever, I thank you."

"Do you know," said Jasper, when he had pushed away his plate and glass, and had sat meditating for a few minutes: "do you know that I find some crumbs of comfort in the communication with which you have so much amazed me?"

"*Do* you?" returned Mr. Grewgious; pretty plainly adding the unspoken clause: "I don't, I thank you!"

"After recovering from the shock of a piece of news of my dear boy, so entirely unexpected, and so destructive of all the castles[1] I had built for him; and after having had time to think of it; yes."

"I shall be glad to pick up your crumbs," said Mr. Grewgious, dryly.

"Is there not, or is there—if I deceive myself, tell me so, and shorten my pain—is there not, or is there, hope that, finding himself in this new position, and becoming sensitively alive to the awkward burden of explanation, in this quarter, and that, and the other, with which it would load him, he avoided the awkwardness, and took to flight?"

"Such a thing might be," said Mr. Grewgious, pondering.

"Such a thing has been. I have read of cases in which people, rather than face a seven days' wonder, and have to account for themselves to the idle and impertinent,[2] have taken themselves away, and been long unheard of."

"I believe such things have happened," said Mr. Grewgious, pondering still.

"When I had, and could have, no suspicion," pursued Jasper, eagerly following the new track, "that the dear lost boy had with-held[3] anything from me—most of all, such a leading matter as this—what gleam of light was there for me in the whole black sky? When I supposed that his intended wife was here, and his marriage close at hand, how could I entertain the possibility of his voluntarily leaving this place, in a manner that

[1] castles] airy castles MS
[2] impertinent] importunate ES (*possibly printed in proof*)
[3] dear lost boy had with-held] dear boy with-held MS

would be so unaccountable, capricious, and cruel? But now that I know
what you have told me, is there no little chink through which day pierces?
Supposing him to have disappeared of his own act, is not his disappearance more accountable and less cruel? The fact of his having just parted
from your ward, is in itself a sort of reason for his going away. It does not
make his mysterious departure the less cruel to me, it is true; but it
relieves it of cruelty to her."

Mr. Grewgious could not but assent to this.

"And even as to me," continued Jasper, still pursuing the new track,
with ardour, and, as he did so, brightening with hope: "he knew that you
were coming to me; he knew that you were entrusted to tell me what you
have told me; if your doing so has awakened a new train of thought in my
perplexed mind, it reasonably follows that, from the same premises, he
might have foreseen the inferences that I should draw. Grant that he did
foresee them; and¹ even the cruelty to me—and who am I!—John Jasper,
Music-Master!—vanishes."

Once more, Mr. Grewgious could not but assent to this.

"I have had my distrusts, and terrible distrusts they have been," said
Jasper; "but your disclosure, overpowering as it was at first—showing me
that my own dear boy had had a great disappointing reservation from me,
who so fondly loved him—kindles hope within me. You do not extinguish
it when I state it, but admit it to be a reasonable hope. I begin to believe
it possible:" here² he clasped his hands: "that he may have disappeared
from among us of his own accord, and that he may yet be alive and well!"

Mr. Crisparkle came in at the moment. To whom Mr. Jasper repeated:

"I begin to believe it possible that he may have disappeared of his own
accord, and may yet be alive and well!"

Mr. Crisparkle taking a seat, and inquiring: "Why so?" Mr. Jasper
repeated the arguments he had just set forth. If they had been less plausible
than they were, the good Minor Canon's mind would have been in a state
of preparation to receive them, as exculpatory of his unfortunate pupil.
But he, too, did really attach great importance to the lost young man's
having been, so immediately before his disappearance, placed in a new
and embarrassing relation towards every one acquainted with his projects
and affairs; and the fact seemed to him to present the question in a new
light.

"I stated to Mr. Sapsea, when we waited on him," said Jasper: as he
really had done: "that there was no quarrel or difference between the two
young men at their last meeting. We all know that their first meeting was,
unfortunately, very far from amicable; but all went smoothly and quietly
when they were last together at my house. My dear boy was not in his
usual spirits; he was depressed—I noticed that—and I am bound henceforth to dwell upon the circumstance the more, now that I know there was

¹ and] *probably* and then MS *blotted*   ² here] and here MS

a special reason for his being depressed: a reason, moreover, which may possibly have induced him to absent himself."

"I pray to Heaven it may turn out so!" exclaimed Mr. Crisparkle.

"*I* pray to Heaven it may turn out so!" repeated Jasper. "You know—and Mr. Grewgious[1] should now know likewise—that I took a great[2] prepossession against Mr. Neville Landless, arising out of his furious conduct on that first occasion. You know that I came to you, extremely apprehensive, on my dear boy's behalf, of his mad violence. You know that I even entered in my Diary, and showed the entry to you, that I had dark forebodings against him. Mr. Grewgious[1] ought to be possessed of the whole case. He shall not, through any suppression of mine, be informed of a part of it, and kept in ignorance of another part of it. I wish him to be good enough to understand that the communication he has made to me has hopefully influenced my mind, in spite of its having been, before this mysterious occurrence took place, profoundly impressed against young Landless."

This fairness troubled the Minor Canon much. He felt that he was not as open in his own dealing. He charged against himself reproachfully that he had suppressed, so far, the two points of a second strong outbreak of temper against Edwin Drood on the part of Neville, and of the passion of jealousy having, to his own certain knowledge, flamed up in Neville's breast against him. He was convinced of Neville's innocence of any part in the ugly disappearance, and yet so many little circumstances combined so woefully against him, that he dreaded to add two more to their cumulative weight. He was among the truest of men; but he had been balancing in his mind, much to its distress, whether his volunteering to tell these two fragments of truth, at this time, would not be tantamount to a piecing together of falsehood in the place of truth.

However,[3] here was a model before him. He hesitated no longer. Addressing Mr. Grewgious, as one placed in authority by the revelation he had brought to bear on the mystery (and surpassingly Angular Mr. Grewgious became when he found himself in that unexpected position), Mr. Crisparkle bore his testimony to Mr. Jasper's strict sense of justice, and, expressing his absolute confidence in the complete clearance of his pupil from the least taint of suspicion, sooner or later, avowed that his confidence in that young gentleman had been formed, in spite of his confidential knowledge that his temper was of the hottest and fiercest, and that it was directly incensed[4] against Mr. Jasper's nephew, by the circumstance of his romantically supposing himself to be enamoured of the same young lady. The sanguine reaction manifest in Mr. Jasper was proof even against this unlooked-for declaration. It turned him paler; but he repeated that he would cling to the hope he had derived from Mr.

[1] Mr. Grewgious] Mr Grewgious here MS   [2] great] strong MS
[3] However,] But MS   [4] directly incensed] undeniably irritated MS

Grewgious; and that if no trace of his dear boy were found, leading to the dreadful inference that he had been made away with, he would cherish unto the last stretch of possibility, the idea, that he might have absconded of his own wild will.

Now, it fell out that Mr. Crisparkle, going away from this conference still very uneasy in his mind, and very much troubled on behalf of the young man whom he held as a kind of prisoner in his own house,[1] took a memorable night walk.

He walked to Cloisterham Weir.

He[2] often did so, and consequently there was nothing remarkable in his footsteps tending that way. But the preoccupation of his mind so hindered him from planning any walk, or taking heed of the objects he passed, that his first consciousness of being near the Weir, was derived from the sound of the falling water close at hand.

"How did I come here!" was his first thought, as he stopped.

"Why did I come here!" was his second.

Then, he stood intently listening to the water. A familiar passage in his reading, about airy tongues that syllable men's names, rose so unbidden to his ear, that he put it from him with his hand, as if it were tangible.[3]

It was starlight.[4] The Weir was full two miles above the spot to which the young men had repaired to watch the storm. No search had been made up here, for the tide had been running strongly down, at that time of the night of Christmas Eve, and the likeliest places for the discovery of a body, if a fatal accident had happened under such circumstances, all lay—both when the tide ebbed, and when it flowed again—between that spot and the sea. The water came over the Weir, with its usual sound on a cold starlight night, and little could be seen of it; yet Mr. Crisparkle had a strange idea that something unusual hung about the place.

He reasoned with himself: What was it? Where was it? Put it to the proof. Which sense did it address?

No sense reported anything unusual there. He listened again, and his sense of hearing again checked the water coming over the Weir, with its usual sound on a cold starlight night.[5]

Knowing very well that the mystery with which his mind was occupied, might of itself give the place this haunted air, he strained those hawk's eyes of his for the correction of his fancy.[6] He got closer to the Weir, and peered at its well-known posts and timbers. Nothing in the least unusual was remotely shadowed forth to the sense of sight.[7] But he resolved that he would come back early in the morning.

[1] house] house, let him gloss it as he would MS
[2] He] no new paragraph in MS
[3] "How did . . . tangible.] not in MS   [4] starlight] starlight, and he stopped MS
[5] He reasoned . . . starlight night.] not in MS
[6] fancy] MS sight 70–75   [7] to the sense of sight] MS om. 70–75

The Weir ran through his broken sleep, all night, and he was back again at sunrise. It was a bright frosty morning. The[1] whole composition before him, when he stood where he had stood last night, was clearly discernible in its minutest[2] details. He had surveyed it closely for some minutes, and was about to withdraw his eyes, when they were attracted keenly to one spot.

He turned his back upon the Weir, and looked far away at the sky, and at the earth, and then looked again at that one spot. It caught his sight again immediately, and he concentrated his vision upon it. He could not lose it now, though it was but such a speck in the landscape. It fascinated his sight. His hands began plucking off his coat.[3] For it struck him that at that spot—a corner of the Weir—something glistened, which did not move and come over with the glistening water-drops, but remained stationary.

He assured himself of this, he threw off his clothes, he plunged into the icy water, and swam for the spot. Climbing the timbers, he took from them, caught among their interstices by its chain, a gold watch, bearing engraved upon its back, E. D.

He brought the watch to the bank, swam to the Weir again, climbed it, and dived off. He knew every hole and corner of all the depths, and dived and dived and dived, until he could bear the cold no more. His notion was, that he would find the body; he[4] only found a shirt-pin sticking in some mud and ooze.

With these discoveries he returned to Cloisterham, and, taking Neville Landless with him, went straight to the Mayor. Mr. Jasper was sent for, the watch and shirt-pin were identified, Neville was detained, and the wildest frenzy and fatuity of evil report arose[5] against him. He was of that vindictive and violent nature, that but for his poor sister, who alone had influence over him, and out of whose sight he was never to be trusted, he would be in the daily commission of murder. Before coming to England he had caused to be whipped to death sundry "Natives"—nomadic persons, encamping now[6] in Asia, now in Africa, now in the West Indies, and now at the North Pole—vaguely supposed in Cloisterham to be always black, always of great virtue,[7] always calling themselves Me, and everybody else Massa or Missie (according to sex), and always reading tracts of the ob- scurest meaning,[8] in broken English, but always accurately[9] understanding them in the purest mother tongue. He had nearly brought Mrs. Crisp- arkle's grey hairs with sorrow to the grave. (Those[10] original expressions

---

[1] morning. The] morning, and the MS   [2] minutest] minute MS
[3] He turned . . . coat.] *not in* MS; *no new paragraph in* MS *here*
[4] body; he] body; but he MS ES   [5] arose] rose 73 75
[6] encamping now] now encamping MS *on verso from* now encamping *to* North Pole
[7] virtue] virtue, always undressed in coarse muslin MS
[8] of the obscurest meaning,] *not in* MS *which has* ⟨and always posing overseers with⟩
[9] accurately] *not in* MS ES   [10] Those] *possibly* These MS

were Mr. Sapsea's.) He had repeatedly said he would have Mr. Crisparkle's
life. He had repeatedly said he would have everybody's life, and become in
effect the last man. He had been brought down to Cloisterham, from
London, by an eminent Philanthropist, and why? Because that Philanthropist had expressly declared: "I owe it to my fellow-creatures that he
should be, in the words of BENTHAM, where he is the cause of the greatest
danger to the smallest number."

These dropping shots from the blunderbusses of blunderheadedness
might not have hit him in a vital place. But he had to stand against a trained
and well-directed fire of arms of precision too. He had notoriously
threatened the lost young man, and had, according to the showing of his
own faithful friend and tutor who strove so hard for him, a cause of bitter
animosity (created by himself, and stated by himself), against that ill-
starred fellow. He had armed himself with an offensive weapon for the
fatal night, and he had gone off early in the morning, after making preparations for departure. He had been found with traces of blood on him;
truly, they might have been wholly caused as he represented, but they
might not, also. On a search-warrant being issued for the examination of
his room, clothes, and so forth, it was discovered that he had destroyed all
his papers, and rearranged all his possessions, on the very afternoon of the
disappearance. The watch found at the Weir was challenged by the
jeweller as one he had wound and set for Edwin Drood, at twenty minutes
past two on that same afternoon; and it had run down, before being cast
into the water; and it was the jeweller's positive opinion that it had never
been re-wound. This would justify the hypothesis that the watch was
taken from him not long after he left Mr. Jasper's house at midnight, in
company with the last person seen with him, and that it had been thrown
away after being retained some hours. Why thrown away? If he had been
murdered, and so artfully disfigured, or concealed, or both, as that the
murderer hoped identification to be impossible, except from something
that he wore, assuredly the murderer would seek to remove from the body
the most lasting, the best known, and the most easily recognizable, things
upon it. Those things would be the watch and shirt-pin. As to his opportunities of casting them into the river; if he were the object of these
suspicions, they were easy. For, he had been seen by many persons, wandering about on that side of the city—indeed on all sides of it—in a miserable
and seemingly half-distracted manner. As to the choice of the spot, obviously such criminating evidence had better take its chance of being
found anywhere, rather than upon himself, or in his possession. Concerning the reconciliatory nature of the appointed meeting between the two
young men, very little could be made of that, in young Landless's favor;
for, it distinctly appeared that the meeting originated, not with him, but
with Mr. Crisparkle, and that it had been[1] urged on by Mr. Crisparkle;

---

[1] had been] was MS ES

and who could say how unwillingly, or in what ill-conditioned mood, his enforced pupil had[1] gone to it? The more his case was looked into, the weaker it became in every point. Even the broad suggestion that the lost young man had absconded, was rendered additionally improbable on the showing of the young lady from whom he had so lately parted; for, what did she say, with great earnestness and sorrow, when interrogated? That he had, expressly and enthusiastically, planned with her, that he would await the arrival of her guardian, Mr. Grewgious. And yet, be it observed, he disappeared before that gentleman appeared.

On the suspicions thus urged and supported, Neville was detained and re-detained, and the search was pressed on every hand, and Jasper laboured night and day. But nothing more was found. No discovery being made which proved the lost man to be dead, it at length became necessary to release the person suspected of having made away with him. Neville[2] was set at large. Then, a consequence ensued which Mr. Crisparkle had too well foreseen. Neville must leave the place, for the place shunned him and cast him out. Even had it not been so, the dear old china shepherdess would have worried herself to death with fears for her son, and with general trepidation occasioned by their having such an inmate. Even had that not been so, the authority to which the Minor Canon deferred officially,[3] would have settled the point.

"Mr. Crisparkle," quoth the Dean, "human justice may err, but it must act according to its lights. The days of taking sanctuary are past. This young man must not take sanctuary with us."

"You mean that he must leave my house, sir?"

"Mr. Crisparkle," returned the prudent Dean, "I claim no authority in your house. I merely confer with you, on the painful necessity you find yourself under, of depriving this young man of the great advantages of your counsel and instruction."

"It is very lamentable, sir," Mr. Crisparkle represented.

"Very much so," the Dean assented.

"And if it be a necessity—" Mr. Crisparkle faltered.

"As you unfortunately find it to be," returned the Dean.[4]

Mr. Crisparkle bowed submissively. "It is hard to prejudge his case, sir, but I am sensible that——"

"Just so. Perfectly. As you say, Mr. Crisparkle," interposed the Dean, nodding his head smoothly, "there is nothing else to be done. No doubt, no doubt. There is no alternative, as your good sense has discovered."

"I am entirely satisfied of his perfect innocence, sir, nevertheless."

"We-e-ell!" said the Dean, in a more confidential tone, and slightly glancing around him, "I would not say so, generally. Not generally.

---

[1] had] might have MS   [2] him. Neville] him and Neville MS
[3] deferred officially] so deferred on all occasions MS
[4] "It is very lamentable . . . returned the Dean.] *not in* MS

Enough of suspicion attaches to him to—no, I think I would not say so, generally."

Mr. Crisparkle bowed again.

"It does not become us, perhaps," pursued the Dean, "to be partizans. Not partizans. We clergy keep our hearts warm and our heads cool, and we hold a judicious middle course."

"I hope you do not object, sir, to my having stated in public, emphatically, that he will reappear here, whenever any new suspicion may be awakened, or any new circumstance may come to light in this extraordinary matter?"

"Not at all," returned the Dean. "And yet, do you know, I don't think," with a very nice and[1] neat emphasis on those two words: "I *don't think* I would state it, emphatically. State it? Ye-e-es! But emphatically? No-o-o. I *think* not. In point of fact, Mr. Crisparkle, keeping our hearts warm and our heads cool, we clergy[2] need do nothing emphatically."

So, Minor Canon Row knew Neville Landless no more; and he went whithersoever he would, or could, with a blight upon his name and fame.

It was not until then that John Jasper silently resumed his place in the choir. Haggard and red-eyed, his hopes plainly had deserted him, his sanguine mood was gone, and all his worst misgivings had come back. A day or two afterwards, while unrobing, he took his Diary from a pocket of his coat, turned the leaves, and with an expressive[3] look, and without one spoken word, handed this entry to Mr. Crisparkle to read:

"My dear boy is murdered. The discovery of the watch and shirt-pin convinces me that he was murdered that night, and that his jewellery was taken from him to prevent identification[4] by its means. All the delusive hopes I had founded on his separation from his betrothed wife, I give to the winds. They perish before this fatal discovery. I now swear, and record the oath on this page, That I nevermore will discuss this mystery with any human creature, until I hold the clue to it in my hand. That I never will relax in my secresy or in my search. That I will fasten the crime of the murder of my dear dead boy, upon the murderer. And That I devote myself to his destruction."

---

[1] and] *not in* MS
[3] expressive] MS impressive 70–75
END OF No. IV

[2] clergy] *not in* MS ES
[4] identification] his identification MS

CHAPTER XVII

PHILANTHROPY, PROFESSIONAL AND UNPROFESSIONAL[1]

FULL half a year had come and gone, and Mr. Crisparkle sat in a waiting-room in the London chief offices of the Haven of Philanthropy, until he could have audience of Mr. Honeythunder.

In his college-days of athletic exercises, Mr. Crisparkle had known professors of the Noble Art of fisticuffs, and had attended two or three of their gloved gatherings. He had now an opportunity of observing that as to the phrenological formation of the backs of their heads, the Professing Philanthropists were uncommonly like the Pugilists. In the development of all those organs which constitute, or attend, a propensity to "pitch into" your fellow-creatures, the Philanthropists were remarkably favored. There were several Professors passing in and out, with exactly the aggressive air upon them of being ready for a turn-up with any Novice who might happen to be on hand, that Mr. Crisparkle well remembered in the circles of the Fancy. Preparations were in progress for a moral little Mill somewhere on[2] the rural circuit, and other Professors were backing this or that Heavy-Weight as good for such or such speech-making hits, so very much after the manner of the sporting publicans that the intended Resolutions might have been Rounds. In an official manager of these displays much celebrated for his platform tactics, Mr. Crisparkle recognized (in a suit of black) the counterpart of a deceased benefactor of his species, an eminent public character, once known to fame as Frosty-faced Fogo,[3] who in days of yore superintended the formation of the magic circle with the ropes and stakes. There were only three conditions of resemblance wanting between these Professors and those. Firstly, the Philanthropists were in very bad training: much too fleshy, and presenting, both in face and figure, a superabundance of what is known to Pugilistic Experts as Suet Pudding. Secondly, the Philanthropists had not the good temper[4] of the Pugilists, and used worse language. Thirdly, their fighting code stood in great need of revision, as empowering them not only to bore their man to the ropes, but to bore him to the confines of distraction; also to hit him when he was down, hit him anywhere and anyhow, kick him, stamp upon him, gouge him, and maul him behind his

Proofs to the printers start here. The symbol P denotes proof as printed. Where a divergence is recorded between P and 70, as at n. 4 below, it is to be understood that the alteration came in as a proof-correction, unless a specific note to the contrary is given. Passages deleted as 'over-matter' in proof are retained in the present text as in 70

[1] PROFESSIONAL AND UNPROFESSIONAL] ⟨IN SEVERAL PHASES⟩ PROFESSIONAL AND UNPRO-
FESSIONAL MS
[2] on] in P
[3] an eminent . . . Fogo] *deleted in* P   [4] temper] tempers MS P

back without mercy. In these last particulars[1] the Professors of the Noble Art were much nobler than the Professors of Philanthropy.

Mr. Crisparkle was so completely lost in musing on these similarities and dissimilarities, at the same time watching the crowd which came and went,[2] always, as it seemed, on errands of antagonistically snatching something from somebody, and never giving anything to anybody:[3] that his name was twice[4] called before he heard it. On his at length responding, he was shown by a miserably[5] shabby and underpaid stipendiary Philanthropist (who could hardly have done worse if he had taken service with a declared enemy[6] of the human race) to Mr. Honeythunder's room.

"Sir," said Mr. Honeythunder, in his tremendous voice, like a schoolmaster issuing orders to a boy of whom he had a bad opinion, "sit down."

Mr. Crisparkle seated himself.

Mr. Honeythunder, having signed the remaining few score of a few thousand circulars, calling upon a corresponding number of families without means to come forward, stump up instantly, and be Philanthropists, or go to the Devil, another shabby stipendiary Philanthropist (highly disinterested, if in earnest) gathered these into a basket and walked off with them.[7]

"Now, Mr. Crisparkle," said Mr. Honeythunder, turning his chair half round towards him when they were alone,[8] and squaring his arms with his hands on his knees, and his brows knitted, as if he added, I am going to make short work of *you*: "Now, Mr. Crisparkle, we entertain different views, you and I, sir, of the sanctity of human life."

"Do we?" returned the Minor Canon.[9]

"We do, sir."

"Might I ask you," said the Minor Canon: "what are your views on that subject?"

"That human life is a thing to be held sacred, sir."

"Might I ask you," pursued the Minor Canon as before: "what you suppose to be my views on that subject?"

"By George, sir!" returned the Philanthropist, squaring his arms still more, as he frowned on Mr. Crisparkle: "they are best known to yourself."

"Readily admitted. But you began by saying that we took different views, you know. Therefore (or you could not say so) you must have set up some views as mine. Pray, what views *have* you[10] set up as mine?"

[1] In these last particulars] In this last particular MS P
[2] went] MS went by P (*with* by *deleted*) 70–75
[3] always, as it seemed . . . anybody:] *deleted in* P
[4] twice] MS *om.* P 70–75   [5] miserably] miserable and P
[6] could hardly have done worse . . . a declared enemy] would have done better, perhaps, . . . an enemy MS P
[7] "Sir," said Mr. Honeythunder . . . off with them.] *deleted in* P
[8] when they were alone] *deleted in* P   [9] Canon] Canon calmly MS P
[10] *have* you] have *you* MS P

"Here is a man—and a young man," said Mr. Honeythunder, as if that made the matter infinitely worse, and he could have easily borne the loss of an old one: "swept off the face of the earth by a deed of violence. What do you call that?"

"Murder," said the Minor Canon.

"What do you call the doer of that deed, sir?"

"A murderer," said the Minor Canon.

"I am glad to hear you admit so much, sir," retorted Mr. Honeythunder, in his most offensive manner; "and I candidly tell you that I didn't expect it." Here he lowered heavily at Mr. Crisparkle again.

"Be so good as to explain what you mean by those very unjustifiable expressions."

"I don't sit here, sir," returned the Philanthropist, raising his voice to a roar, "to be browbeaten."

"As the only other person present, no one can possibly know that better than I do," returned the Minor Canon very quietly. "But I interrupt your explanation."

"Murder!" proceeded Mr. Honeythunder, in a kind of boisterous reverie, with his platform folding of his arms, and his platform nod of abhorrent reflection after each short sentence[1] of a word. "Bloodshed! Abel! Cain! I hold no terms with Cain. I repudiate with a shudder the red hand when it is offered me."

Instead of instantly leaping into his chair and cheering himself hoarse, as the Brotherhood in public meeting assembled would infallibly have done on this cue, Mr. Crisparkle merely reversed the quiet crossing of his legs, and said mildly: "Don't let me interrupt your explanation—when you begin it."

"The Commandments say no murder. NO murder, sir!" proceeded Mr. Honeythunder, platformally pausing as if he took Mr. Crisparkle to task for having distinctly asserted that they said, You may do a little murder and then leave off.

"And they also say, you shall bear no false witness," observed Mr. Crisparkle.

"Enough!" bellowed Mr. Honeythunder, with a solemnity and severity that would have brought the house down at a meeting, "E—e—nough! My late wards being now of age, and I being released from a trust which I cannot contemplate without a thrill of horror, there are the accounts which you have undertaken to accept on their behalf, and there is a statement of the balance which you have undertaken to receive, and which you cannot receive too soon. And let me tell you, sir, I wish, that[2] as a man and a Minor Canon, you were better employed," with a nod. "Better employed," with another nod. "Bet—ter em—ployed!" with another and the three nods added up.

---

[1] sentence] MS sentiment P 70-75
[2] I wish, that] that I wish [both?] MS that I wish, that P

Mr. Crisparkle rose; a little heated in the face, but with perfect command of himself.

"Mr. Honeythunder," he said, taking up the papers referred to: "my being better or worse employed than I am at present is a matter of taste and opinion. You might think me better employed in enrolling myself a member of your Society."

"Ay, indeed, sir!" retorted Mr. Honeythunder, shaking his head in a threatening manner. "It would have been better for you if you had done that long ago!"

"I think otherwise."

"Or," said Mr. Honeythunder, shaking his head again, "I might think one of your profession better employed in devoting himself to the discovery and punishment of guilt than in leaving that duty to be undertaken by a layman."[1]

"I may regard my profession from a point of view which teaches me that its first duty is towards those who are in necessity and tribulation, who are desolate and oppressed," said Mr. Crisparkle. "However, as I have quite clearly satisfied myself that it is no part of my profession to make professions, I say no more of that. But I owe it to Mr. Neville, and to Mr. Neville's sister (and in a much lower degree to myself),[2] to say to you that I *know* I was in the full possession and understanding of Mr. Neville's mind and heart at the time of this occurrence; and that, without in the least coloring or concealing what was to be deplored in him and required to be corrected, I feel certain that his tale is true. Feeling that certainty, I befriend him. As long as that certainty shall last I will befriend him. And if any consideration could shake me in this resolve, I should be so ashamed of myself for my meanness that no man's good opinion—no, nor no woman's—so gained, could compensate me for the loss of my own."

Good fellow! Manly fellow! And he was so modest, too. There was no more self-assertion in the Minor Canon than in the schoolboy who had stood in the breezy playing-fields keeping a wicket. He was simply and staunchly true to his duty alike in the large case and in the small. So all true souls ever are. So every true soul ever was, ever is, and ever will be. There is nothing little to the really great in spirit.

"Then who do you make out did the deed?" asked Mr. Honeythunder, turning on him abruptly.

"Heaven[3] forbid," said Mr. Crisparkle, "that in my desire to clear one man I should lightly criminate another! I accuse no one."

"Tcha!" ejaculated Mr. Honeythunder with great disgust; for this was by no means the principle on which the Philanthropic Brotherhood usually proceeded. "And, sir, you are not a disinterested witness, we must bear in mind."

[1] Mr. Crisparkle rose . . . by a layman."] *deleted in* P
[2] myself] yourself P   [3] Heaven] ⟨Heaven⟩ God MS God P

"How am I an interested one?" inquired Mr. Crisparkle, smiling innocently, at a loss to imagine.

"There was a certain stipend, sir, paid to you for your pupil, which may have warped your judgment a bit," said Mr. Honeythunder, coarsely.

"Perhaps I expect to retain it still?" Mr. Crisparkle returned, enlightened; "do you mean that too?"

"Well, sir," returned the professional Philanthropist, getting up, and thrusting his hands down into his trousers pockets; "I don't go about measuring people for caps. If people find I have any about me that fit 'em, they can put 'em on and wear 'em, if they like. That's their look out: not mine."[1]

Mr. Crisparkle eyed him with a just indignation, and took him to task thus:

"Mr. Honeythunder, I hoped when I came in here that I might be under no necessity of commenting on the introduction of platform manners or platform manœuvres[2] among the decent forbearances of private life. But you have given me such a specimen of both, that I should be a fit subject for both if I remained silent respecting them. They are detestable."

"They don't suit *you*, I dare say, sir."

"They are," repeated Mr. Crisparkle, without noticing the interruption, "detestable. They violate equally[3] the justice that should belong to Christians, and the restraints that should belong to gentlemen. You assume a great crime to have been committed by one whom I, acquainted with the attendant circumstances, and having numerous reasons on my side, devoutly believe to be innocent of it.[4] Because I differ from you on that vital point, what is your platform resource? Instantly to turn upon me, charging that I have no sense of the enormity of the crime itself, but am its aider and abettor! So, another time—taking me as representing your opponent in other cases—you set up a platform credulity: a moved and seconded and carried unanimously profession of faith in some ridiculous delusion or mischievous imposition. I decline to believe it, and you fall back upon your platform resource of proclaiming that I believe nothing; that because I will not bow down to a false God of your making,[5] I deny the true God! Another time, you make the platform[6] discovery that War is a vast[7] calamity, and you propose to abolish it by a string of twisted resolutions tossed into the air like the tail of a kite. I do not admit the discovery to be yours in the least, and I have not a grain of faith in your

---

[1] "Perhaps I expect . . . not mine."] *deleted in* P

[2] platform manners or platform manœuvres] platform morals or platform manners MS P

[3] equally] with equal ruthlessness MS P   [4] it] *om.* P

[5] a false God of your making] P (*with* of your making *as a proof addition*) ES 73 75 a false God MS P a false God of our making 70

[6] the platform] a platform MS P   [7] vast] ⟨great⟩ vast MS *om.* P 70–75

remedy. Again, your platform resource of representing me as revelling in the horrors of a battle-field like a fiend incarnate! Another time, in another of your undiscriminating platform rushes, you would punish the sober for the drunken. I claim consideration for the comfort, convenience, and refreshment, of the sober; and you presently make platform proclamation that I have a depraved desire to turn Heaven's creatures into swine and wild beasts! In all such cases your movers, and your seconders, and your[1] supporters—your regular Professors of all degrees—run amuck like so many mad Malays; habitually attributing the lowest and basest motives with the utmost recklessness (let me call your attention to a recent instance in yourself for which you should blush), and quoting figures which you know to be as wilfully onesided as a statement of any complicated account that should be all Creditor side and no Debtor, or all Debtor side and no Creditor. Therefore it is, Mr. Honeythunder, that I consider the platform a sufficiently bad example and a sufficiently bad school, even in public life; but hold that, carried into private life, it becomes an unendurable nuisance."[2]

"These are strong words, sir!" exclaimed the Philanthropist.

"I hope so," said Mr. Crisparkle. "Good-morning."

He walked out of the Haven at a great rate, but soon fell into his regular brisk pace, and soon had a smile upon his face as he went along, wondering what the china shepherdess would have said if she had seen him pounding Mr. Honeythunder in the late little lively affair. For Mr. Crisparkle had just enough of harmless vanity[3] to hope that he had hit hard, and to glow with the belief that he had trimmed the Philanthropic jacket pretty handsomely.

He betook[4] himself to Staple Inn, but not to P. J. T. and Mr. Grewgious. Full many a creaking stair he climbed before he reached some attic rooms in a corner, turned the latch of their unbolted door, and stood beside the table of Neville Landless.

An air of retreat and solitude hung about the rooms, and about their inhabitant.[5] He was much worn, and so were they. Their sloping ceilings, cumbrous rusty locks and grates, and heavy wooden bins and beams, slowly mouldering withal, had a prisonous[6] look, and he had the haggard[7] face of a prisoner. Yet the sunlight shone in at the ugly garret window which had a penthouse to itself thrust out among the tiles; and on the cracked and[8] smoke-blackened parapet beyond, some of the deluded sparrows of the place rheumatically hopped, like little feathered cripples who had left their crutches in their nests; and there was a play of living

[1] your] *not in* MS P
[2] an unendurable nuisance] a gross offence, and an unendurable nuisance MS P
[3] vanity] variety P (*uncorrected*) ES
[4] betook] MS took P 70–75
[5] inhabitant] inhabitant too MS P
[6] prisonous] poisonous P
[7] haggard] yellow haggard MS P
[8] and] *not in* MS P

leaves at hand that changed the air, and made an imperfect sort of music in it that would have been melody in the country.

The rooms were sparely furnished, but with good store of books. Everything expressed the abode of a poor student. That Mr. Crisparkle had been either chooser, lender, or donor of the books, or that he combined the three characters, might have been easily seen in the friendly beam of his eyes upon them as he entered.

"How goes it, Neville?"

"I am in good heart, Mr. Crisparkle, and working away."

"I wish your eyes were not quite so large, and not quite so bright," said the Minor Canon, slowly releasing the hand he had taken in his.

"They brighten at the sight of you," returned Neville. "If[1] you were to fall away from me, they would soon be dull enough."

"Rally, rally!" urged the other, in a stimulating tone. "Fight for it, Neville!"

"If I were dying, I feel as if a word from you would rally me; if my pulse had stopped, I feel as if your touch would make it beat again," said Neville. "But I *have* rallied,[2] and am doing famously."

Mr. Crisparkle turned him with his face a little more towards the light.

"I want to see a ruddier touch here, Neville," he said, indicating his own healthy cheek by way of pattern; "I want more sun to shine upon you."

Neville drooped suddenly as he replied in a lowered voice: "I am not hardy enough for that, yet.[3] I may become so, but I cannot bear it yet. If you had gone through those Cloisterham streets as I did; and[4] if you had seen, as I did, those averted eyes, and the better sort of people silently giving me too[5] much room to pass, that I might not touch them or come near them, you wouldn't think it quite unreasonable that I cannot go about in the daylight."

"My poor fellow!" said the Minor Canon, in a tone so purely sympathetic that the young man caught his hand:[6] "I never said it was unreasonable: never thought[7] so. But I should like you to do it."

"And that would give me the strongest motive to do it. But I cannot yet.[8] I cannot persuade myself that the eyes of even the stream of strangers I pass in this vast city look at me without suspicion. I feel marked and tainted, even when I go out—as I only do—[9]at night. But the darkness covers me then, and I take courage from it."

Mr. Crisparkle laid a hand upon his shoulder, and stood looking down at him.

"If I could have changed my name," said Neville, "I would have done

[1] If] Well they may! If MS P [2] rallied] rallied all my forces MS P
[3] yet] sir MS P [4] and] MS *om.* P 70–75
[5] too] very P [6] hand] hand and pressed it MS P
[7] thought] said P [8] yet] yet. I cannot bear it MS P
[9] as I only do—] MS as I do—only P as I do only— 70–75

so. But as you wisely pointed out to me, I can't do that, for it would look like guilt. If I could have gone to some distant[1] place, I might have found relief in that, but the thing is not to be thought of, for the same reason. Hiding and escaping would be the construction in either case. It seems a little hard to be so tied to a stake, and innocent; but I don't complain."

"And you must expect no miracle to help you, Neville," said Mr. Crisparkle, compassionately.

"No, sir, I know that.[2] The ordinary fulness of time and circumstance[3] is all I have to trust to."

"It will right you at last, Neville."

"So I believe, and I hope I may live to know it."

But perceiving that the despondent mood into which he was falling cast a shadow on the Minor Canon, and (it may be) feeling that the broad hand upon his shoulder was not then quite as steady as its own natural strength had rendered it when it first touched him just now, he brightened and said:

"Excellent circumstances for study, anyhow! and you know, Mr. Crisparkle, what need I have of study in[4] all ways. Not to mention that you have advised me to study for the difficult profession of the law, specially, and that of course I am guiding myself by the advice of such a friend and helper. Such a good friend and helper!"

He took the fortifying hand from his shoulder, and kissed it. Mr. Crisparkle beamed at the books, but not so brightly as when he had entered.[5]

"I gather from your silence on the subject that my late guardian is adverse, Mr. Crisparkle?"

The Minor Canon answered: "Your late guardian is a—a most unreasonable person, and it signifies nothing to any reasonable person whether he is *ad*verse[6] or *per*verse, or the *re*verse."

"Well for me that I have enough with economy to live upon," sighed Neville, half wearily and half cheerily, "while I wait to be learned, and wait to be righted! Else I might have proved the proverb that while the grass grows, the steed starves!"

He opened some books as he said it, and was soon immersed in their interleaved and annotated passages, while Mr. Crisparkle sat beside him, expounding, correcting, and advising. The Minor Canon's Cathedral duties made these visits of his difficult to accomplish, and only to be compassed at intervals of many weeks. But they were as serviceable as they were precious to Neville Landless.[7]

When they had got through such studies as they had in hand, they stood leaning on the window-sill, and looking down upon the patch of garden.

---

¹ distant] wild distant MS P
² It seems a little hard . . . I know that.] *replaced in* P *by* Well!
³ circumstance] circumstances 73 75   ⁴ in] *om.* P
⁵ and that of course . . . had entered] *deleted in* P *and Neville's speech run on*
⁶ *ad*verse] adverse MS P   ⁷ But they were . . . Landless.] *deleted in* P

"Next week," said Mr. Crisparkle, "you will cease to be alone, and will have a devoted companion."

"And yet," returned Neville, "this seems an uncongenial place to bring my sister to!"

"I don't think so," said the Minor Canon. "There is duty to be done here; and there are womanly feeling, sense, and courage wanted here."

"I meant," explained Neville, "that the surroundings are so dull and unwomanly, and that Helena can have no suitable friend or society here."

"You have only to remember," said Mr. Crisparkle, "that you are here yourself, and that she has to draw you into the sunlight."

They were silent for a little while, and then Mr. Crisparkle began anew.

"When we first spoke together, Neville, you told me that your sister had risen out of the disadvantages of your past lives as superior to you as the tower of Cloisterham Cathedral is higher than the chimnies of Minor Canon Corner. Do you remember that?"

"Right well!"

"I was inclined to think it at the time an enthusiastic flight. No matter what I think it now. What I would emphasize is, that under the head of Pride your sister is a great and opportune example to you."

"Under *all*[1] heads that are included in the composition of a fine character, she is."

"Say so; but take this one.[2] Your sister has learnt[3] how to govern what is proud in her nature. She can dominate it even when it is wounded through her sympathy with you.[4] No doubt she has suffered deeply in those same streets where you suffered deeply. No doubt her life is darkened by the cloud that darkens yours. But bending her pride into a grand composure that is not haughty or aggressive, but is a sustained confidence in you and in[5] the truth, she has won her way through those streets until she passes along them as high in the general respect as any one who treads them. Every day and hour of her life since Edwin Drood's disappearance, she has faced malignity and folly—for you—as only a brave nature well directed can. So it will be with her to the end.[6] Another and weaker kind of pride might sink broken-hearted, but never such a pride as hers: which knows no shrinking, and can get no mastery of her."[7]

The pale cheek beside him flushed under the comparison and the hint implied in it.[8] "I will do all I can to imitate her," said Neville.

"Do so, and be a truly brave man as she is a truly brave woman,"[9]

---

[1] *all*] *probably* all MS

[2] "I don't think so," said the Minor Canon . . . Say so; but take this one.] *deleted in* P

[3] Your sister has learnt] *changed in* P *to* "Your sister:" returned the Minor Canon, "has learnt   [4] She can . . . with you.] *deleted in* P

[5] in] *not in* MS P   [6] Every day and hour . . . to the end.] *deleted in* P

[7] which knows no shrinking . . . of her] MS *deleted in* P which knows no shrinking . . . over her 70–75

[8] it] these words MS P   [9] as she is . . . woman] *deleted in* P

156   THE MYSTERY OF EDWIN DROOD   V

answered Mr. Crisparkle, stoutly. "It is growing dark. Will you go my
way with me, when it is quite dark? Mind! It is not I who wait for darkness."[1]

Neville replied that he would accompany him directly. But Mr. Crisparkle said he had a moment's call to make on Mr. Grewgious as an act of
courtesy, and would run across to that gentleman's chambers, and rejoin
Neville on his own doorstep if he would come down there to meet him.

Mr. Grewgious, bolt upright as usual, sat taking his wine in the dusk
at his open window; his wineglass and decanter on the round table at his
elbow; himself and his legs on the window-seat; only one hinge in his
whole body, like a bootjack.

"How do you do, reverend sir?" said Mr. Grewgious, with abundant
offers of hospitality which were as cordially declined as made.[2] "And how
is your charge getting on over the way in the set that I had the pleasure of
recommending to you as vacant and eligible?"

Mr. Crisparkle replied suitably.

"I am glad you approved[3] of them," said Mr. Grewgious, "because I
entertain a sort of fancy for having him under my eye."

As Mr. Grewgious had to turn his eye up considerably, before he could
see the chambers, the phrase was to be taken figuratively and not literally.[4]

"And how did you leave Mr. Jasper, reverend sir?" said Mr. Grewgious.[5]

Mr. Crisparkle had left him pretty well.

"And where did you leave Mr. Jasper, reverend sir?"[6]

Mr. Crisparkle had left him at Cloisterham.

"And when did you leave Mr. Jasper, reverend sir?"[6]

That morning.

"Umps!" said Mr. Grewgious. "He didn't say he was coming, perhaps?"

"Coming where?"

"Anywhere, for instance?" said Mr. Grewgious.

"No."

"Because here he is," said Mr. Grewgious, who had asked all these
questions, with his preoccupied glance directed out at[7] window. "And he
don't look agreeable,[8] does he?"

Mr. Crisparkle was craning towards the window, when Mr. Grewgious
added:

"If you will kindly step round here behind me, in the gloom of the
room, and will cast your eye at the second-floor landing window, in

---

[1] darkness] the darkness P   [2] made] offered MS P
[3] approved] MS approve P 70–75
[4] As Mr. Grewgious . . . literally.] *deleted in P and Mr. Grewgious's speech run on*
[5] said Mr. Grewgious.] *deleted in P*
[6] sir?"] sir?" said Mr. Grewgious. MS P   [7] at] of the P
[8] agreeable] handsome MS P

yonder house,[1] I think you will hardly fail to see a slinking individual in whom I recognize our local friend."

"You are right!" cried Mr. Crisparkle.

"Umps!" said Mr. Grewgious. Then he added, turning his face so abruptly that his head nearly came into collision with Mr. Crisparkle's: "what should you say that our local friend was up to?"

The last passage he had been shown in the Diary returned on Mr. Crisparkle's mind with the force of a strong recoil, and he asked Mr. Grewgious if he thought it possible that Neville was to be harassed by the keeping of a watch upon him?

"A watch," repeated Mr. Grewgious, musingly. "Ay!"[2]

"Which would not only of itself haunt and torture his life," said Mr. Crisparkle, warmly, "but would expose him to the torment of a perpetually reviving suspicion, whatever he might do, or wherever he might go?"

"Ay!" said Mr. Grewgious, musingly still.[3] "Do I see him waiting for you?"

"No doubt you do."

"Then *would* you have the goodness to excuse my getting up to see you out, and to go out to join him, and to go the way that you were going, and to[4] take no notice of our local friend?" said Mr. Grewgious. "I entertain a sort of fancy for having *him* under my eye to-night, do you know?"[5]

Mr. Crisparkle, with a significant nod,[6] complied,[7] and, rejoining Neville, went away with him. They dined together, and parted at the yet unfinished and undeveloped railway station: Mr. Crisparkle to get home; Neville to walk the streets, cross the bridges, make a wide round of the city in the friendly darkness, and tire himself out.

It was midnight when he returned from his[8] solitary expedition, and climbed his staircase. The night was hot, and the windows of the staircase were all wide open. Coming to the top, it gave him a passing chill of surprise (there being no rooms but his up there) to find a stranger sitting on the window-sill, more after the manner of a venturesome glazier than an amateur ordinarily careful of his neck; in fact, so much more outside the window than inside, as to suggest the thought that he must have come up by the water-spout instead of the stairs.

The stranger said nothing until Neville put his key in his door; then, seeming to make sure of his identity from the action, he spoke:

"I beg your pardon," he said, coming from the window with a frank and smiling air, and a prepossessing[9] address; "the beans."

[1] in yonder house] in the second house from the left corner MS P

[2] "A watch," . . . "Ay!"] *deleted in* P   [3] still] *deleted in* P

[4] to] *om.* P   [5] "I entertain . . . know?"] *deleted in* P

[6] nod] nod of intelligence MS nod of obeyance P

[7] complied] complied immediately MS P   [8] his] *so probably in* MS this P

[9] prepossessing] most agreeable MS P

Neville was quite at a loss.

"Runners," said the visitor. "Scarlet. Next door at the back."

"Oh!" returned Neville. "And the mignonette and wallflower?"

"The same," said the visitor.

"Pray walk in."

"Thank you."

Neville lighted his candles, and the visitor sat down. A handsome gentleman, with a young face, but an older figure in its robustness and its breadth of shoulder; say a man of eight-and-twenty, or at the utmost thirty: so extremely sunburnt that the contrast between his brown visage and the white forehead shaded out of doors by his hat, and the glimpses of white throat below his neckerchief,[1] would have been almost ludicrous but for his broad temples, bright blue eyes, clustering brown hair, and laughing[2] teeth.

"I have noticed," said he; "—my name is Tartar."

Neville inclined his head.

"I have noticed (excuse me) that you shut yourself up a good deal, and that you seem to like my garden aloft here. If you would like a little more of it, I could throw out a few lines and stays between my windows and yours, which the runners would take to directly. And I have some boxes, both of mignonette and wallflower, that I could shove on along the gutter (with a boat-hook I have by me) to your windows, and draw back again when they wanted watering or gardening, and shove on again when they were ship-shape, so that they would cause you no trouble. I couldn't take this liberty without asking permission,[3] so I venture to ask it. Tartar, corresponding set, next door."

"You are very kind."

"Not at all. I beg you will not think so.[4] I ought to apologize for looking in so late. But having noticed (excuse me) that you generally walk out at night, I thought I should inconvenience you least by awaiting your return. I am always afraid of inconveniencing busy men, being an idle man."

"I should not have thought so, from your appearance."

"No? I take it as a compliment. In fact, I was bred in the Royal Navy and was First Lieutenant when I quitted it. But, an uncle disappointed in the service leaving me his property on condition that I left the Navy, I accepted the fortune and resigned my commission."

"Lately, I presume?"

"Well, I had had twelve or fifteen years of knocking about[5] first. I came here some nine months before you; I[6] had had one crop before you came.

[1] his neckerchief] MS the neckerchief P 70–75   [2] laughing] beaming MS P
[3] permission] MS your permission P 70–75
[4] I beg you will not think so.] MS om. P 70–75
[5] knocking about] knocking about on salt water MS P   [6] I] probably I MS

I chose this place, because, having served last in a little¹ Corvette, I knew
I should feel more at home where I had a constant opportunity of knocking my head against the ceiling. Besides: it would never do for a man who
had been aboard ship from his boyhood to turn luxurious all at once. Besides, again: having been accustomed to a very short allowance of land all
my life, I thought I'd feel my way to the command of a landed estate, by
beginning in boxes."

Whimsically as this was said, there was a touch of merry earnestness in
it that made it doubly whimsical.

"However," said the Lieutenant, "I have talked quite enough about
myself. It is not my way I hope; it has merely been to present myself to
you naturally. If you will allow me to take the liberty I have described, it
will be a charity,² for it will give me something more to do. And you are
not to suppose that it will entail³ any interruption or intrusion on you, for
that is far from my intention."

Neville replied that he was greatly obliged, and that he thankfully
accepted the kind proposal.

"I am very glad to take your windows in tow," said the Lieutenant.
"From what I have seen of you when I have been gardening at mine, and
you have been looking on, I have thought you (excuse me) rather too
studious and delicate! May I ask, is your health at all affected?"

"I have undergone some mental distress," said Neville, confused,
"which has stood me in the stead of illness."

"Pardon me," said Mr. Tartar.

With the greatest delicacy he shifted his ground to the windows again,
and asked if he could look at one of them. On Neville's opening it, he
immediately sprang out, as if he were going aloft with a whole watch in
an emergency, and were setting a bright example.

"For Heaven's sake!" cried Neville, "don't do that! Where are you
going, Mr. Tartar? You'll be dashed to pieces!"

"All well!" said the Lieutenant, coolly looking about him on the house-
top. "All taut and trim here. Those lines and stays shall be rigged before
you turn out in the morning. May I take the short cut⁴ home and say,
Good-night?"

"Mr. Tartar!" urged Neville. "Pray! It makes me giddy to see you!"

But Mr. Tartar, with a wave of his hand and the deftness of a cat, had
already dipped through his scuttle of scarlet runners without breaking a
leaf, and "gone below."

Mr. Grewgious, his bedroom window-blind held aside with his hand,
happened at that moment to have Neville's chambers under his eye for
the last time that night. Fortunately his eye was on the front of the house
and not the back, or this remarkable appearance and disappearance might

---

¹ little] *not in* MS P   ² a charity] a charity on the whole MS P
³ entail] inflict MS P   ⁴ the short cut] MS this short cut P 70–75

have broken his rest as a phenomenon. But, Mr. Grewgious seeing nothing there, not even a light in the windows, his gaze wandered from the
windows to the stars, as if he would have read in them something that was
hidden from him. Many of us would if we could; but none[1] of us so much
as know our letters in the stars yet—or seem likely to,[2] in this state of
existence—and few languages can be read until their alphabets are
mastered.[3]

CHAPTER XVIII

A SETTLER IN CLOISTERHAM

A T about this time, a stranger appeared in Cloisterham; a white-haired
personage with black eyebrows. Being buttoned up in a tightish blue
surtout, with a buff waistcoat and grey trousers, he had something of a
military air; but he announced himself at the Crozier (the orthodox hotel,
where he put up with a portmanteau) as an idle dog who lived upon his
means; and he further announced that he had a mind to take a lodging
in the picturesque old city for a month or two, with the view[4] of settling
down there altogether. Both announcements were made in the coffee-room
of the Crozier, to all whom it might, or might not, concern, by the stranger
as he stood with his back to the empty fireplace, waiting for his fried sole,
veal cutlet, and pint of sherry. And the waiter (business being chronically
slack at the Crozier) represented all whom it might or might not concern,
and absorbed the whole of the information.

This gentleman's white head was unusually large, and his shock of
white hair was unusually thick and ample. "I suppose, waiter," he said,
shaking his shock of hair, as a Newfoundland dog might shake his before
sitting down to dinner, "that a fair lodging for a single buffer might be
found in these parts, eh?"

The waiter had no doubt of it.

"Something old," said the gentleman. "Take my hat down for a moment
from that peg, will you? No, I don't want it; look into it. What do you see
written there?"

The waiter read: "Datchery."

"Now you know my name," said the gentleman; "Dick Datchery.

---

[1] but none] but, alas! none MS P
[2] likely to] MS P (*with no alteration*) likely to do it 70–75
[3] Mr. Grewgious, his bedroom window-blind [*p. 159*] . . . are mastered.] P *has both
mark of deletion and* STET *by this paragraph*
CHAPTER XVIII] CHAPTER ⟨XIX⟩ XVIII MS
[4] the view] MS a view P 70–75

Hang it up again. I was saying something old is what I should prefer, something odd and out of the way; something venerable, architectural, and inconvenient."

"We have a good choice of inconvenient lodgings in the town, sir, I think," replied the waiter, with modest confidence in its resources that way; "indeed, I have no doubts that we could suit you that far, however particular you might be.[1] But a architectural lodging!" That seemed to trouble the waiter's head, and he shook it.

"Anything Cathedrally now," Mr. Datchery suggested.

"Mr. Tope," said the waiter, brightening, as he rubbed his chin with his hand, "would be the likeliest party to inform in that line."

"Who is Mr. Tope?" inquired Dick Datchery.

The waiter explained that he was the Verger, and that Mrs. Tope had indeed once upon a time let lodgings herself—or offered to let them; but that as nobody had ever taken them, Mrs. Tope's window-bill, long a Cloisterham Institution, had disappeared; probably had tumbled down one day, and never been put up again.

"I'll call on Mrs. Tope," said Mr. Datchery, "after dinner."

So when he had done his dinner, he was duly directed to the spot, and sallied out for it. But the Crozier being an hotel of a most retiring disposition, and the waiter's directions being fatally precise, he soon became bewildered, and went boggling about and about the Cathedral tower, whenever he could catch a glimpse of it, with a general impression on his mind that Mrs. Tope's was somewhere very near it, and that, like the children in the game of hot boiled beans and very good butter, he was warm in his search when he saw the tower, and cold when he didn't see it.

He was getting very cold indeed when[2] he came upon a fragment of burial-ground in which an unhappy sheep was grazing. Unhappy, because a hideous small boy was stoning it through the railings, and had already lamed it in one leg, and was much excited by the benevolent sportsmanlike purpose of breaking its other three legs, and bringing it down.

" 'It 'im agin!"[3] cried the boy, as the poor creature leaped; "and made a dint in 'is[4] wool!"

"Let him be!" said Mr. Datchery. "Don't you see you have lamed him?"

"Yer lie," returned the sportsman. " 'E went and lamed 'isself. I see 'im do it, and I giv' 'im a shy as a Widdy-warning[5] to 'im not to go a bruisin'[6] 'is master's mutton any more."

"Come here."

"I won't; I'll come when yer can ketch me."

[1] indeed, I have . . . might be] MS *deleted in* P   P 70–75 *print* doubt *for* doubts
[2] with a general impression . . . indeed when] *replaced in* P *by* until at length
[3] agin] again P   [4] 'is] MS his P 70–75
[5] Widdy-warning] caution MS P   [6] a bruisin'] a 'urtin' MS P

8124392   M

"Stay there then, and show me which is Mr. Tope's."

" 'Ow can I stay here and show you which is Topeseses, when[1] Topeseses is t'other side the Kinfreederel,[2] and over the crossings, and round ever so many corners? Stoo-pid! Ya-a-ah!"

"Show me where it is, and I'll give you something."

"Come on, then!"

This brisk dialogue concluded, the boy led the way, and by-and-bye stopped at some distance from an arched passage, pointing.

"Look'ee[3] yonder. You see that there winder and door?"

"That's Tope's?"[4]

"Yer lie; it ain't. That's Jarsper's."

"Indeed?" said Mr. Datchery, with a second look of some interest.

"Yes,[5] and I ain't a goin' no nearer 'IM, I tell yer."

"Why not?"

" 'Cos I ain't a going[6] to be lifted off my legs and 'ave my braces bust and be choked; not if I knows it and not by 'Im. Wait till I set a jolly good flint a flyin' at the back o' 'is jolly old 'ed some day! Now look t'other side the harch; not the side where Jarsper's door is; t'other side."

"I see."

"A little way in, o' that side, there's a low door, down two steps. That's Topeseses with 'is name on a hoval plate."

"Good. See here," said Mr. Datchery, producing a shilling. "You owe me half of this."

"Yer lie; I don't owe yer[7] nothing; I never seen yer."

"I tell you you owe me half of this, because I have no sixpence in my pocket. So the next time you meet me you shall do something else for me, to pay me."

"All right, give us 'old."

"What is your name, and where do you live?"

"Deputy. Travellers' Twopenny, 'cross the green."

The boy instantly darted off with the shilling, lest Mr. Datchery should repent, but stopped at a safe distance, on the happy chance of his being uneasy in his mind about it, to goad him with a demon dance expressive of its irrevocability.[8] Mr. Datchery, taking off his hat to give that shock of white hair of his another shake, seemed quite resigned, and betook himself whither he had been directed.[9]

---

    [1] when] wen MS

    [2] Kinfreederel] ⟨Kinfreedial⟩ Kinfreederel MS *probable not certain*

    [3] Look'ee] MS Lookie P 70–75   [4] That's Tope's] That's Tope's, is it MS P

    [5] "Indeed?" . . . Yes,] *deleted in* P *and Deputy's speech run on with new sentence beginning at* And

    [6] a going] a-goin' 73 75   [7] yer] you MS

    [8] irrevocability] ⟨irrevocability⟩ irrevocable loss MS irrevocable loss P

    [9] Mr. Datchery, taking off . . . directed.] *deleted in* P; *printed as a separate paragraph in* P 70–75, *but not in* MS

Mr. Tope's official dwelling, communicating by an upper stair with Mr. Jasper's (hence Mrs. Tope's attendance on that gentleman), was of very modest proportions, and partook of the character of a cool dungeon. Its ancient walls were massive and its rooms rather seemed to have been dug out of them, than to have been designed beforehand with any reference to them. The main door opened at once on a chamber of no describable shape, with a groined roof, which in its turn opened on another chamber of no describable shape, with another groined roof: their windows small, and in the thickness of the walls. These[1] two chambers, close as to their atmosphere and swarthy as to their illumination by natural light, were the apartments which Mrs. Tope had so long offered to an unappreciative city. Mr. Datchery, however, was more appreciative. He found that if he sat with the main door open he would enjoy the passing society of all comers to and fro by the gateway, and would have light enough. He found that if Mr. and Mrs. Tope living overhead, used for their own egress and ingress a little side stair that came plump into the Precincts by a door opening outward, to the surprise and inconvenience of a limited public of pedestrians in a narrow way, he would be alone, as in a separate residence. He found the rent moderate, and everything as quaintly inconvenient as he could desire. He agreed therefore to take the lodging then and there, and money down, possession to be had next evening on condition that reference was permitted him to Mr. Jasper as occupying the Gate House, of which, on the other side of the gateway the Verger's hole in the wall was an appanage or subsidiary part.

The poor dear gentleman was very solitary and very sad, Mrs. Tope said, but she had no doubt he would "speak for her." Perhaps Mr. Datchery had heard something of what had occurred there last winter?

Mr. Datchery had as confused a knowledge of the event in question, on trying to recall it, as he well could have. He begged Mrs. Tope's pardon when she found it incumbent on her to correct him in every detail of his summary of the facts, but pleaded that he was merely a single buffer getting through life upon his means as idly as he could, and that so many people were so constantly making away with so many other people, as to render it difficult for a buffer of an easy temper to preserve the circumstances of the several cases unmixed in his mind.[2]

Mr. Jasper proving[3] willing to speak for Mrs. Tope, Mr. Datchery, who had sent up his card, was invited to ascend the postern staircase. The Mayor was there, Mrs.[4] Tope said; but he was not to be regarded in the light of company, as he and Mr. Jasper were great friends.

"I beg pardon," said Mr. Datchery, making a leg with his hat under his arm, as he addressed himself equally to both gentlemen; "a selfish

---

[1] roof: their . . . walls. These] roof. Their . . . walls, these P (*uncorrected*) ES
[2] Perhaps Mr. Datchery had heard . . . in his mind.] *deleted in* P
[3] proving] being MS P   [4] Mrs.] Mr. 73 75

precaution on my part and not personally interesting to anybody but myself. But as a buffer living on his means, and having an idea of doing it in this lovely place in peace and quiet, for remaining span of life, beg¹ to ask if the Tope family are quite respectable?"

Mr. Jasper could answer for that without the slightest hesitation.

"That is enough, sir," said Mr. Datchery.

"My friend the Mayor," added Mr. Jasper, presenting Mr. Datchery with a courtly motion of his hand towards that potentate; "whose recommendation is naturally² much more important to a stranger than that of an obscure person like myself, will testify in their behalf, I am sure."

"The Worshipful the Mayor," said Mr. Datchery, with a low bow, "places me under an infinite obligation."

"Very good people, sir, Mr. and Mrs. Tope," said Mr. Sapsea, with condescension. "Very good opinions. Very well behaved. Very respectful. Much approved by the Dean and Chapter."

"The Worshipful the Mayor gives them a character," said Mr. Datchery, "of which they may indeed be proud. I would ask His Honor (if I might be permitted) whether there are not many objects of great interest in the city which is under his beneficent sway?"

"We are, sir," returned Mr. Sapsea, "an ancient city, and an ecclesiastical city. We are a constitutional city, as it becomes such a city to be, and we uphold and maintain our glorious privileges."

"His Honor," said Mr. Datchery, bowing, "inspires me with a desire to know more of the city, and confirms me in my inclination to end my days in the city."

"Retired from the Army, sir?" suggested Mr. Sapsea.

"His Honor the Mayor does me too much credit," returned Mr. Datchery.

"Navy, sir?" suggested Mr. Sapsea.

"Again," repeated Mr. Datchery, "His Honor the Mayor does me too much credit."

"Diplomacy is a fine profession," said Mr. Sapsea, as a general remark.

"There, I confess, His Honor the Mayor is too many for me," said Mr. Datchery, with an ingenuous³ smile and bow; "even a diplomatic bird must fall to such a gun."

Now,⁴ this was very soothing. Here was a gentleman of a great—not to say a grand—address, accustomed to rank and dignity, really setting a fine example how to behave to a Mayor. There was something in that third person style of being spoken to, that Mr. Sapsea found particularly recognizant of his merits and position.

"But I crave pardon," said Mr. Datchery. "His Honor the Mayor will bear with me, if for a moment I have been deluded into occupying his

---

¹ beg] I beg 75   ² naturally] MS *probable not certain* actually P 70–75
³ ingenuous] ingenious 73 75   ⁴ Now] No P

time, and have forgotten the humble claims upon my own, of my hotel, the Crozier."

"Not at all, sir," said Mr. Sapsea. "I too[1] am returning home, and if you would like to take the exterior of our Cathedral in your way, I shall be glad to point it out."

"His Honor the Mayor," said Mr. Datchery, "is more than kind and gracious."

As Mr. Datchery, when he had made his acknowledgments to Mr. Jasper, could not be induced to go out of the room before the Worshipful, the Worshipful led the way down stairs; Mr. Datchery following with his hat under his arm, and his shock of white hair streaming in the evening breeze.

"Might I ask His Honor," said Mr. Datchery, "whether that gentleman we have just left is the gentleman of whom I have heard in the neighbourhood as being much afflicted by the loss of a nephew, and concentrating his life on avenging the loss?"

"That is the gentleman. John Jasper, sir."

"Would His Honor allow me to inquire whether there are strong suspicions of any one?"

"More than suspicions, sir," returned Mr. Sapsea, "all but certainties."

"Only think now!" cried Mr. Datchery.

"But proof, sir, proof, must be built up stone by stone," said the Mayor. "As I say, the end crowns the work. It is not enough that Justice should be morally certain; she must be *im*morally[2] certain—legally, that is."

"His Honor," said Mr. Datchery, "reminds me of the nature of the law. Immoral. How true!"

"As I say, sir," pompously went on the Mayor,[3] "the arm of the law is a strong arm, and a long arm. That is the way *I*[4] put it. A strong arm and a long arm."

"How forcible!—And yet, again, how true!" murmured Mr. Datchery.

"And without betraying what I call the secrets of the prison-house," said Mr. Sapsea; "the secrets of the prison-house is the term I used on the bench."

"And what other term than His Honor's would express it?" said Mr. Datchery.

"Without, I say, betraying them, I predict to you, knowing the iron will of the gentleman we have just left (I take the bold step of calling it iron, on account of its strength), that in this case the long arm will reach, and the strong arm will strike.—This is our Cathedral, sir. The best judges are pleased to admire it, and the best among our townsmen own to being a little vain of it."

---

[1] too] MS   *om.* P 70–75   [2] *im*morally] MS immorally P 70–75
[3] pompously went on the Mayor] *order in* MS *more probably* the Mayor pompously went on   [4] *I*] I 75

All this time Mr. Datchery had walked with his hat under his arm, and his white hair streaming.[1] He had an odd momentary appearance upon him of having forgotten his hat, when Mr. Sapsea now[2] touched it; and he clapped his hand up to his head as if with some vague expectation of finding another hat upon it.

"Pray be covered, sir," entreated Mr. Sapsea; magnificently implying: "I shall not mind it, I assure you."

"His Honor is very good, but I do it for coolness," said Mr. Datchery.

Then Mr. Datchery admired the Cathedral, and Mr. Sapsea pointed it out as if he himself had invented and built it; there were a few details indeed of which he did not approve, but those he glossed over, as if the workmen had made mistakes in his absence.[3] The Cathedral disposed of, he led the way by the churchyard, and stopped to extol the beauty of the evening—by chance—in the immediate vicinity of Mrs. Sapsea's epitaph.

"And by-the-bye," said Mr. Sapsea, appearing to descend from an elevation to remember it all of a sudden; like Apollo shooting down from Olympus to pick up his forgotten lyre; "*that* is one of our small lions. The partiality of our people has made it so, and strangers have been seen taking a copy of it now and then. I am not a judge of it myself, for it is a little work of my own. But it was troublesome to turn, sir; I may say, difficult to turn with elegance."

Mr. Datchery became so ecstatic over Mr. Sapsea's composition that, in spite of his intention to end his days in Cloisterham, and therefore his probably having in reserve many opportunities of copying it, he would have transcribed it into his pocket-book on the spot, but for the slouching towards them of its material producer and perpetuator,[4] Durdles, whom Mr. Sapsea hailed, not sorry to show him a bright example of behaviour to superiors.

"Ah, Durdles! This is the mason, sir; one of our Cloisterham worthies; everybody here knows Durdles. Mr. Datchery, Durdles; a gentleman who is going to settle here."

"I wouldn't do it if I was him," growled Durdles. "We're a heavy lot."

"You surely don't speak for yourself, Mr. Durdles," returned Mr. Datchery, "any more than for His Honor."

"Who's His Honor?" demanded Durdles.

"His Honor the Mayor."

"I never was brought afore him," said Durdles, with anything but the look of a loyal subject of the mayoralty, "and it'll be[5] time enough for me to Honor him when I am. Until which, and when, and where:

---

[1] "Might I ask His Honor," said Mr. Datchery [*p. 165*] . . . white hair streaming.] *deleted in* P *and the passage run on*

[2] now] *deleted in* P   [3] absence] temporary absence MS P

[4] perpetuator] perpetrator P *reading in* MS *not clear*

[5] it'll be] *om.* P

> "Mister Sapsea is his name,
> England is his nation,
> Cloist'rham's[1] his dwelling-place,
> Aukshneer's[2] his occupation."

Here, Deputy (preceded by a flying oyster-shell) appeared upon the scene, and requested to have the sum of threepence instantly "chucked" to him by Mr. Durdles, whom he had been vainly seeking up and down, as lawful wages overdue. While that gentleman, with his bundle under his arm, slowly found and counted out the money, Mr. Sapsea informed the new settler of Durdles's habits, pursuits, abode, and reputation. "I suppose a curious stranger might come to see you, and your works, Mr. Durdles, at any[3] odd time?" said Mr. Datchery upon that.

"Any gentleman is welcome to come and see me any evening if he brings liquor for two with him," returned Durdles, with a penny between his teeth and certain halfpence in his hands. "Or if he likes to make it twice two, he'll be double[4] welcome."

"I shall come. Master Deputy, what do you owe me?"

"A job."

"Mind you pay me honestly with the job of showing me Mr. Durdles's house when I want to go there."[5]

Deputy, with a piercing broadside of whistle through the whole gap in his mouth, as a receipt in full for all arrears,[6] vanished.

The Worshipful and the Worshipper then passed on together until they parted, with many ceremonies, at the Worshipful's door; even then, the Worshipper carried his hat under his arm, and gave his streaming white hair to the breeze.

Said Mr. Datchery to himself that night, as he looked at his white hair in the gas-lighted looking-glass over the coffee-room chimneypiece at the Crozier, and shook it out: "For a single buffer, of an easy temper, living idly on his means, I have had a rather busy afternoon!"

CHAPTER XIX

SHADOW ON THE SUN-DIAL

AGAIN Miss Twinkleton has delivered her valedictory address, with the accompaniments of white wine and pound-cake, and again the young

---

[1] Cloist'rham's] MS Cloisterham's P 70–75   [2] Aukshneer's] Aucshneer's MS P
[3] any] some MS P   [4] double] MS doubly P 70–75
[5] "I shall come . . . go there."] *deleted in* P   [6] as a receipt . . . arrears] *not in* MS P
CHAPTER XIX] CHAPTER ⟨XVIII⟩ XIX MS

ladies have departed to their several homes. Helena Landless has left the Nuns' House to attend her brother's fortunes, and pretty Rosa is alone.

Cloisterham is so bright and sunny in these summer days, that the Cathedral and the monastery ruin show as if their strong walls were transparent. A soft glow seems to shine from within them, rather than upon them from without, such is their mellowness as they look forth on the hot corn-fields and the smoking roads that distantly wind among them. The Cloisterham gardens blush with ripening fruit. Time was when travel-stained pilgrims rode in clattering parties through the city's[1] welcome shades; time is when wayfarers, leading a gipsy life between haymaking time and harvest, and looking as if they were just made of the dust of the earth, so very dusty are they, lounge about on cool doorsteps, trying to mend their unmendable shoes, or giving them to the city kennels as a hopeless job, and seeking others in the bundles that they carry, along with their yet unused sickles swathed in bands of straw. At all the more public pumps there is much cooling of bare feet, together with much bubbling and gurgling of drinking with hand to spout on the part of these Bedouins; the Cloisterham police meanwhile looking askant from their beats with suspicion, and manifest[2] impatience that the intruders should depart from within the civic bounds, and once more fry themselves on the simmering high roads.

On the afternoon of such a day, when the last Cathedral service is done, and when that side of the High Street on which the Nuns' House stands is in grateful shade, save where its quaint old garden opens to the west between the boughs of trees, a servant informs Rosa, to her terror, that Mr. Jasper desires to see her.

If he had chosen his time for finding her at a disadvantage, he could have done no better. Perhaps he has chosen it. Helena Landless is gone, Mrs. Tisher is absent on leave, Miss Twinkleton (in her amateur state of existence) has contributed herself and a veal pie to a picnic.

"Oh why, why, why, did you say I was at home!" cries Rosa, helplessly.

The maid replies, that Mr. Jasper never asked the question. That he said he knew she was at home, and begged she might be told that he asked[3] to see her.

"What shall I do, what shall I do?" thinks Rosa, clasping her hands.

Possessed by a kind of desperation, she adds in the next breath that she will come to Mr. Jasper in the garden. She shudders at the thought of being shut up with him in the house; but many of its windows command the garden, and she can be seen as well as heard,[4] there, and can shriek in the free air and run away. Such is the wild idea that flutters through her mind.

[1] the city's] its MS P   [2] manifest] a manifest MS P
[3] asked] desired MS P   [4] heard,] *comma inserted in* P *but ignored in* 70

She has never seen him since the fatal night, except when she was questioned before the Mayor, and then he was present in gloomy watchfulness, as representing his lost nephew and burning to avenge him. She hangs her garden-hat on her arm, and goes out. The moment she sees him from the porch, leaning on the sun-dial, the old horrible feeling of being compelled by him, asserts its hold upon her. She feels that she would even then go back, but that he draws her feet towards him. She cannot resist, and sits down, with her head bent, on the garden-seat beside the sun-dial. She cannot look up at him for abhorrence, but she has perceived that he is dressed in deep mourning. So is she. It was not so at first; but the lost has long been given up, and mourned for, as the dead.[1]

He would begin by touching her hand. She feels the intention, and draws her hand back. His eyes are then fixed upon her, she knows, though her own see nothing but the grass.

"I have been waiting," he begins, "for some time, to be summoned back to my duty near you."

After several times forming her lips, which she knows he is closely watching, into the shape of some other hesitating reply, and then into none, by turns,[2] she answers: "Duty, sir?"

"The duty of teaching you, serving you as your faithful music-master."

"I have left off that study."

"Not left off, I think. Discontinued. I was told by your guardian that you discontinued it under the shock that we have all felt so acutely. When will you resume?"

"Never, sir."

"Never? You could have done no more if you had loved my dear boy."

"I did love him!" cries[3] Rosa, with a flash of anger.

"Yes; but not quite—not quite in the right way, shall I say? Not in the intended and expected way. Much as my dear boy was, unhappily, too self-conscious and self-satisfied (but I[4] draw no parallel between him and you in that respect) to love as he should have loved, or as any one in his place would have loved—must have loved!"

She sits in the same still attitude, but shrinking a little more.

"Then, to be told that you discontinued your study with me, was to be politely told that you abandoned it altogether?" he suggests.[5]

"Yes," says Rosa, with sudden spirit. "The politeness was my guardian's, not mine. I told him that I was resolved to leave off, and that I was determined to stand by my resolution."

"And you still are?"

"I still am, sir. And I beg not to be questioned any more about it. At all events, I will not answer any more; I have that in my power."

[1] the dead] MS dead P 70–75   [2] by turns,] MS it was, P (deleted) om. 70–75
[3] cries] cried 75   [4] but I] MS I will P I'll 70–75
[5] suggests] MS suggested P 70–75

She is so conscious of his looking at her with a gloating admiration of the touch of anger on her, and the fire and animation it brings with it, that even as her spirit rises,[1] it falls again, and she struggles with a sense of shame, affront, and fear, much as she did that night at the piano.

"I will not question you any more, since you object to it so much; I will confess."

"I do not wish to hear you, sir," cries[2] Rosa, rising.

This time he does touch her with his outstretched hand. In shrinking from it, she shrinks into her seat again.

"We must sometimes act in opposition to our wishes," he[3] tells her in a low voice. "You must do so now, or do more harm to others than you can ever set right."

"What harm?"

"Presently, presently. You question *me*, you see, and surely that is[4] not fair when you forbid me to question you. Nevertheless, I will answer the question presently. Dearest Rosa! Charming Rosa!"

She starts up again.

This time he does not touch her. But his face looks so wicked and menacing, as he stands leaning against the sun-dial—setting, as it were,[5] his black mark upon the very face of day—that her flight is arrested by horror as she looks at him.

"I do not forget how many windows command a view of us," he says, glancing towards them. "I will not touch you again, I will come no nearer to you than I am. Sit down, and there will be no mighty wonder in your music-master's leaning idly against a pedestal and speaking with you, remembering[6] all that has happened and our shares in it. Sit down, my beloved."

She would have gone once more—was all but gone—and once more his face, darkly threatening what would follow if she went, has stopped her. Looking at him with the expression of the instant frozen on her face, she sits down on the seat again.

"Rosa, even when my dear boy was affianced to you, I loved you madly; even when I thought his happiness in having you for his wife was certain, I loved you madly; even when I strove to make him more ardently devoted to you, I loved you madly; even when he gave me the picture of your lovely face so carelessly traduced by him, which I feigned to hang always in my sight for his sake, but worshipped[7] in torment for yours,[8] I loved you madly. In the distasteful[9] work of the day, in the wakeful misery of the

[1] rises] rose P   [2] cries] ⟨cried⟩ cries MS *alteration not clear* cried P
[3] he] Jasper MS P   [4] that is] MS *incompletely altered from* ⟨that's⟩ that's P 70–75
[5] as it were] *not in* MS P
[6] remembering] ⟨after⟩ ⟨remembering⟩ after MS after P
[7] worshipped] worshipped it P   [8] yours] MS years P 70–75
[9] the distasteful] distasteful P

night, girded by sordid realities, or wandering through Paradises and
Hells of visions into which I rushed, carrying your image in my arms, I
loved you madly."

If anything could make his words more hideous to her than they are in
themselves, it would be the contrast between the violence of his look and
delivery, and the composure of his assumed attitude.

"I endured all[1] in silence. So long as you were his, or so long as[2] I supposed you to be his, I hid my secret loyally.[3] Did I not?"

This lie, so gross, while the mere words in which it is told are so true,
is more than Rosa can endure. She answers with kindling indignation:
"You were as false throughout, sir, as you are now. You were false to him,
daily and hourly. You know that you made my life unhappy by your
pursuit of me. You know that you made me afraid to open his generous
eyes, and that you forced me, for his own trusting, good, good sake, to
keep the truth from him, that you were a bad, bad, man!"

His preservation of his easy attitude rendering his working features and
his convulsive hands absolutely diabolical, he returns, with a fierce
extreme of admiration:

"How beautiful you are! You are more beautiful in anger than in
repose. I don't ask you for your love; give me yourself and your hatred;
give me yourself and that pretty rage; give me yourself and that enchant-
ing scorn; it will be enough for me."

Impatient tears rise to the eyes of the trembling little beauty, and her
face flames; but as she again rises to leave him in indignation, and seek
protection within the house, he stretches out his hand towards the porch,
as though he invited her to enter it.

"I told you, you rare charmer, you sweet witch, that you must stay and
hear me, or do more harm than can ever be undone. You asked me what
harm. Stay, and I will tell you. Go, and I will do it!"

Again Rosa quails before his threatening face, though innocent of its
meaning, and she remains. Her panting breathing comes and goes as if it
would choke her; but with a repressive hand upon her bosom, she remains.

"I have made my confession that my love is mad. It is so mad that, had
the ties between me and my dear lost boy been one[4] silken thread less
strong, I might have swept even him from your side when you favored
him."

A film comes over the eyes she raises for an instant, as though he had
turned her faint.

"Even him," he repeats. "Yes, even him! Rosa, you see me and you
hear me. Judge for yourself whether any other admirer shall love you and
live, whose life is in my hand."

---

[1] all] MS it all P 70–75   [2] so long as] *not in* MS P
[3] loyally] loyally and held my breath MS P
[4] one] *possibly* a MS *difficult to read   om.* P

"What do you mean, sir?"

"I mean to show you how mad my love is. It was hawked through the late inquiries by Mr. Crisparkle, that young Landless had confessed to him that he was a rival of my lost boy. That is an inexpiable offence in my eyes. The same Mr. Crisparkle knows under my hand that I devoted[1] myself to the murderer's discovery and destruction, be he who[2] he might, and that I determined to discuss the mystery with no one until I should hold the clue in which to entangle the murderer as in a net. I have since worked patiently to wind and wind it round him; and it is slowly winding as I speak."

"Your belief, if you believe in the criminality of Mr. Landless, is not Mr. Crisparkle's belief, and he is a good man," Rosa retorts.

"My belief is my own; and I reserve it, worshipped of my soul! Circumstances may accumulate so strongly *even against an innocent man*, that, directed, sharpened, and pointed, they may slay him. One wanting link discovered by perseverance against a guilty man, proves his guilt, however slight its evidence before, and he dies. Young Landless stands in deadly peril either way."

"If you really suppose," Rosa pleads with him, turning paler, "that I favor Mr. Landless, or that Mr. Landless has ever in any way addressed himself to me, you are wrong."

He puts that from him with a slighting action of his hand and a curled lip.

"I was going to show you how madly I love you. More madly now than ever, for I am willing to renounce the second object that has arisen in my life to divide it with you; and henceforth to have no object in existence but you only. Miss Landless has become your bosom friend. You care for her peace of mind?"

"I love her dearly."

"You care for her good name?"

"I have said, sir, I love her dearly."

"I am unconsciously," he observes, with a smile, as he folds his hands upon the sun-dial and leans his chin upon them, so that his talk would seem from the windows (faces occasionally come and go there)[3] to be of the airiest and playfullest: "I am unconsciously giving offence by questioning again. I will simply make statements, therefore, and not put questions. You do care for your bosom friend's good name, and you do care for her peace of mind. Then remove the shadow of the gallows from her, dear one!"[4]

"You dare propose to me to——"

"Darling, I dare propose to you. Stop there. If it be bad to idolize you,

---

[1] devoted] MS have devoted P 70–75   [2] who] MS whom P 70–75

[3] there)] there), whence his eyes cannot be seen, MS P

[4] her, dear one] her dear one P *comma barely discernible in* MS

JASPER'S SACRIFICES

I am the worst of men; if it be good, I am the best. My love for you is above all other love, and my truth to you is above all other truth. Let me have hope and favor, and I am a forsworn man for your sake."[1]

Rosa puts her hands to her temples, and, pushing back her hair, looks wildly and abhorrently at him, as though she were trying to piece together what it is his deep purpose to present to her only in fragments.

"Reckon up nothing at this moment, angel, but the sacrifices that I lay at those dear feet, which I could fall down among the vilest ashes and kiss, and put upon my head as a poor savage might. There is my fidelity to my dear boy after death. Tread upon it!"

With an action of his hands, as though he cast down something precious.

"There is the inexpiable offence against my adoration of you. Spurn it!"

With a similar action.

"There are my labours in the cause of a just vengeance for six toiling months. Crush them!"

With another repetition of the action.

"There is my past and my present wasted life. There is the desolation of my heart and my soul. There is my peace; there is my despair. Stamp them into the dust, so that you take me, were it even mortally hating me!"

The frightful vehemence of the man, now reaching its full height, so additionally terrifies her as to break the spell that has held her to the spot. She swiftly moves towards the porch; but in an instant he is at her side, and speaking in her ear.

"Rosa, I am self-repressed again. I am walking calmly beside you to the house. I shall wait for some encouragement and hope. I shall not strike too soon. Give me a sign that you attend to me."

She slightly and constrainedly moves her hand.

"Not a word of this to any one, or it will bring down the blow, as certainly as night follows day. Another sign that you attend to me."

She moves her hand once more.

"I love you, love you, love you. If you were to cast me off now—but you will not—you would never be rid of me. No one should come between us. I would pursue you to the death."

The handmaid coming out to open the gate for him, he quietly pulls[2] off his hat as a parting salute, and goes away[3] with no greater show of agitation than is visible in the effigy of Mr. Sapsea's father opposite. Rosa faints in going up stairs, and is carefully carried to her room, and laid down on her bed. A thunderstorm is coming on, the maids say, and the hot and stifling air has overset the pretty dear; no wonder; they have felt their own knees all of a tremble all day long.

[1] sake] sweet sake MS P
[2] pulls] pulled MS P *corresponding change made in* P *in all the other verbs in this paragraph*
[3] away] away as he had gone out at this gate a thousand times, MS P

CHAPTER XX

A FLIGHT[1]

Rosa no sooner came to herself than the whole of the late interview was before her. It even seemed as if it had pursued her into her insensibility, and she had not had a moment's unconsciousness of it. What to do, she was at a frightened loss to know: the only one clear thought in her mind, was, that she must fly from this terrible man.

But where could she take refuge, and how could she go? She had never breathed her dread of him to any one but Helena. If she went to Helena, and told her what had passed, that very act might bring down the irreparable mischief that he threatened he had the power, and that she knew he had the will, to do. The more fearful he appeared to her excited memory and imagination, the more alarming her responsibility appeared: seeing that a slight mistake on her part, either in action or delay, might let his malevolence[2] loose on Helena's brother.

Rosa's mind throughout the last six months had been stormily confused. A half-formed,[3] wholly unexpressed suspicion tossed in it, now heaving itself up, and now sinking into the deep; now gaining palpability, and now losing it. His[4] self-absorption in his nephew when he was alive, and his unceasing pursuit of the inquiry how he came by his death, if he were dead, were themes so rife in the place, that no one appeared able to suspect the possibility of foul play at his hands. She had asked herself the question, "Am I so wicked in my thoughts as to conceive a wickedness that others cannot imagine?" Then she had considered, Did the suspicion come of her previous recoiling from him before the fact? And if so, was not that a proof of its baselessness?[5] Then she had reflected, "What motive could he have, according to my accusation?" She was ashamed to answer in her mind, "The motive of gaining *me!*" And covered her face, as if the lightest shadow of the idea of founding murder on such an idle vanity were a crime almost as great.

She ran over in her mind again, all that he had said[6] by the sun-dial in the garden. He had persisted in treating the disappearance[7] as murder, consistently with his whole public course since the finding of the watch and shirt-pin. If he were afraid of the crime being traced out, would he not rather encourage the idea of a voluntary disappearance? He had unnecessarily[8] declared that if the ties between him and his nephew had been

---

[1] A FLIGHT] ⟨"LET'S TALK"⟩ DIVERS FLIGHTS MS *unchanged in* P

[2] malevolence] blackest malevolence MS P   [3] half-formed] brief formed P

[4] His] MS P (*with no alteration*) ES Jasper's 70 73 75

[5] baselessness] injustice MS P   [6] said] said of that mystery MS P

[7] the disappearance] it MS P   [8] unnecessarily] MS even P 70–75

less strong, he might have swept "even him" away from her side. Was that like his having really done so? He had spoken of laying his six months' labours in the cause of a just vengeance at her feet. Would he have done that, with that violence of passion, if they were a pretence? Would he have ranged them with his desolate heart and soul, his wasted life, his peace, and his despair? The very first sacrifice that he represented himself as making for her, was his fidelity to his dear boy after death. Surely these facts were strong against a fancy that scarcely[1] dared to hint itself. And yet he was so terrible a man! In short, the poor girl (for what could she know of the criminal intellect, which its own professed students perpetually misread, because they persist in trying to reconcile it with the average intellect of average men, instead of identifying it as a horrible wonder apart), could get by no road to any other conclusion than that he *was* a terrible man, and must be fled from.

She had been Helena's stay and comfort during the whole time. She had constantly assured her of her full belief in her brother's innocence, and of her sympathy with him in his misery. But she had never seen him since the disappearance, nor had Helena ever spoken one word of his avowal to Mr. Crisparkle in regard of Rosa, though as a part of the interest of the case it was well known far and wide. He was Helena's unfortunate brother, to her, and nothing more. The assurance she had given her odious suitor was strictly true, though it would have been better (she considered[2] now) if she could have restrained herself from giving[3] it. Afraid of him as the bright and delicate little creature was, her spirit swelled[4] at the thought of his knowing it from her own lips.

But where was she to go? Anywhere beyond his reach, was no reply to the question. Somewhere must be thought of. She determined to go to her guardian, and to go immediately. The feeling she had imparted to Helena on the night of their first confidence, was so strong upon her—the feeling of not being safe from him, and of the solid walls of the old convent being powerless to keep out his ghostly following of her[5]—that no reasoning of her own could calm her terrors. The fascination of repulsion had been upon her so long, and now culminated so darkly, that she felt as if he had power to bind her by a spell. Glancing out at window, even now, as she rose to dress, the sight of the sun-dial on which he had leaned when he declared himself, turned her cold, and made her shrink from it, as though he had invested it with some awful quality from his own nature.

She wrote a hurried note to Miss Twinkleton, saying that she had sudden reason for wishing to see her guardian promptly, and had gone to him; also, entreating the good lady not to be uneasy, for all was well with her. She hurried a few quite useless articles into a very little bag,

---

[1] scarcely] hardly MS had P
[2] considered] thought MS P
[3] giving] MS so giving P (*with* so *deleted*) 70–75
[4] swelled] swells P
[5] to keep . . . of her] to keep his ghost from following her P

left the note in a conspicuous place, and went out, softly closing the gate[1] after her.

It was the first time she had ever been even in Cloisterham High Street, alone. But knowing all its ways and windings very well, she hurried straight to the corner from which the omnibus departed. It was, at that very moment, going off.

"Stop and take me, if you please, Joe. I am obliged to go to London."

In less than another minute she was on her road to the railway, under Joe's protection. Joe waited on her when she got there, put her safely into the railway carriage, and handed in the very little bag after her, as though it were some enormous trunk, hundredweights heavy, which she must on no account endeavour to lift.

"Can you go round when you get back, and tell Miss Twinkleton that you saw me safely off, Joe?"

"It shall be done, Miss."

"With my love, please, Joe."

"Yes, Miss—and I wouldn't mind having it myself!" But Joe did not articulate the last clause; only[2] thought it.

Now that she was whirling away for London in real earnest, Rosa was at leisure to resume the thoughts which her personal hurry had checked. The indignant thought that his declaration of love soiled her; that she could only be cleansed from the stain of its impurity by appealing against it[3] to the honest and true; supported her for a time against her fears, and confirmed her in her hasty resolution. But as the evening grew darker and darker, and the great city impended nearer and nearer, the doubts usual in such cases began to arise. Whether this was not a wild proceeding after all; how Mr. Grewgious might regard it; whether she would[4] find him at the journey's end; how she would act if he were absent; what might become of her, alone, in a place so strange and crowded; how if she had but waited and taken counsel first; whether, if she could now go back, she would not do it thankfully: a multitude of such uneasy speculations disturbed her, more and more as they accumulated. At length the train came into London over the housetops; and down below lay[5] the gritty streets with their yet un-needed lamps aglow, on a hot light summer night.

"Hiram Grewgious, Esquire, Staple Inn, London." This was all Rosa knew of her destination; but it was enough to send her rattling away again in a cab, through deserts of gritty streets, where many people crowded at the corners[6] of courts and bye-ways, to get some air, and where many other people walked with a miserably monotonous noise of shuffling feet[7] on hot paving-stones, and where all the people and all their surroundings were so gritty and so shabby.

[1] gate] door P   [2] only] but P   [3] against it] MS   *om.* P 70–75
[4] would] MS should P 70–75   [5] lay] there lay MS P
[6] corners] corner 73 75   [7] shuffling feet] shuffling of feet 75

There was music playing here and there, but it did not enliven the case. No barrel-organ mended the matter, and no big drum beat[1] dull care away. Like the chapel bells that were also going here and there, they only seemed to evoke echoes[2] from brick surfaces, and dust from everything. As to the flat[3] wind instruments, they seemed to have cracked their hearts and souls[4] in pining for the country.[5]

Her jingling conveyance stopped at last at a fast-closed gateway which appeared[6] to belong to somebody who had gone to bed very early, and was much afraid of housebreakers; Rosa, discharging her conveyance, timidly knocked at this gateway, and was let in, very little bag and all, by a watchman.

"Does Mr. Grewgious live here?"

"Mr. Grewgious lives there, Miss," said the watchman, pointing further in.

So Rosa went further in, and, when the clocks were striking ten, stood on P. J. T.'s doorsteps, wondering what P. J. T. had done with his street door.

Guided by the painted name of Mr. Grewgious, she went up stairs and softly tapped and tapped several times. But no one answering, and Mr. Grewgious's door-handle yielding to her touch, she went in, and saw her guardian sitting on a window-seat at an open window, with a shaded lamp placed far from him on a table in a corner.

Rosa drew nearer to him in the twilight of the room. He saw her, and he said in an under-tone: "Good Heaven!"[7]

Rosa fell upon his neck, with tears, and then he said, returning her embrace:

"My child, my child! I thought you were your mother!"

"But what, what, what," he added, soothingly, "has happened? My dear, what has brought you here? Who has brought you here?"

"No one. I came alone."

"Lord bless me!" ejaculated Mr. Grewgious. "Came alone! Why didn't you write to me to come and fetch you?"

"I had no time. I took a sudden resolution. Poor, poor Eddy!"

"Ah, poor fellow, poor fellow!"

"His uncle has made love to me. I cannot bear it," said Rosa, at once with a burst of tears, and a stamp of her little foot; "I shudder with horror of him, and I have come to you to protect me and[8] all of us from him. You[9] will?"

¹ beat] sent that P
² only seemed to evoke echoes] seemed to evoke only flat echoes MS P
³ the flat] not in MS P   ⁴ and souls] not in MS P
⁵ There was ... country] paragraph written on verso of MS for insertion
⁶ appeared] seemed MS P   ⁷ Heaven] Heavens P
⁸ me and] not in MS P   ⁹ him. You] MS him, if you P 70–75

"I will!" cried Mr. Grewgious, with a sudden rush of amazing energy. "Damn him!

> "Confound his politics,
> Frustrate his knavish tricks!
> On Thee his hopes to fix?
> Damn him again!"

After this most extraordinary outburst, Mr. Grewgious, quite beside himself, plunged about the room,[1] to all appearance undecided whether he was in a fit of loyal enthusiasm, or combative denunciation.[2]

He stopped and said, wiping his face: "I beg your pardon, my dear, but you will be glad to know I feel better. Tell me no more just now, or I might do it again. You must be refreshed and cheered. What did you take last? Was it breakfast, lunch, dinner, tea, or supper? And what will you take next?[3] Shall it be breakfast, lunch, dinner, tea, or supper?"

The respectful tenderness with which, on one knee before her, he helped her to remove her hat, and disentangle her pretty hair from it, was quite a chivalrous sight. Yet who, knowing him only on the surface, would have expected chivalry—and of the true sort, too: not the spurious—from Mr. Grewgious?

"Your rest too must be provided for," he went on; "and you shall have the prettiest chamber in Furnival's. Your toilet must be provided for, and you shall have everything that an unlimited head chambermaid—by which expression I mean a head chambermaid not limited as to outlay—can procure. Is that a bag?" he looked hard at it; sooth[4] to say, it required hard looking at to be seen at all in a dimly lighted room: "and is it your property, my dear?"

"Yes, sir. I brought it with me."

"It is not an extensive bag," said Mr. Grewgious, candidly, "though admirably[5] calculated to contain a day's provision for a canary bird. Perhaps you brought a canary bird?"

Rosa smiled, and shook her head.

"If you had he should have been made welcome," said Mr. Grewgious, "and I think he would have been pleased to be hung upon a nail outside and pit himself against our Staple sparrows; whose execution must be admitted to be not quite equal to their intention. Which is the case with so many of us! You didn't say what meal, my dear. Have a nice jumble of all meals."

Rosa thanked him, but said she could only take a cup of tea. Mr. Grewgious, after several times running out, and in again, to mention such supplementary items as marmalade, eggs, water-cresses, salted[6] fish, and

---

[1] room,] room brandishing his arms ⟨and⟩ MS room brandishing his arms, and P
[2] denunciation] denunciation, or both MS P
[3] next] to-night P
[4] it; sooth] it—for, sooth MS P
[5] admirably] admirably well MS P
[6] salted] *not in* MS P

MR. GREWGIOUS EXPERIENCES A NEW SENSATION

frizzled ham, ran across to Furnival's without his hat, to give his various directions. And soon afterwards they were realized in practice, and the board was spread.

"Lord bless my soul!" cried Mr. Grewgious, putting the lamp upon it, and taking his seat opposite Rosa; "what a new sensation for a poor old Angular bachelor, to be sure!"

Rosa's expressive little eyebrows asked him what he meant?

"The sensation of having a sweet young presence in the place that whitewashes it, paints it, papers it, decorates it with gilding, and makes it Glorious!" said Mr. Grewgious. "Ah me! Ah me!"

As there was something mournful in his sigh, Rosa, in touching him with his[1] tea-cup, ventured to touch him with her small hand too.[2]

"Thank you, my dear," said Mr. Grewgious. "Ahem! Let's talk."

"Do you always live here, sir?" asked Rosa.

"Yes, my dear."

"And always alone?"

"Always alone; except that I have daily company in a gentleman by the name of Bazzard; my clerk."

"*He* doesn't live here?"

"No, he goes his ways[3] after office hours. In fact, he is off duty here, altogether, just[4] at present; and a Firm down stairs with which I have business relations, lend me a substitute. But it would be extremely difficult to replace Mr. Bazzard."

"He must be very fond of you," said Rosa.

"He bears up against it with commendable fortitude if he is," returned Mr. Grewgious, after considering the matter. "But I doubt if he is. Not particularly so. You see, he is discontented, poor fellow."

"Why isn't he contented?" was the natural inquiry.

"Misplaced," said Mr. Grewgious, with great mystery.

Rosa's eyebrows resumed their inquisitive and perplexed expression.

"So misplaced," Mr. Grewgious went on, "that I feel constantly apologetic towards him. And he feels (though he doesn't mention it) that I have reason to be."

Mr. Grewgious had by this time grown so very mysterious, that Rosa did not know how to go on. While she was thinking about it Mr. Grewgious suddenly jerked out of himself for the second time:

"Let's talk. We were speaking of Mr. Bazzard. It's a secret, and moreover it is Mr. Bazzard's secret; but the sweet presence[5] at my table makes me so unusually expansive, that I feel I must impart it in inviolable confidence. What do you think Mr. Bazzard has done?"

---

[1] his] her 73 75   [2] too] too. He put it to his lips MS P
[3] ways] way 73 75
[4] just] *not in* MS P   MS *at first merely had* off duty at present
[5] sweet presence] sweet presence I have mentioned MS P

"Oh dear!" cried Rosa, drawing her chair a little nearer, and her mind reverting to Jasper, "nothing dreadful, I hope?"

"He has written a play," said Mr. Grewgious, in a solemn whisper. "A tragedy."

Rosa seemed much relieved.

"And nobody," pursued Mr. Grewgious in the same tone, "will hear, on any account whatever, of bringing it out."

Rosa looked reflective, and nodded her head slowly; as who should say: "Such things are, and why are they!"

"Now, you know," said Mr. Grewgious, "*I* couldn't[1] write a play."

"Not a bad one, sir?" asked[2] Rosa, innocently, with her eyebrows again in action.

"No. If I was under sentence of decapitation, and was about to be instantly decapitated, and an express arrived with a pardon for the condemned convict Grewgious if he wrote a play, I should be under the necessity of resuming the block and begging the executioner to proceed to extremities,—meaning," said Mr. Grewgious, passing his hand under his chin, "the singular number, and this extremity."

Rosa appeared to consider what she would do if the awkward suppositious case were hers.

"Consequently," said Mr. Grewgious, "Mr. Bazzard would have a sense of my inferiority to himself under any circumstances; but when I am his master, you know,[3] the case is greatly aggravated."

Mr. Grewgious shook his head seriously, as if he felt the offence to be a little too much, though of his own committing.

"How came you to be his master, sir?" asked Rosa.

"A question that naturally follows," said Mr. Grewgious. "Let's talk. Mr. Bazzard's father, being a Norfolk farmer, would have furiously laid about him with a flail, a pitchfork, and every agricultural implement available for assaulting purposes, on the slightest hint of his son's having written a play. So the son, bringing to me the father's rent (which I receive), imparted his secret, and pointed out that he was determined to pursue his genius, and that it would put him in peril of starvation, and that he was not formed for it."

"For pursuing his genius, sir?"

"No, my dear," said Mr. Grewgious,[4] "for starvation. It was impossible to deny the position that Mr. Bazzard was not formed to be starved, and Mr. Bazzard then pointed out that it was desirable that I should stand between him and a fate so perfectly unsuited to his formation.[5] In that way Mr. Bazzard became my clerk, and he feels it very much."

"I am glad he is grateful," said Rosa.

---

[1] couldn't] cannot P   [2] asked] said 75   [3] you know,] *not in* MS P
[4] Mr. Grewgious] Mr. Grewgious, correctively MS P
[5] formation] formation until he achieved renown MS P

"I[1] didn't quite mean that, my dear. I mean that he feels the degradation. There are some other geniuses that Mr. Bazzard has become acquainted with, who have also written tragedies, which likewise nobody will on any account whatever hear of bringing out, and these choice spirits dedicate their plays to one another in a highly panegyrical manner. Mr. Bazzard has been the subject of one of these dedications. Now, you know, *I* never had a play dedicated to *me!*"

Rosa looked at him as if she would have liked him to be the recipient of a thousand dedications.

"Which again, naturally, rubs against the grain of Mr. Bazzard," said Mr. Grewgious. "He is very short with me sometimes, and then I feel that he is meditating: 'This blockhead my master![2] A fellow who couldn't write a tragedy on pain of death, and who will never have one dedicated to him with the most complimentary congratulations on the high position he has taken in the eyes of posterity!' Very trying, very trying. However, in giving him directions, I reflect beforehand: 'Perhaps he may not like this,' or 'He might take it ill if I asked that,' and so we get on very well. Indeed, better than I could have expected."

"Is the tragedy named, sir?" asked Rosa.

"Strictly between ourselves," answered Mr. Grewgious, "it has a dreadfully appropriate name. It is[3] called The Thorn of Anxiety. But Mr. Bazzard hopes—and I hope—that it will come out at last."

It was not hard to divine that Mr. Grewgious had related the Bazzard history thus fully, at least quite as much for the recreation of his ward's mind from the subject that had driven her there, as for the gratification of his own tendency to be social and communicative. "And now, my dear," he said at this point, "if you are not too tired to tell me more of what passed to-day—but only if you feel quite able—I should be glad to hear it. I may digest it the better, if I sleep on it to-night."

Rosa, composed now, gave him a faithful account of the interview. Mr. Grewgious often smoothed his head while it was in progress, and begged to be told a second time those parts which bore on Helena and Neville.[4] When Rosa had finished, he sat, grave, silent, and meditative, for a while.

"Clearly narrated," was his only remark at last, "and, I hope, clearly put away here," smoothing his head again: "See, my dear," taking her to the open window, "where they live! The dark windows[5] over yonder."

"I may go to Helena to-morrow?" asked Rosa.

"I should like to sleep on that question to-night," he answered, doubtfully. "But let me take you to your own rest, for you must need it."

With that, Mr. Grewgious helped her to get her hat on again, and hung

[1] I] Hem! I MS P
[2] This blockhead my master!] MS This blockhead is my master! P 70–75
[3] It is] It's P   [4] Helena and Neville] Helena and Neville Landless MS P
[5] windows] window P

upon his arm the very little bag that was of no earthly use, and led her by the hand (with a certain stately awkwardness, as if he were going to walk a minuet) across Holborn, and into Furnival's Inn. At the hotel door, he confided her to the Unlimited head chambermaid, and said that while she went up to see her room, he would remain below, in case she should wish it exchanged for another, or should find that there was anything she wanted.

Rosa's room was airy, clean, comfortable, almost[1] gay. The Unlimited had laid in everything omitted from the very little bag (that is to say, everything she could possibly need), and Rosa tripped down the great many stairs again, to thank her guardian for his thoughtful and affectionate care of her.

"Not at all, my dear," said Mr. Grewgious, infinitely gratified; "it is I who thank you for your charming confidence and for your charming company. Your breakfast will be provided for you in a neat, compact,[2] and graceful little sitting-room (appropriate to your figure),[3] and I will come to you at ten o'clock in the morning. I hope you don't feel very strange indeed, in this strange place."

"Oh no, I feel so safe!"

"Yes, you may be sure that the stairs are fire-proof," said Mr. Grewgious, "and that any outbreak of the devouring element would be perceived and suppressed by the watchmen."

"I did not mean that," Rosa replied. "I mean, I feel so safe[4] from him."

"There is a stout gate of iron bars to keep him out," said Mr. Grewgious, smiling,[5] "and Furnival's is specially[6] watched and lighted, and *I* live over the way!" In the stoutness of his knight-errantry, he seemed to think the last-named protection all-sufficient. In the same spirit, he said to the gate-porter as he went out, "If some one staying in the hotel should wish to send across the road to me in the night, a crown will be ready for the messenger." In the same spirit, he walked up and down outside the iron gate for the best part of an hour, with some solicitude: occasionally looking in between the bars, as if he had laid a dove in a high roost in a cage of lions, and had it on his mind that she might tumble out.

[1] almost] and almost P   [2] compact] *not in* MS P
[3] figure)] figure) close to your own chamber MS P
[4] "Yes, you may be sure . . . so safe] *deleted in* P *and Rosa's speech run on*
[5] smiling,] *not in* MS P
[6] is specially] MS P   is fire-proof and specially 70–75   *inserted in* P *when previous* fire-proof *reference deleted*
END OF No. V AS PUBLISHED

CHAPTER XXI

A RECOGNITION

Nothing occurred in the night to flutter the tired dove, and the dove arose refreshed. With Mr. Grewgious when the clocks[1] struck ten in the morning, came Mr. Crisparkle, who had come at one plunge out of the river at Cloisterham.

"Miss Twinkleton was so uneasy, Miss Rosa," he explained to her,[2] "and came round to Ma and me with your note, in such a state of wonder, that, to quiet her, I volunteered on this service by the very first train to be caught in the morning. I wished at the time that you had come to me; but now I think it best that you did *as* you did, and came to your guardian."

"I did think of you," Rosa told him; "but Minor Canon Corner was so near him——"

"I understand. It was quite natural."[3]

"I have told Mr. Crisparkle," said Mr. Grewgious, "all that you told me last night, my dear. Of course I should have written it to him immediately; but his coming was most opportune. And it was particularly kind of him to come, for he had but just gone."

"Have you settled," asked Rosa, appealing to them both, "what is to be done for Helena and her brother?"

"Why really," said Mr. Crisparkle, "I am in great perplexity. If even Mr. Grewgious, whose head is much longer than mine and who is a whole night's cogitation in advance of me, is undecided, what must I be!"[4]

The Unlimited here put her head in at the door—after having tapped,[5] and been authorized[6] to present herself—announcing that a gentleman wished for a word with another gentleman named Crisparkle, if any such gentleman were there. If no such gentleman were there, he begged pardon for being mistaken.

"Such a gentleman is here," said Mr. Crisparkle, "but is engaged just now."

"Oh, is[7] it a dark gentleman?" interposed Rosa, retreating on her guardian.

"No, Miss, more of a brown gentleman."

"You are sure not with black hair?" asked Rosa, taking courage.

"Quite sure of that, Miss. Brown hair and blue eyes."

"Perhaps," hinted Mr. Grewgious, with habitual caution, "it might be well to see him, reverend sir, if you don't object. When one is in a difficulty,

CHAPTER XXI A RECOGNITION] *not in* MS P *no alteration in* P
[1] clocks] MS clock P 70–75   [2] her] Rosa MS P ES
[3] I wished at the time . . . quite natural.] *deleted in* P
[4] "Have you settled . . . must I be!"] *deleted in* P   [5] tapped] MS rapped P 70–75
[6] authorized] invited MS P ES   [7] Oh, is] MS Is P 70–75

or at a loss, one never knows in what direction a way out[1] may chance to open. It is a business principle of mine, in such a case, not to close up any direction, but to keep an eye on every direction that may present itself. I could relate an anecdote in point, but that it would be premature."

"If Miss Rosa will allow me then? Let the gentleman come in," said Mr. Crisparkle.

The gentleman came in; apologized, with a frank but modest grace, for not finding Mr. Crisparkle alone; turned to Mr. Crisparkle, and smilingly asked the unexpected question: "Who am I?"

"You are the gentleman I saw smoking under the trees in Staple[2] Inn a few minutes ago."

"True. There I saw you. Who else am I?"

Mr. Crisparkle concentrated his attention on a handsome face, much sunburnt; and the ghost of some departed boy seemed to rise, gradually and dimly, in the room.[3]

The gentleman saw a struggling recollection lighten up the Minor Canon's features, and smiling again, said: "What will you have for breakfast this morning? You are out of jam."

"Wait a moment!" cried Mr. Crisparkle, raising his right hand. "Give me another instant! Tartar!"

The two shook hands with the greatest heartiness, and then went the wonderful length—for Englishmen—of laying their hands each on the other's shoulders, and looking joyfully each into the other's face.

"My old fag!" said Mr. Crisparkle.

"My old master!" said Mr. Tartar.

"You saved me from drowning!" said Mr. Crisparkle.

"After which you took to swimming, you know!" said Mr. Tartar.

"God bless my soul!" said Mr. Crisparkle.

"Amen!" said Mr. Tartar.

And then they fell to shaking hands most heartily again.

"Imagine," exclaimed Mr. Crisparkle, with glistening eyes: "Miss Rosa Bud and Mr. Grewgious: imagine Mr. Tartar, when he was the smallest of juniors, diving for me, catching me, a big heavy senior, by the hair of my[4] head, and striking out for the shore with me like a water-giant!"

"Imagine my not letting him sink, as I was his fag!" said Mr. Tartar. "But the truth being that he was my best protector and friend, and did me more good than all the masters put together, an irrational impulse seized me either to[5] pick him up, or go down with him."

"Hem! Permit me, sir, to have the honor," said Mr. Grewgious, advancing with extended hand, "for an honor I truly esteem it. I am proud to make your acquaintance. I hope you didn't take cold. I hope you were

1 out] out of it MS P ES
3 *Proof changes from page to galley here*
5 either to] MS rather to P ES to 70 73 75
2 Staple] Staples MS
4 my] MS the P 70–75

not inconvenienced by swallowing too much water. How have you been since?"

It was by no means apparent that Mr. Grewgious knew what he said, though it was very apparent that he meant to say something highly[1] friendly and appreciative.

If Heaven, Rosa thought, had but sent such courage and skill to her poor mother's aid! And he to have been so slight and young then!

"I don't wish to be complimented upon it, I thank you, but I think I have an idea," Mr. Grewgious announced, after taking a jog-trot or two across the room, so very[2] unexpected and unaccountable that they had[3] all stared at him, doubtful whether he was choking, or had the cramp. "I *think* I have an idea. I believe I have had the pleasure of seeing Mr. Tartar's name as tenant of the top set in the house[4] next the top set in the corner?"

"Yes, sir," returned Mr. Tartar. "You are right so far."

"I am right so far," said Mr. Grewgious. "Tick that off," which he did, with his right thumb on his left. "Might you happen to know the name of your neighbour in the top set on the other side of the party-wall?" coming very close to Mr. Tartar, to lose nothing of his face, in his shortness of sight.

"Landless."

"Tick that off," said Mr. Grewgious, taking another trot, and then coming back. "No personal knowledge, I suppose, sir?"

"Slight, but some."

"Tick that off," said Mr. Grewgious, taking another trot, and again coming back. "Nature of knowledge, Mr. Tartar?"

"I thought he seemed to be a young fellow in a poor way, and I asked his leave—only within a day or so[5]—to share my flowers up there with him; that is to say, to extend my flower-garden[6] to his windows."

"Would you have the kindness to take seats?" said Mr. Grewgious. "I *have* an idea!"

They complied; Mr. Tartar none[7] the less readily, for being all abroad; and Mr. Grewgious, seated in the centre, with his hands upon his knees, thus stated his idea,[8] with his usual manner of having got the statement by heart.

"I cannot as yet make up my mind whether it is prudent to hold open communication under present circumstances, and on the part of the fair member of the present company, with Mr. Neville or Miss Helena. I have reason to know that a local friend of ours (on whom I beg to bestow a passing but a hearty malediction, with the kind permission of my reverend

---

[1] highly] *not in* MS P ES
[2] very] MS *om.* P 70–75
[3] had] *om.* 73 75
[4] in the house] *not in* MS P ES
[5] within a day or so] just now MS P ES
[6] flower-garden] flower-gardens P ES
[7] none] more P (*uncorrected*) ES
[8] idea] ideas P ES

friend) sneaks to and fro, and dodges up and down. When not doing so
himself, he may have some informant skulking about, in the person of any[1]
watchman, porter, or such-like hanger-on of Staple.[2] On the other hand,
Miss Rosa very naturally wishes to see her friend Miss Helena, and it
would seem important that at least Miss Helena (if not her brother too,
through her) should privately know from Miss Rosa's lips what has
occurred, and what has been threatened. Am I agreed with generally in
the views I take?"

"I entirely coincide with them," said Mr. Crisparkle, who had been
very attentive.

"As I have no doubt I should," added Mr. Tartar, smiling, "if I understood them."

"Fair and softly, dear[3] sir," said Mr. Grewgious; "we shall fully confide
in you directly, if you will favor us with your permission.[4] Now, if our
local friend should have any informant on the spot, it is tolerably clear
that such informant can only be set to watch the chambers in the occupation of Mr. Neville. He reporting, to our local friend, who comes and goes
there, our local friend would supply for himself, from his own previous
knowledge, the identity of the parties. Nobody can be set to watch all
Staple,[2] or to concern himself with comers and goers to other sets of
chambers: unless, indeed, mine."

"I begin to understand to what you tend," said Mr. Crisparkle, "and I[5]
highly approve of your caution."

"I needn't repeat that I know nothing yet of the why and wherefore,"
said Mr. Tartar; "but I also understood to what you tend, so let me say at
once that my chambers are freely at your disposal."[6]

"There!" cried Mr. Grewgious, smoothing his head triumphantly.
"Now we have all got the idea.[7] You have it, my dear?"

"I think I have," said Rosa, blushing a little as Mr. Tartar looked
quickly towards her.

"You see, you go over to Staple[2] with Mr. Crisparkle and Mr. Tartar,"
said Mr. Grewgious; "I going in and out and out and in, alone, in my
usual way; you go up with those gentlemen to Mr. Tartar's rooms; you
look into Mr. Tartar's flower-garden; you wait for Miss Helena's appearance there, or you signify to Miss Helena that you are close by; and you
communicate with her freely, and no spy can be the wiser."

"I am very much afraid I shall be——"

[1] any] MS a P 70–75
[2] Staple] Staples MS P ES
[3] dear] MS *om.* P 70–75
[4] Am I agreed with generally . . . your permission.] *deleted in P*
[5] I] MS *om.* P 70–75
[6] "I begin to understand . . . disposal."] *deleted in P and Mr. Grewgious's speech run on*
[7] Now we have all got the idea.] *changed in P, in line with the preceding deletion, to* Have
we all got the idea?

"Be what, my dear?" asked Mr. Grewgious, as she hesitated. "Not frightened?"

"No, not that," said Rosa, shyly;—"in Mr. Tartar's way. We seem to be appropriating Mr. Tartar's residence so very coolly."

"I protest to you," returned that gentleman, "that I shall think the better of it for evermore, if your voice sounds in it only once."

Rosa not quite knowing what to say about that, cast down her eyes, and turning to Mr. Grewgious, dutifully asked if she should put her hat on? Mr. Grewgious being of opinion that she could not do better, she withdrew for the purpose. Mr. Crisparkle took the opportunity of giving Mr. Tartar a summary of the distresses of Neville and his sister; the opportunity was quite long enough,[1] as the hat happened to require a little extra fitting on.[2]

Mr. Tartar gave his arm to Rosa, and Mr. Crisparkle walked, detached, in front.

"Poor, poor Eddy!" thought Rosa, as they went[3] along.

Mr. Tartar waved his right hand as he bent his head down over Rosa, talking in an animated[4] way.

"It was not so powerful or so sun-browned when it saved Mr. Crisparkle," thought Rosa, glancing at it; "but it must have been very steady and determined even[5] then."

Mr. Tartar told her he had been a sailor, roving everywhere for years and years.

"When are you going to sea again?" asked Rosa.

"Never!"

Rosa wondered what the girls would say[6] if they could see her crossing the wide street on the sailor's arm. And she feared[7] that the passers-by must think her very little and very helpless, contrasted with the strong figure that could have caught her up and carried her out of any danger, miles and miles, without resting.[8]

She was thinking further, that his far-seeing blue eyes looked as if they had been used to watch danger afar off, and to watch it without flinching, drawing[9] nearer and nearer: when, happening to raise her own eyes, she found that he seemed to be thinking something about *them*.

This a little confused Rosebud, and may account for her never afterwards quite knowing how she ascended (with his help) to his garden in the air, and seemed to get[10] into a marvellous country that came into sudden

---

1 long enough] long enough for the purpose MS P ES
2 on] *not in* MS P ES   3 went] walked MS P ES
4 an animated] his animated MS P ES
5 even] *apparently deleted in* MS   *om.* P ES   6 say] think MS P ES
7 feared] MS *probable not certain*   fancied P 70–75
8 danger . . . resting] danger without resting, miles and miles MS P ES
9 drawing] coming MS P ES
10 seemed to get] got MS P ES

bloom[1] like the country on the summit of the magic beanstalk. May it
flourish[2] for ever!

CHAPTER XXII

A GRITTY STATE OF THINGS COMES ON

MR. TARTAR's chambers were the neatest, the cleanest, and the best
ordered chambers ever seen under the sun, moon, and stars. The floors
were scrubbed to that extent, that you might have supposed the London
blacks emancipated for ever, and gone out of the land for good. Every inch
of brass-work in Mr. Tartar's possession was polished and burnished, till
it shone like a brazen mirror. No speck, nor spot, nor spatter soiled the
purity of any of Mr. Tartar's household gods, large, small, or middle-
sized. His sitting-room was like the admiral's cabin, his bath-room was
like a dairy, his sleeping-chamber, fitted all about with lockers and
drawers, was like a seedsman's shop; and his nicely-balanced cot just
stirred in the midst, as if it breathed. Everything belonging to Mr. Tartar
had quarters of its own assigned to it: his maps and charts had their
quarters; his books had theirs; his brushes had theirs; his boots[3] had
theirs; his clothes had theirs; his case-bottles had theirs; his telescopes
and other instruments had theirs. Everything was readily accessible. Shelf,
bracket, locker, hook, and drawer were equally within reach, and were
equally contrived with a view to avoiding waste of room, and providing
some snug inches of stowage for something that would have exactly fitted
nowhere else. His gleaming little service of plate was so arranged upon
his sideboard as that a slack salt-spoon would have instantly betrayed
itself; his toilet implements were so arranged upon his dressing-table as
that a toothpick of slovenly deportment could have been reported at a
glance. So with the curiosities he had brought home from various
voyages. Stuffed, dried, repolished,[4] or otherwise preserved, according
to their kind; birds, fishes, reptiles, arms, articles of dress, shells, sea-
weeds, grasses, or memorials of coral reef; each was displayed in its
especial[5] place, and each could have been displayed in no better place.
Paint and varnish seemed to be kept somewhere out of sight, in constant
readiness to obliterate stray finger-marks wherever any might become

---

[1] came into sudden bloom] bloomed MS P ES

[2] flourish] *proof to Fildes has* bloom *and* inserted *before* flourish: *proof to printers has
insertion subsequently deleted*
END OF No. V AS PLANNED BY DICKENS   *proofs to printers finish* here
CHAPTER XXII] CHAPTER XXI MS

[3] boots] *possibly* top boots MS

[4] repolished] *possibly* polished MS   [5] especial] *possibly* special MS

perceptible in Mr. Tartar's chambers. No man-of-war was ever kept more spick and span from careless touch. On this bright summer day, a neat awning was rigged over Mr. Tartar's flower-garden as only a sailor could rig it; and there was a sea-going air upon the whole effect, so delightfully complete, that the flower-garden might have appertained to stern-windows afloat, and the whole concern might have bowled away gallantly with all on board, if Mr. Tartar had only clapped to his lips the speaking-trumpet that was slung in a corner, and given hoarse orders to have[1] the anchor up, look alive there, men, and get all sail upon her!

Mr. Tartar doing the honors of this gallant craft, was of a piece with the rest. When a man rides an amiable hobby that shies at nothing and kicks nobody, it is always[2] agreeable to find him riding it with a humorous sense of the droll side of the creature. When the man is a cordial and an earnest man by nature, and withal is perfectly fresh and genuine, it may be doubted whether he is ever seen to greater advantage than at such a time. So Rosa would have naturally thought (even if she *hadn't*[3] been conducted over the ship with all the homage due to the First Lady of the Admiralty, or First Fairy of the Sea), that it was charming to see and hear Mr. Tartar half laughing at, and half rejoicing in, his various contrivances. So Rosa would have naturally thought, anyhow, that the sunburnt sailor showed to great advantage when, the inspection finished, he delicately withdrew out of his admiral's cabin, beseeching her to consider herself its Queen, and waving her free of its[4] flower-garden with the hand that had had[5] Mr. Crisparkle's life in it.

"Helena! Helena Landless! Are you there?"[6]

"Who speaks to me? Not Rosa?" Then a second handsome face appearing.

"Yes, my darling!"

"Why, how did you come here, dearest?"

"I—I don't quite know," said Rosa with a blush; "unless I am dreaming!"

Why with a blush? For their two faces were alone with the other flowers. Are blushes among the fruits of the country of the magic bean-stalk?

"*I* am not dreaming," said Helena, smiling. "I should take more for granted if I were. How do we come together—or so near together—so very unexpectedly?"

Unexpectedly indeed, among the dingy gables and chimneypots of P. J. T.'s connexion, and the flowers that had sprung from the salt sea.

[1] have] heave 75   [2] always] MS only 70–75
[3] *hadn't*] MS hadn't 70–75   [4] its] MS his 70–75
[5] had had] had ES
[6] Mr. Tartar doing the honors . . . Are you there?"] *written in MS on slip pasted over the original reading*

But Rosa, waking, told in a hurry how they came to be together, and all the why and wherefore of that matter.

"And Mr. Crisparkle is here," said Rosa, in rapid conclusion; "and could you believe it? Long ago, he saved his life!"

"I could believe any such thing of Mr. Crisparkle," returned Helena, with a mantling face.

(More blushes in the beanstalk country!)

"Yes, but it wasn't Mr. Crisparkle," said Rosa, quickly putting in the correction.

"I don't understand, love."

"It was very nice of Mr. Crisparkle to be saved," said Rosa, "and he couldn't have shown his high opinion of Mr. Tartar more expressively. But it was Mr. Tartar who saved him."

Helena's dark eyes looked very earnestly at the bright face among the leaves, and she asked, in a slower and more thoughtful tone:

"Is Mr. Tartar with you now, dear?"

"No; because he has given up his rooms to me—to[1] us, I mean. It is[2] such a beautiful place!"

"Is it?"

"It is like the inside of the most exquisite ship that ever sailed. It is like—it is like——"

"Like a dream?" suggested Helena.

Rosa answered with a little nod, and smelled the flowers.

Helena resumed, after a short pause of silence, during which she seemed (or it was Rosa's fancy) to compassionate somebody: "My poor Neville is reading in his own room, the sun being so very bright on this side just now. I think he had better not know that you are so near."

"Oh, I think so too!" cried Rosa very readily.

"I suppose," pursued Helena, doubtfully, "that he must know by-and-bye all you have told me; but I am not sure. Ask Mr. Crisparkle's advice, my darling. Ask him whether I may tell Neville as much or as little of what you have told me as I think best."

Rosa subsided into her state-cabin, and propounded the question. The Minor Canon was for the free exercise of Helena's judgment.

"I thank him very much," said Helena, when Rosa emerged again with her report. "Ask him whether it would be best to wait until any new[3] maligning and pursuing of Neville on the part of this wretch shall disclose itself, or to try to anticipate it: I mean, so far as to find out whether any such goes on darkly about us?"

The Minor Canon found this point so difficult to give a confident opinion on, that, after two or three attempts and failures, he suggested a reference to Mr. Grewgious. Helena acquiescing, he betook himself (with a most

[1] to] *word blotted, possibly deleted in* MS   [2] *is*] is 73 75
[3] new] MS more 70–75

unsuccessful assumption of lounging indifference) across the quadrangle
to P. J. T.'s, and stated it. Mr. Grewgious held decidedly to the general
principle, that if you could steal a march upon a brigand or a wild beast,
you had better do it; he also held decidedly to the special case, that John
Jasper was a brigand *and*[1] a wild beast in combination.

Thus advised, Mr. Crisparkle came back again and reported to Rosa,
who in her turn reported to Helena. She, now steadily pursuing her train
of thought at her window, considered thereupon.

"We may count on Mr. Tartar's readiness to help us, Rosa?" she
inquired.

Oh yes! Rosa shyly thought so. Oh yes, Rosa shyly believed she could
almost answer for that.[2] But should she ask Mr. Crisparkle? "I think your
authority on the point as good as his, my dear," said Helena, sedately,
"and you needn't disappear again for that." Odd of Helena!

"You see, Neville," Helena pursued after more reflection, "knows no
one else here: he has not so much as exchanged a word with any one else
here. If Mr. Tartar would[3] call to see him openly and often; if he would
spare a minute for the purpose, frequently; if he would even do so, almost
daily; something might come of it."

"Something might come of it, dear?" repeated Rosa, surveying her
friend's beauty with a highly perplexed face. "Something might?"

"If Neville's movements are really watched, and if the purpose really
is to isolate him from all friends and acquaintance and wear his daily life
out grain by grain (which would seem to be in[4] the threat to you), does it
not appear likely," said Helena, "that his enemy would in some way communicate with Mr. Tartar to warn him off from Neville? In which case,
we might not only know the fact but might know from Mr. Tartar what
the terms of the communication were."

"I see!" cried Rosa. And immediately darted into her state-cabin
again.

Presently her pretty face reappeared, with a heightened[5] color, and she
said that she had told Mr. Crisparkle, and that Mr. Crisparkle had fetched
in Mr. Tartar, and that Mr. Tartar—"who is waiting now in case you want
him," added Rosa, with a half look back, and in not a little confusion
between the inside of the state-cabin and the out[6]—had declared his
readiness to act as she had suggested, and to enter on his task that very
day.

"I thank him from my heart," said Helena. "Pray tell him so."

Again not a little confused between the flower-garden and the cabin, Rosa
dipped in with her message, and dipped out again with more assurances

---

[1] he also . . . *and*] MS and he also . . . and 70–75   [2] that] ⟨it⟩ that MS it 70–75
[3] would] should ES   [4] in] ⟨part of⟩ in MS *om.* 70–75
[5] heightened] ⟨greatly⟩ heightened MS greatly heightened 70–75
[6] the out] MS out 70–75

from Mr. Tartar, and stood wavering in a divided state between Helena and him, which proved that confusion is not always necessarily awkward, but may sometimes present a very pleasant appearance.

"And now, darling," said Helena, "we will be mindful of the caution that has restricted us to this interview for the present, and will part. I hear Neville moving too. Are you going back?"

"To Miss Twinkleton's?" asked Rosa.

"Yes."

"Oh, I could never go there any more; I couldn't indeed, after that dreadful interview!" said Rosa.

"Then where *are* you going, pretty one?"

"Now I come to think of it, I don't know," said Rosa. "I have settled nothing at all yet, but my guardian will take care of me. Don't be uneasy, dear. I shall be sure to be somewhere."

(It did seem likely.)

"And I shall hear of my Rosebud from Mr. Tartar?" inquired Helena.

"Yes, I suppose so; from——" Rosa looked back again in a flutter, instead of supplying the name. "But tell me one thing before we part, dearest Helena. Tell me that you are sure, sure, sure, I couldn't help it."

"Help it, love?"

"Help making him malicious and revengeful. I couldn't hold any terms with him, could I?"

"You know how I love you, darling," answered Helena, with indignation; "but I would sooner see you dead at his wicked feet."

"That's a great comfort to me! And you will tell your poor brother so, won't you? And you will give him my remembrance and my sympathy? And you will ask him not to hate me?"

With a mournful shake of the head, as if that would be quite a superfluous entreaty, Helena lovingly kissed her two hands to her friend, and her friend's two hands were kissed to her; and then she saw a third hand (a brown one) appear among the flowers and leaves, and help her friend out of sight.

The refection[1] that Mr. Tartar produced in the admiral's cabin by merely touching the spring knob of[2] a locker and the handle of a drawer, was a dazzling enchanted repast. Wonderful macaroons, glittering liqueurs, magically preserved tropical spices, and jellies of celestial tropical fruits, displayed themselves profusely at an instant's notice. But Mr. Tartar could not make time stand still; and time, with his hard-hearted fleetness, strode on so fast, that Rosa was obliged to come down from the beanstalk country to earth, and her guardian's chambers.

"And now, my dear," said Mr. Grewgious, "what is to be done next? To put the same thought in another form; what is to be done with you?"

Rosa could only look apologetically sensible of being very much in her

---

[1] refection] MS 75 reflection 70 ES 73   [2] of] in ES

THE MYSTERY OF EDWIN DROOD

own way, and in everybody else's. Some passing idea of living, fire-proof, up a good many stairs in Furnival's Inn for the rest of her life, was the only thing in the nature of a plan that occurred to her.

"It has come into my thoughts," said Mr. Grewgious, "that the respected lady, Miss Twinkleton, occasionally repairs to London in the recess, with the view of extending her connexion, and being available for interviews with metropolitan parents, if any. Whether,[1] until we have time in which to turn ourselves round, we might invite Miss Twinkleton to come and stay with you for a month?"

"Stay where, sir?"

"Whether," explained Mr. Grewgious, "we might take a furnished lodging in town for a month, and invite Miss Twinkleton to assume the charge of you in it for that period?"

"And afterwards?" hinted Rosa.

"And afterwards," said Mr. Grewgious, "we should be no worse off than we are now."

"I think that might smooth the way," assented Rosa.

"Then let us," said Mr. Grewgious, rising, "go and look for a furnished lodging. Nothing could be more acceptable to me than the sweet presence of last evening, for all the remaining evenings of my existence; but these are not fit surroundings for a young lady. Let us set out in quest of adventures, and look for a furnished lodging. In the meantime, Mr. Crisparkle here, about to return home immediately, will no doubt kindly see Miss Twinkleton and invite that lady to co-operate in our plan."

Mr. Crisparkle, willingly accepting the commission, took his departure; Mr. Grewgious and his ward set forth on their expedition.

As Mr. Grewgious's idea of looking at a furnished lodging was to get on the opposite side of the street to a house with a suitable bill in the window, and stare at it; and then work his way tortuously to the back of the house, and stare at that; and then not go in, but make similar trials of another house, with the same result; their progress was but slow. At length he bethought himself of a widowed cousin, divers times removed, of Mr. Bazzard's, who had once solicited his influence in the lodger world, and who lived in Southampton Street, Bloomsbury Square. This lady's name, stated in uncompromising capitals of considerable size on a brass door-plate, and yet not lucidly stated[2] as to sex or condition, was BILLICKIN.

Personal faintness, and an overpowering personal candour, were the distinguishing features of Mrs. Billickin's organization. She came languishing out from[3] her own exclusive back parlor, with the air of having been expressly brought-to for the purpose, from an accumulation of several swoons.

---

[1] that the respected . . . if any. Whether] MS ES that as the respected . . . if any— whether 70 73 75
[2] stated] MS *om.* 70–75
[3] from] MS of 70–75

O

"I hope I see you well, sir," said Mrs. Billickin, recognizing her visitor with a bend.

"Thank you, quite well. And you, ma'am?" returned Mr. Grewgious.

"I am as well," said Mrs. Billickin, becoming aspirational with excess of faintness, "as I hever ham."

"My ward and an elder[1] lady," said Mr. Grewgious, "wish to find a genteel lodging for a month or so. Have you any apartments available, ma'am?"

"Mr. Grewgious," returned Mrs. Billickin, "I will not deceive you; far from it. I *have* apartments available."

This, with the air of adding: "Convey me to the stake, if you will; but while I live, I will be candid."

"And now, what apartments, ma'am?" asked Mr. Grewgious, cosily. To tame a certain severity apparent on the part of Mrs. Billickin.

"There is this sitting-room—which call it what you will, it is the front parlior,[2] Miss," said Mrs. Billickin, impressing Rosa into the conversation: "the back parlior[2] being what I cling to and never part with; and there is two bedrooms at the top of the 'ouse with gas laid on. I do not tell you that your bedroom floors is firm, for firm they are not. The gas-fitter himself allowed that to make a firm job, he must go right under your jistes, and it were not worth the outlay as a yearly tenant so to do. The piping is carried above your jistes, and it is best that it should be made known to you."

Mr. Grewgious and Rosa exchanged looks of some dismay, though they had not the least idea what latent horrors this carriage of the piping might involve. Mrs. Billickin put her hand to her heart, as having eased it of a load.

"Well! The roof is all right, no doubt," said Mr. Grewgious, plucking up a little.

"Mr. Grewgious," returned Mrs. Billickin, "if I was to tell you, sir, that to have nothink above you is to have a floor above you, I should put a deception upon you which I will not do. No, sir. Your slates WILL rattle loose at that elewation in windy weather, do your utmost, best or worst! I defy you, sir, be you who[3] you may, to keep your slates tight, try how you can." Here Mrs. Billickin, having been warm with Mr. Grewgious, cooled a little, not to abuse the moral power she held over him. "Consequent," proceeded Mrs. Billickin, more mildly, but still firmly in her incorruptible candour: "consequent it would be worse than of no use for me to trapse and travel up to the top of the 'ouse with you, and for you to say, 'Mrs. Billickin, what stain do I notice in the ceiling, for a stain I do consider it?' and for me to answer, 'I do not understand you, sir.' No sir; I will not be so underhand. I *do* understand you before you pint it out. It is the wet, sir. It do come in, and it do not come in. You may lay dry

---

[1] elder] MS elderly 70–75   [2] parlior] MS parlor 70–75
[3] who] MS what 70–75

there, half your lifetime; but the time will come, and it is best that you should know it, when a dripping sop would be no name for you."

Mr. Grewgious looked much disgraced by being prefigured in this pickle.

"Have you any other apartments, ma'am?" he asked.

"Mr. Grewgious," returned Mrs. Billickin, with much solemnity, "I have. You ask me have I, and my open and my honest answer air, I have. The first and second floors is wacant, and sweet rooms."

"Come, come! There's nothing against *them*," said Mr. Grewgious, comforting himself.

"Mr. Grewgious," replied Mrs. Billickin, "pardon me, there is the stairs. Unless your mind is prepared for the stairs, it will lead to inevitable disapintmink.[1] You cannot, Miss," said Mrs. Billickin, addressing Rosa, reproachfully, "place a first floor, and far less a second, on the level footing of a parlior.[2] No, you can not[3] do it, Miss, it is beyond your power, and wherefore try?"

Mrs. Billickin put it very feelingly, as if Rosa had shown a headstrong determination to hold the untenable position.

"Can we see these rooms, ma'am?" inquired her guardian.

"Mr. Grewgious," returned Mrs. Billickin, "you can. I will not disguise it from you, sir, you can."

Mrs. Billickin then sent into her back parlor for her shawl (it being a state fiction, dating from immemorial antiquity, that she could never go anywhere without being wrapped up), and having been enrobed[4] by her attendant, led the way. She made various genteel pauses on the stairs for breath, and clutched at her heart in the drawing-room as if it had very nearly got loose, and she had caught it in the act of taking wing.

"And the second floor?" said Mr. Grewgious, on finding the first satisfactory.

"Mr. Grewgious," replied Mrs. Billickin, turning upon him with ceremony, as if the time had now come when a distinct understanding on a difficult point must be arrived at, and a solemn confidence established, "the second floor is over this."

"Can we see that too, ma'am?"

"Yes, sir," returned Mrs. Billickin, "it is open as the day."

That also proving satisfactory, Mr. Grewgious retired into a window with Rosa for a few words of consultation, and then, asking for pen and ink, sketched out a line or two of agreement. In the meantime Mrs. Billickin took a seat, and delivered a kind of Index to, or Abstract of, the general question.

"Five-and-forty shillings per week by the month certain at the time of year," said Mrs. Billickin, "is only reasonable to both parties. It is not

[1] disapintmink] MS disappointment 70-75   [2] parlior] MS parlor 70-75
[3] can not] MS cannot 70-75   [4] enrobed] MS enrolled 70-75

Bond Street nor yet St. James's Palace; but it is not pretended that it is. Neither is it attempted to be denied—for why should it?—that the Archway[1] leads to a Mews. Mewses must exist. Respectin'[2] attendance; two is kep', at liberal wages. Words *has* arisen as to tradesmen, but dirty shoes on fresh hearth-stoning was attributable, and no wish for a commission on your orders. Coals is either *by*[3] the fire, or *per* the scuttle." She emphasized the prepositions as marking a subtle but immense difference. "Dogs is not viewed with favior.[4] Besides litter, they gets stole, and sharing[5] suspicions is apt to creep in, and unpleasantness takes place."

By this time Mr. Grewgious had his agreement-lines, and his earnest-money, ready. "I have signed it for the ladies, ma'am," he said, "and you'll have the goodness to sign it for yourself, Christian and Surname, there, if you please."

"Mr. Grewgious," said Mrs. Billickin in a new burst of candour, "no, sir! You must excuse the Chris'en[6] name."

Mr. Grewgious stared at her.

"The door-plate is used as a protection," said Mrs. Billickin, "and acts as such, and go from it I will not."

Mr. Grewgious stared at Rosa.

"No, Mr. Grewgious, you must excuse me. So long as this 'ouse is known indefinite as Billickin's, and so long as it is a doubt with the riff-raff where Billickin may be hidin', near the street door or down the airy, and what his weight and size, so long I feel safe. But commit myself to a solitary female statement, no, Miss! Nor would you for a moment wish," said Mrs. Billickin, with a strong sense of injury, "to take that advantage of your sex, if you was[7] not brought to it by inconsiderate example."

Rosa reddening as if she had made some most disgraceful attempt to overreach the good lady, besought Mr. Grewgious to rest content with any signature. And accordingly, in a baronial[8] way, the sign-manual BILLICKIN got appended to the document.

Details were then settled for taking possession on the next day but one, when Miss Twinkleton might be reasonably expected; and Rosa went back to Furnival's Inn on her guardian's arm.

Behold Mr. Tartar walking up and down Furnival's Inn, checking himself when he saw them coming, and advancing towards them!

"It occurred to me," hinted Mr. Tartar, "that we might go up the river, the weather being so delicious and the tide serving. I have a boat of my own at the Temple Stairs."

"I have not been up the river for this many a day," said Mr. Grewgious, tempted.

¹ Archway] MS Arching 70–75   ² Respectin'] MS Respecting 70–75
³ *by*] by ES   ⁴ favior] favor ES
⁵ sharing] snaring ES
⁶ Chris'en] MS Christian 70–75   ⁷ was] were 75   ⁸ baronial] baronical ES

UP THE RIVER

"I was never up the river," added Rosa.

Within half an hour they were setting this matter right by going up the river. The tide was running with them, the afternoon was charming. Mr. Tartar's boat was perfect. Mr. Tartar and Lobley (Mr. Tartar's man) pulled a pair of oars. Mr. Tartar had a yacht, it seemed, lying somewhere down by Greenhithe; and Mr. Tartar's man had charge of this yacht, and was detached upon his present service. He was a jolly favored man, with tawny hair and whiskers, and a big red face. He was the dead image of the sun in old woodcuts, his hair and whiskers answering for rays all round[1] him. Resplendent in the bow of the boat, he was a shining sight, with a man-of-war's man's shirt on—or off, according to opinion—and his arms and breast tattoo'd all sorts of patterns. Lobley seemed to take it easily, and so did Mr. Tartar; yet their oars bent as they pulled, and the boat bounded under them. Mr. Tartar talked as if he were doing nothing, to Rosa who was really doing nothing, and to Mr. Grewgious who was doing this much that he steered all wrong; but what did that matter, when a turn of Mr. Tartar's skilful wrist, or a mere grin of Mr. Lobley's over the bow, put all to rights! The tide bore them on in the gayest and most sparkling manner, until they stopped to dine in some everlastingly green garden, needing no matter-of-fact identification here; and then the tide obligingly turned—being devoted to that party alone for that day; and as they floated idly among some osier beds, Rosa tried what she could do in the rowing way, and came off splendidly, being much assisted; and Mr. Grewgious tried what he could do, and came off on his back, doubled up with an oar under his chin, being not assisted at all. Then there was an interval of rest under boughs (such rest!) what time Mr. Lobley mopped, and, arranging cushions, stretchers, and the like, danced the tight rope the whole length of the boat like a man to whom shoes were a superstition and stockings slavery; and then came the sweet return among delicious odours of limes in bloom, and musical ripplings; and, all too soon, the great black city cast its shadow on the waters, and its dark bridges spanned them as death spans life, and the everlastingly green garden seemed to be left for everlasting, unregainable and far away.

"Cannot people get through life without gritty stages, I wonder!" Rosa thought next day, when the town was very gritty again, and everything had a strange and an uncomfortable appearance on it[2] of seeming to wait for something that wouldn't come. No. She began to think, that, now the Cloisterham school-days had glided past and gone, the gritty stages would begin to set in[3] at intervals and make themselves wearily known!

Yet what did Rosa expect? Did she expect Miss Twinkleton? Miss Twinkleton duly came. Forth from her back parlor issued the Billickin

---

[1] round] around 75   [2] on it] MS *om.* 70–75
[3] begin to set in] begin set in MS; *intended reading may be* begin, set in

to receive Miss Twinkleton, and War was in the Billickin's eye from that fell moment.

Miss Twinkleton brought a quantity of luggage with her, having all Rosa's as well as her own. The Billickin took it ill that Miss Twinkleton's mind, being sorely disturbed by this luggage, failed to take in her personal identity with that clearness of perception which was due to its demands. Stateliness mounted her gloomy throne upon the Billickin's brow in consequence. And when Miss Twinkleton, in agitation taking stock of her trunks and packages, of which she had seventeen, particularly counted in the Billickin herself as number eleven, the B found it necessary to repudiate.

"Things cannot too soon be put upon the footing," said she, with a candour so demonstrative as to be almost obtrusive, "that the person of the 'ouse is not a box nor yet a bundle, nor a carpet bag. No, I am 'ily obleeged to you, Miss Twinkleton, nor yet a beggar."

This[1] last disclaimer had reference to Miss Twinkleton's distractedly pressing two and sixpence on her, instead of the cabman.

Thus cast off, Miss Twinkleton wildly inquired, "which gentleman" was to be paid? There being two gentlemen in that position (Miss Twinkleton having arrived with two cabs), each gentleman on being paid held forth his two and sixpence on the flat of his open hand, and, with a speechless stare and a dropped jaw, displayed his wrong to heaven and earth. Terrified by this alarming spectacle, Miss Twinkleton placed another shilling in each hand; at the same time appealing to the law in flurried accents, and re-counting[2] her luggage this time with the two gentlemen in, who caused the total to come out complicated. Meanwhile the two gentlemen, each looking very hard at the last shilling, as if it might become eighteenpence if he kept his eyes on it, grumblingly descended[3] the doorsteps, ascended their carriages, and drove away, leaving Miss Twinkleton bewildered[4] on a bonnet-box in tears.

The Billickin beheld this manifestation of weakness without sympathy, and gave directions for "a young man to be got in" to wrestle with the luggage. When that gladiator had disappeared from the arena, peace ensued, and the new lodgers dined.

But the Billickin had somehow come to the knowledge that Miss Twinkleton kept a school. The leap from that knowledge to the inference that Miss Twinkleton would[5] set herself to teach *her* something, was easy. "But you don't do it," soliloquized the Billickin; "*I* am not your pupil, whatever she," meaning Rosa, "may be, poor thing!"

Miss Twinkleton on the other hand, having changed her dress and recovered her spirits, was animated by a bland desire to improve the

---

[1] This] *possibly* The MS   [2] re-counting] MS recounting 70–75
[3] shilling, as if . . . grumblingly descended] MS shilling grumblingly, as if . . . descended 70–75   [4] bewildered] MS *om.* 70–75   [5] would] MS *om.* 70–75

occasion in all ways, and to be as serene a model as possible. In a happy compromise between her two states of existence, she had already become, with her workbasket before her, the equably vivacious companion with a slight judicious flavoring of information, when the Billickin announced herself.

"I will not hide from you, ladies," said the B, enveloped in the shawl of state, "for it is not my character to hide neither my motives nor my actions, that I take the liberty to look in upon you to express a 'ope that your dinner was to your liking. Though not Professed but Plain, still her wages should be a sufficient object to her to stimilate to soar above mere roast and biled."

"We dined very well indeed," said Rosa, "thank you."

"Accustomed," said Miss Twinkleton, with a gracious air which to the jealous ears of the Billickin seemed to add "my good woman"—"Accustomed to a liberal and nutritious,[1] yet plain and salutary diet, we have found no reason to bemoan our absence from the ancient city, and the methodical household, in which the quiet routine of our lot has been hitherto cast."

"I did think it well to mention to my cook," observed the Billickin with a gush of candour, "which I 'ope you will agree with me,[2] Miss Twinkleton, was a right precaution, that the young lady being used to what we should consider here but poor diet, had better be brought forard[3] by degrees. For, a rush from scanty feeding to generous feeding, and from what you may call messing to what you may call method, do require a power of constitution, which is not often found in youth, particular when undermined by boarding-school!"

It will be seen that the Billickin now openly pitted herself against Miss Twinkleton, as one whom she had fully ascertained to be her natural enemy.

"Your remarks," returned Miss Twinkleton, from a remote moral eminence, "are well meant, I have no doubt; but you will permit me to observe that they develop a mistaken view of the subject, which can only be imputed to your extreme want of accurate information."

"My informiation,"[4] retorted the Billickin, throwing in an extra syllable for the sake of an emphasis[5] at once polite and powerful:[6] "My informiation,[4] Miss Twinkleton, were my own experience, which I believe is usually considered to be good guidance. But whether so or not, I was put in youth to a very genteel boarding-school, the mistress being no less a lady than yourself, of about your own age or it may be some years younger, and a poorness of blood flowed from the table which has run through my life."

---

[1] liberal and nutritious] liberal, nutritious ES   [2] me] MS *om.* 70–75
[3] forard] MS forward 70–75   [4] informiation] information ES
[5] an emphasis] MS emphasis 70–75   [6] powerful] painful ES

"Very likely," said Miss Twinkleton, still from her distant eminence; "and very much to be deplored. Rosa, my dear, how are you getting on with your work?"

"Miss Twinkleton," resumed the Billickin, in a courtly manner, "before retiring on the 'Int, as a lady should, I wish to ask of yourself as a lady, whether I am to consider that my words is doubted?"

"I am not aware on what ground you cherish such a supposition," began Miss Twinkleton, when the Billickin neatly stopped her.

"Do not, if you please, put suppositions betwixt my lips, where none such have been imparted[1] by myself. Your flow of words is great, Miss Twinkleton, and no doubt is expected from you by your pupils, and no doubt is considered worth the money. *No* doubt, I am sure. But not paying for flows of words, and not asking to be faviored[2] with them here, I wish to repeat my question."

"If you refer to the poverty of your circulation," began Miss Twinkleton again,[3] when again the Billickin neatly stopped her.

"I have used no such expressions."

"If you refer then to the poorness of your blood."

"Brought upon me," stipulated the Billickin, expressly, "at a boarding-school."

"Then," resumed Miss Twinkleton, "all I can say, is, that I am bound to believe on your asseveration that it is very poor indeed. I cannot forbear adding, that if that unfortunate circumstance influences your conversation, it is much to be lamented, and it is eminently desirable that your blood were richer. Rosa, my dear, how are you getting on with your work?"

"Hem! Before retiring, Miss," proclaimed the Billickin to Rosa, loftily cancelling Miss Twinkleton, "I should wish it to be understood between yourself and me that my transactions in future is with you alone. I know no elderly lady here, Miss, none older than yourself."

"A highly desirable arrangement, Rosa, my dear," observed Miss Twinkleton.

"It is not, Miss," said the Billickin, with a sarcastic smile, "that I possess the Mill I have heard of, in which old single ladies could be ground up young (what a gift it would be to some of us!), but that I limit myself to you totally."

"When I have any desire to communicate a request to the person of the house, Rosa, my dear," observed Miss Twinkleton, with majestic cheerfulness, "I will make it known to you, and you will kindly undertake, I am sure, that it is conveyed to the proper quarter."

"Good-evening, Miss," said the Billickin, at once affectionately and distantly. "Being alone in my eyes, I wish you good-evening with best

---

[1] imparted] imported ES   [2] faviored] MS favored 70–75
[3] again] MS *om.* 70–75

wishes, and do not find myself drove, I am truly 'appy to say, into expressing my contempt for any[1] indiwidual, unfortunately for yourself, belonging to you."

The Billickin gracefully withdrew with this parting speech, and from that time Rosa occupied the restless position of shuttlecock between these two battledores. Nothing could be done without a smart match being played out. Thus, on the daily-arising question of dinner, Miss Twinkleton would say, the three being present together:

"Perhaps, my love, you will consult with the person of the house, whether she could[2] procure us a lamb's fry; or, failing that, a roast fowl."

On which the Billickin would retort (Rosa not having spoken a word), "If you was better accustomed to butcher's meat, Miss, you would not entertain the idea of a lamb's fry. Firstly, because lambs has long been sheep, and secondly, because there is such things as killing-days, and there is not. As to roast fowls, Miss, why you must be quite surfeited with roast fowls, letting alone your buying, when you market for yourself, the agedest of poultry with the scaliest of legs, quite as if you was accustomed to picking 'em out for cheapness. Try a little inwention, Miss. Use yourself to 'ousekeeping a bit. Come now, think of somethink else."

To this encouragement, offered with the indulgent toleration of a wise and liberal expert, Miss Twinkleton would rejoin, reddening:

"Or, my dear, you might propose to the person of the house a duck."

"Well, Miss!" the Billickin would exclaim (still no word being spoken by Rosa), "you do surprise me when you speak of ducks! Not to mention that they're getting out of season and very dear, it really strikes to my heart to see you have a duck; for the breast, which is the only delicate cuts in a duck, always goes in a direction which I cannot imagine where, and your own plate comes down so miserable[3] skin-and-bony! Try again, Miss. Think more of yourself and less of others. A dish of sweetbreads now, or a bit of mutton. Somethink[4] at which you can get your equal chance."

Occasionally the game would wax very brisk indeed, and would be kept up with a smartness rendering such an encounter as this quite tame. But the Billickin almost invariably made by far the higher score; and would come in with side hits of the most unexpected and extraordinary description, when she seemed without a chance.

All this did not improve the gritty state of things in London, or the air that London had acquired in Rosa's eyes of waiting for something that never came. Tired of working and conversing with Miss Twinkleton, she suggested working and reading: to which Miss Twinkleton readily assented, as an admirable reader, of tried powers. But Rosa soon made the discovery that Miss Twinkleton didn't read fairly. She cut the love scenes,

[1] any] an 75
[2] could] MS can 70–75
[3] miserable] MS miserably 70–75
[4] Somethink] Something 75

interpolated passages in praise of female celibacy, and was guilty of other glaring pious frauds. As an instance in point, take the glowing passage: " 'Ever dearest and best adored,' said Edward, clasping the dear head to his breast, and drawing the silken hair through his caressing fingers, from which he suffered it to fall like golden rain; 'ever dearest and best adored, let us fly from the unsympathetic world and the sterile coldness of the stony-hearted, to the rich warm Paradise of Trust and Love.' " Miss Twinkleton's fraudulent version tamely ran thus: " 'Ever engaged to me with the consent of our parents on both sides, and the approbation of the silver-haired rector of the district,' said Edward, respectfully raising to his lips the taper fingers so skilful in embroidery, tambour, crochet, and other truly feminine arts; 'let me call on thy papa ere to-morrow's dawn has sunk into the west, and propose a suburban establishment, lowly it may be, but within our means, where he will be always welcome as an evening guest, and where every arrangement shall invest economy, and the constant[1] interchange of scholastic acquirements, with the attributes of the ministering angel to domestic bliss.' "

As the days crept on and nothing happened, the neighbours began to say that the pretty girl at Billickin's, who looked so wistfully and so much out of the gritty windows of the drawing-room, seemed to be losing her spirits. The pretty girl might have lost them but for the accident of lighting on some books of voyages and sea-adventure. As a compensation against their romance, Miss Twinkleton, reading aloud, made the most of all the latitudes and longitudes, bearings, winds, currents, offsets, and other statistics (which she felt to be none the less improving because they expressed nothing whatever to her); while Rosa, listening intently, made the most of what was nearest to her heart. So they both did better than before.

CHAPTER XXIII

THE DAWN AGAIN

ALTHOUGH Mr. Crisparkle and John Jasper met daily under the Cathedral roof, nothing at any time passed between them bearing[2] reference to Edwin Drood after the time, more than half a year gone by, when Jasper mutely showed the Minor Canon the conclusion and the resolution entered in his Diary. It is not likely that they ever met, though so often, without the thoughts of each reverting to the subject. It is not likely that

---

[1] the constant] MS constant 70–75
CHAPTER XXIII] CHAPTER XXII MS
[2] bearing] having 73 75

they ever met, though so often, without a sensation on the part of each that the other was a perplexing secret to him. Jasper as the denouncer and pursuer of Neville Landless, and Mr. Crisparkle as his consistent advocate and protector, must at least have stood sufficiently in opposition, to have speculated with keen interest each[1] on the steadiness and next direction of the other's designs. But neither ever broached the theme.

False pretence not being in the Minor Canon's nature, he doubtless displayed openly that he would at any time have revived the subject, and even desired to discuss it. The determined reticence of Jasper, however, was not to be so approached. Impassive, moody, solitary, resolute, concentrated on one idea, and on its attendant fixed purpose that[2] he would share it with no fellow-creature, he lived apart from human life. Constantly exercising an Art which brought him into mechanical harmony with others, and which could not have been pursued unless he and they had been in the nicest mechanical relations and unison, it is curious to consider that the spirit of the man was in moral accordance or interchange with nothing around him. This indeed he had confided to his lost nephew, before the occasion for his present inflexibility arose.

That he must know of Rosa's abrupt departure, and that he must divine its cause, was not to be doubted. Did he suppose that he had terrified her into silence, or did he suppose that she had imparted to any one— to Mr. Crisparkle himself for instance—the particulars of his last interview with her? Mr. Crisparkle could not determine this in his mind. He could not but admit, however, as a just man, that it was not, of itself, a crime to fall in love with Rosa, any more than it was a crime to offer to set love above revenge.

The dreadful[3] suspicion of Jasper which Rosa was so shocked to have received into her imagination, appeared to have no harbour in Mr. Crisparkle's. If it ever haunted Helena's thoughts, or Neville's, neither gave it one spoken word of utterance. Mr. Grewgious took no pains to conceal his implacable dislike of Jasper, yet he never referred it, however distantly, to such a source. But he was a reticent as well as an eccentric man; and he made no mention of a certain evening when he warmed his hands at the Gate House fire, and looked steadily down upon a certain heap of torn and miry clothes upon the floor.

Drowsy Cloisterham, whenever it awoke to a passing reconsideration of a story above six months old and dismissed by the bench of magistrates, was pretty equally divided in opinion whether John Jasper's beloved nephew had been killed by his passionate rival, treacherously,[4] or in an open struggle: or had, for his own purposes, spirited himself away. It then

[1] each] MS *om.* 70–75
[2] concentrated . . . fixed purpose that] MS so concentrated . . . fixed purpose, that 70–75   [3] The dreadful] *possibly* That dreadful MS
[4] passionate rival, treacherously] MS treacherously passionate rival 70–75

lifted up its head, to notice that the bereaved Jasper was still ever devoted to discovery and revenge; and then dozed off again. This was the condition of matters, all round, at the period to which the present history has now attained.

The Cathedral doors have[1] closed for the night; and the Choir Master, on a short leave of absence for two or three services, sets his face towards London. He travels thither by the means by which Rosa travelled, and arrives, as Rosa arrived, on a hot, dusty evening.

His travelling baggage is easily carried in his hand, and he repairs with it, on foot, to a hybrid hotel in a little square behind Aldersgate Street, near the General Post Office. It is hotel, boarding-house, or lodging-house, at its visitor's option. It announces itself, in the new Railway Advertisers, as a novel enterprise, timidly beginning to spring up.[2] It bashfully, almost apologetically, gives the traveller to understand that it does not expect him, on the good old constitutional hotel plan, to order a pint of sweet blacking for his drinking, and throw it away; but insinuates that he may have his boots blacked instead of his stomach, and maybe also have bed, breakfast, attendance, and a porter up all night, for a certain fixed charge. From these and similar premises, many true Britons in the lowest spirits deduce that the times are levelling times, except in the article of high roads, of which there will shortly be not one[3] in England.

He eats without appetite, and soon goes forth again. Eastward and still eastward through the stale streets he takes his way, until he reaches his destination: a miserable court, specially miserable among many such.

He ascends a broken staircase, opens a door, looks into a dark stifling room, and says: "Are you alone here?"

"Alone, deary; worse luck for me and better for you," replies a croaking voice. "Come in, come in, whoever you be: I can't see you till I light a match, yet I seem to know the sound of your speaking. I am[4] acquainted with you, ain't I?"

"Light your match, and try."

"So I will, deary, so I will; but my hand that shakes, as I can't lay it on a match all in a moment. And I cough so, that, put my matches where I may, I never find 'em there. They jump and start, as I cough and cough, like live things. Are you off a voyage, deary?"

"No."

"Not seafaring?"

"No."

"Well, there's land customers, and there's water customers. I'm a mother to both. Different from Jack Chinaman t'other side the court. He

---

[1] have] had ES

[2] It announces itself . . . to spring up] It announces itself as a novel enterprize in the new Railway Advertisers timidly beginning to spring up MS

[3] be not one] not be one ES   [4] I am] I'm 73 75

ain't a father to neither. It ain't in him. And he ain't got the true secret of mixing, though he charges as much as me that has, and more if he can get it. Here's a match, and now where's the candle? If my cough takes me, I shall cough out twenty matches afore I gets a light."

But she finds the candle, and lights it before the cough comes on. It seizes her in the moment of success, and she sits down rocking herself to and fro, and gasping at intervals, "Oh, my lungs is awful bad, my lungs is wore away to cabbage-nets!" until the fit is over. During its continuance she has had no power of sight, or any other power not absorbed in the struggle; but as it leaves her, she begins to strain her eyes, and as soon as she is able to articulate, she cries, staring:

"Why, it's you!"

"Are you so surprised to see me?"

"I thought I never should have seen you again, deary. I thought you was dead, and gone to Heaven."

"Why?"

"I didn't suppose you could have kept away, alive, so long, from the poor old soul with the real receipt for mixing it. And you are in mourning too! Why didn't you come and have a pipe or two of comfort? Did they leave you money, perhaps, and so you didn't want comfort?"

"No!"

"Who was they as[1] died, deary?"

"A relative."

"Died of what, lovey?"

"Probably, Death."

"We are short to-night!" cries the woman, with a propitiatory laugh. "Short and snappish, we are! But we're out of sorts for want of a smoke. We've got the all-overs, haven't us, deary? But this is the place to cure 'em in; this is the place where the all-overs is smoked off!"

"You may make ready then," replies the visitor, "as soon as you like."

He divests himself of his shoes, loosens his cravat, and lies across the foot of the squalid bed, with his head resting on his left hand.

"Now, you begin to look like yourself," says the woman, approvingly. "Now, I begin to know my old customer indeed! Been trying to mix for yourself this long time, poppet?"

"I have been taking it now and then in my own way."

"Never take it your own way. It ain't good for trade, and it ain't good for you. Where's my ink-bottle, and where's my thimble, and where's my little spoon? He's going to take it in a artful form now, my deary dear!"

Entering on her process, and beginning to bubble and blow at the faint spark enclosed in the hollow of her hands, she speaks from time to time, in a tone of snuffling satisfaction, without breaking[2] off. When he speaks,

[1] as] that ES

[2] breaking] MS leaving 70–75

he does so without looking at her, and as if his thoughts were already roaming away by anticipation.

"I've got a pretty many smokes ready for you, first and last, haven't I, chuckey?"

"A good many."

"When you first come, you was¹ quite new to it; warn't ye?"

"Yes, I was easily disposed of, then."

"But you got on in the world, and was able by-and-bye to take your pipe² with the best of 'em, warn't ye?"

"Ay.³ And the worst."

"It's just ready for you. What a sweet singer you was when you first come! Used to drop your head, and sing yourself off, like a bird! It's ready for you now, deary."

He takes it from her with great care, and puts the mouthpiece to his lips. She seats herself beside him, ready to refill the pipe. After inhaling a few whiffs in silence, he doubtingly accosts her with:

"Is it as potent as it used to be?"

"What do you speak of, deary?"

"What should I speak of, but what I have in my mouth?"

"It's just the same. Always⁴ the identical same."

"It doesn't taste so. And it's slower."

"You've got more used to it, you see."

"That may be the cause, certainly. Look here." He stops, becomes dreamy, and seems to forget that he has invited her attention. She bends over him, and speaks in his ear.

"I'm attending to you. Says you just now, look here. Says I now, I am⁵ attending to ye. We was talking just before of your being used to it."

"I know all that. I was only thinking. Look here. Suppose you had something in your mind; something you were going to do."

"Yes, deary; something I was going to do?"

"But had not quite determined to do."

"Yes, deary."

"Might or might not do, you understand."

"Yes." With the point of a needle she stirs the contents of the bowl.

"Should you do it in your fancy, when you were lying here doing this?" She nods her head. "Over and over again."

"Just like me! I did it over and over again. I have done it hundreds of thousands of times in this room."

"It's to be hoped it was pleasant to do, deary."

"It *was* pleasant to do!"

He says this with a savage air, and a spring or start at her. Quite unmoved, she retouches or⁶ replenishes the contents of the bowl with her

¹ was] *possibly* war MS   ² pipe] *possibly* pipes MS   ³ Ay] Ah 73 75
⁴ Always] *possibly* Allays MS   ⁵ I am] I'm 73 75   ⁶ or] MS and 70–75

little spatula. Seeing her intent upon the occupation, he sinks into his former attitude.

"It was a journey, a difficult and dangerous journey. That was the subject in my mind. A hazardous and perilous journey, over abysses where a slip would be destruction. Look down, look down! You see what lies at the bottom there?"

He has darted forward to say it, and to point at the ground, as though at some imaginary object far beneath. The woman looks at him, as his spasmodic face approaches close to hers, and not at his pointing. She seems to know what the influence of her perfect quietude will[1] be; if so, she has not miscalculated it, for he subsides again.

"Well; I have told you, I did it, here, hundreds of thousands of times. What do I say? I did it millions and billions of times. I did it so often, and through such vast expanses of time, that when it was really done, it seemed not worth the doing, it was done so soon."

"That's the journey you have been away upon?" she quietly remarks.

He glares at her as he smokes; and then, his eyes becoming filmy, answers: "That's the journey."

Silence ensues. His eyes are sometimes closed and sometimes open. The woman sits beside him, very attentive to the pipe, which is all the while at his lips.

"I'll warrant," she observes, when he has been looking fixedly at her for some consecutive moments, with a singular appearance in his eyes of seeming to see her a long way off, instead of so near him: "I'll warrant you made the journey in a many ways, when you made it so often?"

"No, always in one way."

"Always in the same way?"

"Ay."

"In the way in which it was really made at last?"

"Ay."

"And always took the same pleasure in harping on it?"

"Ay."

For the time he appears unequal to any other reply than this lazy monosyllabic assent. Probably to assure herself that it is not the assent of a mere automaton, she reverses the form of her next sentence.

"Did you never get tired of it, deary, and try to call up something else for a change?"

He struggles into a sitting posture, and retorts upon her: "What do you mean? What did I want? What did I come for?"

She gently lays him back again, and, before returning him the instrument he has dropped, revives the fire in it with her own breath; then says to him, coaxingly:

"Sure, sure, sure! Yes, yes, yes! Now, I go along with you. You was too quick for me. I see now. You come o' purpose to take the journey. Why, I might have known it, through its standing by you so."

He answers first with a laugh, and then with a passionate setting of his teeth: "Yes, I came on purpose. When I could not bear my life, I came to get the relief, and I got it. It WAS one! It WAS one!" This repetition with extraordinary vehemence, and the snarl of a wolf.

She observes him very cautiously, as though mentally feeling her way to her next remark. It is: "There was a fellow-traveller, deary."

"Ha ha ha!" He breaks into a ringing laugh, or rather yell.

"To think," he cries, "how often fellow-traveller, and yet not know it! To think how many times he went the journey, and never saw the road!"

The woman kneels upon the floor, with her arms crossed on the coverlet of the bed, close by him, and her chin upon them. In this crouching attitude, she watches him. The pipe is falling from his mouth. She puts it back, and laying her hand upon his chest, moves him slightly from side to side. Upon that he speaks, as if she had spoken.

"Yes! I always made the journey first, before the changes of colors and the great landscapes and glittering processions began. They couldn't begin till it was off my mind. I had no room till then for anything else."

Once more he lapses into silence. Once more she lays her hand upon his chest, and moves him slightly to and fro, as a cat might stimulate a half-slain mouse. Once more he speaks, as if she had spoken.

"What? I told you so. When it comes to be real at last, it is so short that it seems unreal for the first time. Hark!"

"Yes, deary. I'm listening."

"Time and place are both at hand."

He is on his feet, speaking in a whisper, and as if in the dark.

"Time, place, and fellow-traveller," she suggests, adopting his tone, and holding him softly by the arm.

"How could the time be at hand unless the fellow-traveller was? Hush! The journey's made. It's over."

"So soon?"

"That's what I said to you. So soon. Wait a little. This is a vision. I shall sleep it off. It has been too short and easy. I must have a better vision than this; this is the poorest of all. No struggle, no consciousness of peril, no entreaty—and yet I never saw *that* before." With a start.

"Saw what, deary?"

"Look at it! Look what a poor, mean, miserable thing it is! *That* must be real. It's over!"

He has accompanied this incoherence with some wild unmeaning gestures; but they trail off into the progressive inaction of stupor, and he lies a log upon the bed.

The woman, however, is still inquisitive. With a repetition of her cat-

SLEEPING IT OFF

like action she slightly stirs his body again, and listens; stirs it[1] again, and listens; whispers to it, and listens. Finding it past all rousing for the time, she slowly gets upon her feet, with an air of disappointment, and flicks the face with the back of her hand in turning from it.

But she goes no further away from it than the chair upon the hearth. She sits in it, with an elbow on one of its arms, and her chin upon that[2] hand, intent upon him. "I heard ye[3] say once," she croaks under her breath, "I heard ye[3] say once, when I was lying where you're lying, and you were making your speculations upon me, 'Unintelligible!' I heard you say so, of two more than me. But don't ye be too sure always; don't ye be too sure, beauty!"

Unwinking, cat-like, and intent, she presently adds: "Not so potent as it once was? Ah! Perhaps not at first. You may be more right there. Practice makes perfect. I may have learned the secret how to make ye talk, deary."

He talks no more, whether or no. Twitching in an ugly way from time to time, both as to his face and limbs, he lies heavy and silent. The wretched candle burns down; the woman takes its expiring end between her fingers, lights another at it, crams the guttering frying morsel deep into the candlestick, and rams it home with the new candle, as if she were loading some ill-savoured and unseemly weapon of witchcraft; the new candle in its turn burns down; and still he lies insensible. At length what remains of the last candle is blown out, and daylight looks into the room.[4]

It has not looked very long, when he sits up, chilled and shaking, slowly recovers consciousness of where he is, and makes himself ready to depart. The woman receives what he pays her with a grateful "Bless ye, bless ye, deary!" and seems, tired out, to begin making herself ready for sleep as he leaves the room.

But seeming may be false or true. It is false in this case, for, the moment the stairs have ceased to creak under his tread, she glides after him, muttering emphatically: "I'll not miss ye twice!"

There is no egress from the court but by its entrance. With a weird peep from the doorway, she watches for his looking back. He does not look back before disappearing, with a wavering step. She follows him, peeps from the court, sees him still faltering on without looking back, and holds him in view.

He repairs to the back of Aldersgate Street, where a door immediately opens to his knocking. She crouches in another doorway, watching that one, and easily comprehending that he puts up temporarily at that house.

---

[1] it] MS *om.* 70–75   [2] that] MS her 70–75   [3] ye] *possibly* you MS

[4] But she goes no further . . . into the room] *these three paragraphs written on a slip pasted over the original, of which can be read* "So far I might a'most as well have never found out how to set you talking," *is her commentary;* "you are too deep to talk too plain and you hold your secrets tight, you do!"

Her patience is unexhausted by hours. For sustenance she can, and does, buy bread within a hundred yards, and milk as it is carried past her.

He comes forth again at noon, having changed his dress, but carrying nothing in his hand, and having nothing carried for him. He is not going back into the country, therefore, just yet. She follows him a little way, hesitates instantaneously, turns[1] confidently, and goes straight into the house he has quitted.

"Is the gentleman from Cloisterham indoors?"

"Just gone out."

"Unlucky. When does the gentleman return to Cloisterham?"

"At six this evening."

"Bless ye and thank ye. May the Lord prosper a business where a civil question, even from a poor soul, is so civilly answered!"

"I'll not miss ye twice!" repeats the poor soul in the street, and not so civilly. "I lost ye last, where that omnibus you got into nigh your journey's end plied betwixt the station and the place. I wasn't so much as certain that you even[2] went right on to the place. Now, I know ye did. My gentleman from Cloisterham, I'll be there before ye and bide your coming. I've swore my oath that I'll not miss ye twice!"

Accordingly, that same evening the poor soul stands in Cloisterham High Street, looking at the many quaint gables of the Nuns' House, and getting through the time as she best can until nine o'clock; at which hour she has reason to suppose that the arriving omnibus passengers may have some interest for her. The friendly darkness, at that hour, renders it easy for her to ascertain whether this be so or not; and it is so, for the passenger not to be missed twice arrives among the rest.

"Now, let me see what becomes of you. Go on!"

An observation addressed to the air. And yet it might be addressed to the passenger, so compliantly does he go on along the High Street until he comes to an arched gateway, at which he unexpectedly vanishes. The poor soul quickens her pace; is swift, and close upon him in turning[3] under the gateway; but only sees a postern staircase on one side of it, and on the other side an ancient vaulted room, in which a large-headed, grey-haired gentleman is writing, under the odd circumstances of sitting open to the thoroughfare and eyeing all who pass, as if he were toll-taker at[4] the gateway: though the way is free.

"Halloa!" he cries in a low voice, seeing her brought to a standstill: "who are you looking for?"

"There was a gentleman passed in here this minute, sir. A gentleman in mourning."[5]

"Of course there was. What do you want with him?"

---

[1] hesitates instantaneously, turns] MS hesitates, instantaneously turns 70–75
[2] even] *possibly* ever MS   [3] in turning] MS entering 70–75
[4] at] MS of 70–75   [5] A gentleman in mourning.] MS *om.* 70–75

"Where do he live, deary?"

"Live? Up that staircase."

"Bless ye! Whisper. What's his name, deary?"

"Surname Jasper, Christian name John. Mr. John Jasper."

"Has he a calling, good gentleman?"

"Calling? Yes. Sings in the choir."

"In the spire?"

"Choir."

"What's that?"

Mr. Datchery rises from his papers, and comes to his doorstep. "Do you know what a cathedral is?" he asks, jocosely.

The woman nods.

"What is it?"

She looks puzzled, casting about in her mind to find a definition, when it occurs to her that it is easier to point out the substantial object itself, massive against the dark-blue sky and the early stars.

"That's the answer. Go in there at seven to-morrow morning, and you may see Mr. John Jasper, and hear him too."

"Thank ye! Thank ye!"

The burst of triumph in which she thanks him, does not escape the notice of the single buffer of an easy temper living idly on his means. He glances at her; clasps his hands behind him, as the wont of such buffers is; and lounges along the echoing Precincts at her side.

"Or," he suggests, with a backward hitch of his head, "you can go up at once to Mr. Jasper's rooms there."

The woman eyes him with a cunning smile, and shakes her head.

"Oh! You don't want to speak to him?"

She repeats her dumb reply, and forms with her lips a soundless "No."

"You can admire him at a distance three times a day, whenever you like. It's a long way to come for that, though."

The woman looks up quickly. If Mr. Datchery thinks she is to be so induced to declare where she comes from, he is of a much easier temper than she is. But she acquits him of such an artful thought, as he lounges along, like the chartered bore of the city, with his uncovered grey hair blowing about, and his purposeless hands rattling the loose money in the pockets of his trousers.

The chink of the money has an attraction for her greedy ears. "Wouldn't you help me to pay for my travellers' lodging, dear gentleman, and to pay my way along? I am a poor soul, I am indeed, and troubled with a grievous cough."

"You know the travellers' lodging, I perceive, and are making direct¹ for it," is Mr. Datchery's bland comment, still rattling his loose money. "Been here often, my good woman?"

¹ direct] MS directly 70–75

"Once in all my life."

"Ay, ay?"

They have arrived at the entrance to the Monks' Vineyard. An appropriate remembrance, presenting an exemplary model for imitation, is revived in the woman's mind by the sight of the place. She stops at the gate, and says energetically:

"By this token, though you mayn't believe it, That a young gentleman gave me three and sixpence as I was coughing my breath away on this very grass. I asked him for three and sixpence, and he gave it me."

"Wasn't it a little cool to name your sum?" hints Mr. Datchery, still rattling. "Isn't it customary to leave the amount open? Mightn't it have had the appearance, to the young gentleman—only the appearance—that he was rather dictated to?"

"Look'ee here, deary," she replies, in a confidential and persuasive tone, "I wanted the money to lay it out on a medicine as does me good, and as I deal in. I told the young gentleman so, and he gave it me, and I laid it out honest to the last brass farden. I want to lay out the same sum in the same way now; and if you'll give it me, I'll lay it out honest to the last brass farden again, upon my soul!"

"What's the medicine?"

"I'll be honest with you beforehand, as well as after. It's opium."

Mr. Datchery, with a sudden change of countenance, gives her a sudden look.

"It's opium, deary. Neither more nor less. And it's like a human creetur so far, that you always hear what can be said against it, but seldom what can be said in its praise."

Mr. Datchery begins very slowly to count out the sum demanded of him. Greedily watching his hands, she continues to hold forth on the great example set him.

"It was last Christmas Eve, just arter dark, the once that I was here afore, when the young gentleman gave me the three and six."

Mr. Datchery stops in his counting, finds he has counted wrong, shakes his money together, and begins again.

"And the young gentleman's name," she adds, "was Edwin."

Mr. Datchery drops some money, stoops to pick it up, and reddens with the exertion as he asks:

"How do you know the young gentleman's name?"

"I asked him for it, and he told it me. I only asked him the two questions, what was his Chris'en name, and whether he'd a sweetheart? And he answered, Edwin, and he hadn't."

Mr. Datchery pauses with the selected coins in his hand, rather as if he were falling into a brown study of their value, and couldn't bear to part with them. The woman looks at him distrustfully, and with her anger brewing for the event of his thinking better of the gift; but he bestows it on her as if he were abstracting his mind from the sacrifice, and with many servile thanks she goes her way.

John Jasper's lamp is kindled, and his Lighthouse is shining when Mr. Datchery returns alone towards it. As mariners on a dangerous voyage, approaching an iron-bound coast, may look along the beams of the warning light to the haven lying beyond it that may never be reached, so Mr. Datchery's wistful gaze is directed to this beacon, and beyond.

His object in now revisiting his lodging, is merely to put on the hat which seems so superfluous an article in his wardrobe. It is half-past ten by the Cathedral clock, when he walks out into the Precincts again; he lingers and looks about him, as though, the enchanted hour when Mr. Durdles may be stoned home having struck, he had some expectation of seeing the Imp who is appointed to the mission of stoning him.

In effect, that Power of Evil is abroad. Having nothing living to stone at the moment, he is discovered by Mr. Datchery in the unholy office of stoning the dead, through the railings of the churchyard. The Imp finds this a relishing and piquing pursuit; firstly, because their resting-place is announced to be sacred; and secondly, because the tall headstones are sufficiently like themselves, on their beat in the dark, to justify the delicious fancy that they are hurt when hit.

Mr. Datchery hails him with: "Halloa, Winks!"

He acknowledges the hail with: "Halloa, Dick!" Their acquaintance seemingly having been established on a familiar footing.

"But I say," he remonstrates, "don't yer go a making my name public. I never means to plead to no name, mind yer. When they says to me in the Lock-up, a going to put me down in the book, 'What's your name?' I says to them, 'Find out.' Likeways when they says, 'What's your religion?' I says, 'Find out.'"

Which, it may be observed in passing, it would be immensely difficult for the State, however statistical, to do.

"Asides[1] which," adds the boy, "there ain't no family of Winkses."

"I think there must be."

"Yer lie, there ain't. The travellers give me the name on account of my getting no settled sleep and being knocked up all night; whereby I gets one eye roused open afore I've shut the other. That's what Winks means. Deputy's the nighest name to indict me by: but yer[2] wouldn't catch me pleading to that, neither."

"Deputy be it always, then. We two are good friends; eh, Deputy?"

"Jolly good."

"I forgave you the debt you owed me when we first became acquainted, and many of my sixpences have come your way since; eh, Deputy?"

"Ah! And what's more, yer ain't no friend o' Jarsper's. What did he go a histing me off my legs for?"

---

[1] Asides] *possibly* Besides MS   yer] you MS

"What indeed! But never mind him now. A shilling of mine is coming[1] your way to-night, Deputy. You have just taken in a lodger I have been speaking to; an infirm woman with a cough."

"Puffer," assents Deputy, with a shrewd leer of recognition, and smoking an imaginary pipe, with his head very much on one side and his eyes rolling[2] very much out of their places: "Hopeum Puffer."

"What is her name?"

" 'Er Royal Highness the Princess Puffer."

"She has some other name than that; where does she live?"

"Up in London. Among the Jacks."

"The sailors?"

"I said so; Jacks. And Chaynermen. And hother Knifers."

"I should like to know, through you, exactly where she lives."

"All right. Give us 'old."

A shilling passes; and, in that spirit of confidence which should pervade all business transactions between principals of honor, this piece of business is considered done.

"But here's a lark!" cries Deputy. "Where do[3] yer think 'Er Royal Highness is a goin' to, to-morrow morning? Blest if she ain't a goin' to the KIN-FREE-DER-EL!" He greatly prolongs the word in his ecstacy, and smites his leg, and doubles himself up in a fit of shrill laughter.

"How do you know that, Deputy?"

" 'Cos she told me so just now. She said she must be hup and hout o' purpose. She ses, 'Deputy, I must 'ave a early wash, and make myself as swell as I can, for I'm a goin' to take a turn at the KIN-FREE-DER-EL!'" He separates the syllables with his former zest, and, not finding his sense of the ludicrous sufficiently relieved by stamping about on the pavement, breaks into a slow and stately dance, perhaps supposed to be performed by the Dean.

Mr. Datchery receives the communication with a well-satisfied though a pondering[4] face, and breaks up the conference. Returning to his quaint lodging, and sitting long over the supper of bread and cheese and salad and ale which Mrs. Tope has left prepared for him, he still sits when his supper is finished. At length he rises, throws open the door of a corner cupboard, and refers to a few uncouth chalked strokes on its inner side.

"I like," says Mr. Datchery, "the old tavern way of keeping scores. Illegible, except to the scorer. The scorer not committed, the scored debited with what is against him. Humph![5] A very small score this; a very poor score!"

He sighs over the contemplation of its poverty, takes a bit of chalk from one of the cupboard shelves, and pauses with it in his hand, uncertain what addition to make to the account.

"I think a moderate stroke," he concludes, "is all I am justified in scoring up;" so, suits the action to the word, closes the cupboard, and goes to bed.

A brilliant morning shines on the old city. Its antiquities and ruins are surpassingly beautiful, with the lusty[1] ivy gleaming in the sun, and the rich trees waving in the balmy air. Changes of glorious light from moving boughs, songs of birds, scents from gardens, woods, and fields—or, rather, from the one great garden of the whole cultivated island in its yielding time—penetrate into the Cathedral, subdue its earthy odour, and preach the Resurrection and the Life. The cold stone tombs of centuries ago grow warm; and flecks of brightness dart into the sternest marble corners of the building, fluttering there like wings.

Comes Mr. Tope with his large keys, and yawningly unlocks and sets open. Come Mrs. Tope, and attendant sweeping sprites. Come, in due time, organist and bellows-boy, peeping down from the red curtains in the loft, fearlessly flapping dust from books up at that remote elevation, and whisking it from stops and pedals. Come sundry rooks, from various quarters of the sky, back to the great tower; who may be presumed to enjoy vibration, and to know that bell and organ are going to give it them. Come a very small and straggling congregation indeed: chiefly from Minor Canon Corner and the Precincts. Come Mr. Crisparkle, fresh and bright; and his ministering brethren, not quite so fresh and bright. Come the choir in a hurry (always in a hurry, and struggling into their nightgowns at the last moment, like children shirking bed), and comes John Jasper leading their line. Last of all comes Mr. Datchery into a stall, one of a choice empty collection very much at his service, and glancing about him for Her Royal Highness the Princess Puffer.

The service is pretty well advanced before Mr. Datchery can discern Her Royal Highness. But by that time he has made her out, in the shade. She is behind a pillar, carefully withdrawn from the Choir Master's view, but regards him with the closest attention. All unconscious of her presence, he chants and sings. She grins when he is most musically fervid, and—yes, Mr. Datchery sees her do it!—shakes her fist at him behind the pillar's friendly shelter.

Mr. Datchery looks again to convince himself. Yes, again! As ugly and withered as one of the fantastic carvings on the under brackets of the stall seats, as malignant as the Evil One, as hard as the big brass eagle holding the sacred books upon his wings (and, according to the sculptor's presentation[2] of his ferocious attributes, not at all converted by them), she hugs herself in her lean arms, and then shakes both fists at the leader of the choir.

And at that moment, outside the grated door of the choir, having

[1] the lusty] a lusty 73 75
[2] presentation] ⟨re⟩presentation MS representation 70–75

eluded the vigilance of Mr. Tope by shifty resources in which he is an adept, Deputy peeps, sharp-eyed, through the bars, and stares astounded from the threatener to the threatened.

The service comes to an end, and the servitors disperse to breakfast. Mr. Datchery accosts his last new acquaintance outside, when the choir (as much in a hurry to get their bedgowns off, as they were but now to get them on) have scuffled away.

"Well, mistress. Good-morning. You have seen him?"

"*I*'ve seen him, deary; *I*'ve seen him!"

"And you know him?"

"Know him! Better far, than all the Reverend Parsons put together know him."

Mrs. Tope's care has spread a very neat, clean breakfast ready for her lodger. Before sitting down to it, he opens his corner cupboard door; takes his bit of chalk from its shelf; adds one thick line to the score, extending from the top of the cupboard door to the bottom; and then falls to with an appetite.[1]

*   *   *   *   *   *   *

[1] *Below this line in MS is a flourish indicating the end of the chapter*

MANUSCRIPT LIST OF PROJECTED NAMES AND TITLES

Friday Twentieth August, 1869.

Gilbert   Alfred
Edwin
Jasper   Edwyn
Michael   Oswald
Arthur

The loss of James Wakefield   Selwyn
Edwyn   Edgar

Mr Honeythunder
Mr Honeyblast
James's Disappearance   The Dean
Mrs Dean
Flight And Pursuit   Miss Dean

Sworn to avenge it

One Object in Life
A Kinsman's Devotion   The Two Kinsmen

The Loss of Edwyn Brood

The loss of Edwin Brude
The Mystery in the Drood Family
The loss of Edwyn Drood
The flight of Edwyn Drood
Edwin Drood in hiding
The Loss of Edwin Drude
The Disappearance of Edwin Drood
The Mystery of Edwin Drood

Dead? Or alive?

(Mystery of Edwin Drood.— No. IV.)

Chap Cr. XIII

Do it. not their Best.

The last Christmas Now Rachel

Chapter XIV

When shall these three meet again?

How can I possibly tell you?

"Awake?" Is going to the Postern stairs"

Chapter XV.

Impeached

Neville away out? Pursued, or thought to be R

not Sapsea's communicative: Archbishops will Sapsea

Chapter XVI.

Devoted

Once more carry Mr? Edwin and Rosa?

Or Ned & Ned? Last time

Last Meeting of Rosa & Edwin

Rosa / Jack

Jack K

Edwin gives up Rosa.

The Watchful night

The Sun sets and Alarm

Jasper's Failures at 14 miles

Jasper Diary? Yes.

Plan for Number IV
of the novel.
Forster collection, Victoria
and Albert Museum.
(Reduced)

APPENDIX B

NUMBER PLANS

Introductory note

In the following transcript a close reproduction of Dickens's working notes is attempted. All his underlinings and enclosing lines for emphasis are included; but the slight diagonal lines used frequently to separate consecutive items have been omitted. Dickens's arrangement of notes has been observed, but alignment has been adjusted where to follow the angle of the writing would be distracting. The full point after 'Mr' has been omitted and two full points have been used in 'N?', as this is Dickens's usual, though not entirely consistent, practice.

Opium-Smoking
    Touch the Key note
       "When the Wicked Man"—
The Uncle and Nephew:
    "Pussy's" Portrait
You won't take warning then?
_____

Dean   Mr Jasper
    Minor Canon. Mr Crisparkle
                    Verger
     Uncle and Nephew   Peptune
  Gloves for the Nuns' House   change to Tope
    Churchyard
    = =
    Cathedral town running throughout

Inside the Nuns' House
  Miss Twinkleton, and her double existence
        Mrs Tisher
        Rosebud
The affianced young people. Every love scene of theirs, a
                      quarrel more or less
  Mr Sapsea   Old Tory Jackass
             His wife's Epitaph
    Jasper and the Keys
        Durdles down in the crypt and among
  the graves. His dinner bundle

(Mystery of Edwin Drood.—№ I.)

Chapter I

⟨Prologue⟩ The Dawn

> change title to The Dawn
>
> Opium smoking and Jasper
>
> Lead up to Cathedral

Chapter II

A Dean, and a Chapter also[1]

Cathedral and Cathedral town   Mr Crisparkle
and the Dean

> Uncle and Nephew
>
> Murder very far off

Edwin's story and Pussy

Chapter III

The Nuns' House[1]

Still picturesque suggestions of Cathedral Town

The Nuns' House and the young couples first love scene

Chapter IV

Mr Sapsea

Connect Jasper with him (He will want a solemn donkey
bye and bye

> Epitaph brings them together, and
>
> brings Durdles with them.

The Keys.   Stoney Durdles

[1] Title squashed in as if inserted later.

Bring in the other young couple.   Yes

Neville and Olympia Heyridge—or Heyfort?

Neville and Helena Landless

Mixture of Oriental blood—or imperceptibly acquired nature—in them.   Yes

(Mystery of Edwin Drood.—N? II.)

Chapter V

Philanthropy in Minor-Canon Corner[1]

old Mrs Crisparkle

The Blusterous Philanthropist   China Shepherdess

Mr Honeythunder

Minor Canon Corner

Chapter VI

More Confidences than one

Neville's to Mr Crisparkle.

Rosa's to Helena

Piano scene with
Jasper.   She singing;
he following her lips.

Chapter VII

Daggers Drawn

Quarrel (Fomented by Jasper).   Goblet.   And then
confession to Mr Crisparkle
Jasper lays his ground

Chapter VIII

Mr Durdles and friend

Deputy engaged to stone Durdles nightly

No

Carry through the woman of the 1st chapter

Carry through Durdles's calling—and the
bundle & the Keys

John Jasper looks at Edwin asleep.

[1] Title inserted in balloon.

Pursue Edwin Drood and Rosa?

Lead on to final scene between them in N? V? IV?

Yes

How many more scenes between them?

Way to be paved for their marriage—

_____and parting instead.   Yes.

Miss Twinkleton's?   No. Next N?

Rosa's Guardian?   Done in N? II.

Mr Sapsea?   Yes.   Last chapter

Neville Landless at Mr Crisparkle's │   Yes
                    And Helena? │

Neville admires Rosa. That comes out
from himself

(Mystery of Edwin Drood.—N.º III.)

Chapter ⟨I⟩ Xᴵ

Smoothing The Way

That is, for Jasper's plan, through Mr Crisparkle:
who takes new ground on Neville's new
confidence.

Minor Canon Corner.   The closet I
remember there as a child

Edwin's appointment for Xmas Eve

Chapter X Iᴵ

A Picture and a Ring

$$J \overset{P}{-} T$$
$$1747$$

Dinner in chambers
   Bazzard the clerk

┌─────────────────┐
│ The two waiters │
└─────────────────┘

Mr Grewgious's past story
"A ring of diamonds and rubies delicately set in gold.[2]
                    Edwin takes it

Chapter XI Iᴵ

A Night with Durdles

Lay the ground for the manner of the Murder, to
come out at last.

Keep the boy suspended
Night picture of the Cathedral.

---

[1] Dickens had already written these figures as IX, X, and XI, and had to alter them
to allow for the new ch. ix in No. II.
[2] This last note is squashed in: Dickens had presumably not left himself sufficient
space.

Once more carry through Edwin and Rosa?

or, Last time?   Last time.

⟨Last scene but one between them⟩

Then

outside

Last Meeting of Rosa and Edwin ⟨in⟩ ∧ the Cathedral?   Yes

Kiss at parting

"Jack.

Edwin goes to the dinner.

The Windy night.

The Surprise and Alarm

Jasper's failure in the one great
object made known by Mr Grewgious

Jasper's Diary?   Yes

(Mystery of Edwin Drood.—N° IV.)

Chapter XIII

Both at their Best

The Last Interview

And Parting

Chapter XIV

When shall these three meet again?

How each passes the day

Watch and shirt pin
all Edwin's jewellery

Neville
Edwin
Jasper

Watch to the
Jeweller

"And so he goes up the Postern stair"

Storms of wind

Chapter XV

Impeached

Neville away early

Pursued and brought back

Mr Grewgious's communication:

And his scene with Jasper

Chapter XVI

Devoted

Jasper's artful use of the communication on his recovery.

Cloisterham Weir, Mr Crisparkle, and the Watch and pin.

Jasper's artful turn

The Dean. Neville cast out

Jasper's Diary. "I devote myself to his destruction"

Edwin and Rosa for the last time?   Done already

Kinfrederel

Edwin Disappears

The Mystery   Done already

(Mystery of Edwin Drood.—N.º V.)

Chapter XVII

Philanthropy ⟨in several phases⟩ professional and unprofessional

Chapter XVIII

⟨Shadow on the Sun Dial⟩
A Settler in Cloisterham

Chapter XIX

⟨A Settler in Cloisterham⟩
Shadow on the Sun Dial

Chapter XX

⟨Let's talk⟩
⟨Various Flights⟩   Divers Flights

APPENDIX B

[Number VI Plan—no left-hand]

(Mystery of Edwin Drood.—N? VI.)

Chapter XXI

A Gritty state of things comes on

Chapter XXII

The Dawn again

Chapter XXIII

[THE SAPSEA FRAGMENT[1]]

Wishing to take the air, I proceeded by a circuitous route to the Club, it being our weekly night of meeting. I found that we mustered our full strength. We were enrolled under the denomination of The Eight Club. We were eight in number; we met at eight o'clock during eight months of the year; our annual subscription was eight shillings each;[2] we played eight games of four handed cribbage at eightpence the game; our frugal supper was composed of eight rolls, eight mutton chops, eight pork sausages, eight baked potatoes, eight marrow bones with eight toasts, and eight bottles of ale. There may or may not be a certain harmony of colour in the ruling idea of this (to adopt a phrase of our lively neighbours) reunion. It was a little idea of mine.

A somewhat popular member of the Eight Club was a member by the name of Kimber. By profession dancing-master.[3] A common-place hopeful sort of man, wholly destitute of dignity or knowledge of the world.

As I entered the Club-room, Kimber was making the remark: "And he still half believes him to be very high in the Church."

In the act of hanging up my hat on the Eighth peg by the door, I caught Kimber's visual ray. He lowered it, and passed a remark on the next change of the moon. I did not take particular notice of this at the moment, because the world was often pleased to be a little shy of Ecclesiastical topics in my presence. For I felt that I was picked out (though perhaps only through a coincidence) to a certain extent to represent what I call our glorious constitution in church and state. The phrase may be objected to by captious minds; but I own to it as mine. I threw it off in argument some little time back. I said, Our Glorious Constitution in Church and State.

Another member of the Eight Club was Peartree, also member of the Royal College of Surgeons. Mr Peartree is not accountable to me for his opinions, and I say no more of them here than that he attends the poor gratis, whenever they want him, and is not the parish doctor. Mr Peartree

---

Dickens's spelling, and punctuation, so far as it can be discerned, are retained. Substantive differences between manuscript and Forster are given. For description of the manuscript and comment on the probable relation of the 'Sapsea fragment' to Edwin Drood *see Introduction, pp. xxvii–xxviii, xlviii.*

[1] *Forster gives as title:* HOW MR. SAPSEA CEASED TO BE A MEMBER OF THE EIGHT CLUB. TOLD BY HIMSELF.

[2] our annual . . . each] *om.* Forster

[3] dancing-master] MS a dancing-master Forster

may justify it to the grasp of *his* mind thus to do his republican utmost to bring an appointed officer into contempt. Suffice it that Mr Peartree can never justify it to the grasp of *mine*.

Between Peartree and Kimber there was a sickly sort of feeble-minded alliance. It came under my particular notice when I sold off Kimber by auction. (Goods taken in execution.) He was a widower in a white under waistcoat and slight shoes with bows, and had two daughters not ill-looking. Indeed, the reverse. Both daughters taught dancing in Scholastic Establishments for Young Ladies—had done so at Mrs Sapsea's; nay, Twinkletons—and both, in giving lessons, presented the unwomanly spectacle of having little fiddles tucked under their chins. In spite of which the younger one might, if I am correctly informed—I will raise the veil so far as to say I KNOW she might—have soared for life from this degrading taint, but for having the worst[1] class of mind alloted to what I call, the common herd, and being so incredibly devoid of veneration as to become painfully ludicrous.

When I sold off Kimber without reserve, Peartree (as poor as he can hold together) had several prime household lots knocked down to him. I[2] am not to be blinded, and of course it was as plain to me what he was going to do with them, as it was that he was a brown hulking sort of revolutionary subject who had been in India with the soldiers and ought (for the sake of society) to have his neck broken.[3] I saw the lots shortly afterwards in Kimber's lodgings—through the windows[4]—and I easily made out that there had been a sneaking pretence of lending them 'till better times. A man with a smaller knowledge of the world than myself might have been led to suspect that Kimber had held back money from his creditors and fraudulently bought the goods. But besides that I knew for certain he had no money, I knew that this would involve a species of forethought not to be made compatible with the frivolity of a caperer, innocculating other people with capering, for his bread.

As it was the first time I had seen either of those two since the Sale, I kept myself in what I call Abeyance. When selling him up, I had delivered a few remarks—shall I say a little homily?—concerning Kimber, which the world did regard as more than usually worth notice. I had come up into my pulpit, it was said, uncommonly like; and a murmur of recognition had repeated his (I will not name whose) title, before I spoke. I had then gone on to say that all present would find, in the first page of the Catalogue that was lying before them, in the last paragraph before the first lot, the following words: 'Sold in pursuance of a Writ of execution issued by a Creditor.' I had then proceeded to remind my Friends that however frivolous, not to say contemptible, the pursuits[5] by which a man

[1] worst] MS *probable reading om.* Forster   [2] *I*] I Forster
[3] broken] *possibly* broke *as in* Forster   [4] windows] window Forster
[5] pursuits] business Forster

got his goods together, still his goods were as dear to him, and as cheap to society (if sold without reserve) as though his pursuits had been of [a][1] character that would bear serious contemplation. I had then divided my text (if I may be allowed so to call it) into three heads; firstly, Sold; secondly, In pursuance of a writ of execution; thirdly, Issued by a creditor; with a few moral reflections on each and winding up with "Now to the first Lot" in a manner that was complimented when I afterwards mingled with my hearers.

So not being certain on what terms I and Kimber stood, I was grave, I was chilling. Kimber however, moving to me, I moved to Kimber. (I was the creditor who had issued the writ. Not that it matters.)

"I was alluding, Mr Sapsea," said Kimber, "when you came in,[2] to a stranger who entered into conversation with me in the street as I came to the club. He had been speaking to you just before, it seemed, by the churchyard; and though you had told him who you were, I could hardly persuade him that you were not high in the Church."

"Idiot!" said Peartree.

"Ass!" said Kimber.

"Idiot and Ass!" said the other five members.

"Idiot and Ass, gentlemen," I remonstrated, looking around me, "are strong expressions to apply to a young man of good appearance and address." My generosity was roused. I own it.

"You'll admit that he must be a Fool," said Peartree.

"You can't deny that he must be a Blockhead," said Kimber.

Their tone of disgust amounted to being offensive. Why should the young man be so calumniated? What had he done? He had only made an innocent and natural mistake. I controlled my generous indignation, and said so.

"Natural," repeated Kimber. "*He*'s a Natural!"

The remaining six members of the Eight Club laughed unanimously. It stung me. It was a scornful laugh. My anger was roused in behalf of an absent friendless stranger. I rose (for I had been sitting down.)

"Gentlemen," I said with dignity, "I will not remain one of this club allowing opprobrium to be cast on an unoffending person in his absence. I will not so violate what I call the sacred rites of hospitality. Gentlemen, until you know how to behave yourselves better, I leave you. Gentlemen, until then I withdraw from this place of meeting whatever personal qualifications I may have brought into it. Gentlemen, until then you cease to be the Eight Club, and must make the best you can of becoming the Seven."

I put on my hat and retired. As I went down stairs I distinctly heard them give a suppressed cheer. Such is the power of demeanour and knowledge of mankind.—I had forced it out of them.

[1] *Considerable deletion here*   [2] when ... in,] *om.* Forster

II.

Whom should I meet in the street, within a few yards of the door of the inn where the Club was held, but the selfsame young man whose cause I had felt it my duty so warmly—and I will add so disinterestedly—to take up!

"Is it Mr Sapsea," he said doubtfully, "or is it—"

"It is Mr Sapsea," I replied.

"Pardon me, Mr Sapsea; you appear warm, Sir."

"I have been warm," I said, "and on your account." Having stated the circumstances at some length (my generosity almost overpowering[1] him), I asked him his name.

"Mr Sapsea," he answered, looking down, "your penetration is so acute, your glance into the souls of your fellow men is so penetrating, that if I was hardy enough to deny that my name is Poker, what would it avail me?"

I don't know that I had quite exactly made out to a fraction that his name *was* Poker, but I dare say I had been pretty near doing it.

"Well, Well," said I, trying to put him at his ease by nodding my head, in a soothing way. "Your name is Poker, and there is no harm in being named Poker."

"Oh Mr Sapsea!" cried the young man in a very well-behaved manner. "Bless you for those words!" He then, as if ashamed of having given way to his feelings, looked down again.

"Come Poker," said I, "let me hear more about you. Tell me. Where are you going to, Poker, and where do you come from?"

"Ah Mr Sapsea!" exclaimed the young man. "Disguise from you is impossible. You know already that I come from somewhere, and am going somewhere else. If I was to deny it, what would it avail me?"

"Then don't deny it," was my remark.

"Or," pursued Poker, in a kind of despondent rapture, "or if I was to deny that I came to this town to see and hear you Sir, what would it avail me? Or if I was to deny

[1] overpowering] ⟨overpowered⟩ overpowering *probable* MS *reading* overpowered Forster

APPENDIX D

THE DESCRIPTIVE HEADLINES ADDED
IN 1875[1]

Chapter i — ——

Chapter ii — Mr. Jasper is taken poorly
A Welcome Visitor
A little Talk about Pussy
Mutual Confidences

Chapter iii — Miss Twinkleton's Seminary
A delightful Birthday
Lumps of Delight

Chapter iv — Mr. Sapsea
The late Mrs. Sapsea
Durdles

Chapter v — A Cock-shy
The Mysteries of Durdles's Craft

Chapter vi — Muscular Christianity
Mrs. Crisparkle receives a Letter
A Model Philanthropist

Chapter vii — The Reverend Septimus's New Inmate
A Mutual Understanding
Helena and Rosa

Chapter viii — High Words
The Stirrup Cup
A Bad Beginning

Chapter ix — Strange News penetrates into the Nuns' House
Rosa's Guardian
An Angular Subject
Rosa confers an Honour on her Guardian
Mr. Grewgious does his Duty

Chapter x — Mr. Crisparkle indulges in a Reverie
A Capital Place for an Explanation
Mr. Crisparkle exacts a Pledge
Mr. Jasper's Diary

Chapter xi — A Mysterious Inscription
Dinner for Three
Mr. Grewgious paints the Portrait of a Lover
A Trust fulfilled

[1] Probably by W. H. Wills: see Clarendon *Oliver Twist*, p. xxx n.

THE ILLUSTRATIONS

CHARLES COLLINS, the illustrator originally chosen, worked on the novel between September and December 1869, producing an 'excellent' cover and at least six preliminary sketches before he was constrained by ill-health to give up work.[1] Not unnaturally his evidence was sought by the speculators anxious to know the novel's conclusion. Kate Perugini, his wife at the time when he was working on the novel, was under the impression that he knew little of the total design,[2] and this is borne out by his letter to Daly, 4 May 1871, when the latter was contemplating a dramatized version of *Edwin Drood*.[3] His interesting comment on the staircase emblem apart, most of his speculations are very close to Forster's, and could have been deduced from an intelligent reading of the novel:

The late Mr. Dickens communicated to me some general outlines for his scheme of 'Edwin Drood', but it was at a very early stage in the development of the idea, and what he said bore mainly upon the earlier portions of the tale.

Edwin Drood *was never to reappear*, he having been murdered by Jasper. The girl Rosa not having been really attached to Edwin, was not to lament his loss very long, and was, I believe, to admit the sailor Mr. Tartar to supply his place. It was intended that Jasper himself should urge on the search after Edwin Drood and the pursuit of his murderer, thus endeavoring to direct suspicion from himself, the real murderer. This is indicated in the design, on the right side of the cover, of the figures hurrying up the spiral staircase emblematical of a pursuit. They are led on by Jasper who points unconsciously to his own figure in the drawing at the head of the title. The female figure at the left of the cover reading the placard 'Lost' is only intended to illustrate the doubt entertained by Rosa Budd as to the fate of her lover Drood. The group beneath it indicates the acceptance of another suitor.[4]

[1] These six sketches were reproduced for the *Dickensian*, xxv (June 1929), with a commentary, 'New Facts Concerning "Edwin Drood" ', by Professor C. F. Lehmann-Haupt. See also Felix Aylmer, *The Drood Case* (1964), pp. 18–20. When Lehmann-Haupt and Aylmer saw the original drawings, in the possession of Sir Henry and Lady Dickens, there was apparently a seventh sketch, a back view of a single figure, possibly Jasper, which was not included in the *Dickensian*. None of the originals can now be traced.

[2] Perugini, p. 650. See also Fildes's letter, *Times Literary Supplement*, Nov. 1905: 'Collins told me he did not in the least know the significance of the various groups in the design; that they were drawn from instructions personally given by Charles Dickens and not from any text. . . .'   [3] See Appendix G below.

[4] Mrs. Perugini, in her article, p. 650, expressed her belief that this figure was meant for Tartar, but she also thought the higher figure on the stairs was his, perhaps in this following Forster's suggestion about Tartar's part in the unmasking of Jasper, but thus losing her husband's impression of symbolical significance in the effect of self-denunciation.

As to any theory further it must be purely conjectural. It seems likely that Rosa would marry Mr. Tartar and possible that the same destiny might await Mr. Crisparkle and Helena Landless. Young Landless himself was to die perhaps, and Jasper certainly would, though whether by falling into the hands of justice or by suicide or through taking an overdose of opium, which seems most likely, it is impossible to say. . . .[1]

When Collins had to give up the illustrating, Fildes took over, supplying all the accompanying illustrations for the monthly parts, and either redrawing or touching up the cover. What one gathers about Fildes's knowledge of the story bears out the impression that the illustrators were told all that was necessary for their sketches, and no more. Fildes's conjecture about the long black scarf has already been referred to:[2] clearly, then, that was one most important feature of the story Dickens had not intended to disclose to him. W. H. Chambers gave insight into the method of procedure by which author and illustrator worked together:

Fildes told me he used to go down to Gadds Hill and Dickens would act the scenes he wanted illustrating, and Fildes would get his models in London and so complete the picture.[3]

As time went on, it appears, Dickens grew to place more confidence in his illustrator.[4] Even so, the amount that Fildes knew seems to have been little beyond what anyone might deduce from the story. One fact does emerge from his recollections, namely that the last illustration of the book had been decided on before Dickens's death, presumably well in advance of some of the preceding scenes:

I remember well the twenty-fourth and last was decided on, and we were to visit the scene, where he told me he himself had not been since he was a child. Only twelve drawings were made, and six of them after Dickens' death. I was going down to Gad's Hill on the 10th of June, and my luggage was packed ready to go, when I read his death in the morning paper.[5]

This twenty-fourth sketch, we learn elsewhere, was to be of the condemned cell, presumably with Jasper as its occupant.[6]

[1] Joseph Francis Daly, *The Life of Augustin Daly* (N.Y., 1917), pp. 107–8.
[2] See p. xxvi.
[3] Letter to Howard Duffield, 28 Nov. 1927. This bears out what Fildes elsewhere said as to there being no necessity for local accuracy in his sketches: 'I never felt the necessity or propriety of being locally accurate to Rochester or its buildings. Dickens, of course, meant Rochester; yet, at the same time, he chose to be obscure on that point, and I took my cue from him. . . .' Quoted by W. R. Hughes, *A Week's Tramp in Dickensland* (1891), p. 129.
[4] D. Croal Thompson, *The Life and Work of Luke Fildes, R.A.* (1895), p. 27. See also Alice Meynell, 'How Edwin Drood Was Illustrated', *Century Magazine* (Feb. 1884).
[5] D. Croal Thompson, pp. 27–8.
[6] W. R. Hughes, p. 140; and Harry How, *Strand Magazine* (Aug. 1893).

As for the actual illustrations, presumably Dickens had already discussed with Fildes those which the artist was subsequently able to produce
for the last three Numbers, or at least those for Numbers IV and V of
which Dickens saw proofs. According to Kitton, the titles for the last six
sketches were supplied by Fildes. Proofs of the first two Numbers were
not received from the printers until 1 December, by which time Charles
Collins had given up the illustrating.[1] It is clear, therefore, that Collins
had no text to work from while he was trying out sketches, but the
correspondence in general subject-matter between his sketches and those
subsequently produced by Fildes indicates that certain scenes were
selected already in Dickens's mind.[2] The opium den scene was an obvious
choice for an exciting opening, and two preliminary sketches of this are
found in Collins's work, each showing Princess Puffer, the Chinaman,
and the Lascar, in addition to Jasper, whose appearance varies from an
impression of diffidence (perhaps intended for revulsion or temporary
remorse) in the one, to a more menacing, decisive air in the other, as he
bends over the bed. The figure in the latter sketch is altogether a darker,
more clearly defined individual, and seems rather less like Collins's Jasper
on the cover than does the other. These were, however, only sketches
and it is rash to make precise differentiations of significance. A second
chosen subject was obviously the Crisparkle dinner party, and here again
we have two tentative illustrations, one with the party gathered round the
table, the other depicting the later scene at the piano. The third pair of
illustrations cannot be located in the story so precisely: they obviously
represent some members of the 'Cathedral' group—the Cathedral can be
seen in the background each time—and may signify Dickens's looking
ahead to Number III; but he probably did not begin to write this Number
until Collins had retired, and it seems more likely that this was tentatively
tried out as the second illustration for Number I, and that the two
prominent figures are the Dean and Minor Canon Crisparkle, with Tope
in the background in one, and possibly Jasper and another, unidentified,
walking away in the other. (The little dog is a mystery in itself: it appears
to be in attendance on the clerical figures, but could hardly have been
present at vespers, and it has no part in the story unless it provided the
dismal howl on Durdles's last Christmas Eve.) These identifications can
only be conjectural, made on the basis of our knowledge of the content
of chapter ii. If it were the case that these 'Cathedral' figures were intended
for Number I, presumably Dickens relegated them to a later Number

[1] See p. xxi.
[2] Until proofs arrived, Dickens would not be certain of the material for each Number.
In fact, the only major substantial change at proof stage in *Edwin Drood*, the transference
of a chapter from Number II to Number I, has not affected the illustrations. We do not
know whether Dickens had discussed four possible scenes with Collins: there are sketches
for three, but it seems likely that Dickens would have already chosen the quarrel scene
for illustration, and that Collins had not had time to attempt it.

Sketches for early scenes in the novel, by Charles Collins. From photographs at Dickens House

where Sapsea and Durdles could be added to the picture, in favour of an illustration of Rosa and Edwin to counterbalance the grimness of the Jasper picture and interest the readers in the young hero and heroine from the start.

As regards the cover, Fildes was presumably responsible for altering some of Collins's drawing, though nothing, it would appear, of great significance.[1] The centre of the picture in both drawings contains the title, but in Fildes's more finished production a small sketch of certain significant items is added below the wording, namely Durdles's dinner-bundle, key, and spade. The surrounding scenes are virtually the same on both covers, but on the earlier one the second and third of the three figures rushing up the staircase, with a glimpse of a fourth in the background, are police officers. Unless Collins mistook Dickens's intention here, Fildes's drawing denotes a later change of plan, possibly with a view to the greater concentration and interest to be achieved by keeping the whole mystery and detection essentially private. Datchery may have been a later invention when this notion took shape, a compromise between the two ideas, a known character masquerading as an unknown for the purpose of spying on Jasper. There is some slight alteration in appearance or positioning in other sketches, but the only one which shows difference in any marked particular is the lower right, in Fildes's cover depicting the Chinaman in the opium den. The corresponding figure in Collins's sketch is not so clearly defined, nor does it bear marked resemblance to the Chinaman in Collins's sketches for Number I. In fact there is something feminine and youthful about this cover figure, though one would be ill-advised to build conjectures in relation to the story on this possibility, as Collins's sketches are not so precisely finished as those of Fildes and some of his men are rather effeminate in face. The garment in the sketch could be either a woman's skirt or the loose, short trouser legs of the Chinaman, and the vague lines between the left foot and the chair may be intended for the round hat the Chinaman is wearing in Collins's other sketches.[2] The placing of this figure on the right, balancing the opium woman on the left, is interesting. The other left-hand sketches seem to

---

[1] For discussion of Fildes's share in the cover drawing see *Dickensian*, xxv (1929), p. 323, letter from S. M. Ellis; *Dickensian*, xxxi (1935), pp. 233, 299–300, letter from M. H. Spielmann, article by C. F. Lehmann-Haupt.

[2] Some commentators build up for Jasper and the opium woman a sinister past relationship, often involving seduction, usually of her daughter, sometimes with an illegitimate child as the issue. This figure could be pressed into service in this role, as daughter or grand-daughter to Princess Puffer. (There have been many speculations as to the opium woman's age: see, for example, Philip Collins, 'Inspector Bucket Visits the Princess Puffer', *Dickensian*, lx (1964), pp. 88–90.) Another line of detection foresees a visit to the opium den by Helena on the track of Jasper. It is a remote possibility that the references in chapter i to the 'contagion' of the opium smokers—'His form of cheek, eye, and temple, and his color, are repeated in her'—have some bearing on the two lower cover sketches.

depict innocence; those on the right villainy and retribution, and this is confirmed by the symbolic figures at the top and by the garland surrounding the title, in which roses on the left are contrasted with thorns and falling petals on the right.[1] One wonders if an echo of this suggestion was intended in the name 'Rosa Bud' and the title of Bazzard's play, 'The Thorn of Anxiety', which it is hoped will 'come out at last'.

The cover illustration which has given rise to the greatest number of conjectures is basically the same in both drawings, and would therefore appear to have been part of a definite and clearly visualized plan in Dickens's mind. It is the only illustration occupying a central position, and the eye is obviously intended to linger on it finally at the foot of the page. It depicts a man, presumably Jasper, just emerging from a doorway and shining a lantern on a motionless figure in coat and hat, with left hand raised towards his coat fastenings, possibly holding something small momentarily concealed from view. This figure certainly looks like Edwin, particularly in Collins's pair of figures. (The sketch of Edwin at the top left, with its air of negligent condescension, is Collins's most individual figure.) Fildes may have been instructed to make the resemblance less obvious, to preserve some air of mystery, but this is pure conjecture and nothing can be deduced from it, as the lantern-bearer is clearly intended to be making some startling discovery, and nothing could be more startling than the reappearance of Edwin, whether genuine or faked. It has been pointed out that, in Fildes's drawing, the coat appears to be fastened right over left, indicating a female—Helena—in disguise; but this is disputable, and certainly not clear in Collins's sketch. The main conclusion one can draw about this illustration, from its prominent position, its clear depiction of a specific, not a general or symbolic, situation, and the close resemblances between the two artists' sketches, is that it formed an extremely important part of Dickens's plot from the outset.

[1] Cf. the similar device on the cover of *Martin Chuzzlewit*.

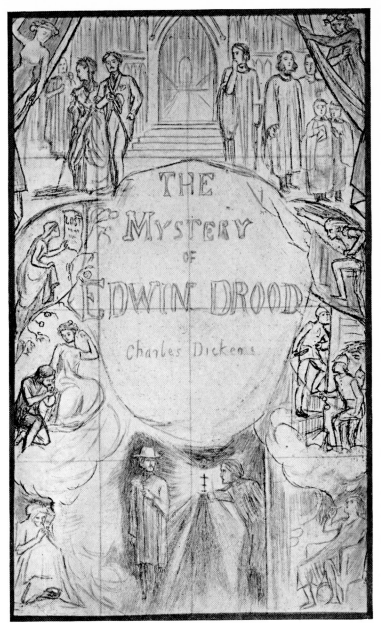

Sketch for wrapper of monthly parts, by Charles Collins. From a photograph at Dickens House

APPENDIX F

EVERY SATURDAY AND FIELDS, OSGOOD AND COMPANY'S ONE-VOLUME EDITION, 1870

In addition to publishing *Edwin Drood* in the weekly journal, *Every Saturday*, Fields, Osgood and Company of Boston published a one-volume edition of the novel in two separate issues in 1870.[1] One of these, in paper covers with the Monthly Numbers cover illustration, but in pinkish-brown, not green, bears at the top of the cover the words 'Author's Edition', and was probably a reissue within one cover of a monthly-parts supplement advertised in the pages of *Every Saturday*. Printed in the preliminaries is the letter of April 1867 from Dickens announcing the firm as his 'only authorized representatives in America', and the cover illustration is repeated in black and white. Unlike *Every Saturday*, this issue contains all the illustrations. It follows *Every Saturday*'s captions where they differ from those of the English text, except on one occasion: 'Mr. Crisparkle is Overpaid', which is used as frontispiece, is correctly titled. A new caption, 'The Young Ladies say Good By for the Holidays', is provided for '"Good-bye, Rosebud, darling!"', missing from *Every Saturday*, and a mistake is made in the caption for the final illustration (also lacking in *Every Saturday*): 'Sleeping it Off' appears as 'Sleeping it out'. The text is printed in two columns and ends on p. 127. This pagination includes the unnumbered preliminaries. The other one-volume issue of 1870, referred to in a note of 17 September in *Every Saturday*, appeared both in paper covers (plain cover) and in green cloth. In addition to *Edwin Drood* the volume contains 'Some Uncollected Pieces': namely, *George Silverman's Explanation*, *Holiday Romance*, *Sketches of Young Couples*, *New Uncommercial Samples*, *The Will of Charles Dickens*. The 1867 letter is omitted; added to the preliminaries is *Some Memories of Charles Dickens* by J. T. F. (Fields), dated July 1870. Illustrations and text are identical in the two issues, even to pagination. (The eight pages of Fields's *Memories* are numbered, but the preliminaries are not included in pagination in this issue.)

    Collation of ES with MS and 70 reveals divergences varying considerably in interest from one Number to another. Where ES and MS agree against 70, the evidence suggests that further changes for 70 were made on a proof later than that sent to America; where MS and 70 agree against ES, the ES reading is clearly in error. Examination of the

[1] Presumably on or about 17 Sept., the date of the final instalment in *Every Saturday*.

one-volume American text (for which the abbreviation FO is here adopted) at the points where ES differs from MS and 70 offers evidence for a distinction between those errors peculiar to ES and those made on the advance sheets and corrected at a later stage for 70;[1] but collation of the American readings provides a new problem, peculiar to the American texts in part of Number VI, where ES is clearly printed from an uncorrected proof and FO from a corrected one.

Numbers I and II present no points of special interest: in Number I there are four errors of substance peculiar to ES, four which the American texts have in common; in Number II there is one common error and one divergence, possibly deliberate, peculiar to ES. (It is found also in Harper and Brothers, 1870.)

Number I

Ch. i, p. 2	three shillings] shilling ES
Ch. ii, p. 5	look] looked ES FO
Ch. ii, p. 7	recognition and greeting] greeting and recognition ES FO
Ch. ii, p. 8	*I*] I ES FO
Ch. iv, p. 23	in mistake] by mistake ES
Ch. iv, p. 24	the cool . . . evening] a cool . . . evening ES FO
Ch. iv, p. 29	and he lives] and lives ES
Ch. v, p. 37	over] above ES

Number II

| Ch. vi, p. 39 | bent head] head bent ES FO |
| Ch. vi, p. 44 | Reverend] Rev. ES (*twice*) (*also in* Harper and Brothers, 1870) |

Number III contains five errors peculiar to ES; one variant common to both, which may have been a proof error or a deliberate American 'improvement'; one instance of known proof error where ES and FO follow proof, and one where they make their own correction; and, the most interesting case, one reading at the end of the Number where MS, ES, and FO agree against 70. This is the first clear evidence of a stage of proof-alteration, whether deliberate or in error, after the sheets were set aside for America.

Number III

| Ch. x, p. 79 | Peach] Pear ES |
| Ch. x, p. 81 | he, who] he that ES |

---

[1] In the list of variants for Number I, for example, 'three shillings'] 'shilling' (ch. i, p. 2) appears to be an error on the part of ES, whereas 'recognition and greeting'] 'greeting and recognition' (ch. ii, p. 7) probably originated in an error on the advance sheets.

Ch. x, p. 81	fear of his outliving] fear of his not outliving ES FO
Ch. xi, p. 88	Constitution . . . us Britons, the odd . . . institution] *corrected by Dickens in a letter to the printer*: constitution . . . us Britons. The odd . . . institutions 70: constitution . . . us Britons; the odd . . . institutions ES FO
Ch. xi, p. 96	lip] lips ES
Ch. xii, p. 100	tickling his ears:—figuratively long enough] MS: tickling his ears—figuratively, long enough 70 ES FO
Ch. xii, p. 105	turn] turned ES
Ch. xii, p. 105	passes] passed ES
Ch. xii, p. 110	on the watch there!] on the watch! MS ES FO

In Number IV, with eight readings common to MS, ES, and FO, the evidence for a second stage of proof-revision becomes conclusive, and on three of these occasions we can even see two stages of change within a single phrase. In this Number there are two errors common to both American readings; no mistakes peculiar to ES.

Number IV

Ch. xiii, p. 113	met] meet ES FO
Ch. xiii, p. 117	and moddley-coddleys] molly-coddles MS: and molly-coddles ES FO (*change in form of word might have been made, not by Dickens, but by the printers, for consistency with ch. ii, p. 7*)
Ch. xiii, p. 118	or other records] or records MS ES FO
Ch. xiii, p. 120	She pulled hurriedly at the handle] She pulled very hurriedly at the pendent handle MS: She pulled hurriedly at the pendent handle ES FO
Ch. xiv, p. 124	his lot in life] his fortune MS: his fortune in life ES FO
Ch. xvi, p. 139	impertinent] importunate ES FO
Ch. xvi, p. 143	find the body; he only found] find the body; but he only found MS ES FO
Ch. xvi, p. 143	always accurately understanding] always understanding MS ES FO
Ch. xvi, p. 144	had been urged on] was urged on MS ES FO
Ch. xvi, p. 146	we clergy need] we need MS ES FO

Number V affords interest of a different kind. We know what was printed in proof and what corrections Dickens made. (In one instance the American printers transcribed Dickens's alteration correctly; the English ones made nonsense of it.) There are in 70 three new readings which have no authority from MS or from correction on existing proof,[1] and one reading which

[1] See p. xxxiv n. for reason for supposing that these later alterations were not made by Dickens.

came in as a proof error which Dickens corrected, but not very clearly. This perpetuated error and two of the new readings were transmitted on the copy to America; the third new reading, and two corrections not made on this proof, were not. There is evidence here of three stages between MS and 70: first proof with Dickens's corrections; second stage of alterations made in time for American copy; third stage of alterations of which the first record is 70.

Number V

Ch. xvii, p. 151   a false God of your making] P (*with* of your making *as a proof addition*) ES FO: a false God of our making 70

Ch. xvii, p. 152   vanity] MS 70: variety P (*uncorrected*) ES FO

Ch. xvii, p. 155   mastery of her] MS P (*no alteration: part of a passage deleted in* P): mastery over her 70 ES FO

Ch. xvii, p. 160   seem likely to] MS P (*with no alteration*): seem likely to do it 70 ES FO

Ch. xviii, p. 163   another chamber . . . with another groined roof: their windows . . . walls. These two chambers] MS 70: another chamber . . . with another groined roof. Their windows . . . walls, these two chambers P (*with no alteration*) ES FO

Ch. xx, p. 174   His self-absorption] MS P (*with no alteration*) ES FO: Jasper's self-absorption 70

Ch. xx, p. 175   from giving it] MS: from so giving it P (*with* so *deleted*) 70 ES FO

Number VI introduces the problem peculiar to the American texts. For the first chapter, which was written as part of Number V, proof exists, and both ES and FO perpetuate an obvious error uncorrected on proof. (See also 'vanity'] 'variety' in Number V.) This was corrected in 70, and the obvious inference is that both ES and FO were printed from the advance sheets. The unusual feature here is that ES has none of Dickens's proof-corrections for this chapter,[1] whereas FO has corrections. It seems, therefore, that two copies of advance sheets, one uncorrected, one corrected, were sent to America. The fact that chapter xxi was printed for Number V gives some probability to the hypothesis of such a mistake on the part of the English publishers. Copy for Number V clearly must have indicated where the Number should end; but conceivably the surplus material, uncorrected because not yet needed, was not removed.

For the rest of Number VI, there are eleven errors peculiar to ES (an unusually high number) and five common to ES and FO.[2] In these

---

[1] ES has the new chapter-division and title, and the reinstated passages which Dickens deleted because of over-matter.

[2] One might be tempted to suppose the ES errors to be proof errors, were it not for

chapters, again, there are two occasions, difficult to account for, on which MS and ES agree against 70 and FO. In the first of these cases,[1] it is possible that FO and 70 came independently to the same reading, a more grammatical one than that of MS; in the second, again the MS reading is not entirely satisfactory, but it is less likely that FO and 70 independently reached the same reading here. The other possibility is that the publishers, dissatisfied with the reading, waited for the English publication of Number VI, in order to check this construction.[2]

Number VI

(i) *Chapter xxi, written for Number V* (P *refers to proof as printed; unless otherwise stated, the* 70 *readings came in as proof-corrections*)

Ch. xxi, p. 183   he explained to her] he explained to Rosa MS P ES (Rosa, *oddly enough, is found also in* Harper and Brothers, 1870, *which otherwise is clearly based on* 70)
Ch. xxi, p. 183   authorized] invited MS P ES
Ch. xxi, p. 184   a way out] a way out of it MS P ES
Ch. xxi, p. 184   either to pick him up, or go down with him] MS: rather to pick him up, or go down with him P ES: to pick him up, or go down with him 70 FO
Ch. xxi, p. 185   something highly friendly and appreciative] something friendly and appreciative MS P ES
Ch. xxi, p. 185   the top set in the house next the top set in the corner] the top set next the top set in the corner MS P ES
Ch. xxi, p. 185   only within a day or so] only just now MS P ES
Ch. xxi, p. 185   my flower-garden] my flower-gardens P ES
Ch. xxi, p. 185   none the less readily] more the less readily P (*uncorrected*) ES FO
Ch. xxi, p. 185   his idea] his ideas P ES
Ch. xxi, p. 186   Staple] Staples MS P ES (*three times*)
Ch. xxi, p. 187   quite long enough] quite long enough for the purpose MS P ES
Ch. xxi, p. 187   a little extra fitting on] a little extra fitting MS P ES
Ch. xxi, p. 187   as they went along] as they walked along MS P ES

the additional group of common errors in ES and FO. Four out of these five errors are mistakes in spelling, and could conceivably be errors which the American printers made twice; the fifth, like the occurrence of 'more' for 'none' in ch. xxi, presents a more difficult problem. If these two errors appeared in any copies of Number VI, one could assume that Number VI of FO was printed from an English published text.

[1] A punctuation change, not recorded in the notes to the text.
[2] This is quite a different case from those in ch. xxi. There, the American publishers would have no cause to wait for the English published text, as their readings were perfectly satisfactory.

Ch. xxi, p. 187   in an animated way] in his animated way MS P ES
Ch. xxi, p. 187   steady and determined even then] steady and deter-
                   mined then MS *probable reading* P ES
Ch. xxi, p. 187   what the girls would say] what the girls would think
                   MS P ES
Ch. xxi, p. 187   out of any danger, miles and miles, without resting] out
                   of any danger without resting, miles and miles MS
                   P ES
Ch. xxi, p. 187   drawing nearer and nearer] coming nearer and nearer
                   MS P ES
Ch. xxi, p. 187   seemed to get] got MS P ES
Ch. xxi, p. 188   came into sudden bloom] bloomed MS P ES

(ii) *Chapters xxii and xxiii, written for Number VI*

Ch. xxii, p. 189   the hand that had had Mr. Crisparkle's life in it] the
                   hand that had Mr. Crisparkle's life in it ES
Ch. xxii, p. 190   said Rosa, in rapid conclusion; "and could] 70 FO:
                   said Rosa, in rapid conclusion; "And could MS ES
Ch. xxii, p. 191   If Mr. Tartar would call] If Mr. Tartar should call ES
Ch. xxii, p. 192   the spring knob of a locker] the spring knob in a locker
                   ES FO
Ch. xxii, p. 193   that the respected lady . . . if any. Whether] MS ES:
                   that as the respected lady . . . if any—whether 70 FO
Ch. xxii, p. 196   *by* the fire] by the fire ES
Ch. xxii, p. 196   favior] favor ES
Ch. xxii, p. 196   sharing suspicions is apt to creep in] snaring suspicions
                   is apt to creep in ES (*probably an attempt to improve
                   the reading*)
Ch. xxii, p. 196   in a baronial way] in a baronical way ES FO
Ch. xxii, p. 199   stimilate] stimulare ES stimulate FO
Ch. xxii, p. 199   a liberal and nutritious . . . diet] a liberal, nutritious . . .
                   diet ES
Ch. xxii, p. 199   informiation] information ES FO (*twice*) (*same mistake
                   in* Harper and Brothers, 1870)
Ch. xxii, p. 199   polite and powerful] polite and painful ES
Ch. xxii, p. 200   none such have been imparted by myself] none such
                   have been imported by myself ES
Ch. xxiii, p. 204 The Cathedral doors have closed for the night] The
                   Cathedral doors had closed for the night ES
Ch. xxiii, p. 204 there will shortly be not one] there will shortly not be
                   one ES
Ch. xxiii, p. 205 Who was they as died, deary?] Who was they that
                   died, deary? ES

THE MYSTERY OF EDWIN DROOD
AFTER-HISTORY 1870–1878

W HEN it was known that Dickens had died leaving the novel unfinished, there was naturally much speculation as to the possibility of its completion by another hand. It is hardly surprising, in view of the frequent collaborations between the two, that rumour suggested the name of Wilkie Collins,[1] and both Collins himself and Chapman and Hall had to issue disclaimers. *The Times* on 23 June carried the announcement from the publishers:

We find that erroneous reports are in circulation respecting *The Mystery of Edwin Drood*, the novel on which Mr. Dickens was at work when he died. It has been suggested that the tale is to be finished by other hands. We hope you will allow us to state in your columns that Mr. Dickens has left three numbers complete, in addition to those already published, this being one-half of the story as it was intended to be written. These numbers will be published, and the fragment will so remain. No other writer could be permitted by us to complete the work which Mr. Dickens has left.

Wilkie Collins, too, later denied all connection with any attempt to complete the novel, and there is no evidence that he had any particular knowledge as to the story's intended development. Collins and Dickens had been close friends for several years, but recent biographers of Collins seem to detect signs of a growing literary rivalry between the two. Dickens's initial enthusiasm for *The Moonstone* gave way to strictures on its 'vein of obstinate conceit', 'wearisome beyond endurance',[2] and if rumour of this criticism reached Collins, he was perhaps retaliating in his summing-up of *Edwin Drood*: 'Dickens' last laboured effort, the melancholy work of a worn out brain.'[3] It seems possible that *Edwin Drood*, with its clear recollection, in the passage about the misplaced watch in chapter iii, of *The Moonstone*'s similar passage about the

---

[1] Some years earlier, in a letter of 14 Oct. 1862, Dickens had offered to perform a similar office for Collins, in case he was too ill to keep up with the instalments of *No Name* (N, iii. 310).

[2] See letters to Wills, 30 June 1867 and 26 July 1868 (N, iii. 534, 660).

[3] *Pall Mall Gazette*, 20 Jan. 1890. See also Kenneth Robinson, *Wilkie Collins, A Biography* (1951), pp. 245, 257–60; and Nuel Pharr Davis, *The Life of Wilkie Collins* (Urbana, Ill., 1956), pp. 257–8, 270, 289–90. According to Davis, when the sales of *The Moonstone* far outsoared those of *Our Mutual Friend* and *Great Expectations*, Dickens and Wills 'communed with each other on Wilkie's story like two jealous children'.

misplaced parcel,[1] was Dickens's answer to the problem of how to write a successful mystery novel, and that Collins's 1871 Christmas story, *Miss or Mrs?*, was his version, with no acknowledgements of debt, of how the unfinished threads of *Edwin Drood* might be utilized.[2] Some years later Collins was vigorous in his repudiation of *John Jasper's Secret*; Charles Dickens junior, whose name was also associated with this book, was equally emphatic in his denial of any authorized continuation:

> I have frequently been asked by unknown correspondents for particulars of a continuation of *Edwin Drood* which is supposed to have been written by Wilkie Collins 'at the request of the Dickens family'. Of course there is no such book. Neither the 'Dickens family' nor Wilkie Collins would have entertained such an idea for a moment.[3]

However, though Collins was thus specifically dissociated from *Edwin Drood*, Charles Dickens junior mentioned another as a potential collaborator in a different way. According to him, his father had made arrangements for dramatizing *Drood* with the co-operation of Dion Boucicault. After Dickens died, Boucicault proposed that his son should join him in the work with a view to a production at the Lyceum Theatre[4] with Henry

---

[1] *The Moonstone*, Second Period, Third Narrative, Section 10. Collins's passage is itself derived from the work of a friend of Dickens, Dr. Elliotson's *Human Physiology* (5th edn., 1840, p. 646).

[2] *Miss or Mrs?* first appeared in the 1871 Christmas number of the *Graphic*, and was later included with other 'Stories in Outline' in a volume published by Chatto and Windus in 1875. In the 1875 Dedication, Collins refers to Dickens but gives no hint of indebtedness for the details of his Christmas story. *Miss or Mrs?*, one of Collins's notably inferior works, has the following plot elements in common with *Edwin Drood* or with a hypothetical ending for *Edwin Drood*: a young girl with two suitors, the older of whom, the villain of the story, fills her with terror; the latter's employment as his accomplice of an opium addict from a den in East London; the appearance of a disguised stranger in the locality of the crime on Christmas Eve; the plan for the accomplice to rob the victim of jewellery to make that appear the motive of the crime, and to burn his own clothes in a lime cauldron before escaping; the subsequent failure of this plan owing to the opium addict's being seized by a fit at the very moment of his murder attempt.

[3] Introduction to Macmillan's 1923 edn., p. xv. See also pp. xvi–xviii.

[4] This is interesting in view of Irving's later success in *The Bells* (first night 25 Nov. 1871, Royal Lyceum Theatre). Leopold Lewis adapted *The Bells* from a French original, *Le Juif polonais*, by Erckmann–Chatrian (Émile Erckmann and Pierre-Alexandre Chatrian), which had appeared in print as early as 1867 and was acted at 'le petit théâtre de Cluny' in 1868. See Erckmann–Chatrian, *Contes et romans populaires* (Paris, 1867); and Jules Claretie, *Erckmann–Chatrian* (Paris, 1883), p. 21. There is no evidence that Dickens knew this work, but he certainly moved in theatrical circles in France (Forster, vii. 5), and he was in Paris in the summer of 1868 to see the French version of *No Thoroughfare*. The resemblances between *Le Juif polonais* and *Edwin Drood* are striking: the disappearance of the body, the date of the crime—Christmas Eve, the respected figure of the criminal, the probable use of lime in each case, the centring of interest on the question of how the murderer will eventually betray himself. The mixed feelings of revulsion and necessity with which Mathis awaits the approach of his victim can easily

Irving as John Jasper. For some reason this production fell through, and Charles Dickens junior blamed Forster in part for the failure:

But, shortly after we had commenced our labours, a foolish version of the book was brought out at the Surrey Theatre, with Henry Neville as Jasper—and with a live Edwin Drood turning up, disguised as a barrister, at Neville Landless's trial. The production of this piece—it was called the *Mystery of Cloisterham*— with the express sanction and approval of Mr. Forster, who declined to take any notice of the remonstrances which Boucicault and I addressed to him, of course put a stop to our play. The book has been dramatised more than once since, but always, I believe, with the same altogether erroneous idea as to what was really meant by the mystery of Edwin Drood.

The writer here appears to be confusing two adaptations of the novel: one at the Britannia Theatre, Hoxton, 22 July 1872 and week, by G. H. MacDermott, and one by Walter Stephens at the Surrey Theatre, around 20 November 1871.[1] In the former of these Drood escapes; in the latter he is murdered. The play by Stephens appears with various titles: on the poster it is called *The Mystery of Edwin Drood*; the copy at Dickens House has as its title *Lost*.[2] Allardyce Nicoll, who records two entries at the Surrey Theatre within two weeks, *The Mystery of Cloisterham*, author unknown, 26/10/71, and *The Mystery of Edwin Drood*, Walter Stephens, 4/11/71, admits that several plays in his lists are probably recorded twice be imagined as present in Jasper, and the manner of the crime, the repeated blows, the horrified gazing at the body, both recall Jasper's 'Look down, look down! You see what lies at the bottom there? . . . Look at it! Look what a poor, mean, miserable thing it is!', and suggest speculation on the possibility of the victim's escape, if the murderer were not so thorough as the burgomaster. More striking than any of this, however, is the manner of the crime's revelation: the influence of the mesmerist and the unconsciousness of the criminal that he is revealing his crime. There is no suggestion, with regard to *Edwin Drood*, of a place for the doubly ironic retribution of *Le Juif polonais*, in which Mathis merely dreams that he has given himself away, and dies of an imagined, self-inflicted sentence; but the resemblances are sufficient to rouse speculation as to whether Dickens had seen or read the French work. The dramatization of *No Thoroughfare* also is interesting in view of the suggestion that Dickens was considering a dramatic adaptation of *Edwin Drood*. Both Dickens and Boucicault were enthusiastic over Fechter's performance as the villain Obenreizer (see Dickens's letter to Fechter, 24 Feb. 1868; *N*, iii. 623), a role which has elements in common with that of Jasper, and Dickens was particularly struck by Fechter's success in arousing the audience's sympathies for an unsympathetic character: 'Of course I knew that Fechter would tear himself to pieces rather than fall short, but I was not prepared for his contriving to get the pity and sympathy of the audience out of his passionate love for Marguerite' (letter of 15 Jan. to Fields; *N*, iii. 604). Dickens's later tribute to Fechter's acting—'in the highest degree romantic . . . fervour in his love-making . . . passionate vehemence . . . always united to a true artist's intelligence . . .' (*Atlantic Monthly* (Aug. 1869); here quoted from *The Works of Charles Dickens*, Standard Edition, vol. xix, pp. 576–9)—indicates those qualities which served him in the part of Obenreizer and would make him a suitable model for a dramatic conception of Jasper.

[1] See play-bill posters, Duffield collection, Dickens House.
[2] *Lost. A drama in 4 acts* . . . by Walter Stephens. Printed by J. W. Last, Princess Street (n.d., but written above the title in ink is 'H. Vaughan. Prompt Copy. 1871').

under different titles, as 'the kaleidoscopic change in titles (a favourite device of the time) renders available records uncertain or ambiguous.'[1] We have thus no accurate means of knowing how many versions of *Edwin Drood* were staged in the year or two following the novel's publication, but it is likely that the book afforded dramatists a popular subject. This is not the only mystery which surrounds the play version of Dickens's last novel. There is also the question as to how much really was known about the proposed ending. Boucicault, as has already been mentioned,[2] was reported to have been told by Dickens himself that he did not know how to end the novel. Another prospective dramatizer was Augustin Daly, the adapter for the American stage of works by Dickens, Wilkie Collins, and Boucicault among others, in some of whose productions Fechter appeared. Daly's version was announced in the *London Figaro*, 20 October 1870, as having just been entered for copyright at Washington and as being prepared for speedy production at the Fifth Avenue Theatre, New York, but this, too, seems to have been fated. Assuming that Dickens would have left some clue to the mystery, Daly wrote to Charles Dickens junior for information, only to be told that 'it was as great a mystery to him as to the public at large'. This hardly squares either with the latter's indignation at erroneous representations of the ending or with his assertion that his father told him Drood was murdered. Daly thereupon wrote to Fildes, who put him on to Charles Collins, who eventually replied on 4 May 1871, giving all the information he had, the most important being that 'Edwin Drood was never to reappear, he having been murdered by Jasper'.[3] Daly then considered inventing his own conclusion, somewhat on the lines of *Le Juif polonais*, but before he could get to work on it the English version, *The Bells*, appeared and effectually deterred him.[4]

The impression that Edwin Drood was murdered may have been fairly widespread: Charles Dickens junior may not have been evasive in implying he knew no more than anyone else. On one other matter, however, he appears to have been curiously silent. There is no indication in his Preface to the novel that he did eventually collaborate in a dramatization, but the evidence seems to be fairly conclusive that he did, in partnership with Joseph Hatton.[5] An article from Hatton in the *People*, 19 November 1905, refers to Dickens's own thoughts of dramatization with Boucicault, to

[1] *XIX Century Drama, 1850–1900* (1946), Appendix B and Preface, vol. 2, p. 16. See also J. Cuming Walters, *The Complete Mystery of Edwin Drood, History, Continuations and Solutions (1870–1912)* (1912), tabulated list of conclusions; F. Dubrez Fawcett, *Dickens the Dramatist* (1952), pp. 103–4; *Dickensian*, xx (1924), pp. 100–1, note by J. C. L. Clark.   [2] See p. xxvii.
[3] See Appendix E above.
[4] Joseph Francis Daly, *The Life of Augustin Daly* (N.Y., 1917), pp. 107–8.
[5] According to a letter in the Duffield collection, written by D. E. Grant, Charles Dickens junior was said to have actually disclaimed connection with this play.

Boucicault's subsequent consideration and later rejection of the idea of writing the play himself, and, admittedly in rather vague terms, to the authenticity of the version ultimately written by himself and Charles Dickens junior. He claimed, for example, that much of the son's version of the finale was proved by the instructions which the author had given to the illustrator in regard to certain of the unwritten chapters, and we know how non-committal these instructions were. A letter in the Duffield collection from Bessie Hatton, the playwright's daughter, more categorical in its assurance that her father told her they knew how the story was to end, enclosed in support one from Mary Angela Dickens,[1] apparently conclusive, but presumably merely taking us back to the one occasion already referred to by her father in his Preface:

> Miss Hatton has asked whether we have any reason for believing that my father, Charles Dickens, the eldest son of my grandfather, knew what was to be the end of *Edwin Drood*.
>
> My father told me more than once that when *Edwin Drood* was being written he went with his father for a country walk. After walking for a long time in dead silence my grandfather suddenly began to talk of the book with which he was evidently completely preoccupied. Almost as if he were talking to himself, my father said, he described the murder, standing still and going through the scene in rapid action. Then he mapped out the means by which the murderer was to be identified.
>
> All that my grandfather thus told my father is embodied in the play in which my father collaborated with Mr. Hatton.

It seems that several years elapsed before the Dickens–Hatton version was ready for the public—a brief preliminary notice appeared in the *Theatre*, 1 March 1880, announcing its forthcoming appearance at the Princess's Theatre, with Mr. Charles Warner in the lead—and even then it failed to find favour in the theatre world. There were difficulties with the stage-manager and the play was never acted.[2] It was, however, published by Charles Dickens and Evans, Crystal Palace Press, and a copy exists at Dickens House. It is a melodramatic affair, with nothing distinctive to recommend it in the dialogue, though with possibilities in the situation, which may owe something to the success of *The Bells*: Jasper in an opium vision 'sees' his crime and its discovery; as he does so, the knocking on his door in Cloisterham in his vision merges with actual knocking on the opium den door. He poisons himself and dies with a defiant confession on his lips. There is no place in the play for Tartar and Datchery: Neville presumably marries Rosa.

There were, in the 1870s, two attempts to pass off as 'authentic' continuations of *The Mystery of Edwin Drood*. The first of these, *John Jasper's Secret*, originally appeared, anonymously, in the American weekly, *Frank Leslie's Illustrated Newspaper*, from 29 April to 2 September

---

[1] Dated 3 Mar. 1929.   [2] Hatton, article in the *People*.

1871, and subsequently in the London weekly, *Chimney Corner*, from 19 August to 16 December 1871. The first American instalment claimed that the writers were English, and the tone of the Preface certainly suggests this, without directly stating so. It also suggests acquaintance-ship with Dickens and inside knowledge of how the story would have ended. There were four early issues of *John Jasper's Secret*, two in volume form, two in eight monthly parts running from October 1871 to May 1872, all published by Petersons of Philadelphia, two in England, two in America.[1] Three of these were published anonymously, but the American monthly-parts issue was apparently ascribed to Henry Morford and wife.[2] In 1878 a French edition, published by E. Dentu and called *Le Crime de Jasper*, ascribed the authorship to 'Charles Dickens and Wilkie Collins'. This elicited an outraged denial from Collins:

I am bringing an action against the man who has written (or translated) a con-clusion to *Edwin Drood*, and put my name to the published French book, with Dickens's. It is an outrage offered to Dickens's reputation to associate his great name with rubbish which is utterly unworthy of it—setting my own injury out of the question. The formal declaration which I enclose *may* be wanted at the trial. If you feel the slightest hesitation about signing it, tear it up and say nothing about it.[3]

That Georgina supported Collins in his protest is indicated by a subse-quent letter, 28 March, from Collins to Frederic Chapman, which is preserved inside the British Museum's copy of the novel:

Miss Hogarth agrees with me that the book which I send to you with this note ought to be seen by your firm.

The person responsible for the fraudulent use made of Dickens's name and of mine is one Bernard Derosne—employed as a translator.[4] I have never written a line of the work attributed to me, and I am bringing an action against Derosne in Paris which will be probably decided in two or three days' time.

The agent (and friend) who is managing the matter for me in Paris has recently compared the French book with *Edwin Drood*—and finds that there is not even a pretence of translating Dickens's uncompleted story. His name also has been used to sell a book which contains nothing of his writing.

I should add that M. Dentu (the publisher) has undertaken to remove my name from the title-page and cover of *Le Crime de Jasper*.

This would seem to have been decisive enough, but it was not the end of

---

[1] According to Howard Duffield, the English monthly-parts version commands a higher price than *Edwin Drood* itself. His collection contains a Heffers' catalogue, no. 337, dated in pencil 1930, citing the price for it as £47. 10s.

[2] Letter in Duffield collection from James B. Russell of Lowell, Mass., 13 Nov. 1926. Russell also gives information about the later American editions of *John Jasper's Secret*. His letter seems to be more accurate in its statements than the pamphlet by 'A Dicken-sian': *The Case for Wilkie Collins and Charles Dickens, Jnr., Authors of 'John Jasper's Secret'*, also in the Duffield collection.

[3] Extract from a letter to Georgina Hogarth, 18 Mar. 1879, quoted by Nuel Pharr Davis, p. 290.   [4] Derosne translated *Edwin Drood* into French (1874).

the story. Twenty years later the ascription was being made to Wilkie
Collins and, not Dickens himself, but his son. In 1898,[1] 1901, and 1905
R. F. Fenno and Company of New York published editions of *John
Jasper's Secret*, attributing the authorship to Charles Dickens junior and
Wilkie Collins, but on the third occasion, although Collins's name
appeared on the spine, a fly-leaf note gave the authorship as 'Henry
Morford—formerly attributed to Wilkie Collins and Charles Dickens
Junior'. A note from H. Snowden Ward in *Notes and Queries*, 23 April
1904, stated, apparently on Mrs. Morford's authority, that she had
arranged with Fenno and Company that her husband's name should
appear on any new edition.

   The second 'authentic' continuation far outstripped *John Jasper's
Secret* in the audacity of its claim, being nothing less than an attempt to
foist off on the public a completion by Dickens himself, in spirit. *The
Mystery of Edwin Drood Complete by Charles Dickens*, published by T. P.
James at Brattleborough, Vermont, towards the end of 1873, soon, no
doubt, became, as a subsequent (1874) cover proclaimed, 'The Novel
of the Season'. It was later denounced by Charles Dickens junior as
a 'disgraceful and impudent American imposture',[2] by a young man
fraudulently posing as an illiterate mechanic. The author was elsewhere
said to be a printing-office foreman at the *Vermont Record and Farmer*,[3]
and this seems in keeping with the product of his pen, a not altogether
unskilful, but far from sophisticated, imitation of Dickens.

   There were two early continuations of *Edwin Drood* which did not
claim authority for their solutions. The first of these, begun while Dickens
was still alive, took the form of an ingenious burlesque of Dickens's art,
under the pretence of illustrating why American authors could not hope
to reach the literary eminence of English ones. It appeared in *Punchinello*,
a comic weekly published in New York, from 11 June to 5 November
1870, under the title of *The Mystery of Mr. E. Drood* by 'Orpheus C.
Kerr' (R. H. Newell), and was subsequently published in volume form
under its better-known title, *The Cloven Foot*. The second continuation,
A Great Mystery Solved (1878) by Gillan Vase (Elizabeth Newton), was
a straightforward, rather sentimental attempt to provide an ending in
keeping with Dickens's delineation of the characters. In the same year
Richard A. Proctor was beginning his series of articles, later to appear in
book form as *Watched by the Dead* (1887). Since that time speculations
on the *Edwin Drood* mystery have been prolific. The latest in the series,
The Drood Case by Felix Aylmer (1964), gives a brief bibliography of
major works on the subject.

   [1] By this date neither writer was alive to disprove the claim. Collins died in 1889,
Charles Dickens junior in 1896. Morford had died in 1881.
   [2] Introduction to Macmillan's 1923 edn., p. xiii.
   [3] See *Rifts in the Veil, A Collection of Inspirational Poems and Essays Given Through
Various Forms of Mediumship* (1878).

THE PROOF SENT TO THE ILLUSTRATOR

THE Fildes proof is, according to usual practice, page-proof. It is complete, with a fragment of over-matter attached to the end of Number II and a long galley of over-matter accompanying page-proofs for Number V. There are very few written alterations made by Dickens. Apart from three corrections of proof error at the beginning of Number IV, ch. xiii, these are confined to the proof for Number V as written by Dickens (chs. xvii–xxi), that is, the one Number for which we also have the evidence of the proof corrected for the printers (see p. xlix). Proof to Fildes is here far less extensively corrected: most of the alterations which are marked are deletions of over-matter. These would naturally be of concern to the illustrator; but even so, there are only eighteen passages marked for deletion, as compared with about thirty on the proof prepared for the printers. Of the other changes, including punctuation, the Fildes proof has only seven (one apparently deleted later: see p. 188, n. 2) as compared with approximately 200 on the proof for the printers. The obvious inference is that Dickens did not consider it essential to make full detailed corrections on the proof for Fildes, which he would presumably wish to make available for the illustrator as early as possible. This is borne out by the evidence of proof for Numbers III and IV, which are virtually uncorrected, and for Number II, not a first proof, where several changes still to be made for 70 are not recorded.

Thus, the main value of the Fildes proof as evidence is that it helps to establish a distinction between changes which were deliberately made by Dickens between MS and 70, and changes which originated in printers' errors. Had the material been available from the outset, more MS readings would have been restored on the grounds that the 70 reading was, initially, unintentional on Dickens's part; a few of the emended readings which have been incorporated on the assumption of a printer's error, would have been seen to be unwarranted. The parts particularly affected are Numbers III and IV, chs. x–xvi, for which the proof sent to the illustrator is evidently first proof; and the deductions about proof errors perpetuated in the American texts (see Appendix F) need to be reconsidered in the light of the new evidence.

In the commentary and collation which follow, each Number will be treated separately except for the problems raised by the American texts, which are dealt with together at the end. Page and footnote references are given to the text and footnotes of the present edition, in order to facilitate cross-reference. The abbreviation [MS] or [70] denotes the reading now preferred, where the new material provides evidence for a change. In all other cases the reading of the text is confirmed.

Number I

When Dickens received proof for Numbers I and II from the printers, he realized that considerable reorganization of the material would be necessary. Moreover, he was at this point faced with the problem of finding a new illustrator to replace Charles Collins (see pp. xxi–xxii). One would, therefore, not expect Fildes to be given first proof for these Numbers. The proof for Number I confirms this supposition. The chapter which had to be transferred from Number II is in its new place, and the thoroughness of the correction, compared with that on Number II, suggests the possibility that this is third proof, not second. Proof tallies with 70 in all significant detail, except for two instances which show an intermediate stage in a change of reading:

Ch. i, p. 3, n. 4   a-bed] MS   in bed 70   in a bed P
Ch. v, p. 38, n. 3   his unlighted pipe in his hand, for some time, with a fixed
                      and deep attention] unlighted pipe in hand, for a long
                      time, with a fixed attention MS with his unlighted pipe
                      in his hand, for some time, with a fixed and deep
                      attention P

In the first instance, where MS reading has already been restored in the present text, on the assumption of a printer's error, proof evidence is inconclusive either way. All that can be deduced is that Dickens's final decision was against the retention of both 'in' and 'a'. In the second instance the proof reading may be a printer's misinterpretation of Dickens's correction, but the more likely supposition is that Dickens made a further slight change for 70, after seeing his revised reading in print. The same argument holds for all readings throughout Number I: since this is not a first proof, we are no nearer knowing what the printers originally printed and what Dickens deliberately altered. Fildes's proof offers no evidence for changing any of the readings already established for Number I.

The proof differs in a few minor particulars from 70. The running headlines throughout Number I are 'The Mystery of' [verso] 'Edwin Drood' [recto]; an occasional decision as to the use of a hyphen has still to be taken, or a spelling to be corrected; and one clear proof error survives to this stage, yet to be corrected for 70. Directions in ink on the proof are confined to one or two directions to the printers referring to spacing and indentation.

Number II

As in Number I, this is not first proof, even for ch. ix: the chapters have their final numbering and many alterations from MS have already taken effect in print. This includes most of the deletions which had to be made because the newly written chapter was too long; but Dickens had still not calculated exactly, and there is a fragment of over-matter—the last six lines of the Number, following p. 64, are printed separately, with the printed heading 'Henry Drood', and numbered 65. No correction on the proof indicates the six lines still to be deleted, but it is, of course, clear from a comparison with 70 where the last cuts were to be made. Number II has not at this stage undergone such thorough revision as Number I: many MS readings still remain, obviously to be changed later by Dickens. It is possible that none of the material has yet gone beyond the second proof stage. (The slight cut at the end of ch. viii might have been made early, for other reasons than saving space.) The argument as to the establishment of text remains for Number II as for Number I: since this is not first proof there is no clear evidence, where a change has already been made from MS, to distinguish printers' errors from deliberate changes. There is, however, one instance (ch. viii, p. 61, n. 4) where restoration of MS reading in the present text is shown to be unwarranted: the agreement between proof and MS indicates that the subsequent change was deliberately made by Dickens. In other cases where MS reading has been restored, proof agrees with 70, and there is no reason for changing any of the readings already established for Number II.

The following list supplements the textual apparatus in indicating which of the substantive corrections found in 70 were yet to come. (This set of proofs bears no corrections in Dickens's hand; presumably all such corrections were made on a duplicate set for the printers.)

Ch. vi,	p. 38, n. 8	his] his very MS P	
	n. 9	tenderness] the gentlest tenderness MS	gentle tenderness P
	p. 39, n. 1	feign] pretend MS P	
	p. 42, n. 3	Add] Now, add MS P	
	p. 46, n. 3	with] and MS P	
	n. 6	at] as MS P	
	n. 7	with whom they sympathized] *not in* MS P	
	n. 8	fervent] ardent and fervent MS P	
Ch. vii,	p. 48, n. 1	Quite the contrary] Quite the contrary, quite the contrary MS P	
	n. 3	inclined me] made me inclined MS P	

Ch. vii, p. 49, n. 2   the commonest] and the commonest MS P
         p. 52, n. 2   Helena] Helena Landless MS P
         p. 54, n. 1   in which] when MS P
             n. 2   side] side, with a dropped jaw MS P
Ch. viii, p. 55, n. 2   his] this MS P
         p. 56, n. 2   pretend] feign MS P
             n. 5   host] host here MS P
         p. 57, n. 4   red hot] blaze MS P
             n. 5   rooms] room MS P
             n. 6   an imperfect] a very imperfect MS P
         p. 58, n. 2   compounding] blending MS P
             n. 3   Jasper] He MS P
             n. 4   rallyingly] rallying MS P
         p. 61, n. 2   said] *not in* MS P
             n. 4   you to it] MS P   it to you 70   [70]
Ch. ix, p. 65, n. 3   hem! —] *not in* MS P
         p. 72, n. 2   to say so] *not in* MS P
         p. 74, n. 5   want of] *not in* MS P
             n. 9   nephew] nephew. Duty in the abstract must be done,
                   even if it did; but it did not, and it does not. I like
                   your nephew very much. I hope you are satisfied
                   MS P
             n. 10 handsomely.] handsomely. Can I be less than satis-
                   fied? MS P
         p. 75, n. 5   observed Jasper. "I see!... my nephew and me, that]
                   proof reads observed Jasper. "Mr. Grewgious, as
                   you quite fairly said just now, my affection for my
                   dear boy makes me quick to feel in his behalf, and
                   I cannot allow any approach to a slight to be put
                   upon him. There is such an exceptional attachment
                   between him and me, that
         p. 76, n. 1   their] the MS P

There are eight errors still to be corrected on this proof, two of them
literal misprints, the others slight variations from copy; there is also a
blank space at the beginning of the line, three lines from the end of ch. vii,
where the word 'intense' should be. In one instance (p. 67, l. 35: as if
... were] 70 as if ... was P) proof may have MS support: the word could
be read either way, and the change from MS 'was' to 70 'were' in such
expressions is found elsewhere.

Proof for Number II and subsequent Numbers shows the kind of
deliberate punctuation change which was made for 70. Punctuation is
lighter on MS and proof than in 70, where additional commas are inserted,
colons replace commas in certain constructions, and dashes are frequently
eliminated. On the other hand, there is an occasional removal of a comma
between two epithets, as in the phrase 'scanty flat crop of hair' on p. 66.

The first page of proof for Number II is numbered '(33)' at the top centre of the page, and there is no heading other than the chapter heading. Thereafter proof headings agree with 70: 'The Mystery of Edwin Drood' [verso], the appropriate chapter title [recto].[1]

Number III

There is strong evidence for supposing the Fildes proof to be a first proof. In ch. x there are seventeen clear cases where proof and MS agree against 70, and nine where proof agrees with 70 against MS. There is none of this latter group which could not be accounted for as a proof error. A similar situation is discernible in chs. xi and xii. Ch. xi has fourteen instances where proof still retains MS reading, as against seven of agreement with 70, again conceivable proof errors. Ch. xii has approximately thirty-eight instances of agreement between MS and proof (counting only once each the 'Jarsper] Jasper' variant and the references to Mr. Sapsea as Mayor) as opposed to eight where proof has the reading of 70. In addition, there are one or two cases where the proof reading marks a stage between MS and 70, leading to a further change by Dickens. Of the twenty-four instances of agreement between proof and 70, proof error has already been assumed in ten cases, and the MS reading restored, in the present edition. There is now good reason for restoring the other fourteen MS readings. In the two cases where proof represents a half-way stage, the 70 reading should probably still be preferred, as in one instance the MS reading is not absolutely clear, and in each case Dickens might as easily have restored the original reading. Instances where MS reading is too uncertain for restoration to be contemplated, and proof agrees with 70, have not been considered here, as the correspondence of proof to 70 is not significant.

There are four instances in Number III where MS reading has been restored in this edition and proof agreement with MS indicates that a printer's error was wrongly supposed here. In these cases the reading of 70 should have been retained.

One other point of interest on proof concerns the correction which Dickens had to make near the beginning of ch. xi (p. 88) in a letter to the printers. This folio of MS is missing, and proof supplies what presumably was the original reading. The construction here was unsatisfactory and was obviously altered by Dickens on the proof for the printers.

The following list includes all readings of significance for the present edition: namely, those where proof and 70 agree, either confirming, or offering evidence for, the restoration of MS reading; those where proof represents a half-way stage; those where proof and MS agree and MS reading has been wrongly restored; and the original reading for the passage in ch. xi.

[1] This is a departure from Dickens's usual practice and has not been followed in the present edition.

Ch. x,   p. 77, n. 3   Ma] P 70   Ma dear MS   [MS]
         n. 5   lights."] P 70   lights," observed the Minor Canon.
                MS *with lengthy deletions between* lights," *and*
                observed   [MS]
         p. 80, n. 1   unlike] P 70   *un*like MS   [MS]
         n. 3   one great bowl . . . the other] MS   the great bowl
                . . . the other P 70
         p. 82, n. 1   concessions] P 70   concessions here MS   [MS]
         n. 2   full] P 70   with full MS   [MS]
         p. 83, n. 4   undeserving] P 70   undeserving of MS   [MS]
         p. 84, n. 2   are] P 70   were MS   [MS]
         p. 85, n. 2   *you*] MS P   you 70   [70]
         p. 86, n. 3   unformed] MS   unfounded P 70
Ch. xi, p. 88, n. 1   Constitution . . . us Britons, the odd . . . institution]
                proof reads constitution, the property of us
                Britons whose odd fortune
         p. 89, n. 1   at] P 70   in the black basement at MS *with* in the
                black basement *written above the line*   [MS]
         p. 90, n. 1   It is] MS   It's P 70
         p. 91, n. 1   my] MS   any P 70
         p. 92, n. 1   are] P 70   were MS   [MS]
         n. 4   in secret nudges] MS P   *om.* 70   [70]
         p. 93, n. 7   stolid] MS P   *om.* 70   [70]
         p. 94, n. 3   near] MS   nearly P 70
         n. 4   get —] P 70   get — Mr Edwin, MS   [MS]
         p. 96, n. 2   dry] MS   *om.* P 70
Ch. xii, p. 100, n. 1   ears: — figuratively long] MS   ears — figuratively,
                long P 70
         p. 104, n. 4   is] MS   there is P 70
         p. 105, n. 1   reply] P 70   reply to him MS   [MS]
         p. 106, n. 1   frames . . . cast] P 70   framing . . . casts MS [MS]
         n. 2   just as] P 70   as MS   [MS]
         n. 3   Durdles . . . step.] 70   As Durdles . . . step, MS
                Durdles . . . step, P
         p. 107, n. 4   everywheres] MS   everywhere P 70
         n. 5   so emerges] 70   ⟨so⟩ emerges first MS *deletion of*
                so *is not absolutely certain*   so emerges first P
         n. 6   and] MS   so to P 70
         p. 109, n. 1   in] P 70   ⟨in⟩ on MS   [MS]
         p. 111, n. 1   with one defensive leg up] MS P   *om.* 70   [70]

There are, in addition to the twenty-four errors perpetuated in 70, and
setting aside an occasional wrong spelling and literal misprint, twenty-
five proof errors subsequently corrected to the MS reading. These include
several cases of omission of single words, and one of omission of a
sequence of three words; insertion of single words; misplacing of words;
misreading of words and phrases; substitution of adverb for adjective,
of one tense for another, of plural for singular, and of formal expression

for colloquial contraction. On the other hand, where MS mistakenly has 'Edwin' for 'Neville', on two occasions close together on p. 86, printers have corrected the second error, though without noticing the first. The total number of substantive printers' errors in Number III is approximately fifty, about half the total for Number V.

Number IV

This also appears to be a first proof. All the readings where proof agrees with 70 against MS can be accounted for as proof errors. These include two unusual, though not inconceivable, cases of word substitution: 'paper' for 'writing' (p. 121, n. 4) and 'great' for 'strong' (p. 141, n. 2). In ch. xiii there are thirteen cases in which the alteration for 70 is not yet made, eight of agreement between proof and 70 against MS. In addition, there is one proof misreading which leads to a further change in 70. In ch. xiv there are eleven cases where a change for 70 is still to be made, four of agreement between proof and 70 against MS, and one misreading which leads to a further change. Ch. xv has six readings where a change is still to be made, one where proof agrees with 70 against MS. Ch. xvi has twenty-seven cases where a change has still to be made, four of agreement between proof and 70 against MS, and two where proof misreading leads to a further change. The large number of changes still to be made in this chapter includes the insertion of extra passages at the end of the Number, possibly because Dickens felt he was not giving his readers full measure on the final page. In four of the seventeen instances where proof and 70 agree against MS, proof error has already been assumed and MS reading restored. Twelve of the remaining thirteen cases should now revert to MS reading. The one exception is proof insertion of the word 'had' in the second of two verbs using this tense ('had grown used to me, and had grown used to the idea', p. 116, n. 1). Changes of this kind are found in 70; indeed, there is an example two pages earlier (p. 114, n. 1) where neither MS nor proof has the second 'had'. There is apparently clear support for the restoration of one of the MS readings which proof misprinted. This proof contains three corrections in Dickens's hand: the word 'met' (p. 113, n. 1), printed as 'meet', has the second 'e' deleted; the word 'incorrigible', wrongly inserted in the phrase 'to say to [incorrigible] mankind' (p. 113) is deleted (MS had several words above the line here, all crossed out but not very clearly, one of which could be read as 'incorrigible'); and the MS phrase 'here, general depression' (p. 113, n. 2), wrongly printed as 'here a general depression', has a comma substituted for the word 'a'. For some reason this last correction has not taken effect in 70: either it was omitted, or ignored, on the corrected proof for the printers, or Dickens subsequently changed his mind. In view of the evidence of this proof it would seem wrong not to restore MS reading here.

In the four cases where proof misreading leads to further alteration for 70, the decision is more difficult. The last of these (p. 141, n. 4) offers the strongest case for preferring the 70 reading. Two words were changed by Dickens, whereas proof had misread only the first of the two. The second alteration was, therefore, deliberate on Dickens's part and should stand; and to restore MS reading for the first word would establish a combined reading lacking Dickens's authority. On p. 118, n. 2 the change from 'method' to 'shape' in the phrase 'into shape' would, without proof evidence, have been accepted as Dickens's later preference for the more usual expression; but 'shape' was, in fact, introduced by the printer who misread an unmistakable 'method' (badly written above the line) as 'some shape'. The less usual word is appropriate to Mr. Grewgious and should be restored. On p. 127, n. 2 there is a slight preference for restoration of MS reading in the series of phrases describing the haunting effect of the opium woman's words in Edwin's imagination. In MS the four phrases are paired: 'in the rising wind and in the angry sky, in the troubled water and in the flickering lights'. Originally 'and' introduced the three phrases, but the one before 'in the troubled water' is scribbled over. There is a blot on the first 'and' and the printers omitted it, giving a conventional sequence of 'in . . . in . . . in . . . and in'. Dickens presumably preferred a form drawing more attention to the words, and deleted the final 'and'. He could, of course, have made the alteration either way; the original expression is preferred here as being slightly more rhetorical and noticeable than the 70 reading. On p. 139, n. 1, the last instance of proof misreading leading to further change, the preference for MS reading is strong. Jasper's reference to 'all the airy castles' he had built for Edwin was printed as 'any castles'. Dickens clearly wanted the emphatic 'all' and restored it at the expense of 'airy', perhaps forgetting what his original reading had been.

First proofs for Numbers III and IV provide some evidence to suggest that, in making corrections, Dickens considered the printer. There are a few noticeable occasions where word removal is balanced by word insertion within two or three lines, with resulting disturbance to only a few lines of type. Examples from Number IV are the change from 'was' to 'had been' balanced by one from 'might have' to 'had' (p. 144, n. 1, 145, n. 1) where only two lines were disturbed, and the changes in the already much rewritten passage presenting Cloisterham's view of "Natives" (p. 143, nn. 7, 8, 9) where only three lines were disturbed.

There are two cases in Number IV where proof agreement with MS reading indicates that a MS reading has been wrongly restored.

The following list includes readings where proof and 70 agree, those where proof and MS agree and MS has been wrongly restored, and those where proof represents a stage between MS and 70.

Ch. xiii, p. 111, n. 5   strictly] P 70   chastely MS   [MS]
         p. 112, n. 1   finest] MS   first P 70
         p. 113, n. 2   here a general] P 70   here, general MS *and proof-*
                              correction   [MS]
         p. 114, n. 2   hand] P 70   hands MS   [MS]
         p. 115, n. 3   our own] P 70   our MS   [MS]
         p. 116, n. 1   had] P 70   *not in* MS
         p. 117, n. 3   and moddley-coddleys] 70   and molly-coddles P
                              molly-coddles MS *reading should be* moddley-
                              coddleys (*cf. p.* 7)
         p. 118, n. 1   fond] P 70   fond old MS   [MS]
               n. 2   shape] 70   method MS   some shape P   [MS]
Ch. xiv, p. 121, n. 4   paper] P 70   writing MS   [MS]
         p. 125, n. 2   a very] P 70   very MS   [MS]
         p. 126, n. 3   weak] MS   weakly P 70
         p. 127, n. 1   I am] P 70   I'm MS   [MS]
               n. 2   in] 70   and in MS (*twice*) *proof has only second* and [MS]
Ch. xv, p. 132, n. 2   that little] MS P   it 70   [70]
         p. 134, n. 1   intently] MS   intensely P 70
Ch. xvi, p. 138, n. 5   that has] P 70   that's MS   [MS]
         p. 139, n. 1   all the castles] 70   all the airy castles MS   any
                              castles P   [MS]
         p. 141, n. 2   great] P 70   strong MS   [MS]
               n. 4   directly incensed] 70   undeniably irritated MS
                              immediately irritated P
         p. 142, n. 6   fancy] MS P   sight 70   [70]
         and n. 7   to the sense of sight] MS P   *om.* 70   [70]
         p. 146, n. 3   expressive] MS   impressive P 70
               n. 4   identification] P 70   his identification MS   [MS]

In addition to the proof errors listed above which were perpetuated in 70, there were twenty-three of which proof is the only record. One of these perhaps contributed towards a further slight change of emphasis in the final reading (p. 118, n. 3 'like old letters or old vows, or other records' 70. MS had '. . . or old vows, or records', and proof accidentally omitted 'or', throwing 'records' into apposition to 'letters' and 'vows'). The proof errors are similar to those found elsewhere, and include instances of misreading of difficult writing and printing of words intended to be deleted in MS.

Number V

The proof for chs. xvii–xx adds nothing to the information already afforded by the proof corrected for the press. In printed matter the two are identical. The less extensive correction of the proof for Fildes perhaps roughly indicates stages of revision, as Dickens calculated the amount of over-matter to be removed. Not only are there fewer corrections, but some of them are incomplete: for example, when a deletion needed to be accompanied by an inserted direction as to the speaker of the following lines, as at p. 155, nn. 2, 3, the added explanation is not recorded on the proof to Fildes. On one occasion the matter deleted on this proof differs slightly from that deleted on printers' copy: in the Minor Canon's speech on p. 155 (nn. 4, 6, 7) the deletion recorded for Fildes is merely of one continuous passage, from 'Every day and hour' to 'mastery of her'. In other respects corrections on this proof are as on proof for the printers.

Number VI

As for Number V, this proof offers no new evidence affecting readings. For ch. xxi the proof corrected for the printers as part of the original Number V (see p. xxix) establishes authoritative readings. (The one occasion where proof for Fildes changes a reading which was subsequently restored on the printers' copy has already been noted: p. 188, n. 2.) For chs. xxii and xxiii MS is the authority. The proof received by Fildes does, however, throw new light on the stages of the printers' work on Number VI. We know that Number V originally ended at 'May it flourish for ever!' (end of ch. xx in MS; end of ch. xxi in 70) and that the matter extending beyond the required thirty-two pages was printed on a galley numbered 161. Fildes received this proof (thirty-two pages plus a galley) as the original printing for Number V. We also know that when the over-matter was restored to the text, and additional arrangements were devised (see p. xxix, n. 2) to make the necessary thirty-two pages for Number V end at 'and had it on his mind that she might tumble out', the last part of the original ch. xx, beginning 'Nothing occurred in the night to flutter the tired dove', became the new ch. xxi, the first chapter for Number VI as eventually printed (see pp. 183, 188). Proof sent to Fildes shows us a draft of the new chapter in print. It is headed 'Chapter xxi. A Recognition' and is numbered 161–5, but its material, apart from an occasional misprint, is otherwise identical with that of the corresponding section of first proof printed for Number V: for some reason it incorporates none of Dickens's corrections. It is possible that the printers were trying out the redivision of material to see how many pages this would supply for the deficient Number VI. Proof-corrections were presumably not a priority at this stage. Fildes possessed two identical copies of this draft chapter, three copies in all, therefore, of the material from 'Nothing occurred in the night' to 'May it flourish for ever!' (ch. xxi of 70).

The main interest of proof for chs. xxii and xxiii is that it establishes which deviations from MS were printers' errors and which were later deliberate changes. As we should expect, practically all the 70 readings originated in proof error. The exceptions, also predictable, are the passage

in ch. xxiii (p. 204, n. 2) where MS and proof reading involved a misleading construction; the passage in ch. xxii (p. 193, n. 1) in which the MS
and proofreading is awkward, though not impossible; and, a change which
is part error and part deliberate, the reading at the beginning of ch. xxiii
(p. 203, n. 2) where proof's accidental insertion of a comma after the word
'purpose' perhaps helped to confirm the proof-reader in his view that the
insertion of the word 'so' would give a better reading. The successive
readings are thus:

> concentrated on one idea, and on its attendant fixed purpose that   MS
> concentrated on one idea, and on its attendant fixed purpose, that   P
> so concentrated on one idea, and on its attendant fixed purpose, that   70

In addition to the proof errors which were perpetuated in 70, there were,
excluding literal misprints, twelve which were corrected to MS reading.
One odd feature of the printing is that, for no obvious reason, proof
leaves a blank for the rest of the line following the opium woman's speech
ending ' "wore away to cabbage-nets!" ' (p. 205, l. 8); the next word of
the sentence, 'until', is at the beginning of the next line. At one point
(p. 213, n. 2) proof has corrected a mistake which Dickens made in
MS: it was the printers who restored Deputy's characteristic 'yer' for
'you'.

Printed proof also indicates that the kinds of punctuation change noticed
in earlier Numbers from proof to 70 were also made at this stage for the
last Number.

In addition to the two copies of ch. xxi, Fildes possessed two copies
of ch. xxii, but in this case, although in printed matter they are identical,
the second is not an exact replica of the first. It is the second which follows
the normally expected pattern of continuous pagination, ch. xxii ending
on p. 177 of 70, ch. xxiii beginning on verso (p. 178). The first proof has
a blank verso here. The only obvious explanation of this irregularity is
that Dickens sent ch. xxii to the printer before he had written ch. xxiii.
(There is evidence that the material for some earlier Numbers was sent
to the printer in stages: see p. xxii, n. 1, p. xxiv.) Presumably there was
not time to set up this material before Dickens's death. It is scarcely conceivable that he could have seen it in this form: certainly, if he did, he
corrected none of its obvious errors. Moreover, the chapter is numbered
xxii, whereas Dickens wrote it as xxi, and, with the new ch. xxi, it forms,
up to p. 176 of 70, one complete sheet of sixteen pages. The remaining
material, forming p. 177, was obviously set up separately. It seems likely
that, as already suggested in respect of the uncorrected printing of the
new ch. xxi, the printers wished to estimate how much material was
available for the two Numbers, before ch. xxiii, which Dickens completed
just before his death, was made available. It might even be that Forster
wished to read the last pages before handing them over for printing.

The American Texts (Appendix F)

In view of the extensive alterations which Dickens made on proof, it would seem unlikely that the advance sheets which were sent to America would be an early proof with the corrections laboriously written in. Yet there is good reason to suppose that this was the case, at least for Numbers IV and V. The proof given to Fildes for Number IV incorrectly prints 'meet' for 'met' (ch. xiii, p. 113, n. 1) and this has been corrected in ink. Both the American texts print 'meet', and the inference must be, unless this correction was accidentally omitted by Dickens on the proof returned to the printers, that Fields, Osgood and Company received a first proof incompletely corrected. For Number V, proof corrected for the printers exists and it bears an insertion ('of your making', ch. xvii, p. 151, n. 5) which the printers of 70 misread as 'of our making', but the American printers transcribed correctly. Proof for Number V, admittedly, is in a different category from earlier proofs, as Dickens corrected only one stage of proof here, but still it confirms the impression that what was sent to America was, habitually, a proof with hand-written corrections. It is possible that the American reading common to ES and FO in Number III, for which MS is missing (ch. xi, p. 88, n. 1), represents, not as was first supposed (p. 244) an attempt by the American firm to correct an unsatisfactory reading, but a slightly inaccurate rendering of Dickens's hand-written correction. If the hypothesis of sheets corrected by hand is accepted, an occasional omission in such lengthy corrections is understandable: occasions where the American texts agree with MS against 70 may be due to sheer omission, or they may indicate a later stage of alteration after the sheets for America had been set aside.

The supposition outlined above is the only one which would satisfactorily explain the origin of the errors common to ES and FO in Numbers I and II (p. 244). If they were proof errors, no trace of them survives in the proof given to Fildes (second or even third proof), yet the American texts have thoroughly revised copy here, and this includes several alterations not made on the Fildes proof.

The readings common to ES and FO listed in Appendix F for Number III present no problems as regards origin. The reading in ch. xii (p. 100, n. 1) was printed on proof and survives, uncorrected, in 70; the reading in ch. x (p. 81, n. 3) was not a proof error but, presumably, a deliberate American improvement; and the reading at the end of ch. xii (p. 110, n. 4), which has MS authority, was, as assumed, printed on proof and the correction to the 70 reading either accidentally omitted from American copy or made after the sheets for America were set aside.

In Number IV proof errors were responsible for the two variant readings common to ES and FO but not originating in MS: 'meet' for 'met' and 'importunate' for 'impertinent' (ch. xvi, p. 139, n. 2). The American readings on p. 117, n. 3, p. 143, n. 4 and n. 9, p. 144, n. 1, and p. 146, n. 2 are as printed on proof; the remaining three either indicate the stage which proof-revision had reached at this point or, a less likely supposition, are the result of carelessly corrected copy. We now know that for the reading in ch. xiii (p. 118, n. 3) proof accidentally omitted the word 'or'. This was obviously written in on the advance sheets but the further insertion, of the word 'other', was not.

No new evidence is provided by the Fildes proof for Number V.

Proof for Number VI disposes of at least one of the problems raised by the American readings. We now have positive evidence of the existence of an uncorrected proof with the new heading and title, 'Chapter xxi. A Recognition', and there can be no doubt that this was the copy from which ES was printed (see p. 246 and n. 1). Possibly a corrected proof was sent later and used in the printing of FO. Since the error 'more' for 'none' was unnoticed on the proof Dickens corrected for the printers, this could account for its perpetuation in FO (see p. 246, n. 2, p. 247). With regard to chs. xxii and xxiii, we now have evidence that some of the mistakes in ES were proof errors (including two not listed in Appendix F: p. 196, l. 7, 'propositions' for 'prepositions' and p. 201, l. 29, 'sweet-bread snow' for 'sweetbreads now'). The fact that FO prints some of these readings correctly indicates that the two American texts were not printed from the same copy. The problem of the FO errors remains, but there now seems a possible explanation other than that some copies of 70 perpetuated at least one of these (see p. 246, n. 2). Apart from the reading 'baronical' for 'baronial', which does not appear in proof and can only be explained as an aberration of the American printers (the same firm printed ES and FO), the variations in the American readings could be accounted for by the supposition that, as for ch. xxi, two sets of proof for ch. xxii were sent to America, one uncorrected, and one corrected but with an occasional error unnoticed. (Both American texts on occasions agree with proof punctuation against 70.) The problematical readings are all in ch. xxii and we know that this was set up more than once. ES has all the proof errors in this chapter. An odd feature of the printing of ch. xxii in ES lends support to the possibility that the trial printing of chs. xxi and xxii was sent to America. The first instalment of Number VI, which appeared on 3 September, stops short within one page of the end of ch. xxii, p. 176 in 70, at the words 'get your equal chance'. Admittedly ch. xxiii is also subsequently split, but in a more equal division. It is possible that the odd page over the sixteen which make up a sheet was not sent with the rest.

The following list of proof readings supplements list ii, Appendix F, p. 248:

Ch. xxii, p. 189 had had P   p. 190 conclusion; "And could P
          p. 191 should P   p. 192 in P

Ch. xxii, p. 193 if any. Whether P   p. 196 by P
       p. 196 favour P   p. 196 snaring P
       p. 196 baronial P   p. 199 stimulare P
       p. 199 liberal and nutritious P   p. 199 information P
       p. 199 painful P   p. 200 imported P
       p. 204 have P   p. 204 be not one P
       p. 205 as P

Fildes's Annotations

There are occasional comments and markings on the proof, presumably by the illustrator himself. Fildes's signature on the illustrations for 70 bears close resemblance to the writing of one or two of these comments, and the remainder are sufficiently similar to be conceivably by the same hand. Sometimes the comment is a straightforward reference to a possible subject for illustration. The passage in ch. i beginning 'He rises unsteadily from the bed' (p. 2), of which the word 'curtain' is underlined in ink, is marked in the margin and the word 'Illustration' written at the side. Beneath this, deleted but legible, are the words 'Bed in Window' and a large question mark. At the end of ch. iii the word 'illustration?' is written beside the five lines beginning 'retaining it and looking into it'; and in ch. vii there is a line in the margin by the two paragraphs from 'Mr. Jasper was seated at the piano' to ' "Take me away!" ' (pp. 50–1). At the end of ch. i, in the space between the two chapters, is the word 'Bristol?', perhaps indicating a possible model in the illustrator's mind for the Cathedral sketches. More enigmatically, alongside the passage in ch. ii in which Edwin explains his delaying of Jack's drinking: ' "Asks why not . . . Happy returns, I mean." ' (p. 9) the word 'Brothers' is written, and earlier in the same chapter the words characterizing Mr. Crisparkle, 'and perpetually pitching himself . . . deep running water in' (p. 6) are underlined. Finally, against the passage in ch. xiv referring to the setting of Edwin's watch in the jeweller's shop on Christmas Eve (p. 125, ll. 8–18), are written, one beneath another, the notes: '20 Thurs. Friday 7Pm Saturday Sunday', possibly a reckoning of the number of days before the watch was found.